THE FRONTIERSMAN
THE DARKEST WINTER

THE FRONTIERSMAN
THE DARKEST WINTER

WILLIAM W. JOHNSTONE
with J. A. Johnstone

PINNACLE BOOKS
Kensington Publishing Corp.

www.kensingtonbooks.com

PINNACLE BOOKS are published by

Kensington Publishing Corp.
119 West 40th Street
New York, NY 10018

PUBLISHER'S NOTE
Following the death of William W. Johnstone, the Johnstone family is
working with a carefully selected writer to organize and complete Mr.
Johnstone's outlines and many unfinished manuscripts to create additional
novels in all of his series like The Last Gunfighter, Mountain Man, and
Eagles, among others. This novel was inspired by Mr. Johnstone's superb
storytelling.

All Kensington titles, imprints, and distributed lines are available at special quantity discounts for bulk purchases for sales promotions, premiums,
fund-raising, educational, or institutional use. Special book excerpts or
customized printings can also be created to fit specific needs. For details,
write or phone the office of the Kensington sales manager: Kensington
Publishing Corp., 119 West 40th Street, New York, NY 10018, attn: Sales
Department; phone 1-800-221-2647.

ISBN-13: 978-0-7860-4036-0
ISBN-10: 0-7860-4036-X

First printing: August 2017

10 9 8 7 6 5 4 3 2 1

Printed in the United States of America

First electronic edition: August 2017

ISBN-13: 978-0-7860-4037-7
ISBN-10: 0-7860-4037-8

The Moving Finger writes; and, having writ,
Moves on: nor all thy Piety nor Wit
Shall lure it back to cancel half a Line,
Nor all thy Tears wash out a Word of it.

—*The Rubáiyát of Omar Khayyám*
(translated by Edward FitzGerald)

Chapter 1

Breckinridge Wallace had no doubt that the men following him intended to rob him. Probably planned on killing him, to boot. Breck figured he'd have something to say about that.

A cloudy day had given way to a starless night, so the darkness was thick around Breckinridge as he walked along a St. Louis street toward Red Mike's tavern. Enough of a chill lingered from the recently departed winter to make the air dank this close to the river. The Mississippi lay like a giant serpent gliding past the settlement.

Breckinridge walked through a small patch of light that spilled from a window in one of the buildings he passed. That brief illumination revealed a giant of a man in buckskins, tall, broad shouldered, heavy with muscle. His face, too rugged to be called handsome, was clean-shaven. A wide-brimmed, gray felt hat was shoved down on unruly, shaggy red hair that hung almost to those brawny shoulders. Breck carried a long-barreled flintlock rifle in his left hand. A pair of flintlock pistols were shoved behind the broad leather belt strapped around his waist, as well as a bone-handled, wickedly keen hunting knife in a fringed leather scabbard. Even a glimpse was enough to confirm that he was a dangerous man.

Tonight he was even more dangerous than usual, because he felt like he had nothing left to lose and just didn't give a damn.

He slowed as he passed the light and entered an even thicker patch of shadow, willing the three men behind him to go ahead and catch up. He *wanted* them to make their move. Whatever happened might prove to be a welcome distraction.

His keen ears picked up the faint scuff of boot leather on cobblestones from the darkness ahead of him. A grim smile tugged at the corners of Breckinridge's wide mouth. The would-be robbers were smarter than he had taken them for at first. One of them had circled around through the alleys and gotten ahead of him.

Either that, or they'd had a confederate laying an ambush for him all along. Three enemies or four—it didn't really matter. Breckinridge didn't care either way. He strode on, to all appearances completely unaware of the threat.

Then he heard a grunt of effort, along with a whisper of sound as something swung through the air, likely a club aimed at his head. He took a quick step to the side and felt the bludgeon brush against the buckskin sleeve on his upper left arm. He dropped the rifle and reached out blindly as the missed blow made his attacker stumble. Breckinridge's big hands closed over the man's shoulders. His long legs drove them toward the wall of a building that was only a few swift steps away. Breck rammed the man against it with such force that his skull shattered. He heard the soggy thud, like a dropped gourd.

Rapid footsteps sounded as Breckinridge let go of the man and stepped back, turning to meet the new threat.

"Get him!" a harsh voice grated. "Kill the son of a bitch!"

That was plenty to tell Breckinridge his hunch was right. He didn't have to hold back—which was good since he'd already killed a man. He drew both pistols from behind his belt. The weapons were loaded and primed, so all Breck had to do was loop his thumbs around the hammers and pull them back. Then he squeezed the triggers and twin deafening booms filled the street as the guns went off.

Flame shot nearly a foot from the muzzle of each pistol. In that split-second glare, Breckinridge saw one of the heavy lead balls from the right-hand gun tear into the throat of a man charging him. The pistols were double-shotted. The second ball punched into the man's chest. His momentum carried him forward as blood spurted from both wounds.

Breckinridge had aimed at the sound of footsteps, and his accuracy with the left-hand pistol wasn't quite as good. One of the balls missed entirely and skipped off down the street. The other struck the man in the right shoulder, shredding flesh and smashing bone. The impact twisted him halfway around and caused him to stumble. He crashed to the street, hurt badly enough that Breck knew he was out of the fight.

In a matter of a dozen heartbeats, three of the four men who had intended to rob and kill him were down and no longer a threat. That left only one man, who had been slightly behind the two Breckinridge had just shot. Most thieves would have turned and run, since the odds were no longer on their side, but not this one. He let out a furious yell as he continued his charge.

Breckinridge saw a glint of light reflect off a blade as it sliced through the air at his face. He flung up his left hand. The empty pistol it held clashed with the knife. Metal rang against metal. Breck took a quick step back, knowing the attacker would try to catch him on the backswing. For a split second, the man was silhouetted against the patch of light Breck had walked through a minute earlier.

The bastard didn't have a knife, Breckinridge realized during that glimpse.

He had a damn sword!

Probably a former soldier, an officer, judging by the fact he had a saber. Or maybe just a thief who'd taken the weapon off the body of some victim. That was the more likely explanation. Either way, Breckinridge had to keep retreating as the varmint lunged at him, whipping the long, slightly curved blade back and forth.

Then Breckinridge's foot came down on the barrel of the rifle he had dropped. That was enough to throw him off-balance. He tried to right himself, but the rough cobblestones tripped him and he fell over backward.

The attacker leaped in to take advantage of Breckinridge's bad luck. The saber swung high and then flashed down. Breck still had hold of both pistols. He crossed the barrels and shoved them up. The V formed by the pistols caught the saber and stopped it with its edge scant inches from Breck's face.

Breckinridge swung his right leg high in a kick

aimed at the man's groin. It missed, but the toe of his boot sunk into the attacker's belly instead, which was almost as effective. The breath *whoofed* out of the man's lungs as he doubled over. Breck lashed out with his left leg and swept the man's feet from under him.

The thief tumbled to the ground. Breckinridge dropped the empty pistols and yanked his knife from its sheath. He rolled onto his side, powered halfway up, and leaped at the other man, who seemed momentarily stunned.

The varmint managed to angle the saber around in a protective arc. In the poor light, Breckinridge caught sight of it just in time to twist aside. The blade raked across the top of his left shoulder but cut only the buckskin without slicing into the flesh beneath. Breck hooked his knife toward the man's midsection, aiming to rip his guts open. Instead, the man got out of the way somehow, and the knife scraped hard against one of the cobblestones and tore itself out of Breck's grip.

Unarmed now, he didn't take the time to feel around for the knife. Instinct guided him as he grabbed his attacker's right wrist with his left hand. That allowed him to hold the sword off while he sought for the man's throat with his other hand.

As they rolled and wrestled in the street, Breckinridge could tell that the other man was big and muscular as well. It would take daylight to determine which of the two combatants was larger. All that mattered on this dark night was that they were evenly matched. The first one to slip or make a slight mistake would probably die in the next instant.

Something unexpected altered the balance of power. Breckinridge heaved himself up, looming over his opponent for a second. As he did, a heavy blow slammed down on his back.

"Hold him, Gordie!" a man shouted. "I'll bash his brains out!"

The thief Breckinridge had shot in the shoulder must have overcome the pain and loss of blood enough to find the dropped club and get back in the fight. That surprised Breck. He had figured the man would bleed to death or at least pass out. As it was, he now had two of the bastards to deal with.

Hearing the wounded man scrambling to get in position for another blow, Breckinridge let go of the man with the sword and rolled aside. The man with the club grunted as it swept down and hit the cobblestones. Breck could make out the man's dim shape. He kicked the fellow in the chest and sent him sprawling backward. The club clattered away. The man tried to get up, then sighed and fell back, his injury finally catching up with him.

Breckinridge leaped to his feet. He heard someone running away. The man with the saber had given up and decided it was best to escape while he could. The better part of valor, somebody had called it once, Breck recalled. To him, it was just turning tail, something he would never do.

But actually, he had done exactly that, one time not that long ago. The thought stabbed into him sharper than any saber ever could.

He shoved it away and took stock. He was barely breathing hard, even after all the desperate exertion. His big hands slapped over his body. No blood. He hadn't thought he'd been stabbed or cut, but it was good to make sure. Sometimes a man could be hurt and not feel it in the heat of battle.

A low groan came from somewhere not far off. That would be the wounded man. Breckinridge listened, heard a faint rattle. A death rattle. Loss of blood had finally done the bastard in.

So he was standing in the street with three dead men, Breckinridge thought. So far, no one had come to investigate the gunshots, but a constable might show up sooner or later. This close to the waterfront, the authorities in St. Louis expected violence. The men who worked the riverboats were a hardy, proddy breed. So were the fur trappers and mountain men who used the settlement as the jumping-off point for their expeditions to the Rocky Mountains. Bloody clashes were inevitable.

Despite that, there had to be *some* semblance of law and order, Breckinridge knew. This was just about the farthest western outpost of civilization, but the folks who lived here still considered it civilized and would tolerate only so many corpses in the streets. It would be better, Breck thought, if he wasn't anywhere around when these particular carcasses were found.

Besides, the letter he had gotten from his friend Morgan Baxter said that Morgan would be waiting for him every evening in Red Mike's until he showed up. So Breckinridge searched in the street until he found his rifle, his knife, and the two pistols, then turned his steps in that direction again.

Chapter 2

Red Mike's was one of the most notorious taverns in a settlement known for them. Its big, redheaded, hard-fisted Irish proprietor kept trouble from breaking out most of the time, but whenever a brawl did erupt, it was always a spectacular, furniture-shattering, blood-spilling brouhaha.

Other ruckuses went on in the street and alleys just outside the tavern night and day. Mountain men gravitated toward the place, and so did riverboaters. That was a recipe for trouble, often with booming guns and the flash of blades.

Tonight, however, the tavern was so blamed peaceful that Mike had to stifle a yawn as he stood behind the bar. He straightened from his casual pose, though, when he saw the big fella come in.

He recognized Breckinridge Wallace, of course. It was impossible to miss somebody that tall and massive. The hair on Breck's head was a distinctive flaming red, brighter than Mike's own shaggy, rust-colored thatch.

Breck looked a little disheveled tonight, as if he'd recently run into trouble.

It would be a lot more surprising if Breckinridge Wallace *hadn't* gotten into a scrape. The youngster attracted folks trying to kill him like a lodestone drew iron filings.

Maybe this would liven up the evening, Mike thought. He just hoped the tavern would still be standing when Breckinridge left.

Red Mike wasn't the only one who immediately took note of Breckinridge's entrance. At one of the tables in a rear corner, a young man in high-topped boots, whipcord trousers, and a corduroy jacket over a woolen shirt stood up and lifted a hand to catch Breck's attention. A grin stretched across his face. Brown-haired and well-built—although he would appear small next to Breck—he was the big redhead's best friend and trapping partner, Morgan Baxter.

Breckinridge spotted Morgan and started through the room toward the table. He ignored the glances of recognition—and sometimes resentment and dislike—directed at him by the tavern's other patrons.

Breckinridge had made some enemies in the past, but he didn't waste time worrying about that. No sense in dwelling on what had already happened when he never had to wait long for some new problem to crop up right in front of him.

Trouble had dogged Breckinridge's trail for a couple of years now. He had grown to manhood on a farm near Knoxville, Tennessee, in the shadow of the Blue Ridge Mountains, where he had spent most of his time hunting and fishing, to the great annoyance of his pa, who figured Breck should be plowing and planting, instead.

Things might have continued like that indefinitely if Breckinridge hadn't fallen in love with the wrong woman. That had led to violence and tragedy and forced Breck to leave home as a fugitive.

He had headed west, thinking that he might like to see the Rockies, but along the way he had encountered plenty more danger. He had made some friends, though, the best of whom was Morgan Baxter. An easterner from a wealthy family, Morgan had put that behind him to live the life of a fur trapper, in partnership with Breck.

A threat from Breckinridge's past had followed him west, though, and another beautiful woman had complicated things even more. Breck figured on marrying her, but first he had to return home to settle things at last with an old enemy.

He had taken his intended bride with him so she could meet his family. The plan was that they would rendezvous with Morgan in St. Louis in the spring and then head up the Missouri River again, bound for the bright and shining mountains that Breck now considered his true home. Morgan came out from behind the table to throw his arms around Breckinridge and repeatedly slap his old friend on the back.

"Damn it, you big galoot," he said, "if you're not a sight for sore eyes! I sort of expected you before now."

Breckinridge pounded Morgan on the back, too, then had to catch him to keep him from being knocked to the floor by the exuberant greeting. Breck took hold of Morgan's shoulders and set him upright, then said, "I ran into a little fracas on the way here tonight."

"Well, that doesn't surprise me, but I didn't mean tonight in particular. I just thought you and Dulcy might reach St. Louis before now." Morgan frowned slightly and leaned to the side to peer around

Breckinridge's looming form. "Where *is* Dulcy? Did you leave her at a hotel or a boardinghouse? I wouldn't blame you. Red Mike's is hardly the sort of place you'd want to bring a woman you plan on marrying!"

The grin that had appeared on Breckinridge's rugged face as he and Morgan exchanged greetings vanished in an instant.

"She ain't with me," he said.

Morgan's frown deepened. "What? She's all right, isn't she? That bullet wound she got—"

Breckinridge shook his head. "That healed up just fine. Last time I saw her, she was hale and hearty. It's just that her and me . . . well, we ain't gettin' married after all."

"Not getting married? Breck, what the hell? You love that girl, and I'm pretty sure she loves you, too."

"Maybe so, but that ain't all there is to it." Breckinridge pulled out one of the chairs at the table. "I don't plan on talkin' about it, Morgan, and I'd sure appreciate it if we could just leave things at that."

"Well . . . well, sure, Breck." Morgan was visibly flustered, but he shook his head and went on, "We're partners, and if that's the way you want it, that's the way it'll be." He went back to his chair. "We're still heading for the mountains, though, aren't we?"

"Derned right we are. You got an outfit put together for us?"

"I sure do. Two fine canoes that we can bring back down the river in the fall stacked high with pelts. I have plenty of supplies for us, too."

Breckinridge sat down and reached for the jug that sat on the table. "I sure appreciate you doin' all that. I reckon you probably had to pay more than your fair share for all of it, since I didn't have a whole heap of money to leave with you when I headed back to Tennessee."

Morgan waved a hand and said, "Don't worry about that. The money I inherited from my father would last us a long time even if we weren't making more trapping. But we had a decent season last year, and I'm sure this season will be even better. If we keep it up, you'll be a rich man one of these days, Breck."

Breckinridge shook his head. "I don't care a lick about bein' rich. I never seen anything to make me think a lot of money really makes folks happy. I just want to get back to the high country, breathe some of that air, and see an eagle soarin' way up in that blue sky, free as he can be."

He tipped the jug to his mouth and took a long swallow of the fiery liquor it held. The whiskey kindled a small fire in his belly, but other than that he didn't feel any effect from it. With his size, he could drink all night and not get drunk.

Morgan picked up the jug when Breckinridge slid it back across the table to him.

"To the high country," he said. He downed a slug of the liquor, too, coughed a little, and wiped the back of his hand across his mouth. "When do you want to get started?"

"The sooner the better," Breckinridge said.

The next morning, Breckinridge sold the horse he had ridden to St. Louis to the livery where he had stabled the animal. Morgan had rented some space in a shedlike warehouse near the waterfront for the canoes and supplies.

He and Breck carried the sturdy but lightweight craft to the river, one at a time, and tied them to one of the docks. Then they went back to fetch the supplies and toted them to the canoes. Sugar, flour, salt, coffee, and salted pork were the staples they were taking with them.

They also had some tobacco, although Breck didn't use the stuff and Morgan puffed on a pipe only occasionally. It was good for trading with friendly Indians, though.

They also had a few bolts of cloth and some assorted knickknacks and geegaws to use as trade goods. Many of the tribes were hostile to the white trappers coming into what they considered their lands, but often such wrath could be turned aside by something shiny or colorful.

And for the times when that didn't turn out to be the case, Breckinridge and Morgan were taking along plenty of powder and shot, too.

The previous summer they'd had a couple of partners, but this year it would be just the two of them. They wouldn't be able to take as many pelts that way, but they would have to split the profits only two ways.

Breckinridge intended to see to it that Morgan recouped every bit of his investment before they started divvying up the rest of the money. Morgan would probably argue about that, but Breck intended to stand firm.

Morgan hadn't mentioned Dulcy again. Breckinridge was thankful for that. He didn't want to dwell on what had happened between them, and it would be easier to put the whole thing behind him if he didn't have to go around explaining it.

He wanted to look forward instead of back.

As always, the riverfront was a busy place this morning. Dozens of steamboats were tied up at the wharves that stretched for more than a mile along the western bank.

Scores of burly dockworkers loaded the boats with cargo to be carried back downriver to New Orleans. Later in the day, northbound vessels would be arriving, and they would be heavily laden with cargo that had to be unloaded.

Breckinridge watched the men—a mixture of white, black, and even a few Indians—struggling with the crates and was glad he didn't have to work at a job like that.

The labor wouldn't bother him much; he was big and strong and could carry heavy loads all day without getting too tired. But being stuck there, going back and forth between the wharves and the decks of the riverboats all day, would drive him mad. Going back and forth, plowing the rows in a field, had affected him the same way. Something inside him had to be up and moving, but he wanted to actually get somewhere.

He and Morgan weren't the only ones preparing to head for the mountains. About fifty yards up the riverfront, a group of men in buckskins and homespun were loading supplies onto half a dozen canoes.

Some wore felt hats like Breckinridge and Morgan, while others sported coonskin caps or knit toques like northern backwoodsmen Breck had met in the Rockies. They were armed to the teeth with rifles, pistols, knives, and tomahawks. Trapping was dangerous work.

A man with a bushy black beard extending halfway down his chest seemed to be the leader. He wasn't very tall and gave the appearance of being almost as wide as he was high.

None of his bulk appeared to be fat, though. Thick slabs of muscles coated his arms, shoulders, chest, and back, and bulged against the tight buckskin shirt he wore. His stubby legs were as big around as tree trunks.

When he'd skinned the raccoon to make the cap he wore, he had left the creature's head on, so its snout pointed the same way as the bearded man's face was turned, and its dead eyes peered the same direction as its owner's deep-set, beady ones.

A steady stream of shouted orders and profanities made its way past the huge chaw of tobacco that distended the man's cheek. His voice was deep and powerful enough to carry up and down the riverfront, over the normal hubbub.

Breckinridge looked at the bearded man and asked Morgan, "Who's that big bag o' wind over yonder? I don't recollect seein' him last year."

"I think his name's Carnahan. I've heard a few men mention him. He's supposed to be quite the ring-tailed roarer." Morgan chuckled. "If you don't believe me, you can ask him. I'm sure he'd be happy to tell you."

"No, that's all right. I've never been that comfortable around fellas who like to beat their own drum. That's a pretty rough-lookin' bunch he's got with him."

"They look like cutthroats and brigands to me. I'd just as soon not run into them, once we're out there hundreds of miles from anywhere."

Breckinridge's broad shoulders rose and fell in a

shrug. "I never worried overmuch about such things. They leave me alone and I'll leave them alone."

"That's the way I'd like it, too."

Carnahan, if that was actually the bearded man's name, had climbed into one of the canoes, which were larger than the ones Breckinridge and Morgan were using. Each held three men, except a lone canoe with only two occupants.

A man came hurrying along the dock at the last minute and climbed into that canoe, filling out its complement. Carnahan yelled something at him, causing him to turn half around and lift a hand in acknowledgment of what sounded like a reprimand, although Breckinridge couldn't make out the words this time.

Breckinridge frowned at the sight of the new-comer. The man was dressed in black and had an old-fashioned tricorne hat on his head. His craggy, lantern-jawed face was made even more striking by the black patch over his left eye.

There was something else about him that had really caught Breck's attention, though, and he pondered it as he watched the men begin to paddle, sending the canoes arrowing out into the broad, sluggish stream.

The latecomer wore a scabbarded saber that had bounced against his thigh as he hurried along the dock.

Chapter 3

Breckinridge had no way of knowing if the man who had joined Carnahan's party at the last minute was the same one who had attacked him the previous night. Certainly, it was possible that more than one man in St. Louis carried a saber.

The man with the eye patch, though, looked like somebody who would try to rob and kill a stranger. And Morgan had said that Carnahan's men were cutthroats.

If the situation had been different, Breckinridge might have confronted the man and tried to find out the truth, just to satisfy his own curiosity, if for no other reason. But if his hunch was right, such a confrontation might have afforded him the opportunity to finish that fight, and he would have welcomed that.

The other canoes were well out of sight by the time Breckinridge and Morgan pushed off from the dock. Better to just forget about it, Breck told himself.

Anyway, they were all headed in the same direction. They were liable to encounter each other somewhere out there on the frontier. Breckinridge didn't think it was very likely he would forget a fella who looked like that and carried a sword.

For the moment he was content to be out on the great river, the muscles in his arms and shoulders working smoothly as he stroked with the paddle he held.

Switching from side to side with each stroke, he propelled the canoe against the current. Its sharply pointed prow cleaved the muddy water and sent it bubbling and splashing past the craft. A few yards to Breckinridge's right and slightly behind, Morgan paddled his canoe.

Time meant little in a situation like this. The hours drifted past, much like the landscape on both sides of the river. By midmorning, Breckinridge and Morgan had made the turn into the Missouri River, where the Big Muddy flowed into the Father of Waters.

The banks on both sides of the broad stream were low and covered with trees and brush. Away from the river, the terrain rolled away endlessly in gentle hills.

This was the heartland of the continent, and it beat in a slow, steady rhythm . . . just like the paddles wielded by the two men dipped into the water and propelled them onward.

Now and then they put in to shore and stopped to rest. Breckinridge didn't need the respites so much, but Morgan did. The months he had spent on the frontier had toughened him, especially compared to his previous soft existence back East, but he still didn't possess Breck's almost supernatural strength and stamina and never would.

During one of those breaks, Breckinridge could tell

that Morgan wanted to ask him about Dulcy. Morgan frowned, started several times to say something inconsequential without finishing, and seemed generally uncomfortable.

Breckinridge didn't want to talk about it, though, so after a few minutes he went to his canoe and got ready to shove it back into the water.

"Let's get goin'," he said. "Them beaver ain't gonna trap and skin themselves."

"That's true," Morgan said. He seemed almost relieved that he hadn't forced the issue. As they paddled back out into the river, Breckinridge hoped Morgan would just put the past completely out of his thoughts.

That's what he was trying to do.

They camped that night in what seemed like a vast, dark emptiness. Breckinridge knew that in another day or so, they would start seeing Indian villages along the river. Other trappers would be making their way toward the mountains, too, but on this night, no other campfires were in sight.

Breckinridge was a mite wary of kindling one himself, but Morgan wanted hot food and coffee. Anyway, they hadn't come very far from St. Louis. There shouldn't be any real danger along this stretch of the river.

He kept his rifle close at hand, regardless. The pistols behind his belt were loaded and ready to belch fire and leaden death.

Breckinridge's blue eyes narrowed in concentration and searched the darkness intently every time he heard the faintest sound. A man could grow weary of being so cautious all the time, he thought, but if he ever let his guard down, sure enough *that* would be the time when he needed to be most alert.

The prospect of death didn't bother him as long as he could go out fighting, as he knew he was meant to, but to be taken by surprise was unacceptable.

The night passed without incident, and the two canoes were back on the river when the sun came up the next morning.

Two more days went by in much the same fashion. On the fourth day after leaving St. Louis, Breckinridge spotted a tendril of gray smoke rising into the sky ahead of them and pointed it out to Morgan.

"Injun camp," he called across the water. "Ioways, most likely. You remember, we spent a night with one band of 'em last fall, somewhere upriver."

"That's right," Morgan replied. "Are we going to stop again?"

Breckinridge thought his friend sounded hopeful that they would stop and visit with the Indians. Three days of not seeing anyone else probably had Morgan a little restless. He was a fella who genuinely liked being around people.

For the most part, Breck could take 'em or leave 'em.

"We'll put in and visit for a spell," he said. "The Ioways are friendly folks. As I recollect, they've moved around a lot. Every time the whites start crowdin' in where they live, they up and move instead of fightin'. One of these days they're liable to have to do the same thing here."

"Do you really think civilization will expand past St. Louis? I had the idea that that might be the end of it, despite any talk about manifest destiny."

Breckinridge shook his head. "Reckon it's only a matter of time. One of these days, there'll be people shovin' in all over the dang country, until there won't be room for a fella to spit. I'm just glad I probably won't live to see it."

They came within sight of two dozen earthen lodges scattered on the left-hand bank of the river. The Ioway were horse Indians who did a certain amount of wandering and hunting, but they built semipermanent villages like this one, too, where some of them lived year-round and planted crops. When they were on the move, they lived in buffalo-hide tipis like their cousins farther west. In the villages, they dwelled in these moundlike lodges made of mud and brush.

As Breckinridge and Morgan angled their canoes toward the shore, dogs gathered and began to bark at them. That commotion drew a large number of the Indians, who stood watching the two white men paddle closer.

Most of the men had feathers sticking up at angles from their greased topknots. Colorful blankets were draped around their shoulders over their buckskins.

The women, squat and round-faced, chattered among themselves. Excited children whooped and hollered. Added to the dogs' barking, it made for quite a racket.

When the water was shallow enough, Breckinridge and Morgan stepped out of the canoes and dragged the craft halfway up onto the shore. Breck lifted his right hand, palm out, and said, "Howdy, folks."

This was a different village from the one where he and Morgan had stopped the previous fall. He didn't see anyone he recognized. He wondered if any of the Ioway spoke the white man's tongue.

That question was put to rest quickly by an older

man who stepped forward and said in good English, "Welcome to our home, my friends. I am Mohasca, the chief of these people."

"Breckinridge Wallace," Breck introduced himself. "This is Morgan Baxter."

Morgan nodded and said, "I'm mighty pleased to meet you, Chief."

Breckinridge heard some giggles coming from the young women of the tribe. He knew they were looking at Morgan and whispering to each other about him. Gals always seemed to think he was a right handsome fella.

Most females didn't react the same way to him. Other than his red hair and blue eyes, he bore a distinct resemblance to a grizzly bear, or at least he figured that was so.

"You are on your way to the Shining Mountains?" Mohasca asked.

"That's right," Breckinridge said. "We're fur trappers and traders."

The chief still looked solemn, but Breckinridge thought he saw amusement twinkling in the man's dark eyes.

"What will you do when the beaver are gone?"

"Oh, that day won't ever come," Morgan said. "There are millions and millions of them up in the mountains."

"There is an end to everything," Mohasca said. "But come, visit with us. We will smoke and eat and talk."

The crowd parted when Mohasca turned and walked toward the largest of the lodges, accompanied by the rest of the older men and several young, brawnier warriors. Breckinridge and Morgan fell in with them.

Some of the women reached out and poked fingers against Breckinridge and Morgan as they walked by, then laughed. Breck grinned back at them. He knew they didn't mean any harm.

"A friendly bunch," Morgan commented quietly.

"Yep. Too bad bein' friendly hasn't done much for 'em except to make certain they have to move on every few years."

That was a problem he couldn't solve, Breckinridge mused. He had done some Indian fighting in his life and expected to have to do more before he crossed the divide. But he would just as soon get along with them as much as he could.

The two visitors and the group of elders sat on buffalo robes around the fire in the middle of the lodge. Smoke from the crackling, burning wood drifted through the hole in the center of the roof above them.

They passed around a pipe. Breckinridge puffed on it when his time came, although he didn't really care for it. When they were done with that, women brought bowls of thick stew that he liked better.

While they were eating, Breckinridge asked, "Are we the first white men who have stopped here this season?"

"Yes," Mohasca replied. "Although a group of them camped across the river last night."

"Is that so? How many?"

"Six canoes. Three men in each canoe."

Carnahan's bunch, Breckinridge thought.

As if to confirm that, Mohasca went on, "Their chief was a little man with a long beard, like the ones who dwell underneath the earth."

Breckinridge wasn't sure what he meant by that,

but Morgan said, "A dwarf, like the ones in the old folktales from Europe. As short and wide as Carnahan is, with that beard, I can understand that."

"I do not know what you mean, my friend, but their chief did look like that. You know these men?"

Mohasca's lips pursed a little, as if his future attitude toward Breckinridge and Morgan might depend on their answer.

"We know who they are," Breckinridge said. "Saw them back in St. Louis. They ain't friends of ours."

"This is good. They were very loud. We could hear them all the way across the water." Mohasca's wrinkled face creased even more in a stern frown. "They spoke ugly things. I was glad that few of my people have an understanding of the white man's tongue. We seek no trouble, but if our young men had known what was being said about our women, they might have wanted to cross the river and fight."

"I'm mighty sorry, Chief. We won't cause you any problems like that."

"No, I can tell that you are decent young men who will not abuse my people. You are welcome to spend the night in the village of the Ioway."

Breckinridge glanced at Morgan. A couple hours of daylight remained. They could get a few more miles upstream if they pushed on after finishing the meal with their hosts.

But Breckinridge could tell Morgan wanted to stay, and what difference would a couple of hours make, anyway?

"We're obliged to you for the hospitality, Chief," Breckinridge said, "and we'll sure take you up on it."

Chapter 4

Some of the tribes were known to provide visitors with female companionship to warm their robes at night, but the Ioway weren't *that* hospitable.

Actually, Breckinridge was just fine with that development, although he suspected Morgan might have been a tad disappointed. Breck thought it was unlikely that he had sworn off women for good, but right now he didn't need any of them complicating his life, even temporarily.

He and Morgan talked long into the night with Mohasca and the other elders. The chief translated for those who didn't speak English, which was most of them. During the conversation, Mohasca explained that he had learned the language from a black robe—a Jesuit priest—who had come down the Mississippi River from Canada with a party of French trappers some forty years earlier. The padre had spoken not only French but also English and Spanish and had taught all three languages to the young boy, who was eager to learn. In those days, the Ioway had lived far to the east of their current hunting grounds, on the other side of the great river.

Finally, an older woman who Breckinridge figured was one of the chief's wives had led the two white men to one of the smaller lodges. A fire had been built and buffalo robes were laid out around it. Breck and Morgan turned in as the flames burned down to embers.

Breckinridge wasn't sure how long he had been asleep when something woke him. As always, he was awake instantly, fully alert, ready for trouble if any threatened.

But as he lay there with his eyes open, he didn't hear anything except Morgan's deep, regular breathing on the other side of the fire's faintly glowing remains. He looked around the lodge's dimly lit interior. Nothing was moving or out of place. Breck's rifle, pistols, knife, powder horn, shot pouch, hat, and boots were right beside him.

He stiffened as he caught the sound of a quiet cry from somewhere outside. It lasted only a second and then cut off abruptly, as if someone had clapped a hand over the mouth from which the outcry issued.

The sound came from a woman; Breckinridge was sure of that. But it didn't necessarily *mean* anything. Some wife could have been arguing with her husband. The noise might have even been an outburst of passion, although that wasn't the way it had sounded to Breck.

But whatever was going on, it was none of his business, and he was trying to convince himself to roll over and go back to sleep when a dog suddenly began barking angrily, then yelped and fell silent.

That wasn't right, and every instinct in Breckinridge's body told him so.

He slid out of the robes and reached for his boots.

Without making any noise, he pulled them on and then stood up. He picked up the pistols and the sheathed knife and shoved them behind his belt. Leaving everything else where it was, he went to the entrance and eased aside the deer-hide flap that covered the opening.

A few desultory barks came from other dogs in the village, but none of them seemed really upset about anything. Maybe he was jumping to conclusions, Breckinridge told himself.

Then he heard the brush rustle a little, not far from the lodge he and Morgan shared, which was on the edge of the village away from the river. The growth in that direction was thick. It would be difficult to move through there without making some sort of racket.

It would be even harder to do so if you were dragging a prisoner along, Breckinridge thought.

Now he was *really* jumping to conclusions. A muffled cry, a bark, a yelp . . . those things didn't add up to a woman being kidnapped.

But they didn't rule out the possibility, either. Breckinridge knew he had to make sure nothing bad was going on. The Ioway had extended their hospitality to him and Morgan. He owed them that much.

He glanced over his shoulder at the vague shape Morgan made under the buffalo robe and thought about waking his friend. Since he wasn't certain about what was going on, he decided to let Morgan sleep. He didn't expect to run into anything he couldn't handle himself.

Moving with uncanny stealth for such a big man, Breckinridge drifted out of the lodge and let the flap fall closed behind him. He cat-footed his way to the brush and glided into it.

He was good in the darkness and was able to move fairly swiftly without making much noise. Every minute or so he stopped briefly to listen. The first couple of times he didn't hear anything, but the third time, the crackle of branches again came to his ears, followed by something unmistakable.

A curse, grated softly in a low, guttural voice. It came from a white man, no doubt about that.

Another voice hissed what sounded like a command, although Breckinridge couldn't make out the words. He went forward again, moving like a ghost.

The village was at least a hundred yards behind him now, maybe more. Whomever he was following must have believed they'd put enough distance between themselves and the lodges that they didn't have to be as careful. They started making more noise as they pushed through the brush.

Once Breckinridge heard a soft little cry of pain or fear—or both—but again it was quickly stifled. Two men, at least, and they had a prisoner.

Could some of Carnahan's bunch have doubled back to steal a woman from the Ioway village? That seemed to be the likeliest explanation. From what Breckinridge had seen of the men, he wouldn't put much of anything past most of them.

Too many trappers seemed to regard Indians as less than human. It wouldn't bother them to kidnap an Ioway woman so they could have their sport with her and then eventually, when they tired of her, kill her or abandon her in the wilderness. They might even plan on trading her as a slave to some other tribe.

Those thoughts filled Breckinridge with fury. He started moving faster in an attempt to catch up, then when he stopped to listen again and heard nothing but a somehow ominous silence, he realized he might have made a mistake.

The tiny snap of a branch was the only warning he had. He turned as a dark shape hurtled at him from behind. In that split second, he knew the men he was following had heard him, and at least one of them had stopped to lie in wait for him.

It was too dark for anything except instinct to guide him. He twisted aside and felt something sharp rake along his side, leaving behind a fiery line of pain. Breckinridge knew he had just been cut by a knife, and whoever was wielding the blade had intended to plunge it into his back.

He struck out straight ahead with his right fist, putting all the massive strength of his arm and shoulders into it. The pile-driver blow landed solidly against what felt like a man's chest.

The unseen attacker grunted and fell back. Breckinridge whipped his own knife from its sheath and slashed the shadows in front of him. The blade bit into flesh. A man loosed a thin cry of pain and then sobbed and cursed.

"He cut me, Harlan!" the wounded man gasped. "Get the damn redskin!"

So they thought one of the Indians had followed them from the village. Breckinridge didn't see any reason to disabuse them of the notion.

He turned and ducked low as footsteps rushed at him from behind. The second man blundered into him and fell right over him. Breck straightened, picking up the man and flinging him away like a rag doll. The man yelled until flying flesh and bone collided with something, a tree trunk, by the sound of it. That shut him up in a hurry.

Then a third man yelled in pain and exclaimed, "The bitch bit me!" A blow thudded. Breckinridge saw red, knowing that the third man had just struck the female captive.

He bellowed his rage, since there was no longer any need for stealth, and shoved the knife back in its sheath. Guided by the sounds of a struggle, he charged blindly and hoped he wouldn't bash his brains out against a tree.

Instead he crashed into two wrestling figures. The impact was enough to knock them apart. Breckinridge flailed around until he caught hold of somebody's throat with his left hand. A bristly beard tickled the back of his hand, so he knew he hadn't grabbed the woman. Aiming by that, he swung a huge fist that slammed into the face of the man he grappled with.

Breckinridge felt the satisfying crunch of cartilage when the blow landed and knew that he had just flattened the varmint's nose. Maintaining his hold on the man's neck, he bent and grabbed a thigh.

With only a slight grunt of effort, he heaved the struggling man into the air, lifted him high, and tossed him into the trees with enough force to break bones.

"That . . . that ain't a Injun!" a man gasped somewhere nearby. "It's a monster!"

"Forget about the squaw!" another man said. "Let's get outta here!"

Breckinridge stood there, fists clenched and poised to strike again, but no one else came near him. Instead he heard the violent rustling of several men fleeing through the brush.

From the other direction, back toward the Ioway village, came the sounds of men heading this way to find out what all the shouting was about. When his temper was up, Breckinridge could be a mite loud.

Somewhere close by, a woman spoke tentatively in the Ioway tongue. Breckinridge didn't understand but a few words of it and couldn't make out what she was saying.

She probably wouldn't understand him, either, he thought, but he said, "It's all right now, ma'am. I think them low-down skunks have done took off for the tall and uncut."

She moved closer to him, then took him by surprise by throwing her arms around him and hugging him tightly.

Awkwardly, Breckinridge rested a hand on the back of the buckskin dress she wore and then patted it a couple of times. She began to sob. From the feel of her, she was a little bit of a thing and didn't quite come up to the middle of his chest. She seemed to be built sturdy, though.

"Here, now," Breckinridge said. "It's all right. You ain't got nothin' else to be scared of."

Light began to flicker in the woods. Breckinridge looked around and saw that one of the men approaching from the village held a torch.

To make sure none of them took him for a kidnapper and launched arrows at him, he called out, "Chief Mohasca, over here! It's Breckinridge Wallace. Everything's all right."

"Breck!" That startled exclamation came from Morgan. "What's going on?"

The red glare from the burning brand fell over Breckinridge and the young Ioway woman who still clung to him. A dozen warriors from the village, along with Morgan and Chief Mohasca, gathered around them. Breck saw the grim faces of the men and the way they held their bows ready with arrows nocked and was glad he had called out.

The woman finally let go of Breckinridge and rushed over to hug Mohasca and chatter at him.

Morgan said, "I knew when there was a commotion and I woke up to find you gone, that you'd be right in the middle of whatever the trouble was, Breck. Then I heard what sounded like a mad bull out here and I was sure of it."

"Some fellas snuck into the village and grabbed that gal," Breckinridge said. "I don't know how many there was—three or four, I reckon. I had a hunch somethin' was up, followed 'em, and when I knew for certain, I laid into 'em."

"At odds of three or four to one," Morgan said.

Breckinridge shrugged. "You know me, Morgan. When I'm riled up, I never stop to think about things like that."

"And we are very grateful that you do not, friend Breckinridge," Mohasca said. He turned the still-shaken young woman over to some of the other men so they could take her back to the village. "That is my brother's daughter. Those men intended to treat her very badly."

"No doubt about that. I'm glad I could help."

Morgan said, "Do you figure the bastards came from Carnahan's party?"

"That's the first thing I thought," Breckinridge said. "Some of 'em could've doubled back easy enough and then caught up to the rest of the bunch later. But I don't know because I never really got a good look at 'em."

"Whoever they were," Mohasca said, "they will not trouble us again. Not after the punishment you dealt to them."

"I hope that's true," Breckinridge said. He felt a warm, sticky wetness on his left side and put his hand to it, remembering now that he had been wounded during the fight. It had completely slipped his mind. "Speakin' of punishment, I seem to be bleedin' pretty good here . . ."

Chapter 5

The young woman was called Sunflower, and when a smile wreathed her round face, she was as bright and pretty as her namesake.

She fussed mightily over Breckinridge when they all got back to the village and insisted on being the one to clean the knife slash in his side and apply a poultice of herbs to it. He had to take off his shirt for her to do that, of course, and while she was busy with the chore her hands kept straying up to brush against his broad, muscular chest.

On the other side of the fire that had been built up in the lodge, Morgan tried not to grin as he said, "I've got a hunch you could just stay right here and become a member of the Ioway tribe if you wanted to, Breck. You've got yourself a ready-made wife right there and everything."

"And let you go on to the mountains by yourself? You wouldn't last a week."

Sunflower said something Breckinridge couldn't make out, but her shy smile and coy, downcast gaze told him she was declaring something along the same lines Morgan had hinted at.

The last thing Breckinridge wanted right now was a wife. That feeling had nothing to do with the fact that she was an Indian. If he'd been in the market for a bride, Sunflower would have made a good one.

Since he couldn't think of anything to say and she wouldn't have understood him anyway, he just sat there in stolid silence while she placed a piece of deer hide over the poultice and tied it in place with several rawhide strips.

Breckinridge flexed his left arm, then smiled and nodded at Sunflower. Despite being messy, the wound wasn't deep and the poultice had already taken some of the sting out of it. Breck was confident it would heal just fine and leave nothing but yet another scar on his body, which was already considerably marked up despite his young age.

"You done a mighty fine job," he told Sunflower. "I'm sure obliged to you."

Sunflower said something, then glanced across the fire at Morgan. She reached up and started unlacing the rawhide that held her dress closed at the throat.

"Reckon I ought to go find somewhere else to finish my night's sleep," Morgan said as he started to get up. "Although I'm not sure Sunflower would mind all that much if I stayed."

"Damn it!" Breckinridge said as he reached out to take hold of Sunflower's wrists and stop what she was doing. "Morgan, sit yourself back down." Looking at the young woman, he shook his head and continued, "You don't have to do that. I appreciate you patchin' me up, but that's plenty. We're all square, understand? You don't need to do nothin' else."

She said something in the Ioway tongue, then added tentatively, "Breck . . . in . . . ridge." Her lower lip started to quiver.

Morgan fell over on his side on the buffalo robes. His body shook with suppressed laughter.

"Blast it, I'll come over there and wallop you," Breckinridge said through clenched teeth. He managed to put a smile on his face as he moved his hands from Sunflower's wrists to her shoulders. He held her as he leaned forward and planted a chaste kiss on her forehead, the same way he would have kissed a little sister. He hoped she would get the message from that.

Judging by the sudden flare of anger in her dark eyes, she did. She let out a little snort, shrugged his hands off her shoulders, and backed away, then stood up. She barked something at him and gestured toward the wound in his side.

Breckinridge nodded and said, "I'll be careful with it, I sure will. And thank you again for takin' care of me."

Sunflower sniffed, then turned to leave the lodge. She flung the deer-hide flap closed behind her with enough force that if it had been a door, it would have slammed.

When she was gone, Morgan let out a whoop of laughter, then sat up, controlled himself, and said, "I reckon it's a good thing we'll be moving on in the morning. I'm not sure how friendly the Ioway will be toward us now that you've turned down that expression of Sunflower's gratitude."

"Aw, go to hell," Breckinridge muttered. He picked up his buckskin shirt from where it lay beside him and frowned at the rip and the bloodstain that the knife had left behind. "She probably wouldn't be interested in mendin' this shirt and tryin' to wash some of the blood outta it, would she?"

Morgan started laughing and fell over again.

The dog that had tried to warn the village about the kidnappers the night before had been knocked out by a butt stroke from a rifle but seemed to be fine the next morning. Breckinridge was glad of that. He had always liked dogs.

Mohasca told him about that when the chief showed up at the lodge, along with a couple of older women who brought breakfast for Breckinridge and Morgan. One of the women also changed the poultice on Breck's side and bound it up again. There was no sign of Sunflower, so Breck figured she didn't want to see him anymore.

"You will go on to the mountains this morning?" Mohasca asked as he sat cross-legged on one of the robes.

"We plan on startin' in that direction," Breckinridge replied. "It'll be a few weeks before we get there, though."

"Sunflower was very grateful to you for saving her from those evil men."

"Yeah, I, uh, know she was," Breckinridge said. He looked down at the fire. "I tried to make her understand I was glad to do it and that she didn't owe me nothin' in return."

"She does not agree." Mohasca cocked his head a little to the side. "But considering everything, it is good that you and your friend will be leaving soon. It would cause unhappiness for you to remain for very long."

"Well, we sure ain't plannin' to cause anybody to be unhappy, are we, Morgan?"

"No, we never intended to do anything but spend the night, anyway," Morgan said. "We thank you for making us welcome, Chief."

"The spirits brought you here to save Sunflower," Mohasca said solemnly. "Now they call you on to the Shining Mountains."

"They sure do," Breckinridge agreed. "That's where our destiny is waitin' for us."

A little later, as they were preparing to leave, Morgan said quietly, "Destiny? That's a pretty strong word for a fur trapping expedition, isn't it?"

"You never know what's waitin' for you on the other side of the hill until you go and see for yourself," Breckinridge said.

As they were about to get into their canoes, many of the village's inhabitants gathered on the shore to watch the departure. Mohasca stepped out of the crowd and said to the two white men, "Those evil men are probably ahead of you on the river. You would be wise to watch for them."

"They won't know me and Morgan had anything to do with what happened," Breckinridge said. "I don't reckon they got any better look at me than I did at them."

His size might give him away, though, he thought. After all, one of them *had* called him a monster.

"Men such as those have a dark shadow in their hearts," Mohasca said. "They need no reason to do evil other than the fact that they can."

Breckinridge nodded and said, "Reckon you're

right about that. We'll keep our eyes open for 'em, won't we, Morgan?"

"Of course," Morgan said. "Breck's always alert for trouble." He chuckled. "But it seems to find him anyway."

They pushed the canoes out until the craft were floating, then climbed in and took up the paddles. As they stroked away from the shore, a commotion broke out among the watching Ioway. The crowd parted and Sunflower broke through. She stood at the edge of the water and called after Breckinridge and Morgan. When Breck looked back, she smiled and waved.

"Appears that she forgives you," Morgan commented from the other canoe.

"And I'm glad of it," Breckinridge said as he returned the wave. "No need for any hard feelin's."

"What about those fellows who tried to kidnap her?"

Breckinridge's face hardened as he turned forward again and stroked away from the village. "Now, them varmints, I might have a grudge against," he said.

The journey upriver continued. As Breckinridge expected, within a few days the wound in his side was almost completely healed. He had been blessed with great recuperative powers to go along with his strength.

Sometimes he wondered if his physical prowess meant that, to balance things out, he had gotten less than his fair share of thinking ability. But then he remembered that he could read and write and cipher fairly well, while a lot of folks couldn't. He might not have a lot in the way of book learning, but he figured he wasn't exactly a fool, neither.

They passed other Ioway villages but didn't stop at any of them. Leaving that territory behind, they traveled through the lands of the Omaha, the Pawnee, and the Ponca, tribes that were peaceful enough as long as no one threatened them.

Breckinridge and Morgan stuck to the river, making camp on its banks when they stopped at night and staying away from the Indian villages. They even paddled out to the center of the broad stream whenever they passed one of the collections of lodges or tipis.

They hadn't seen any other white men, which came as a bit of a surprise to Breckinridge. Of course, it was still early in the season, he reminded himself. He and Morgan had been among the first trappers to leave St. Louis and head for the Rockies. There would be hundreds more coming upriver behind them.

One evening as they sat next to their small campfire, Breckinridge said, "We'll be gettin' into Sioux country in the next day or two. Be best if we stop early, get some hot food and coffee in us, then push on for a spell and make cold camps. I'd just as soon not show a light at night."

"They're hostile?" Morgan asked.

"More so than the tribes downriver. Of course, you can't never tell what a Injun's gonna do. He might act friendly as can be one day and try to lift your hair the next."

Morgan's eyes widened. "They take scalps?"

"From what I hear, they've started to. Didn't used to be that way. I reckon they picked up the habit from them damn Frenchies who come down from Canada. Heard a fella back in St. Louis talkin' about how the

French trappers put out a bounty on Injun scalps. I can believe it."

"I'm kind of attached to my hair. If you think cold camps are best, that's what we'll do."

The terrain had gotten a bit more rugged, the hills to the west more pronounced. The next day, as Breckinridge and Morgan paddled along, Breck called to his friend, "Look over yonder. On top of that hill about five hundred yards away."

"I don't see anything," Morgan said. "You have sharper eyes than I do. What is it?"

"Couple of fellas on horseback, just sittin' there and lookin' in this direction."

Morgan lifted his paddle out of the water and paused in his stroke. "Sioux?"

Breckinridge did likewise and said, "Can't think of nobody else it could be. Best go back to paddlin'. We don't want 'em knowin' that we saw 'em."

The two men resumed their powerful strokes and sent the canoes forward against the current. Morgan said, "Do you think they're going to attack us?"

"I ain't spent enough time out here to be sure about things like that. I'm hopin' they're just curious. We'll keep on bein' careful. Might ought to start takin' turns standin' guard at night."

"That sounds like a good idea to me," Morgan said. "I don't like the idea of being watched."

"Better than bein' shot at," Breckinridge said.

They stopped in the late afternoon, made a tiny, almost smokeless fire from buffalo chips, and had a brief meal before starting upriver again. After they had paddled for a couple of miles, Breckinridge started looking for a good place to make camp. He hadn't found one yet when he suddenly lifted his head and gazed intently ahead of them.

Morgan saw the reaction and said, "What is it?"

"Listen," Breckinridge said. "Hear it?"

From somewhere upriver came the sharp rattle of gunfire.

Chapter 6

For a moment the two men sat there with the current pushing the canoes slightly downstream. Morgan asked, "Are we going to get mixed up in this, Breck?"

"I don't reckon we've got much choice," Breckinridge replied. "If we were in a tight spot, we'd want somebody to come along and give us a hand."

"We don't know anything about what's going on up there."

A fighting grin flashed across Breckinridge's face. "Like I said back in that Ioway village, the only way to find out is to go and see."

He dug his paddle into the water and sent the canoe ahead again. A few yards away, Morgan sighed and did likewise.

Up ahead, the river made a long, lazy curve to the left. As Breckinridge and Morgan drew closer to it, Breck could tell the shots came from the other side of the bend. He pointed to some trees that grew down close to the water. Shadows were already starting to gather underneath them.

"Let's put in to shore over yonder and go ahead on foot," he told Morgan as he angled his canoe toward the trees. "If we go paddlin' around that bend, we'll be out in the open where we'd be spotted."

Morgan nodded his agreement and followed Breckinridge toward the tree-lined bank.

It took only a few minutes for them to reach the edge of the river. They got out, boots splashing in the shallow water, and hauled the canoes up onto the bank. Then, taking their rifles, they trotted through the grove.

Breckinridge led the way, weaving around tree trunks. When he approached the edge of the growth, he halted and dropped to one knee, staying in the shadows. Morgan came up on his right and knelt behind one of the trees.

"Can you tell what's going on?" he asked in a whisper.

Breckinridge's eyes scanned the scene before him. The ground sloped gently to a wide, parklike area along the river before rising again to a tree-covered hill. Off to the left, a thick stand of brush blocked the end of that swale.

To the right lay a large campfire. Six canoes were pulled up on the bank near it. That would have been enough to identify Carnahan's party, even if Breck hadn't spotted the squat, bearded leader stretched out in a shallow depression, aiming a rifle at the brush. Flame belched from the weapon's muzzle as Jud Carnahan fired.

The rest of the men were scattered around the

camp, trying to take advantage of whatever meager cover they could find. A few lay among the canoes, for what little good that would do. The thin hulls of the craft wouldn't stop a rifle ball.

Luckily for them, the attackers hidden in the brush didn't seem to have any rifles, Breckinridge realized after watching the battle for a moment. Instead, arrows flew through the fading light, arching in to land among the besieged trappers. Breck couldn't tell if any of the men had been hit yet.

"Looks like Carnahan and his bunch run smack-dab into an ambush," Breckinridge said.

"Why don't they just get in their canoes and push off?" Morgan asked. "They could get far enough out in the river that arrows wouldn't reach them."

"Because the damn fools unloaded a goodly portion of their supplies before the Injuns jumped 'em," Breckinridge said as he nodded to the crates and sacks sitting around the camp. "If they pull out, the Sioux will get their hands on those goods. What they can't use themselves, they'll destroy so the trappers can't use 'em."

"And Carnahan doesn't want to push on to the Rockies without provisions. Well, I guess that makes sense. Like you said, though, it was foolish of them not to just take what they needed out of the canoes and leave the rest."

"This fella Carnahan must be a greenhorn," Breckinridge speculated. "Might be his first trip west. A fella can be plenty tough back East and not know the first blessed thing about survivin' out here on the frontier."

"I wasn't the least bit tough, and I've survived out here."

"That's because you and me sorta learned together," Breckinridge said with a grin. "Now, let's figure out what we're gonna do."

"I'd say we can go back to our canoes, paddle all the way over to the other side of the river, and keep going. Carnahan's party is large and well armed. That's probably why they thought they could build such a big campfire and get away with it. They weren't worried about drawing the attention of the Indians."

"You mean we ought to leave 'em to fight their own way outta this mess?"

"Some of them are the ones who tried to kidnap Sunflower!"

"We don't know that for sure," Breckinridge said. "Even if that's true, the others might not've known anything about it."

"You saw them back in St. Louis. Did any of them look innocent to you?"

Morgan had a point. Breckinridge hadn't liked the look of the men with Carnahan, especially that fella with the saber. All of them had looked perfectly capable of stealing an Indian woman away from her people and having their brutal way with her.

But Breck and Morgan didn't *know*. Breckinridge had been forced to go on the run because he'd been blamed for something he hadn't done. It stuck in his craw to turn the other way and let somebody come to grief when they might be blameless in this instance— no matter how much of a sorry son of a bitch they might have been otherwise.

Anyway, he'd always had a hard time turning his back on a fight.

"Here's what we're gonna do," he said. "We're gonna work our way west through these woods until we can get behind those Injuns and come in through the brush. We'll set up a big ruckus, and maybe they'll think they're caught between two forces and will light a shuck outta there."

"Do you really think that'll work?" Morgan asked.

"Well, we'll probably have to kill a few of 'em. But there's at least a chance we can spook 'em into runnin'. As long as they ain't cornered, Injuns won't fight when the odds are against 'em. They'd rather call it a day and come back to fight some other time." Breckinridge glanced at the sky. "There ain't a whole lot of light left, neither, and they don't like to fight in the dark. Some folks'll tell you they *won't* fight at night, which is a damn lie, but they don't cotton to it much."

Morgan sighed and said, "All right, you've persuaded me. I just hope we're not making a huge mistake."

"Me, too," Breckinridge said. "If you want, you can go back to the canoes and wait for me. If I don't come back after a while, you can head on without me."

"Blast it, Breck, you know me better than that!"

"Yeah, I reckon I do," Breckinridge said. "Come on."

They stole through the grove of trees, staying deep enough that the gathering shadows concealed them. The Indians in the brush probably weren't paying any attention in this direction, anyway. Their wrath was focused on the group of trappers who had made camp beside the river.

After they had gone a quarter of a mile, Breckinridge motioned to Morgan. In some open ground behind the brush thicket, a couple of young braves stood holding the woven bridles of a dozen ponies.

They were looking toward the battle, and in their excitement, they weren't aware of anything else going on around them. Breck and Morgan could have killed both of them with rifle shots before the Sioux youth knew what had happened. Morgan hefted his weapon and gave Breck an inquiring look. Breck thought about it for a second, then shook his head. He gestured for Morgan to follow and burst out of the trees, charging toward the two youngsters holding the horses.

The white men had to cross about thirty yards to reach the two Sioux. Breckinridge hoped to cover most of that distance before the horse-holders heard him and Morgan coming.

However, they had made it only halfway before one of the young men glanced over his shoulder. Breckinridge saw the Indian's eyes widen in surprise. He let out a startled yelp to his companion. Both of them swung around to meet this unexpected threat.

Unfortunately for them, they hesitated in taking action, evidently unsure whether to let go of the ponies' leads and grab for their bows. That gave Breckinridge the time he needed to take two more huge bounds. He dropped his rifle, spread his arms wide, and launched himself in a diving tackle that swept both young men off their feet. As they all sprawled on the ground, Breck grabbed both Indians by the throat and banged their heads together hard enough to knock them out.

The ponies, loose now and spooked by the commotion, stampeded, scattering in several different directions as they charged away.

Morgan had paused to pick up Breckinridge's rifle

and now thrust it back into his friend's hands as Breck got to his feet. "The rest of them will have heard those horses take off," Morgan said. "Some of them will come to see what happened."

"Let's go meet 'em," Breckinridge said. He plunged into the brush with Morgan right behind him.

Breckinridge had gone only a few feet when a burly Sioux painted for war loomed up in front of him. The man yelled angrily and swung a tomahawk at Breck's head. Breck ducked under the weapon and lashed out with his rifle stock as he came up. The brass butt plate slammed into the Indian's jaw. Breck both heard and felt bone shatter under the powerful blow. The warrior dropped, out cold.

An arrow whipped past his left ear. Breckinridge turned and saw a painted savage nocking another missile. Before the Indian could draw the bow back and loose the arrow, Breck shot him in the chest with the rifle. The man flew backward as the heavy lead ball drove into his body.

Morgan's rifle blasted as well, but Breckinridge didn't have time to see how his friend was doing. Two more warriors appeared and charged him. One had an arrow ready and fired it as he ran. Breck reacted instinctively and with blinding speed, sweeping the rifle barrel around in time to hit the flying shaft and deflect it.

Then Breckinridge dropped the rifle and yanked out both pistols. They boomed in unison and the powerful charge in each made it kick against his strong grip. The Sioux tumbled off their feet as the balls tore through them.

Breckinridge heard several angry yips from the

Indians. He let out a bellow of his own and followed it by shouting, "Come on, boys! Let's get 'em!" He ran back and forth, crashing around in the brush so much that he sounded like a dozen men. At least, that was the impression he was trying to create.

It must have worked. No one else attacked him or Morgan, who appeared at Breckinridge's side and exclaimed, "I think they're running away!"

"That was the idea," Breckinridge said. He shoved the pistols behind his belt again, picked up his rifle, and reloaded it with swift, practiced efficiency. Then he led the way to the rear edge of the thicket and looked out to see half a dozen buckskin-clad figures running away from the river. The two youngsters he had knocked out were gone, so he figured they had regained consciousness and fled with the others. He asked Morgan, "How many of 'em did you get?"

"Just one. What about you?"

"Three, I reckon. And busted another one's jaw. I didn't see him layin' where I knocked him down, though, so he must've got up and took off for the tall and uncut with the others."

"That's about right. You're at least four times as dangerous as me, Breck."

"I ain't keepin' score," Breckinridge said. "Do we head back to our canoes, or you reckon we ought to go talk to Carnahan and his bunch?"

"They're bound to be curious about who pulled their fat out of the fire," Morgan said. "If we don't want to have to deal with them, we'd best be moving."

That was Breckinridge's opinion, too. They turned to head toward the trees and work their way back through the growth to where they had left the canoes, but before they could do so, several men stepped out of the brush and pointed rifles at them.

"Stand right where you are," one of the men ordered in a harsh voice.

Those tones sounded a little familiar to Breckinridge, so when he looked around, he wasn't particularly surprised.

The man who had just issued the command was the rawboned son of a bitch with the eye patch and the saber, which rested in a scabbard hung from his belt. Now he held a rifle, as well. That weapon was trained on Breckinridge's chest.

Chapter 7

"Take it easy, fellas," Breckinridge said. "In case you hadn't noticed, I reckon we're all on the same side."

The rifle pointed at him didn't budge. The man with the eye patch said, "How do we know that? It could have been you two shooting those arrows at us. A white man can pull a bow the same as a savage. English longbowmen changed history at the battle of Agincourt."

"I wasn't there, so I'll have to take your word for it."

One of the other men called, "Hey, Ralston, got a couple of dead redskins over here."

"And here's another one," a second man added. "Looks like he's been shot."

The man with the eye patch finally lowered his rifle slightly. "You two did that?" he asked.

"We did," Morgan said. "We saw some fellow trappers in trouble and stepped in to help."

"How many of them were there?"

"Counted a dozen ponies," Breckinridge said.

"How did the two of you manage to defeat a dozen men?"

"We took 'em by surprise. Anyway, we didn't kill 'em all, just made 'em believe they was trapped in a crossfire, so they'd skedaddle." Breckinridge shrugged. "Seems to have worked."

The man pointed his rifle at the ground. "Where are the horses?"

"They got scattered when we jumped the young fellas holdin' 'em."

One of the men asked, "Why are you actin' so suspicious, Ralston? These gents saved our hides, seems to me, like."

Ralston frowned. "We would have been all right without their help. We had the savages outnumbered, remember? And they were armed with bows and arrows. They wouldn't have been able to overcome our rifles."

"Mebbe so, but we might've lost a man or two first, since they had good cover and we didn't. We couldn't even see what we was shootin' at. I reckon we ought to be obliged to . . . ?"

The man who spoke looked at Breckinridge and Morgan and raised his eyebrows quizzically.

"Breckinridge Wallace," Breck introduced himself. "This here is my partner, Morgan Baxter."

"Name's Al Nusser," said the man who had defended them to Ralston. He was stocky, dressed in buckskin trousers, a homespun shirt, and a coonskin cap. Brown whiskers stuck out on his jaw like the bristles of a brush. He jerked a thumb at his companions and went on, "Bart Coogan, Fred Norton, Deke Simms, and Gordie Ralston."

"That's Major Gordon Ralston," the man with the eye patch snapped.

After listening to the man talk for the past few

minutes, Breckinridge was convinced that Ralston had been one of the would-be thieves back in St. Louis. Hearing him called Gordie just now confirmed that. One of the other robbers had called out that name in the dark street near Red Mike's.

Breckinridge didn't let on about that. He didn't see any point in revealing that he knew what Ralston had done—or tried to do. He hadn't told Morgan about the incident. Best just to let it stay in the past.

He didn't intend for the two of them to spend much time with Carnahan's bunch, anyway.

"You ain't an officer anymore, Ralston," Nusser said. Evidently there was little or no love lost between the two men. "Your army days are behind you."

"Jud made me his second-in-command," Ralston protested.

"Still don't make you a major anymore. But shoot, it ain't any o' my business. You can call yourself the Queen of the May as far as I'm concerned." Nusser turned to Breckinridge and Morgan, either unaware or unconcerned that Ralston was glaring at him behind his back. "You fellas ought to come on to camp with us. After the way you pitched in and ran off those Injuns, least we can do is feed you a good meal."

One of the other men suggested, "Maybe Jud'd let us crack open one o' them jugs of corn liquor."

"There's an idea," Nusser said with a grin. "Come on, boys, we'll introduce you to Jud Carnahan. He's the one who put this little trappin' expedition together."

Breckinridge leaned his head toward the trees and said, "We left our canoes over yonder around the bend."

"Well, go get 'em and paddle on to where we're camped. We'll be waitin' for you."

Breckinridge and Morgan exchanged a glance. There was no way they could turn down the invitation without creating hard feelings, and they didn't want to go out of their way to do that, especially outnumbered eighteen to two.

The idea of sitting down to break bread with at least one son of a bitch who'd tried to rob and kill him less than a week earlier rubbed Breckinridge the wrong way, but he'd had to put up with a lot of unpleasantness in his life. He supposed he could stand a little more.

"We'll see you in a few minutes," he said.

As they walked through the trees toward their canoes, Morgan said quietly, "I suppose we had to help them, but that doesn't mean I want to befriend those brigands."

"I ain't too happy about that, neither," Breckinridge said. "But we'll just share a meal with 'em and then push on. Probably never see 'em again after today."

"You really think so?" Morgan asked dubiously. "They strike me as the sort that might decide to kill us and take our canoes and all our supplies."

"They can try, but they'll play hell doin' it," Breckinridge said. "Keep your powder dry, Morgan."

They paddled around the bend and then put in to shore again. The campfire had been built up even more as night settled down. The flames leaped high and cast flickering, reddish light over a large circle. The men had left cover and were on their feet again, some moving around, others just standing near the fire.

Breckinridge and Morgan pulled their canoes up onto the bank, not too near the canoes belonging to the larger party. They took their rifles, now reloaded, and walked toward the fire.

Jud Carnahan was easy to pick out among the trappers. He was a head shorter and much broader than any of them. He walked out to meet the two newcomers. His long beard jutted out in front of him.

"Howdy," he greeted Breckinridge and Morgan. "Welcome to our camp." He put out a hand with short, thick fingers. "Name's Jud Carnahan. I'm heading up this bunch."

Breckinridge clasped the man's hand. Carnahan's grip was strong. "I'm Breckinridge Wallace," Breck said.

Carnahan nodded and said, "Seems like I've heard of you, Wallace. Weren't you mixed up in some ruckus at a rendezvous last year?"

"It didn't really amount to much," Breckinridge said, which was stretching the truth more than a mite. "Ruckus" was an understatement.

"And you're Morgan Baxter," Carnahan went on as he turned to Morgan and shook hands with him. "You boys come on over to the fire. We'll have some grub here in a bit, but the coffee's ready now. We even have some white lightning you can use to sweeten it, if you want."

Breckinridge didn't think it was a good idea for him and Morgan to be drinking much while they were around these men, but he just nodded noncommittally and glanced at Morgan. He could tell his friend shared the same thought.

"You met the major and some of the other boys already," Carnahan said as he ushered Breckinridge and Morgan toward the fire. "I'll introduce you to the rest of them."

Breckinridge didn't think that was necessary but didn't argue. Breck knew he wouldn't remember most of the names Carnahan spouted. He had to wonder, though, if some of them were the would-be robbers he had battled back in St. Louis.

One of the trappers was preparing a meal of biscuits, beans, and salt pork. He grinned up at the newcomers and nodded pleasantly when Carnahan introduced him as Chet Bagley. Round-faced, with thinning blond hair, he didn't seem to be quite as much of a hard case as the others. He said, "Pleased to meet you, boys. Hope you brought an appetite with you."

Breckinridge returned the grin, patted his belly, and said, "I carry one around with me, permanent-like. My ma always said I ate like I've got two hollow legs, not just one."

Bagley laughed. "I'll do my best to fill 'em up."

Men were starting to sit down cross-legged near the fire. Carnahan gestured that Breckinridge and Morgan should join them. They sank onto the ground and accepted clay mugs of hot, strong coffee that Bagley handed to them.

Breckinridge took a sip of his, nodded in appreciation, and said, "What did you do with the bodies of them Sioux we killed?"

"Left them for the scavengers, of course," Ralston answered immediately from where he had sat down on the other side of the fire. "What else would we do with them? They can rot, as far as I'm concerned."

"Their friends are liable to come back for 'em. Might've been a good idea to move your camp on upriver a ways."

"This is a good campsite," Ralston said. "Plus we've already built a fire. I see no reason to waste it."

"Take it easy, Major," Carnahan said. "Our new friends are just trying to be helpful. They're old hands, and we're just getting started in the trapping business."

Breckinridge knew that he and Morgan had only limited experience at living on the frontier, but even so, they weren't greenhorns like Carnahan and his men appeared to be. He said, "It'll probably be all right. Just post plenty of guards tonight."

"We always do. Admittedly, the savages took us by surprise this time." Carnahan's voice took on a grim note as he added, "But they won't again."

Bagley began passing around plates of food. The men dug in, hungry after a long day of paddling upriver.

As he ate, Breckinridge said, "We should've shared some of our supplies with you fellas."

"No need for that," Carnahan said. "We have plenty. And you two already contributed by chasing off those redskins."

"I still say we didn't need help," Ralston muttered.

Carnahan let out a harsh laugh. "The major's used to being in command. I don't reckon he likes it much when he isn't giving the orders."

Ralston's face paled with anger, making the black eye patch stand out even more against his face. He didn't say anything, though. He just reached for a jug that sat on the ground near him, picked it up, pulled the cork with his teeth, and added a dollop of the clear liquid inside to his coffee.

"Don't get pie-eyed, Major," Carnahan warned. "You'll be standing a turn at guard duty tonight like the rest of us. I know you aren't used to that, but it's only fair."

Ralston still didn't say anything. Breckinridge saw his angular jaw clench. There would be trouble between those two before this expedition was over, Breck thought.

He wouldn't have wanted to bet on who would come out on top, though. Ralston was a thief and a killer, Breck knew that for a fact, but Carnahan's eyes, set deep in pits of gristle under bushy black brows, were as cold and hard as agate, despite his outwardly jovial manner.

The men passed around the jug, some of them adding the liquor to their coffee, others tilting it to their mouths and downing long swallows of the raw stuff.

Breckinridge handed the jug along to Morgan when it came to him. Morgan took just a small nip before passing the jug to the next man. Breck thought Carnahan's eyes narrowed a bit at that, but he wasn't sure. Maybe Carnahan just didn't like the idea that his hospitality wasn't being accepted in full.

"You fellas are gonna spend the night with us, aren't you?" Carnahan asked after a while.

"We don't want to be any bother—" Morgan began.

"No bother," Carnahan said.

"We didn't figure to join up with a big company," Breckinridge said.

"A larger group's safer from the Injuns," bristle-bearded Al Nusser pointed out.

"Maybe these two are just unfriendly," Ralston said.

Carnahan frowned. "Nobody said anything about you joining our company, Wallace, although after what you and Baxter did today, you'd certainly be welcome. But the decision is entirely up to you."

"Two more men would make all our shares smaller," Ralston said.

"No need to worry about that," Breckinridge said. "Me and Morgan will be movin' on in the mornin'. You boys seem like a fine bunch of fellas"—that was a lie, but a prudent one—"but we like to strike out on our own, don't we, Morgan?"

"That's the plan," Morgan said.

Carnahan nodded and said, "All right. You'll stay the night, though?"

"It's too late to be pushin' on now, so I reckon we will," Breckinridge said. There were snags in the river that made traveling at night dangerous. It would be too easy to rip out the bottom of a canoe in the dark.

He just hoped they would both still be alive to see the sun come up in the morning.

Chapter 8

Carnahan put the cork back in the jug before any of the men could get drunk. Breckinridge had to give the man credit for that. With the threat of the Sioux looming over the expedition, having the men too liquor sodden to be alert could be fatal.

After supper, Breckinridge and Morgan went back to the canoes for their bedrolls and spread them not far from the craft. None of the others seemed to care or even notice. Breck wanted to be able to leave these parts in a hurry if he and Morgan needed to.

So far, he didn't see any real reason to be suspicious of the group of trappers. True, at least one of them—Gordon Ralston—had tried to rob and kill him back in St. Louis. But that didn't mean Ralston intended to continue his lawless ways out here away from the settlement. Surrounded by all the dangers of the frontier, the man might be more interested in having allies than victims.

Even so, Breckinridge figured it would be a good idea for him and Morgan to take turns staying awake during the night. If nothing else, one of them would be alert in case the Sioux tried a sneak attack to get their revenge. Breck was convinced that sooner or later, the Indians *would* try to get payment in blood for the men they had lost.

"I'll take the first watch," Morgan volunteered when Breckinridge made his low-voiced suggestion. "You go ahead and get some sleep."

Breckinridge didn't put up an argument. He rolled in his blankets and dozed off almost immediately, like the healthy animal he was.

His was a deep and dreamless slumber, the sleep of a young man with a clear conscience. He woke up easily, long after midnight, when Morgan laid a light touch on his shoulder.

Breckinridge sat up and asked, "Anything?"

"Quiet as can be," Morgan reported. "Other than a considerable amount of snoring from those other fellows."

Breckinridge grinned in the darkness. He heard the racket coming from some of Carnahan's men as they slept. The campfire had burned down to embers, but those embers still glowed brightly enough for him to see the blanket-wrapped shapes scattered around on the ground.

He turned his head and picked out the dark figures of two men standing near the canoes, rifles cradled in their arms. He whispered, "Where are the other guards?"

"There's a man in the trees on each side of the clearing," Morgan replied in equally low tones. "They changed shifts a while back, and I assume they will again before morning, since they have the luxury of more men."

Breckinridge nodded, even though Morgan might

not be able to see the gesture. "All right. Head for your soogans. I'll keep an eye on things."

"I'll be glad when morning comes and we can set off on our own again. I feel sort of like we're trying to sleep in a den of wolves."

"Same here," Breckinridge said. He patted the stock of the rifle he had picked up and placed across his lap. "But I got somethin' here to scare 'em off if need be."

Morgan let out a little grunt of grim amusement, then curled up in his blankets, put his hat under his head for a pillow, and soon was breathing deeply and regularly.

Breckinridge sat there, all his senses fully awake and engaged. His gaze roved around the camp, searching for any suspicious movement. His hearing reached out into the night, alert for anything that sounded wrong. He even sniffed the air, aware that Indians often coated their hair with bear grease, which had a distinctive odor when it turned rancid.

His thoughts, however, roamed here and there and inevitably turned back toward the past. Several months earlier, if anyone had told him how things were going to turn out and mentioned the situation in which he found himself now, he wouldn't have believed them. Everything had seemed clear-cut in his mind, almost preordained. He had been certain of all the things he was going to do—and the person who was going to be at his side while he was doing them.

Then all that had been turned on its head with no warning.

Well, that wasn't *completely* true, he mused. Dulcy had tried. She had hinted that things might not go as smoothly as he'd expected. But with his enormous confidence in himself and in fate, he had brushed that aside. Things would turn out the way he wanted them to because he, Breckinridge Wallace, said so.

Funny how the world didn't pay any attention to that. It kept turning and things played out the way they had, and Breckinridge hadn't been able to stop them any more than he would have been able to put his shoulder to a mountain and stop it from falling if it took a mind to.

Most of the time, he was able to push all that away and not allow it to bother him. His belief in himself might have been shaken a little, but it hadn't been broken. He could accept the past and carry on.

It was only at moments such as this, when he didn't have enough to occupy his thoughts, that the memories and the doubts crept in, and he understood why philosophers referred to the dark night of the soul. Some of those nights were pretty damned dark, sure enough.

But thankfully, morning always came.

Breckinridge woke Morgan when the sky was gray in the east. He leaned close and said, "Time to go."

Morgan sat up and knuckled his eyes. "Carnahan and his men aren't up yet?"

"Nope, but I reckon they will be soon. The guards will see us leavin', but I don't think they'll try to stop us." Breckinridge's voice hardened as he added, "If they're plannin' to cause trouble for us, I'd just as soon get it over with."

"I suppose you're right."

Both young men got to their feet and began gathering their gear. The dim, predawn light grew stronger as they worked. Breckinridge could see the guards over by the Carnahan party's canoes, so he knew the men could see him and Morgan as well.

While they were stowing their things in the canoes, one of those men started stalking toward them. Breckinridge saw the long, thin shape swinging against the man's leg and knew it had to be the saber carried by Ralston. The major came to a stop and demanded, "Where do you think you're going?"

"Figured we'd head on upriver," Breckinridge said. "Get a good start on the day. It's light enough now to see where we're goin'."

The rifle in Ralston's hands moved slightly as he said, "Then it's light enough for you to see this."

"What's goin' on here, Ralston?" Breckinridge asked. He deliberately made his voice louder this time.

"You're not going anywhere yet," the major rasped.

A faint smile ghosted over Breckinridge's face. "You figure on shootin' me if I try?" he asked. "If you do, you might take a look at Morgan over there. See how he's got his hand on his pistol? If you shoot me, he'll have plenty of time to put a ball in you before you can reload your rifle or draw that pigsticker o' yours."

It was light enough now for Breckinridge to see the sneer on Ralston's face. He said, "If Baxter tries to shoot me, one of the other guards will kill him."

"You'll be bettin' your life they'll be fast enough to do it—and that they won't miss in this poor light."

"You're running a bluff, and it's a damned poor one."

"There's one way for you to find out," Breckinridge said.

A few seconds of tense silence ticked past. Then it

was broken by Jud Carnahan saying, "Ralston, what the hell are you doing?"

"These two were about to leave," Ralston said without taking his eyes off Breckinridge as Carnahan came up behind him. "I think they were trying to sneak off before anyone was up because they've stolen some of our supplies."

Anger flared up inside Breckinridge. "By God, we ain't thieves!" he exclaimed. "There may be some no-good robbers in this camp, but it ain't Morgan and me!"

That might not have been the smartest thing to say, he realized, but when he was mad, his mouth sometimes got ahead of his brain. Anyway, he'd said it, and he couldn't call the words back now.

"I think we should search their canoes," Ralston said.

Breckinridge gave a contemptuous snort and waved a hand toward the craft. "Go ahead. You won't find a damn thing 'cept what we brought with us."

Ralston smiled then, and the confident expression was like a sudden punch in Breckinridge's gut. Something was wrong here, and Breck had a hunch he knew what it was.

Some of the other men had wandered up behind Carnahan to see what was going on. He turned and motioned to a couple of them. "Brady, Hanks, take a look in those canoes."

The two men went over to the canoes and started poking around in them. It annoyed Breckinridge to have strangers messing with his gear, but it was too late to stop it now. He hadn't caught on to what was happening in time, and now the hand had to play out. He looked at Morgan, who wore a worried frown.

Maybe he had started to figure things out, too, Breck thought.

The man who was looking through Morgan's canoe suddenly straightened from the task and said, "Jud, there's a keg of powder and a bag full of shot here with your mark on them. They had to come from that store back in St. Louis where we outfitted."

Carnahan's bushy brows drew down severely. "Is that so?" he rumbled. He turned a suspicious glare on Breckinridge. "How do you reckon that happened?"

"I'll tell you exactly how it happened," Breckinridge replied without hesitation. He pointed at Gordon Ralston. "The major snuck up durin' the night and put those things there. Either that, or he got somebody else to do it for him, to make Morgan and me look like thieves." Breck started to add something about the pot calling the kettle black, but he managed to control the urge this time.

He also didn't mention that the trick must have been carried out while Morgan was standing guard, because he knew no one had approached the canoes while he was watching. He didn't see any point in casting blame and making his friend feel bad about it, though.

"That's insane," Ralston said in response to the accusation. "Why in the world would I do such a thing?"

"Because you and me have rubbed each other wrong from the beginning, Major," Breckinridge said. "I figure you just want to cause trouble for me and Morgan."

And to have an excuse for killing us and taking our canoes and gear, he thought, just like he and Morgan had discussed the day before. If Ralston suspected that Breckinridge was the one he and his confederates had attacked back in St. Louis, he might want to make sure that story didn't ever get out, as well.

"That seems like a flimsy story to me, Wallace," Carnahan said. "The evidence says you got caught trying to steal powder and shot from us. That's a mighty unfriendly thing to do, especially after we invited you into our camp last night."

"In return for us helping you drive off those hostiles," Morgan reminded him.

"You just did that so you'd have a chance to steal from us," Ralston said.

Even though he knew it probably wouldn't do any good, Breckinridge said, "Hold on and think about this for a minute. You had guards posted all night, Carnahan. Wouldn't at least one of them have spotted us rummagin' around in your goods and raised the alarm if it was really us who took those things?"

"I suppose that depends on how stealthy you were about it," Carnahan said.

Breckinridge gestured at his massive form and said, "I ain't exactly built for stealth."

That was what most people would think, anyway. In reality, he could move through the woods like a phantom when he wanted to, making no more noise than an Indian on the prowl.

Ralston nodded toward Morgan and said, "Maybe the weasely one did it."

"Weasely?" Morgan exclaimed. "Why, I—"

Breckinridge held up a hand to stop him. In a flat, hard voice, he said, "We've told you the truth, Carnahan. That powder and shot were planted. You can believe that, or you can go to hell. Your men took it out, so you've got your goods back. Now Morgan and me are leavin' like we planned."

"I was planning to ask you to stay for breakfast," Carnahan said, "but I reckon that's not gonna happen now."

"Fine by us." Breckinridge jerked his head toward the canoes. "Come on, Morgan."

"Wait just a damn minute!" Ralston yelled. "Just because they didn't get away with it doesn't make it all right that they tried to steal from us. They ought to pay for that, by God!"

"What do you suggest?" Carnahan asked as he watched Ralston with a sly frown on his face.

Ralston's lip curled in a sneer. "If they were in my command, I'd order them whipped and then sending them slinking back downriver like the thieving curs they are. A taste of the lash would teach them not to try to steal from their betters."

"If you want to try to whip them . . ." Carnahan's broad shoulders rose and fell in a shrug. "Nobody's going to stop you, Major."

"Except me," Breckinridge said. "Nobody's takin' a whip to me."

Ralston licked his lips. His arrogance had gotten him into a dilemma. Carnahan hadn't backed him up the way Ralston obviously expected he would. If everything had gone according to Ralston's plan, Breckinridge and Morgan would have put up a fight when they were accused of stealing. As outnumbered as they were, it would have been easy to make sure they wound up dead.

Instead, Breckinridge was about half-convinced now that Carnahan hadn't been aware of the trick. It was all Ralston's doing. And if Ralston was going to press the issue, he would have to do it by himself, or at least with fewer allies than he'd counted on. Breck could tell that his logic had convinced some of the men he was telling the truth.

The smartest thing Ralston could do was to accept that his ploy had failed. For a moment Breckinridge thought that was what the major was going to do. He could almost see the wheels turning in Ralston's brain.

However, the former officer's pride wouldn't allow him to admit defeat. His face hardened, and his single eye blazed with hatred. He handed his rifle to Al Nusser and then said, "Wallace not only tried to steal from us, he accused *me* of the crime. He as much as called me a liar. I won't stand for that, Jud."

"Then do something about it," Carnahan said in a faintly mocking tone.

"I intend to." Metal rasped against metal as Ralston drew the saber from its scabbard. He pointed the blade at Breckinridge and said, "Prepare yourself, Wallace. I intend to kill you right now, before the sun comes up."

Chapter 9

For a moment, Breckinridge fixed Ralston with a hard, cold stare. Then he said, "If you're figurin' on havin' a sword fight with me, mister, you're outta luck. I don't have one o' them frog-giggers."

Ralston smiled thinly. "You're the one out of luck. I happen to have a second saber, and I'd be happy to loan it to you."

Morgan said, "Wait just a damned minute! This isn't fair. Breck's never used a saber." He glanced at his friend. "You haven't, have you?"

Breckinridge shrugged. "No, but I've fought with knives plenty of times. Reckon it's pert near the same thing, only the blade's longer."

"No, it's not," Morgan argued. He looked at Carnahan. "Surely you can see this isn't right."

"The fellow who gets challenged to a duel has the choice of weapons," Carnahan said. "Wallace didn't actually challenge the major, but he *did* call him a liar, which is pretty close to the same thing."

"Close enough," Ralston said. "How about it, Wallace? Are you going to do the honorable thing—or be a craven coward and get gutted like a hog?"

Breckinridge surprised all the men gathered on the bank of the Missouri River by throwing back his head and laughing. "You're askin' me if I'm gonna back down from a fight? Mister, you don't know the Wallaces very well, and you sure as hell don't know this one!"

He set the rifle in his canoe, then pulled the brace of pistols from his belt and placed them beside the long-barreled flintlock. He tossed the sheathed hunting knife into the canoe as well, then turned back to face Ralston.

"Fetch your other *sw–ord*," he said, mockingly pronouncing the *w* in the word this time.

"I'll be right back," Ralston promised. He stalked toward the other canoes.

"Breck, don't do this," Morgan urged in a low voice. "He knows how to use one of those things. He's going to kill you."

"He's gonna try," Breckinridge said, "but I reckon I'm gonna have somethin' to say about that."

Morgan continued to look anxious as Ralston returned with a second saber. He held it in his left hand and slashed back and forth with it, making a hissing sound in the air.

"You can see that this is a fine, sturdy blade," the one-eyed major said. "It belonged to one of my fellow officers who was killed in battle against the Seminoles. I was with him when he died, and he bequeathed the weapon to me almost with his last breath. I hate to see it dishonored by being used by the likes of you, Wallace, but *my* honor demands satisfaction."

"Mighty fond of the sound of your own voice, ain't you?" Breckinridge held out his hand. Ralston gave him the sword.

Carnahan waved his arms and said in a loud voice, "You fellows back up now. Give 'em room."

Morgan put a hand on Breckinridge's arm and said, "I still think this is a bad idea, Breck."

"Yeah, there's more than just my hide ridin' on this, ain't there?" Breckinridge muttered. "If Ralston kills me, the rest of this bunch is liable to turn on you next." He brightened. "Oh well, I'll just have to make sure he don't kill me."

Ralston raised his saber in front of him and said, "Let's get on with this, Wallace."

Breckinridge took off his hat and tossed it into the canoe with his weapons, then turned to face Ralston. The sun was coming up now, and the major was positioned so that the bright red orb was behind him. Breck didn't figure that was an accident, but he didn't think it mattered much, either. Likely they would be moving around enough as they fought that the sun wouldn't be in his eyes all the time.

He said, "Whenever you're ready, mister."

Ralston might have wanted Breckinridge to attack first, so that he could gauge his opponent's level of speed and skill. But his urge to kill got the better of him. As his face twisted with hatred, he lunged forward, the blade glinting redly in the dawn light as he thrust it in front of him.

Breckinridge twisted his wrist and used his sword to slap aside Ralston's. It was a neat parry, but as Breck launched a thrust of his own as part of the same move, Ralston darted aside from it. His blade flashed downward, but it was only a feint. When Breck went to block the attack, the tip of Ralston's sword came up again with blinding speed. Breck had to leap backward to keep it from ripping his throat.

That put him off-balance for a second, and his guard was down as well. Ralston leaped at him, hacking with the sword as if he intended to chop Breckinridge into little pieces. Breck gave more ground and flung up his blade. Steel rang against steel once, twice, three times in little more than the blink of an eye. Ralston's assault was furious and deadly. Breck barely fought it off.

Fighting with sabers really was different from a knife tussle, he realized now. Morgan had been right about that. A knife fight was close-quarters combat. To survive, a man sometimes had to strike with fist or foot as well as blade.

A sword fight took place at longer range. It wouldn't be as easy to kick an opponent in the belly, and you couldn't grab him and hold him close while you drove your blade in and out of his chest half a dozen times. Speed and finesse were more important than brute strength, which was what Breckinridge had in abundance.

However, he wasn't exactly slow, which he proved by catching his balance and counterattacking. His blade jabbed at Ralston, who had to hurry to parry the thrusts.

The tide of battle surged back and forth. As Breckinridge expected, he and Ralston turned and circled enough that the rising sun didn't prove to be an advantage for either of them. Shouts rang out from the men who had formed a rough circle around them. Most were words of encouragement directed at Ralston by his fellow members of Carnahan's expedition. The only one rooting for Breck was Morgan. Carnahan himself, though, stood with arms crossed over his broad chest and watched the fight with avid interest.

He wanted to see who was going to win, but he didn't seem to be rooting for one man over the other.

The biggest advantage Breckinridge had was his stamina. He fought tirelessly as the minutes stretched on. He wasn't breathing hard, and he hadn't lost any speed. The same wasn't true of Ralston. His moves weren't as swift and crisp as they had been when the combat began, and his chest began to heave a little as he fought harder for breath. Ralston had expected to kill him within a minute or so, Breck thought. The major had counted on his skill being enough to accomplish that deadly goal. Now, the longer it took, the more Ralston would begin to suffer.

That was just fine with Breckinridge. He could keep this up all day.

With his lips pulled back from his teeth in a grimace, Ralston attacked again. The way he slashed back and forth with the blade had a frenzied, desperate quality. Breckinridge blocked the blows again and again. Sparks leaped from the sabers as they clashed. Spittle flew from Ralston's mouth as he cursed bitterly.

Breckinridge felt that moisture strike his face and knew Ralston's bloodlust had made him careless. He had finally come close enough. Breck's left arm shot out. His hand closed on the front of Ralston's jacket. The muscles of his arms, shoulders, and back bunched as he pivoted at the waist and heaved.

Taken by surprise, Ralston left his feet and flew through the air. Shocked cries came from the onlookers.

Ralston landed hard and rolled over a couple of times. The men on that side of the circle jumped back to give him room. Breckinridge was right after him, and as Ralston stopped and tried to lift himself from the ground, Breck's right foot lashed out and the toe of his boot smashed into Ralston's wrist. Ralston yelled in pain as the sword flew out of his grip.

Breckinridge then put his foot on Ralston's chest and pinned the major to the ground. The tip of his saber hovered over Ralston's throat but didn't drive downward in a killing stroke.

Panting, Ralston stared up at Breckinridge. His single eye was wide and bulging. After a couple of tense heartbeats, he cried, "End it! Go ahead and end it, you son of a bitch!"

Breckinridge shoved the sword down, but as he did, he turned the point so that the blade sunk into the ground less than an inch from the side of Ralston's neck. He stepped back.

The sound of a gun being cocked made him look over his shoulder. Jud Carnahan had lifted a pistol and aimed it at him.

"You figure on shootin' me?" Breckinridge asked.

"I might have, if you'd killed Ralston," Carnahan said. "Maybe you should have. You'd have had the satisfaction of seeing him die before you did."

"That don't strike me as bein' all that satisfyin'. You and all these fellas saw it, Carnahan. I beat him fair and square, usin' his choice of weapons."

"I'm not sure how fair it was. There at the end it was more like wrestling instead of a sword fight."

"If you don't want to get grabbed, don't get close enough that the fella you're fightin' can grab you."

Carnahan let a second go by, then abruptly laughed. "Simple, yet profound," he said as he eased his pistol's hammer back down and lowered the weapon. "All right, Wallace. You acquitted yourself well. I'm still not certain exactly what happened here this morning, but whether you and Baxter stole that powder and shot or not, the matter is closed. The two of you get in your canoes and leave."

"You're lettin' 'em go?" Al Nusser asked.

"That's right." Carnahan looked around at the others. "Anybody object to that?"

No one did, not even Ralston, who had rolled onto his side and was lying there breathing heavily.

"But I'm putting you on notice," Carnahan went on to Breckinridge and Morgan. "Ralston's going to bear a grudge against you, and if he sees you again, I probably won't be able to stop him from indulging it. I'm not sure I'd even *want* to. I'm sure some of the other men don't trust you, either, and aren't that fond of you."

The hostile glares many of the trappers directed at them told Breckinridge and Morgan that Carnahan was right about that.

"The frontier is a big place," Carnahan went on. "Steer clear of us. If you don't, there'll be more trouble, and I won't be responsible for what happens."

"I've always had a hard time with bein' told what to do," Breckinridge said.

"For your own sake, learn to swallow it this time."

Breckinridge glanced at Morgan. If he had been on his own, Breck might have told Carnahan to go to hell. But he had a friend and partner to consider. Morgan's life was every bit as much at risk here as his.

"Maybe you'd best steer clear of *us*," Breckinridge said.

Carnahan laughed again. "Your balls are as big as the rest of you, Wallace. Call it what you want, just get the hell out of here."

"That sounds good to me," Morgan muttered. He went to his canoe.

Breckinridge backed away from Carnahan and the others. He didn't trust the squat, bearded man, and he sure didn't trust Ralston, who by now was sitting up on the ground. The former officer could put more hate in one eye than most could in two, and he proved that with the baleful gaze he directed at Breck.

Morgan pushed the canoes out into the river while Breckinridge watched Carnahan and the others. Breck stepped into his canoe, sat down, and picked up the paddle in his left hand, one of the pistols in his right. He looped his thumb over the gun's hammer, ready to cock and fire if need be. Using the paddle in his other hand, he pushed the canoe even farther offshore.

"You head out," he told Morgan. "Stop while you're still in rifle range, and you can cover me whilst I join you."

Carnahan called from the bank, "No one's going to harm you, Wallace. I already told you that you could leave safely."

"Bein' careful's a habit o' mine," Breckinridge said. "No offense."

Oddly enough, he actually meant that.

Within a few minutes, both young men were out in the middle of the broad river, propelling their canoes upstream with short, swift strokes of their paddles. Back on the shore, the members of Carnahan's expedition were moving around, busily getting ready to break camp.

"We should have let those Sioux wipe them out," Morgan called across to Breckinridge.

"Aw, we couldn't do that," Breckinridge said. "Anyway, they prob'ly ain't all so bad. Those fellas Bagley and Nusser seemed like decent sorts."

"And I guess Carnahan was fair enough, in his way."

"Yeah, maybe," Breckinridge said. He was still convinced that Carnahan had played him and Ralston against each other, at least to a certain extent. Carnahan hadn't wanted Breck to kill the major, but he wouldn't mind at all that Ralston had been defeated and taken down a notch. That would keep him from getting too ambitious in the future, at least for a while.

Carnahan was cunning, all right, and Breck had seen enough of the man to believe that he was more dangerous than Ralston in the long run. Ralston's pride and temper were likely to cause him to make mistakes. Carnahan, on the other hand, was calculating and cold-blooded.

Sort of like a snake.

"Are we really going to try to avoid them?" Morgan asked.

"Don't know about that. Like I told Carnahan, bein' told what to do sort of rubs me the wrong way. But it's true the frontier is a big place. I reckon we'll have to wait and see where the beaver are."

"But if they decide to trap in an area where we already are . . . ?"

"Then there'll be trouble," Breckinridge said.

Chapter 10

Breckinridge and Morgan pushed on, paddling upstream for an hour before stopping to boil some coffee and have a quick breakfast.

By now the sun was well up in the sky, glowing brightly. Breckinridge kept the fire small so there wouldn't be much smoke to attract attention. The trouble they'd had with Carnahan's bunch didn't mean they could forget about the continuing threat of the Sioux.

They didn't see any Indians, or any other white men, for that matter, for the rest of that day. Other than deer, antelope, and birds, they saw no life at all.

Breckinridge didn't let that fool him. The vast landscape that surrounded them was teeming with life, both animal and human. He wouldn't be at all surprised to find out that Sioux warriors had been keeping an eye on him and Morgan all day. But as long as the Indians chose not to attack, Breck didn't see any reason not to keep going.

That night they made a cold camp, and for the next three nights as well. By that time, Breckinridge judged that they were past the area where they had to worry the most about the Sioux jumping them.

Such an attack still wasn't beyond the realm of possibility, but the odds were against it. They would be passing through Arikara and Mandan territory for a while, and those two tribes were peaceful for the most part, according to everything Breck had heard.

There had still been no sign of Carnahan's party behind them. Evidently the larger group wasn't in any hurry, and Breckinridge and Morgan were setting a brisk pace.

Being the first ones into a particular area was important to fur trappers, but since there were only two of them, Carnahan probably didn't consider the two young men much of a threat to the number of pelts his group would take this season.

Breckinridge didn't mind putting a bigger gap between them, although the way things had been left rankled him a little. Unfinished business had a way of coming back to plague a fella.

Late in the afternoon, they began searching for a good place to camp. The clouds had been thicker in the sky all day, and now the heavens were a solid gray, darkening almost to black in places.

"I don't like the looks of that," Morgan called across to Breckinridge as they paddled near the shore.

"Yeah, I reckon a storm's comin', all right," Breckinridge agreed. "Look up yonder on the left. See that sandstone bluff stickin' up? That might give us some shelter from the weather."

They angled in and pulled the canoes up onto the bank. The bluff Breckinridge had pointed out rose twenty feet and ran out to form a point that extended a short distance into the river. The ground in front of it was relatively level and clear. A gusty wind had started to blow out of the northwest. The bluff would block most of it.

As they got out of the canoes, Breckinridge sniffed the air for a moment, then said, "Smells like snow to me."

"Snow!" Morgan repeated. "It's the middle of spring."

"Yeah, but we're gettin' pretty far north now. Sometimes there'll be a snowstorm that blows through these parts even when it's almost summer. I've heard old-timers talk about such things. If there's any snow, it probably won't last very long, but we could sure get some."

Morgan shivered. "All the more reason to get a fire going and some hot coffee inside us."

They unloaded the few supplies they would need for the night and began gathering broken branches from the brush to use for firewood. There were no trees growing close by, although Breckinridge could see some dark smudges in the distance that he thought might be small groves. In the rapidly fading light, it was hard to tell for sure.

Even with the main threat from the Sioux behind them, Breckinridge thought it would be wise not to show a fire after dark. They brewed coffee and heated up salt pork, not worrying much about the smoke this time because it would be almost invisible against the leaden sky.

Breckinridge built the fire up and let the flames leap high. He piled rocks around the fire, knowing they would capture some of the heat and release it slowly during the night. That would be better than nothing.

The wind began to blow harder. Breckinridge saw something fly in front of his face and looked up to see more snowflakes whipping down.

"Here it comes," he said. "With the wind blowing like this, it'll seem like a blizzard, no matter how much of the stuff actually comes down."

Morgan sighed and cradled his coffee cup in his hands. "I feel half-frozen already."

"It'll be all right. We've got plenty of blankets."

"One of those buffalo robes like our friends the Ioway had would sure feel good right about now."

Breckinridge nodded. "The Injuns are mighty smart about a lot of things, and that's one of 'em."

The wind increased to a howl that drove curtains of snow through the air. It was a mournful sound, Breckinridge thought. He and Morgan were out of the worst of it, with their camp up against the bluff.

"Maybe we should have waited a couple more weeks before starting for the mountains," Morgan said as he drew a blanket around his shoulders.

"Aw, this is nothin' to worry about," Breckinridge assured him. "It'll blow over by mornin', I expect, and it won't get anywhere near cold enough for the river to freeze. It'll be a chilly night, but it won't slow us down."

"I hope you're right."

They allowed the fire to burn down. The shrieking wind stole much of the heat from it. Thick darkness settled over the countryside.

Breckinridge and Morgan wrapped multiple blankets around themselves and stretched out to make the best of this miserable situation. Under the circumstances, Breck didn't believe it was necessary for either of them to stand guard. Any Indians nearby would be in their lodges or tipis, snug in buffalo robes like the one Morgan longed for.

Breckinridge fell asleep quickly, but despite his slumber, something deep inside him remained aware and alert. Sometime during the night, an unknowable time after he'd dozed off, his eyes snapped open abruptly. He lay there motionless, all his senses keened to a high level, trying to figure out what had roused him.

He heard a snatch of a voice, so faint and obscured by the wind that at first he thought he'd imagined it. Breckinridge knew he wasn't given to imagining things, though. It came again, and this time Breck was able to isolate the sound. It was above them.

Somebody was on top of the bluff that loomed over them.

Guided by his instincts, Breckinridge flung his blankets aside, grabbed the tightly wrapped bundle that was the sleeping Morgan, and rolled hard against the face of the bluff.

At that moment, spurts of orange flame split the darkness above them. Breck heard rifle balls thud into the ground where he and Morgan had been mere instants earlier.

Startled by being grabbed like that, Morgan let out a yell. The wind, still blowing hard, caught the noise and whirled it away, just as it had the rifle reports. Breckinridge had been able to hear the balls striking the ground only because they were so close.

He reached out blindly, unable to see much because of the darkness and the blowing snow, and tried to find the pistols he had left lying on the ground beside him when he went to sleep.

His fingers brushed a gun barrel, slid along it, and closed around the grip. The pistol was loaded and primed, so all he had to do was pull back the hammer as he lifted it. As he squeezed the trigger, he hoped snow hadn't gotten into the lock to foul it and cause a misfire.

The pistol boomed and bucked in his hand as he pointed it at the top of the bluff. He couldn't see what he was shooting at, of course, but he had a pretty good idea where those muzzle flashes he had seen were located. Mostly he wanted to spook whoever was up there and give him and Morgan a chance to retrieve the rest of their guns.

Instead, a man screamed and an instant later came plummeting down out of the storm to land on the remains of the fire, scattering ashes and coals. He struck the ground with a decisive thump that told Breckinridge he probably wouldn't be getting up again.

By now Morgan had fought free of his blankets. Breckinridge took hold of his arm and dragged him to his feet. They both pressed their backs against the sandstone bluff.

Breckinridge put his mouth close to his friend's ear and said, "Edge along the bluff to your left. I'll go right. They won't be able to see us to shoot at us."

He hoped he was right about that.

Even though the pistol was empty, he shoved it behind his belt. A hard enough blow while holding a gun would stove in a man's head. Breckinridge still wore the knife, so he slid it out of its sheath and gripped the handle tightly as he moved along the bluff.

He knew there had to be at least one more bushwhacker up there. He had heard a man's voice, and it was just too unlikely that the varmint would have been talking to himself.

The bluff was about fifty yards long. When Morgan came to his end of it, he'd be at the river and couldn't go any farther. Breckinridge, though, would be able to climb up onto it. That was what he did, feeling his way along in the darkness.

The wind was harder and colder on top of the bluff. It felt like talons clawing at every exposed inch of Breckinridge's skin. Breck was able to ignore the discomfort and concentrate on locating the other man—or men—who had tried to kill him and Morgan. He crouched low as he advanced toward the river.

It was possible that whoever was up here had already fled, especially since Breckinridge's wild shot had actually found a target. They might have lingered, though, hoping for another shot.

Breckinridge intended to deny them that chance if he could.

The heavy bump against his shoulder came with no warning. As soon as it happened, though, Breckinridge knew he had run right into his quarry. The other man knew it, too, and let out a wild, angry yell.

Breckinridge ducked and lunged. A pistol went off practically in his face. Burning bits of powder stung his cheek. The explosion was so loud it pounded his ears like giant fists.

None of that stopped him from crashing into the other man and driving him off his feet. Breckinridge could have stabbed him then, but he didn't want to kill the varmint just yet. He would rather find out who the would-be murderers were and why they had come after him and Morgan.

As they sprawled on top of the bluff, the man lifted a knee into Breckinridge's belly. It was a vicious blow that left Breck gasping for breath, but it was a long way from incapacitating. He ignored the discomfort and felt for his opponent's throat. If he could grab it, he could use his other hand to clout the man on the head with the brass ball at the end of his knife's handle. That would knock him senseless.

Instead, a wildly swung blow with the man's empty pistol clipped Breckinridge on the side of the head and made red explosions go off behind his eyes. He was confident he had the advantage in size and strength, but at the moment he was disoriented and couldn't put those advantages to good use. The man he was battling suddenly writhed away from him.

Breckinridge surged to his feet and felt the sting of a blade that scraped along his side. The other man had a knife, too. That changed things. Breck couldn't afford to be too careful now. He slashed in front of him with his blade but didn't hit anything.

"Now!" a man shouted. "Hit him high!"

So there were *two* of them—at least. And they weren't Indians, because it was unlikely they would be yelling commands in English. That left Breckinridge with a strong suspicion about who was behind this attack.

That thought flashed through his mind, but he didn't have any more time to devote to it because at that instant a heavy weight crashed into his torso. The impact was enough to drive him backward. His feet scrambled for purchase in the snow that had collected on top of the bluff.

Then, suddenly, there was nothing underneath those feet except empty air . . .

Chapter 11

Breckinridge knew he was going to fall. There was nothing he could do about that now.

But his left arm reached out instinctively and his hand closed on the coat worn by the man who had just rammed into him. The man yelled in fear as Breckinridge jerked *him* off the top of the bluff, too. Breck didn't let go. He hung on tightly as he twisted in midair.

That swung the man around underneath him. It all happened in a second, and Breckinridge's lightning-fast reaction was all that saved him. The other man struck the ground first, and Breck crashed down on top of him.

Even with that human cushion, it was a stunning, bone-jarring impact. Breckinridge thought he blacked out for a second, but on a night like this, who could tell for sure? He wasn't stunned for long, though. He rolled to the side and came up on a knee with the knife—which he had managed to hang on to—held out in front of him.

Nothing happened. The expected attack from the man still on top of the bluff didn't materialize.

Maybe if the other ambusher was alone now, he had decided to cut his losses and flee into the snowstorm. As shaken up as Breckinridge was, that would be all right with him.

He found his way over to the bluff and moved along it, guiding himself with a hand on the sandstone wall, until he judged that he was close to the river. Then he called quietly, "Morgan! Morgan, you there?"

"Here, Breck," Morgan replied from a few feet away. "Are you all right?"

"Yeah, I reckon. I fell off the dang bluff. Actually, I got knocked off, but I took the fella who done it down with me."

"Where is he?"

"Back yonder somewhere. I, uh, landed on top of him, so I figure he's probably busted up pretty good. Did you run into any trouble?"

"No, I've been waiting here to see what was going to happen. Do you know how many of them there were?"

"At least one more," Breckinridge replied. "But I've got a hunch he's already turned tail and run. I'm gonna gather up my guns and make sure."

He found his rifle and the other pistol and reloaded the pistol he had fired, working by feel in the darkness but having no trouble performing an action he had done so many times before. Then, with a pistol in each hand, he climbed to the top of the bluff again and cast back and forth—being careful not to topple off a second time—until he was sure there wasn't anyone lurking up there.

When he came back into camp, Morgan must have heard him, because he said, "Breck, is that you?"

"Yeah. Didn't find anybody else."

"I checked these two as best I could. They're both dead. I have no idea who they were, though."

"Reckon we'll find out come morning, when we can see again. I don't want to build another fire. Their partner could still be lurkin' around out there, hopin' to take a rifle shot at us if he gets the chance."

"That's a good idea. I don't think we should risk it, either."

Breckinridge found his blankets and said, "We might as well get some more sleep."

"You can sleep with a couple of corpses lying only a few yards away?"

"If they're dead, they won't be hurtin' nobody else."

Morgan let out a humorless laugh. "I can't argue with your logic, but I don't think I'll be sleeping any more tonight."

"Up to you," Breckinridge said, "but I reckon I'll sleep just fine."

The snow had stopped by morning, as Breckinridge predicted, but enough fell after the attack so that the faces of both corpses had a light dusting of white on them. When Breck brushed the flakes off features that had gone pallid with death, he and Morgan recognized both men.

"That's Hanks," Morgan said as he gestured toward the man Breckinridge had shot. "The other one was called . . . was it Magnuson?"

"Yeah, I think so," Breckinridge said. He hunkered

on his heels next to the bodies. "Don't reckon I'll ever make a blind shot that lucky again."

He pointed to the wound in Hanks's neck. The pistol ball had entered under the man's chin and bored up through his brain before exploding out the top of his head. When checking on him the night before, Morgan had rolled him onto his back, so the damage that had been done when he fell face-first onto the rocks around the fire was visible, too. His features were so battered and swollen, it was a wonder they recognized him.

Magnuson's face was unmarked, although the back of his head was a bloody ruin where it had been crushed by the fall and by Breckinridge's weight coming down on top of the man. He probably had some broken ribs, too, although it was unlikely he had experienced any pain from them. The shattered skull would have killed him almost instantly.

"Do you think Carnahan sent them after us?" Morgan asked as Breckinridge got to his feet.

"Could have. Hard to say. The other man I heard up on the bluff could've been Ralston. I wouldn't put it past him to sneak off and try to settle the score with me. He could've talked these fellas into comin' along with him."

"If that's true, it was the worst mistake they ever made."

"And the last one," Breckinridge said.

Morgan heaved a sigh. "What are we going to do with them?"

"Reckon the decent thing would be to bury 'em. I ain't in much of a mood to do it, but sometimes you have to do things you don't really want to."

Breckinridge had learned that over the past few years, often the hard way.

They had a shovel among their gear and took turns using it to scrape out a shallow grave big enough for both corpses. When the bodies were covered up, Breckinridge found some slabs of sandstone that he placed on top of the mounded dirt as a further bar to predators. The rocks would serve as a makeshift marker as well. Morgan got out his knife and carved the names of both men into one of the slabs. Weather would erode the sandstone quickly, but at least the dead men would have a monument for a while.

As Morgan stepped back after finishing that chore, he said, "When Carnahan and the others come along, they're liable to see these rocks and investigate. That'll be another mark against us, Breck. They'll try to kill us on sight from now on."

"They were probably gonna do that anyway," Breckinridge pointed out. "So we already knew to be careful and watch out for 'em."

"I suppose that's one way to look at it." Morgan shook his head. "And here I thought this would be a nice, peaceful fur trapping expedition."

"Should've known better'n that," Breckinridge said.

They moved out a short time later. The delay caused by the burial of Hanks and Magnuson might give Carnahan's party a better chance to catch up to them, Breckinridge thought, so he set a fast pace as he paddled up the river. The sky was still overcast, although no snow fell, and the air was cold.

After a while, Morgan said from the other canoe,

"Breck, you're going to have to slow down. I can't keep this up."

"All right," Breckinridge said. "We'll take it easy for a spell. I just wanted to put some distance betwixt us and them other fellas." He spat over the side. What they were doing felt like running away, and that galled him. But as long as he had Morgan's life to think of, too, he had to be more careful. He had a history of being reckless, no matter what the odds against him, and sometimes that tendency had wound up hurting other people more than it did him.

During the afternoon, the clouds finally broke up, the sun came out, and the temperature warmed somewhat. By that night, when they made camp in a clump of aspen not far from the river, the wind had turned around to the south. Winter's last gasp was over, Breckinridge thought.

The pleasant days continued as they traveled northward, through the lands of the Arikara, the Mandan, and the Hidatsa. Several times they stopped at Indian villages, where they were made welcome, especially when they proved willing to trade some of the goods they had brought along with them. Morgan enjoyed these intervals so much he might have been willing to stay with the Indians for a while, but Breckinridge knew they had to push on.

The Missouri River made its great, arching curve to the west. Snowcapped peaks were visible now, far in the distance, along with ranges of low hills that were much closer. The mountains seemed to recede every day, so that no matter how long Breckinridge and Morgan paddled, their destination was no closer when they stopped in the evening than it had been when they started that morning.

Breckinridge knew that was just an illusion, though. He and Morgan *were* getting closer, and it was just a matter of time until they reached the mountains.

They veered off into another stream that Breckinridge thought was the Yellowstone and followed it, traveling southwest now. After a couple of days they turned due south into yet another tributary. "I reckon this is the river they call the Bighorn," Breck told Morgan. To the left rose a range of good-sized mountains. Farther off to the right were more mountains, larger and more rugged.

In between, in front of Breckinridge and Morgan, lay a broad, rolling, beautiful green valley abundantly watered by the creeks that flowed from the mountains on both sides. Wildflowers, coaxed into blooming by the increasingly warm weather, were scattered in colorful profusion. From where they paddled in the stream, the two young men saw plenty of deer, antelope, and moose. Breck even spotted a couple of bears, gaunt from their winter's hibernation, pawing through thickets in search of something to break their long fast. Eagles perched in the upper branches of tall trees or soared through the blue sky.

Even though Breckinridge had never been in this particular valley before, he felt like he had come home at last.

He pointed to the mouth of a creek and said, "I got a feelin' there's a bunch of fat, sassy beavers up that stream, just waitin' for us to come get their pelts."

"If you think that's a good place for us to start, it's all right with me. I trust your judgment, Breck."

"Let's go take a look." Breckinridge dipped his paddle in the water and sent the canoe gliding toward the creek mouth.

The smaller stream was a couple of feet deep and thirty feet wide in most places. The water was crystal clear as it flowed swiftly over a rocky bed. Breckinridge reached over the side of the canoe and scooped up a handful, brought it to his mouth. The water was cold and tasted good. These mountain streams were fed by springs and snowmelt, and both those sources provided good water.

After a couple of miles, they came to a sand and gravel bank that would be a good place for them to go ashore, Breckinridge thought. He paddled over to it with Morgan right behind him. They got out and dragged the canoes onto a stretch of grassy, level ground. Breck looked around. Trees grew nearby, but there was enough open area for a camp.

"If there are any beaver dams close by, we can make this our headquarters for a while," Breckinridge said.

"It'll do fine for tonight's camp, anyway," Morgan said. "Why don't you scout around a little while I unload our gear?"

Breckinridge picked up his rifle out of the canoe and nodded. "Sounds like a good idea to me."

He tramped toward the trees that grew all the way up to the bank farther south. They weren't so dense that he had any trouble making his way through them, although the shadows were fairly thick under the branches. Breckinridge was watchful. He didn't expect to run into any real trouble, but a man could never be too careful.

When he had gone half a mile through the trees, he spotted something between the rough-barked trunks. As he came closer, he realized that the creek had curved and now ran more in front of him. And across that creek stretched a humped, brown, irregular barrier made of branches. It was a beaver dam, Breckinridge thought as he grinned. Proof positive that he and Morgan would find good trapping in these parts.

The noise of the creek as it bubbled and danced over the rocks filled the air, but that wasn't enough to keep Breckinridge from hearing a faint snap from somewhere behind him. Someone or something had just stepped on a twig. He turned sharply and lifted the rifle, although he didn't bring it to his shoulder just yet.

Instead he stood stock-still and looked through the trees at a buckskin-clad figure who held a bow with its string pulled back and an arrow nocked. The arrow was aimed straight at Breckinridge.

Chapter 12

It was an even bet what would happen next. Breckinridge thought he stood a good chance of being able to leap aside, out of the arrow's path, before it could strike him. Then he'd have a heartbeat, at most, to raise the rifle and shoot the Indian before the man could launch another shaft at him. It would be close.

On the other hand, the Indian hadn't loosed that first arrow yet, so Breckinridge steeled his muscles to control the reaction that urged him to move. He just stood there, looking across the twenty feet or so that separated him from the Indian.

Seconds crawled past. Breckinridge's impatient nature got the better of him. He said, "If you're figurin' on killin' me, son, you've done missed your best chance already. Try it now and I'll get lead in you before I go down, that's for damn sure. On the other hand, if you put that bow down, neither of us has to shoot anybody."

He had no way of knowing if the Indian spoke any English. Probably not, considering how far from civilization they were. But trappers and missionaries had been trekking into these mountains for more than twenty years now, Breckinridge told himself, so it was possible the young warrior understood what he said.

And the Indian *was* young, probably around the same age as him. He wore no war paint on his face, but that didn't make him any less dangerous. Breckinridge didn't recognize the markings and decorations on the warrior's buckskins. He knew that both the Crow and the Arapaho could be found in this region, so he figured the man came from one of those tribes.

Finally, the warrior let off on the pressure he'd been putting on the bowstring. He lowered the arrow toward the ground but left it nocked. He spoke in a harsh voice to Breckinridge, who couldn't make out any of the words. Some things were universal, though. At least Breck hoped so as he let go of the rifle with his right hand and raised it in front of him, palm out toward the young Indian.

"Friend," Breckinridge said. "I'm not lookin' for trouble."

The Indian stared at him for a long moment, then grunted and took the arrow off the bowstring. He slid it into the hide quiver slung on his back. He seemed to have gotten the idea and didn't want any trouble, either. To show he went along with that, Breckinridge pointed the rifle at the ground.

The young warrior walked toward him and lifted a hand in a gesture of peace, too. "Friend," he said in a guttural voice, proving that he knew at least one word in the white man's tongue. He put that hand against his chest and went on, "Running Elk."

Breckinridge nodded, rested a hand against his own chest, and said, "Breckinridge Wallace."

That was a mouthful for the Indian. He managed, "Breck . . . ridge," then said again, "Friend."

"That's right. We're friends. Running Elk"—and he pointed to the Indian—"and Breckinridge." Pointing to himself. "Friends."

Running Elk looked as solemn as ever, but he nodded. Breckinridge was pleased by how well they were communicating. He tried to remember some of the sign language he had seen old scouts and trappers use in the past. He hoped he was making the correct sign as he asked out loud, "Is your village close by?"

Evidently he must have gotten it right, because Running Elk half turned and pointed toward the east as he said something. Breckinridge couldn't make out any of it except the last two words, which surprised him by being in English.

"Dawn Wind."

"Dawn Wind," Breckinridge repeated. "Is that somebody's name?"

Running Elk didn't answer. He just pointed again and motioned for Breckinridge to follow him.

Breckinridge shook his head, pointed back downstream, and said, "My friend is there. His name's Morgan. Come on with me, and I'll introduce you to him."

Running Elk frowned and gestured again, more insistently this time. "Dawn Wind," he said again.

"Yeah, I reckon so, but I don't want to go off with you and leave Morgan behind. He'd wonder where I'd gotten off to. Come with me, and we'll get him. Then we can pay a visit to your village."

Running Elk shook his head, even though judging by his expression he didn't understand much, if anything, of what Breckinridge had just said. Stubbornly, he motioned again for Breck to follow him.

"Sorry," Breckinridge said. "I reckon I'll have to

visit your village some other time. I need to get back to camp 'fore my partner gets worried and starts lookin' for me."

Running Elk glared, turned, and stalked off through the trees without looking back.

"Well, shoot," Breckinridge said aloud. "That started out pretty good, leastways after he quit aimin' that arrow at me. Didn't really turn out that way, though. Hope that didn't make an enemy out of him."

He wasn't going to spend too much time worrying about whether Running Elk would hold a grudge against him. If that turned out to be the case, he would find out about it sooner or later. Instead he scouted around the beaver dam a little more, looking for good places to set traps, and then headed back toward the clearing on the river where he had left Morgan.

He heard voices before he got there and realized that something was wrong. Morgan shouldn't have been talking to anybody.

Unless some of Running Elk's people had found *him*, too. At least there hadn't been any shooting so far, Breckinridge thought as he began to hurry.

He paused before he reached the clearing, not wanting to leave the trees and burst out into the open before he knew what was going on. Crouching, he advanced at a more deliberate pace and used the tree trunks for cover until he knelt at a spot where he could look out at the camp Morgan had been in the process of setting up when he was interrupted.

Breckinridge's jaw tightened as he saw Jud Carnahan and two other men standing on the bank with Morgan. They had Breck's partner sort of surrounded, and they looked like they were ready to use the rifles they held.

"—warned you boys," Carnahan was saying. "You crossed us, and the men don't like that."

"You mean that one-eyed son of a bitch Ralston doesn't like us," Morgan shot back defiantly. He didn't lack for courage, even when he was outnumbered. "You know good and well he was behind what happened, Carnahan."

"The major's my second-in-command. I'm not going to turn on him without a mighty good reason, and nobody's given me one. You're right about one thing, though." Carnahan laughed. "He won't like it if he finds out you and Wallace are squatting where we aim to do our trapping."

"You've got no right to run us off," Morgan said. "Breck and I got here first."

"You're outnumbered. I figure that gives us all the right we need." Carnahan paused and smiled. "I'm not an unreasonable man, though. I don't want any more bloodshed than necessary. So I'll make you a proposition, Baxter. You and Wallace pack up and get out of here. Head back upriver until you're completely out of the Bighorn country. I won't say anything to Ralston about you being here, and everybody gets to go on about their business without any more killing. What do you think?"

"I think you can go to hell," Morgan said. Breckinridge was proud of him for that. Running away would stick in Morgan's craw, too.

Carnahan's smile disappeared. He said, "That's a damned foolish attitude to take. It's not going to accomplish anything except to get the two of you killed. But I might lose some men, too, and I'd just as soon not do that. I've already had a couple of them disappear."

That sounded genuine to Breckinridge. Carnahan didn't know what had happened to Hanks and Magnuson. That convinced Breck more than ever that Gordon Ralston had been the third man who'd tried to kill them at the bluff during the snowstorm. Ralston and the other two had slipped away from the party on their mission of vengeance without Carnahan knowing. Ralston hadn't said anything about what happened once he rejoined the group, either, and they must not have noticed the grave where Hanks and Magnuson were buried. Ralston had put it over on Carnahan again.

"This is a big country," Morgan said. "Why don't *you* go somewhere else, and take Ralston and the others with you?"

"Because that's not the way it works. You can do as you're told and get out, or I won't be responsible for what happens next."

Breckinridge decided he had waited long enough. He straightened, stepped out of the trees, and eared back the hammer of his rifle as he lifted the weapon and aimed it at Carnahan.

"You'll be responsible, Carnahan," he said, "but you won't have to worry about it because you'll be dead."

Carnahan had already stiffened at the telltale sound of the flintlock being cocked. He didn't move for a second after Breckinridge spoke. Then he looked back over his shoulder and said, "If you shoot me, Wallace, my men will kill Baxter."

"You won't know for sure, because—"

"Yes, yes, I'll be dead," Carnahan interrupted him. "Don't waste my time with threats, Wallace. You're not the sort to shoot me down in cold blood."

"You're bettin' an awful lot on bein' right about me."

"Of course I am. If a bet's worth making, it's worth going all in on, isn't it?"

Their cool stares met over the sights of Breckinridge's rifle. Carnahan didn't seem the least bit concerned, Breck thought, and he realized that was a warning.

Before he could do anything else, however, he caught a glimpse of movement from the corner of his eye. Breckinridge had good peripheral vision. He could tell that a rifle barrel was sticking out from behind a tree trunk at the edge of the woods—and it was pointed right at him.

Carnahan chuckled and said, "We have more of a standoff than you believed, don't we, Wallace? My man over there could have killed you without you ever knowing he was there. But I made it clear that no one was to die here today unless I gave the order—or unless I was dead myself. So you see, if you shoot me, you'll be dead a second later, and Baxter will follow along immediately. So what do you have to gain by bloodshed?"

"Not a blasted thing, it seems like," Breckinridge admitted. "But neither do you."

"That's true. What you have to consider is this: Is my death worth the both of you dying?"

Damn all this talk, Breckinridge thought. It was making his head hurt. He was built for fighting, not negotiating. He had a hunch he could duck back into the cover of the trees before Carnahan's bushwhacker could kill him, but that would leave Morgan on his own. Breck wasn't going to desert his friend.

Morgan was close to the canoes. He could use them for cover if he could reach them, which would mean getting past Carnahan's two men. They were watching the showdown between Breckinridge and Carnahan, though, and not really paying much attention to Morgan. Breck was still undecided what to do when he saw Morgan's eyes flick toward the canoes and knew the same thoughts were running through his head.

Breckinridge did the last thing any of them would have expected. He swung around to his right, dropped to a knee, and yelled, "Morgan, go!" as he pressed the rifle's trigger.

The flintlock boomed and kicked. A fraction of a second later, the hidden rifleman fired as well, but Breckinridge's move had caught him by surprise and he wasn't as quick getting off his shot. Breck had spotted a narrow bit of leg sticking out from behind the tree where the man was hidden, and that was his target. Blood flew as the rifle ball nicked the man's thigh. The ball from his weapon hummed harmlessly past Breck's head.

At the same time, Morgan lowered his shoulder and rammed into the nearest of Carnahan's men. The trapper yelled and went over backward. Morgan leaped past him and then left his feet in a dive that carried him behind one of the canoes. The other man twisted and fired at him, but the ball went high and splashed into the river.

Carnahan jerked a pistol from behind his belt and triggered it at Breckinridge. Breck was already flinging himself aside, though. He rolled behind one of the trees while Carnahan's ball chewed splinters from the trunk.

"By God, Wallace, I'll kill you now!" Carnahan roared. He ran for cover.

Then everyone froze as a man screamed in agony. Breckinridge looked at the man who had just taken the missed shot at Morgan and saw that he had dropped his rifle as he staggered along the bank. He reached down to his thigh . . .

And clutched the shaft of the arrow protruding from it.

Chapter 13

As the trapper's wounded leg gave out under him and he collapsed to the grass to lie there whimpering, at least a dozen warriors in buckskin stepped out of the trees and completely surrounded the campsite. Each man held a bow and arrow ready to fire. One of them aimed his shaft at the man Breckinridge had wounded, while the others covered Carnahan and the two men with him, including the one whose thigh was already skewered.

Breckinridge stood up, stared at one of the Indians, and exclaimed, "Running Elk?"

From behind the canoe where he had taken cover, Morgan called nervously, "Do you know these fellows, Breck?"

"Yeah, I met one of 'em a few minutes ago," Breckinridge replied. He pulled one of the pistols from behind his belt and pointed it at Carnahan, who clenched his jaw so tightly in anger that his jutting beard shivered a little. "Fella there on your left with the big nose is called Running Elk."

To his surprise, a laugh came from the woods

behind him. Even more surprising, it was a woman's laugh. Breckinridge turned sharply and saw a distinctly feminine figure emerge from the shadows under the trees. She wore a buckskin dress decorated with colorful beadwork. Her raven hair was done into two long braids that hung down over her shoulders.

"My brother is a sensitive soul," she said in English. "He would be hurt if he knew that you had identified him by the size of his nose."

"Well, then, don't tell him," Breckinridge replied. A thought occurred to him. "Your name wouldn't happen to be Dawn Wind, would it, ma'am?"

"That is how I am called in your tongue," she admitted. "And you must be Breck'ridge Wallace."

"It's Breckinridge, actually, or just Breck. Your brother had a little trouble wrappin' his tongue around the whole moniker. I think he wanted me to come back to his village with him so I could talk to you."

Carnahan said, "Damn it, Wallace, stop palavering with that squaw and tell your redskin friends not to point those arrows at us. I have wounded men who need to be tended to."

Breckinridge turned back to him and said, "They ain't really my friends yet, although I hope they will be. I can't tell 'em to do nothin', Carnahan. They're their own bosses. I'll bet that if you put your men in your canoes and got the hell outta here, they'd let you go in peace." He glanced around at Dawn Wind. "How about it?"

She spoke in her native language. Running Elk responded with a curt nod. Dawn Wind said to Breckinridge, "These men can leave. But they are not welcome in the land of the Crow. They should not return, else it be at the cost of their lives."

Carnahan sputtered a little as he said, "You can't do that! We have as much right to trap in this region as anybody else."

"You can take that up with the Crow," Breckinridge said, "as long as you're willin' to risk your lives doin' it. Right now, I reckon it'd be smart for you to git while the gittin's good."

Carnahan glared at him for a moment longer, then gestured to his man who hadn't been hit and said, "Come on. Let's load these boys into the canoes."

One at a time, they helped the injured men into the craft that were pulled up on the bank near the canoes belonging to Breckinridge and Morgan. Both wounds were bloody but not life-threatening, Breck thought. The men did a lot of angry cursing as they were lifted into the canoes.

Running Elk and his fellow warriors didn't lower their bows until the canoes were out in the stream and Carnahan and the other unwounded man were paddling away from there. Breckinridge worried that they might try some rifle shots from out there on the creek, but evidently they didn't want to risk it, as outnumbered as they were.

When the canoes went out of sight around a bend, the Indians finally relaxed. Running Elk came over to Breckinridge and pointed at the woman, who was a year or two younger than him.

"Dawn Wind," he said.

"Yeah, I figured that out," Breckinridge said. "We're obliged to you and your friends for your help."

Dawn Wind translated that for her brother, who

nodded solemnly. She turned to Breckinridge again and said, "Those men are your enemies?"

"Yeah, you could sure say that. One of 'em, especially, who wasn't even here right now. But none of 'em like us, and the feelin' is more than mutual. I wouldn't trust any of that bunch as far as I could throw 'em."

Morgan had come up to join them. He grinned as he said, "And as big as Breck is, he could probably throw one of them a pretty good distance. I'm Morgan Baxter, by the way."

"This here's Dawn Wind. Turns out Runnin' Elk is her brother. Them and these other fellas are from a Crow village not far from here." Breckinridge looked at Dawn Wind. "That's right, ain't it?"

"It is," she said. "And we can take you there now, if you'd like."

"How do you know we're friendly?" Breckinridge asked.

Dawn Wind laughed. "My brother said you were as big and solid as a mountain. He trusts you, and the rest of us trust him. He knows a good man when he sees him. So do I."

Breckinridge felt his face warming a little at that comment. He'd been accused of many things in his life, but being called a good man wasn't all that common.

"It'd be our pleasure to visit your village," he told Dawn Wind. "We'll leave our gear here."

"Two of our men will stand guard, just in case your enemies try to return and cause mischief."

"That's a good idea. We'll be obliged to you."

Running Elk and Dawn Wind led the way through the trees. Breckinridge and Morgan were right behind them, followed by the other Crow warriors who had come back with Running Elk in time to give the two white men a hand.

Their path curved to follow the bend of the creek, and after a mile they came to an even larger clearing, this one big enough to accommodate more than three dozen tipis. A pack of barking dogs came running to meet them. On the heels of the dogs, a number of children appeared, excitedly clamoring to see the two white visitors. More warriors came forward as well and eyed them warily.

"White trappers have come among my people many times in the past," Dawn Wind explained to Breckinridge and Morgan. "Many were friendly, but some were not, so we remain cautious."

"It never hurts to be careful," Breckinridge said.

Running Elk called out to the men of the village in the Crow tongue. They seemed to relax slightly, although they remained watchful. One of them, older and sturdy, with his gray hair in braids and a feather adorning it, met the group and spoke to Running Elk in solemn tones. Running Elk replied in the same manner.

"That is my father," Dawn Wind said quietly to Breckinridge. "In your language, he would be called White Owl. He is our chief."

After talking with Running Elk for a moment, White Owl turned to Breckinridge and Morgan and nodded to them, his seamed face grave and expressionless. He spoke in his language.

"My father welcomes you to our village," Dawn Wind translated. "As long as you are friends to the Apsáalooke, the Apsáalooke will be friends to you."

She paused. "That is our name for ourselves. It means *children of the large-beaked bird.*"

"Reckon that's where Running Elk gets it, then," Breckinridge said. For a second he thought Dawn Wind was going to laugh, but she controlled the impulse.

"That is why the whites decided to call us the Crow," she said instead.

"Tell your father that we're mighty pleased to be here and that we'll try to be good friends to the Apsáalooke."

Dawn Wind passed along that sentiment, which drew a nod from White Owl. He gestured toward the largest of the tipis. Dawn Wind said, "He wishes for you to join him. You and the elders of our people will eat and smoke."

"That sounds mighty good to me," Breckinridge said. He and Morgan had found a good area for trapping and had fallen in with this bunch of Indians who welcomed them in peace.

Seemed like all the luck was running their way for a change.

Nothing happened over the next week to change Breckinridge's opinion on that matter. After sharing a meal and smoking a pipe with White Owl and the other Crow elders, he and Morgan returned to their camp to find that nothing had been disturbed. The two warriors who had been standing guard went back to the village, and the white men slept well and undisturbed, then got up the next morning to begin running their traplines.

These mountain streams remained icy even during

the summer, so wading out into them to set the traps was chilly work. The bright sunlight warmed the men quickly, though. The work began to pay dividends almost immediately, as they found several beaver in the traps the next morning. They skinned the animals and cleaned the pelts, then stretched them out to dry.

That pattern repeated itself every day for a week. Breckinridge didn't want to wipe out all the beaver along this stretch of the stream, so he and Morgan began ranging farther up the creek and extending their line in that direction. That meant they were away from camp more.

Running Elk and some of the other warriors from the Crow band came by now and then. Although Breckinridge and Morgan couldn't talk their language, they shared food with the Indians and spent time in companionable silence, occasionally communicating a little in sign language. Running Elk brought them food as well, berries and dried meat. After several such visits, Breck asked about Dawn Wind, hoping she would be coming to see them soon, but Running Elk just shook his head curtly and offered no explanation for her absence, even in sign language.

Morgan observed that and said with a smile, "You were hoping that gal was sweet on you, weren't you, Breck?"

"What? No! I never thought that. Just figured it might be nice to have somebody else to talk to who speaks the same lingo."

"Yeah, I'm sure that's all it was," Morgan said. He chuckled as Breckinridge growled in annoyance.

But the only reason he was annoyed, he realized,

was because Morgan was right. Nobody back where Breckinridge came from would have considered Dawn Wind pretty, but to him she was strikingly attractive. She seemed smart, too, and he would have liked to know more about her, including how she had come to speak such good English.

At the same time, he felt uneasy because of the feelings she stirred in him. He had enjoyed some good times with a few tavern wenches, but all the women he'd had serious feelings for had either betrayed him or let him down in some other way. Breckinridge wasn't foolish enough to believe that *all* women were like that, but he did wonder sometimes if he was destined—or cursed—to run into the ones who were.

In this case, he was probably getting ahead of himself, and he knew it. He hadn't spent all that much time with Dawn Wind. It was crazy to think there would ever be anything between them.

The ever-expanding trapline meant that he and Morgan had to split up sometimes to cover all the traps. Breckinridge worried on those occasions. Not so much for himself, but for his friend. Although there had been no sign of Carnahan, Ralston, or any of the other trappers from Carnahan's party, Breck knew there was no guarantee they wouldn't show up again, looking for trouble. It was possible the encounter with the Indians had spooked them away from the area, but he and Morgan couldn't count on that.

Still, they had come here to trap beaver, and that's what they were doing. It was a job, sure, but Breckinridge enjoyed being out here in the wilderness. Honestly, although he missed his family back in

Tennessee at times, there was no place else he would rather be.

One afternoon he was the farthest distance upstream he had ever been when he spotted some rocky cliffs rearing up nearby. As he approached them, he began to hear a low, roaring sound. It got louder as he continued along the creek, which turned sharply to the left up ahead.

When he came to that bend, he stopped and looked at the cliffs, which lay a couple of hundred yards away. The creek plunged down from those heights in a glittering waterfall. That was where the roaring sound he'd heard came from. The cascading water was silver and gold in the sunlight. Shining spray hung in the air around it. On top of the cliffs, majestic evergreens reared toward the sky. It was as beautiful a natural sight as Breckinridge had ever seen.

He felt drawn to investigate the waterfall and tramped toward it. His long rifle was held in the crook of his left arm. His keen blue eyes searched the landscape and saw nothing threatening. Birds flitted through the trees, small animals made rustling sounds in the brush, but there was no sign of anything larger, human or animal.

When he neared the base of the cascade, he saw a large pool dotted with rocks at the base of the cliffs. The cliffs themselves weren't as sheer as they had appeared from a distance. Not only that, a path wound upward to the left of the waterfall. Breckinridge figured it was a game trail worn into the rock by deer, antelope, and mountain goats, but it looked like a man could use it, too.

He decided to find out.

The path was a little slippery because of the spray that drifted over to it from time to time. Breckinridge felt the tiny droplets of water brushing his face as he began to climb. He had to take the rifle in his left hand and use his right to grasp places where the rock protruded. These handholds were smooth with use, and that told him plenty of men had climbed these cliffs in the past. Maybe for hundreds of years, or however long the Indians had lived in these parts. That thought made him wonder if he was the first white man to come along here. That was doubtful, he decided, considering how many trappers had journeyed to the frontier over the past few decades . . . but it was possible.

He wasn't winded by the time he reached the top of the path. He stepped from it onto the level ground at the edge of the cliff and turned to look around. He had climbed fifty or sixty feet. That was enough to let him see for a long way out over the valley between the mountain ranges. To the south, those ranges came together into a formidable barrier. Northward, the valley stretched back to the flatter territory along the Missouri and Yellowstone rivers, which from Breckinridge's point of view was a hazy brown and tan expanse in the far, far distance. Closer, the valley was a deep, rich green dotted with clumps of color from the wildflowers that still bloomed in profusion.

The creek brawled along and tumbled over the brink almost at Breckinridge's feet. It made for nice music accompanying some of the most beautiful, spectacular scenery he had ever laid eyes on. Breck's massive chest expanded as he drew in a deep breath.

How could anybody ever choose to live all crowded up in some stinking city when there were places like *this* in the world . . . ?

That was the thought going through his mind when something smashed into his head like a hammerblow and sent him toppling outward into empty space.

Chapter 14

The terrible impact might have caused him to black out, but if it did, that senselessness lasted only a split second. Then Breckinridge was aware that he was falling. He saw rocks flash below him and twisted instinctively in midair. A wild heartbeat later, he struck the water.

He hadn't had time to gulp down any air, so as he went under he had to fight the impulse to take a breath. Pain rampaged through his head and filled it so full it felt like his skull was going to burst. But after a second the iciness of the water in which he was submerged dulled the agony somewhat.

His brain was working well enough for him to realize that the pool had saved his life, at least for now. Even though he had struck the water hard, it was more forgiving than the jagged rocks would have been. He had knifed below the surface, and it was deep enough that he hadn't hit the bottom.

Now, though, he had to have air. At the same time, he felt consciousness slipping away and struggled to hang on to it. If he passed out, he would drown. No two ways about it.

However, that wasn't the only danger. Someone must have taken a shot at him. That was the only explanation that made sense. No one had been close enough to hit him with a club—Breckinridge knew that. Someone had tried to kill him, but the ball had only clipped his head.

Did the would-be murderer know that? Or had he taken his shot, seen Breckinridge topple off the cliff after being hit in the head, and assumed that he was dead? Would the varmint try to find him and check? If he made it out of the pool, would he just be exposing himself to another gunshot?

Those questions flashed through Breckinridge's brain. He had no answers for them, nor did he have the luxury of pondering them. If he didn't get air, he was going to die—that was certain. He had dropped the rifle when he fell, so both arms were free. His muscles resisted the command at first, but then he stroked hard and broke the pool's surface. Breck opened his mouth and hauled in a lungful of sweet, life-giving air. He got some water in his mouth, too, and sputtered a little as he floated there.

Everything spun crazily around him. The sky, the pool, and the cliffs in between traded places with each other in rapid succession. The pain in his head blossomed again. He knew he was still on the verge of passing out. Another man without his incredible vitality would have lost consciousness before now. Breckinridge knew he had to get out of the pool while he had the chance. He struggled to reach the edge, but the growing weakness inside him held him back.

It seemed like the water was trying to pull him under again.

Suddenly, something took hold of his right arm. Breckinridge looked up, but his vision had gone so blurry he couldn't make out anything except varying patches of light and darkness. A shape moved in front of him. The hands fastened on his sleeve hauled him forward. His feet brushed something. The bottom of the pool? Breck couldn't think of what else it could be, so he shoved against it at the same time as his rescuer fought to pull him out of the pool. He flopped forward, his muscles limp and useless now. Faintly, he heard what sounded like grunts of effort.

The world receded around him and he couldn't hold on to it anymore. Blackness rose up and swallowed him whole.

The first thing he was aware of was a frigid chill that went all the way through him and froze his bones and guts. He felt a feeble bit of warmth pressed against him, but it wasn't enough to keep him from shaking. Every movement, even those shivers, made pain explode in his head. Breckinridge wanted to go back to the oblivion in which he had floated for a time beyond knowing. Nothingness wasn't nearly as unpleasant as what he was experiencing right now.

On top of everything else, he was wet. That just made him colder. Water sheened his face and dripped into his eyes, nose, and mouth. It was an even bet whether he would freeze to death or drown first. Assuming, of course, that his pounding head didn't just split apart like a dropped melon . . .

"Be quiet," a voice said in his ear. "They are out there."

The words didn't make sense to Breckinridge at first, but then their meaning soaked into his stunned consciousness. So did the fact that the voice belonged to a woman. He still didn't know where they were and he wasn't clear on everything that had happened, but for now he supposed all that could wait. He clamped his jaw shut to keep his teeth from chattering and lay there as still and quiet as he could. Gradually he realized that the woman lay beside him and had her arms around him, trying to share the warmth of her body with him.

Breckinridge still had no sense of time passing. Finally, the woman whispered, "I think they are gone now. I will look. Stay here."

She didn't have to tell him that. He wasn't going anywhere. He couldn't.

He groaned softly, though, as the warmth that came from her went away. The deadly chill began to seep through him again.

Then she was back, saying in a low but urgent voice, "Come with me. You must help me, Breckinridge. You are too big for me to drag alone."

She knew his name. Breckinridge had already started thinking fuzzily that he must know this woman. Something about her voice was familiar. Now that he knew she was aware of who he was, that left only one answer.

Dawn Wind.

His eyes were still closed. He forced them open and saw a curtain of water falling only a couple of feet away. He was lying on a rock ledge behind the waterfall. How she had gotten him back here, he had no idea. He must not have completely lost consciousness earlier, when everything had faded away around him. With his help, she had gotten both of them into hiding, although he didn't remember it happening.

She knelt in the shallow water next to him, tugging at his buckskin shirt. Breckinridge groaned again, put a hand on the ledge, and pushed himself halfway up into a sitting position. That made his head spin worse, so he had to wait until it settled down. When it did, he lifted his other hand and touched his head with shaking fingers. He found a tender spot.

"That is where the ball struck you," Dawn Wind said over the constant roar of the water. "The water washed away all the blood. I do not think the bone is broken, Breckinridge."

"I got . . . a hard head." The raspy sound of his voice surprised him. But as soaked and half-frozen as he was, what did he expect?

"This way," she said as she urged him to slide along the ledge to his left. "It stays shallow this way. I cannot pull you out of the deeper water again."

She had saved his life. Breckinridge had no doubt about that. What she was doing here, why she had been close by when he was shot, he didn't know, but right now that wasn't important. He hunched and scraped and crawled, and the waterfall pounded at him, and once again for a dizzying second he thought he was going to drown. Then he rolled onto another flat, hard surface and lay with his face pointed upward as an enormous light blazed down at him, bringing with it warmth.

That was the sun, he thought. He lay there with his chest heaving and soaked in as much of the heat as he could.

He sensed as much as felt someone lying down beside him. Had to be Dawn Wind, he thought. Her shoulder nudged against his with a comfortable intimacy. When he felt like he wasn't about to die after all, he shaded his eyes with a hand, turned his head, and looked at her. Her eyes were closed as the sunlight washed over her face. The soaked buckskin dress she wore clung to every curve of her body, which was made more obvious by the way her chest rose and fell rapidly.

"Are you . . . looking at me . . . Breckinridge?" she asked without opening her eyes.

The question caught him a little by surprise. "I, uh . . . Yeah, I am."

"Good. Then you probably . . . will not die. A man on the verge of death . . . does not look at a woman . . . with desire in his heart."

He pushed himself up on an elbow. "I never said I had desire in my heart."

"It is all right if you do." She didn't sound quite so breathless now. Even though her eyes were closed, she turned her head so her face was pointed away from him, as if she were embarrassed. She went on, "When you first came to our village . . . I looked at how large and strong you are . . . and thought about what it would be like if you took me in your arms."

Well, if that didn't beat all, Breckinridge thought. Shot in the head, falls off a cliff, damn near drowns, and still winds up lying on a rock beside a mountain pool with a good-looking woman talking desire at him.

If Morgan was here, he would probably give his old friend a good swift kick in the rear right about now, just out of sheer jealousy.

Breckinridge put that thought out of his head and sat up. He asked, "Did you see who shot me?"

Dawn Wind rolled onto her side facing him and opened her eyes. "No. I saw you on top of the cliff and was looking at you when I heard the shot. Then you fell. I thought you must be dead. I hurried toward the waterfall to be sure. Then you began to thrash around in the pool and I knew you lived. So I jumped in to help you."

"I reckon you saved my life. I don't see how you got me up on that little ledge behind the waterfall. What made you decide to do that?"

"I was afraid the man who shot you would come to make certain you were dead. I thought it would be best if you were hidden." One shoulder rose and fell in a graceful shrug. "A person can do more than they believe is possible, when there is enough danger."

"You're right about that." Breckinridge frowned. "And I recollect you sayin' somebody was out here. Did you see who it was?"

Dawn Wind shook her head. "It is difficult to see anything through the waterfall. That is why I decided we should hide there. I could tell there were two men moving around, that is all."

"A couple of Carnahan's men, I'll bet. Maybe Carnahan his own self."

"The short, ugly man with the long beard?"

"Yeah, that's him. He's got a grudge against me. All of that bunch do. Especially one fella who wears a patch over his left eye. If you ever see somebody like that, you'd best steer well clear of him. He's pure poison."

"I avoid every white man," she said, "until I know he can be trusted."

"And you know that about me?"

"I would not have risked my life to help you, otherwise."

"And I'm mighty obliged to you for that." Breckinridge paused. "How'd you come to be in this neck o' the woods, anyway? Are your brother or any more of your people close by?"

She shook her head. "Running Elk is with a hunting party that left our village going in a different direction. Our band of the Apsáalooke consider all the land on both sides of this creek, all the way to the mountains, as our hunting grounds. I like to explore it."

"By yourself?"

Dawn Wind sat up and pushed her wet braids back from her face. "I am not afraid to be alone. I can run fast, and I can fight if I need to."

"I'll bet you can," Breckinridge said. He wondered if she had spotted him traipsing up here and followed him, or if it actually was just a pure accident she had been nearby when he was ambushed. Either way, he was a mighty lucky fella.

She was sitting close enough to him on the big slab of rock that she could lean over just slightly and reach up to touch his head. He started to draw back, then steeled himself to stay still as her fingertips gently explored the area around the wound.

"Does that hurt?" she asked.

"A mite. But it feels a hell of a lot better than it did just a little while ago."

That was true. The pain had subsided to a dull ache. His vision was clear. The icy water had stopped the bleeding from the wound and washed away the gore that had already seeped out. He could already feel his iron constitution starting to heal him.

"Yes," Dawn Wind said as if she knew what he was thinking. "You will live. If you do not grow sick from being so wet and chilled. The sun is warm. We should let it dry our bodies and our clothes."

Before he could say or do anything, she got lithely and gracefully to her feet, reached down to catch hold of the bottom of her buckskin dress, and peeled the sodden garment up and over her head.

Chapter 15

That left Dawn Wind nude except for her moccasins. She kicked those off as well, then moved to spread her wet dress over a rock to dry. Breckinridge couldn't take his eyes off her sleek body. She turned to him with a complete lack of self-consciousness and asked, "Are you not going to take your clothes off?"

Breckinridge swallowed hard. "Well, I, uh . . . I reckon they'd dry quicker that way, wouldn't they?"

"Yes, they would," she said in a calm and steady voice.

Breckinridge scrambled to his feet and started trying to yank the soaked buckskin shirt off. He moved too fast, though, and his head started spinning again. He put out a hand to balance himself and said, "Whoa."

Dawn Wind took his hand and used her other hand to clasp his elbow and support him. Having her standing that close to him, as naked as the day she was born, didn't do all that much to help his mental state, but at least after a moment his dizziness subsided.

"Let me help you," she said.

"Yeah, that might be a good idea," Breckinridge

admitted. He had thought at first that she was trying to seduce him, but maybe she was just being practical. Their clothes really would dry faster this way, and so would their bodies. She didn't have to worry about him getting too carried away, either. He was weak as a kitten right now, and if he tried anything, she could probably fight him off without too much trouble, even as big as he was.

Besides, if he exerted himself too much, more than likely he'd just pass out again before things could get too out of hand.

So maybe for once in his life, he ought to just act like a gentleman, naked gal or no naked gal.

Despite that resolve, his heart pounded along at a pretty good pace as Dawn Wind helped him get his clothes and boots off. The wet buckskin stubbornly resisted her efforts. Eventually, working together, they got him into as much of a jaybird state as she was. Her gaze roamed over his body, frankly assessing him, and she appeared to be pleased by what she saw. Breckinridge felt himself turning red all over.

"Does the warm sun not feel good?" she asked.

"Yeah, it does."

Dawn Wind gestured toward the rock slab at their feet. "We should sit down again."

"Yeah, that's a, uh, good idea."

Breckinridge sat down, pulled his knees up a little, and rested his arms on them. Dawn Wind sank to the rock beside him, stretched her legs out in front of her, and leaned back, placing her hands slightly behind her to support herself.

"Where do you come from, Breckinridge Wallace?" she asked.

"I was born and raised in Tennessee. My folks had a farm there."

"Why did you leave and come west?"

He didn't want to tell her that he'd been fleeing a murder charge, even a false one. So he said, "I always liked bein' out in the woods, huntin' and explorin', better than I did farmin'." There was a large measure of truth to that statement. "When I got a chance to be part of an army expedition that was mappin' the frontier, I was glad to go along. From there I moved on to fur trappin'."

"I am glad you decided to come to our land. I think you will always be a friend to my people."

"I'd sure like that," Breckinridge said. "I'm the peace-lovin' sort and never go lookin' for trouble."

She glanced over at him, then laughed. "You sound like you really believe that."

"Well . . . it's my intention, anyway. It don't always turn out like that, though."

"No, I am sure it does not."

They sat in easy silence for a few minutes. Breckinridge kept stealing looks at her, but he had to stop because she was having too great an effect on him. He frowned slightly and concentrated on the pool in front of them instead. To get his mind off their nudity, he asked, "How'd you learn to talk English so good?"

"A white trapper taught me, many moons ago when I was a little girl. He was a good man who never grew annoyed when the children of the village followed him around. A very good friend to my people. He was called Preacher."

Breckinridge's shaggy red eyebrows rose in surprise. "Preacher!" he repeated. "I know that fella."

"He is still alive?" Dawn Wind seemed surprised, too.

"Sure. At least, he was last year when I met him. When it comes to bein' a mountain man, there ain't nobody more famous than Preacher. He's like Colter, Bridger, Beckwourth, fellas like that." Breckinridge waved a hand at the mountains. "Probably wouldn't even be a fur trade without men like Preacher. That old varmint might just live forever."

"That would be a good thing. He has helped the Apsáalooke many times, especially in their wars against the Blackfeet."

"Yeah, I remember your people don't get along with them."

"*No one* gets along with the Blackfeet, as you put it, Breckinridge."

"I'll be sure to watch out for them, then."

"They are mostly north of here. They should not trouble you. But from what I have seen, it is your own people who are the greatest threat."

Breckinridge frowned. "Carnahan and his bunch ain't my people. I'd hoped they had moved on. Nobody else in these parts would have any reason to take a shot at me, though. Wonder if it was an accident they spotted me and decided to try to kill me, or if they been followin' me and waitin' for a chance like this."

"You should not be alone. You and your friend Morgan should stay together."

Breckinridge rubbed his jaw and nodded. "Yeah, you're right. And I've got to worryin' . . . Those fellas who took that shot at me know Morgan's out there somewhere by himself. What if they go to look for him?"

"Do you know where he is?" Dawn Wind asked.

"I know where he started out for. He was gonna

work his way up the other side of the creek. I don't figure he got this far, because he had more traps to check than I did. I was mostly lookin' for new places to set 'em."

"We must go and make sure he is all right. Our clothes should be mostly dry by now." She stood up and reached for her dress. She nodded as she felt it. "Yes, it is fine."

"Yeah, we should go," Breckinridge said.

But even though he knew she was right, he still felt a pang of disappointment go through him as she slipped the dress over her head and pulled it down, hiding her body from him once again.

They left the pool behind and started back downstream, staying on the other side of the creek this time. Despite the distraction of Dawn Wind's nudity, Breckinridge had tried to remain alert while they were sitting beside the pool, just in case whoever shot him had doubled back. He was watchful now as they made their way through the trees and stayed in the cover of the woods whenever possible.

His head still hurt some, but he was able to ignore it. The dizziness and weakness had gone away. He wouldn't be at his best in a fight right now, but he hoped that if they ran into trouble, his best wouldn't be needed to cope with it.

Before setting out, he had searched among the rocks surrounding the pool and found his rifle. It appeared to have been undamaged by the fall except for a nick in the stock from where it had landed on a jagged stone. Breckinridge felt better with the weapon in his hands. Since his pistols had been submerged in the pool, he had also unloaded, cleaned, and dried them before reloading them.

Dawn Wind's only weapon was a small knife she carried in a deer-hide sheath. Breckinridge didn't intend to put her in harm's way, though, so he told himself it didn't matter how she was armed.

When they reached the bend in the creek, he paused and turned to look back at the waterfall. As things had turned out, it was a place of both beauty and danger, but he didn't think he would ever forget what had happened there today. It had been memorable . . . in more ways than one.

They had gone perhaps another mile back toward the camp when Breckinridge and Dawn Wind both paused suddenly at the same time. Breck heard some popping sounds in the distance, and when he looked at Dawn Wind he knew that she had heard them, too.

"Gunshots," he said. "And not just from one man, either."

"Your friend Morgan must be in trouble."

He jerked his head in a nod. "I got to get there as quick as I can."

"I can keep up," Dawn Wind vowed. "Let us go."

They plunged ahead through the forest at a much faster pace now, throwing caution to the wind. The exertion made Breckinridge's head hurt worse, but he didn't care about that. He just wanted to reach Morgan in time to help his friend.

If anything happened to Morgan, Breckinridge would see to it that the men responsible paid for it, no matter how long it took. He would track them down and settle the score, and his vengeance would be terrible to behold.

But it would be better to save Morgan than to

have to avenge him, so Breckinridge practically flew through the trees. He heard Dawn Wind panting behind him as she tried to keep up, but he didn't slow down for her. Honestly, it would have been fine with him if she weren't so stubborn. He would rather deal with the trouble without having to worry about her.

He figured nothing he said would make her hang back, though. She had saved his life earlier. She probably felt responsible for him now.

The gunfire got louder, although sometimes it was difficult to hear it over the pounding in his head. They came in sight of a mostly bare knoll that stuck up about fifty yards from the creek. A few trees grew on top of the little hill. A figure knelt there among them, trying to take advantage of the meager cover as he fired his rifle down toward some thick brush at the bottom of the knoll. A thin gray cloud of powder smoke hung over the brush as men concealed in it returned the fire at the man on the hill.

Breckinridge thrust out an arm to stop Dawn Wind as she came running up behind him. He pointed and said, "They got Morgan trapped up there, the sons o' bitches."

"At least he is still fighting them. That means he is alive."

"Yeah, I thought of that." Breckinridge stiffened as he caught a glimpse of a couple of men darting through the brush. "But he may not be for long. Those varmints are gonna try to get around and come up behind him."

"We must stop them."

"That's what I figure on doin'."

Breckinridge lifted his rifle and aimed at a gap in the brush. The men attempting to flank Morgan would have to cross that gap to reach the other side of the knoll. He wouldn't have time to drop both of them, but he hoped if he could down one of the bastards, the other man would turn back and not risk it. Even doing that much was going to take quick reflexes and dead aim, though. Breck wished his head wasn't throbbing quite so much.

A flicker of movement from within the brush near the gap caught his eye. Getting even that much warning was a stroke of luck. He took up some of the pressure on the trigger. A heartbeat later, one of the men emerged into the open and started across at a crouching run.

Breckinridge fired.

The distance was at least a hundred yards. It was going to take a hell of a shot. And that was what Breckinridge made at that moment. The running man stumbled, threw up his hands, and pitched forward on his face.

The other man had just broken out of the brush when his companion dropped. He stopped short and scrambled backward so abruptly that his feet went out from under him and he fell to his knees. He dived back into cover, obviously afraid that a rifle ball might come looking for him at any instant.

Breckinridge started reloading. He performed the task swiftly and efficiently as he said, "That'll stop 'em for a minute, anyway."

"But now they know someone has come to help Morgan," Dawn Wind pointed out.

"Yeah, and if it's Carnahan's bunch—and I don't see who else it could be—they'll probably figure it's me, too. Carnahan will split his force and send some of 'em after us." Breckinridge looked over at Dawn

Wind. "You got to get outta here now, while you still got the chance."

She regarded him just as steadily and said, "I will not leave you, Breckinridge Wallace."

"Now, damn it, Dawn Wind—"

"You are wasting your breath *and* your time. Time that would be better spent giving me one of those pistols you carry."

"You know how to use a pistol?"

"I have shot a gun before. Cock it, point it, and pull the trigger. Is this not correct?"

Breckinridge fought down the impulse to grin at the matter-of-fact way she put it. He still wanted her to flee, not to encourage her to stay.

But then a gun cracked somewhere not far away, and a ball clipped through the branches not far above their heads. He bit back a curse, yanked one of the pistols from behind his belt, and pressed the butt into her waiting hands.

"Don't shoot it unless you have to," he told her.

"And if I have to?"

"Then make sure you kill the son of a bitch you're pointin' it at," Breckinridge said.

Chapter 16

More shots blasted. Breckinridge put a hand on Dawn Wind's shoulder. They knelt as the rifle balls tore through the undergrowth and thudded into tree trunks. Splinters flew.

"They're tryin' to soften us up for a charge," Breckinridge said in a low voice. "There might still be time for you to get outta this mess. You'd have to crawl—"

"And have them hunt me down after they kill you?" Dawn Wind shook her head. "We will fight them together, Breckinridge. We will live or die together."

Damn, she was one hell of a gal, he thought, and then he exclaimed, "Here they come!"

Four men rushed forward, firing pistols as they charged. The balls hummed perilously close. Breckinridge didn't let that distract him. He took aim and pressed the rifle's trigger. The flintlock boomed. One of the attackers doubled over as the shot tore into his midsection. Breck dropped the rifle, pulled his second pistol, and fired. A man twisted around and blood flew from a wounded arm.

The other two turned and ran. The man Breckinridge had just shot stumbled after them, his injured arm flopping at his side.

"They run like dogs!" Dawn Wind said.

"Yeah, varmints like that don't have much stomach for fightin'," Breckinridge said. "They're only brave when everything's goin' their way."

More shots searched through the forest for them, but Breckinridge and Dawn Wind were able to pull back slightly and take cover behind some pines. The tang of fresh sap hung in the air from the places where rifle balls had blown away the rough bark. Breck reloaded his rifle and pistol, then slid the flintlock's long barrel around the tree trunk and drew a bead on the brush where the men firing at Morgan were hidden. He sent a ball into that growth and was rewarded by a pained yelp.

Dawn Wind said, "We have them in a . . . what do you call it? A cross fire?"

"Yep," Breckinridge said. "Morgan's got the high ground in front of 'em, and we got their backsides. That ain't a good place to be. They've tried bustin' out past us, and that didn't work for 'em. Now they can keep fightin' or—" He paused and let out a hearty laugh. "Yeah, that's what I thought. Look over yonder, to the right of where they were. See that brush wavin' around? They're lightin' out!"

"But two of their men are dead," Dawn Wind said, clearly puzzled. "Do they intend to leave those bodies behind?"

"That bunch ain't got the same sort of honor that your folks do," Breckinridge told her. "Right now, all they want to do is cut their losses. Those dead fellas ain't worth nothin' to them anymore."

Wary of a trick of some sort, he watched and waited for quite a while before venturing out from cover. On top of the knoll, Morgan did likewise. Breckinridge could see his friend up there, kneeling behind one of the few trees on the hill.

Eventually, Morgan stood up and waved his hat over his head. Since Morgan had the better vantage point, Breckinridge took that to mean he was sure the attackers were gone. Breck stepped out, took off his hat, and returned the signal. Then he said over his shoulder to Dawn Wind, "Stay here whilst I have a look around. And hang on to that pistol I give you. You might still need it."

The first thing he did was check the bodies of the two men he had shot. Both were dead. When he used a boot toe to roll them onto their backs, Breckinridge recognized their faces, although he couldn't recall their names. They were two of Jud Carnahan's men, though, no doubt about that.

Morgan came down from the hill and walked toward him, still looking around warily and holding his rifle ready for instant use. As he came up to Breckinridge, he said, "I'm mighty glad to see you, you big redheaded rascal."

"You don't appear to be shot to doll rags."

Morgan grinned. "No, I'm not hurt. They tried to sneak up on me, but either they're not very good at it or else I'm starting to turn into a halfway decent frontiersman myself. I heard them coming and was able to take cover on that hill." He shrugged. "Unfortunately, once I got up there the cover wasn't as good as I'd hoped and there was nowhere for me to go."

"Why didn't you go down the other side?"

"Then they would have just pursued me. I thought it was better to make a stand." Morgan grew more solemn. "Actually, when Carnahan yelled up at me and demanded that I surrender, he claimed you were dead. That just made me more determined than ever to put up a fight." He smiled again. "I'm glad to see that he was wrong."

"Yeah, but not for lack of tryin'." Breckinridge took off his hat and pointed at the gash on the side of his head, which had oozed enough blood that now it was starting to scab over. "That's how close they come to blowin' my brains out."

"Son of a—It's a good thing you have a rock for a skull, Breck. Are you all right?"

"A mite light-headed now and then, but I'll be fine . . . thanks to Dawn Wind."

He turned and gestured for her to come out of the trees. Morgan's smile widened into a grin as she did so.

"She just happened to come along after you got shot?"

"That's right," Breckinridge said. He tried not to sound defensive about it.

"Well, I've always said you were a lucky man, Breckinridge."

Morgan didn't know *how* lucky, Breckinridge thought as he remembered the time he and Dawn Wind had spent beside that pool at the bottom of the waterfall. Breck didn't intend to tell him about it, either.

Instead, Breckinridge said, "I figure a couple of those varmints spotted me, took a shot at me, thought I was dead, and went back to tell the others. Then they came a-huntin' you, knowin' that you were gonna be by yourself."

"That makes sense," Morgan agreed. "I was hoping that Carnahan and his party had left the country, since we hadn't seen them in a good while."

"Perhaps they will leave now," Dawn Wind said. "You have killed several of them and wounded others, is this not true?"

"Yep, we've done some damage to 'em," Breckinridge said.

"Will they not . . . how did you put it? Cut their losses and leave?"

"We can hope," Breckinridge said.

But somehow in his bones he doubted it.

Morgan wanted to know more about Breckinridge getting bushwhacked and Dawn Wind's involvement in the incident. Breck told him an abbreviated version as they headed back to the Crow village, leaving out most of the details. Breck wanted to make sure Dawn Wind was safe among her people before he and Morgan returned to their camp.

When they got there, Running Elk and the men who had been hunting with him were already back. The young warrior was glad to see his sister. He cast a few suspicious glances at Breckinridge when he heard about the ambush and how Dawn Wind had come to his aid. Breck kept his description of the day's events pretty sketchy in this case, as well.

Running Elk didn't bother concealing his anger when he spoke after Breckinridge had concluded the story. Breck looked over at Dawn Wind, who translated, "He says he and the other warriors should find this man Carnahan and his friends and kill them all."

White Owl spoke in a cautionary tone. Again Dawn Wind provided the translation for Breckinridge and Morgan. "My father says that killing white men just leads to more trouble." Running Elk replied sharply. "And my brother says that some white men need killing."

"I can't argue with him about that," Breckinridge said. "Carnahan and Ralston fit that description, I reckon."

Running Elk and White Owl wrangled about it some more, then Running Elk stalked off, obviously angry. Breckinridge didn't need a translation to know that the Crow chief had prevailed in the argument. The warriors would not try to hunt down the party of trappers . . . at least not yet.

Dawn Wind suggested to Breckinridge, "You and Morgan should move your camp here to our village. You will be safer that way."

"I never figured our safety would be guaranteed when we come to the Rocky Mountains," Breckinridge said. "Nobody in his right mind would. And if we were stayin' here, that might just bring trouble down on you and your people."

Morgan said, "Carnahan and Ralston have more of a grudge against us than they do against you folks. Breck's right. The best thing for you is if we just go our own way from now on. It might be even better if we found another creek to do our trapping."

"No," Breckinridge and Dawn Wind said at the

same time. Breck went on hastily, "I don't reckon we have to go that far."

Morgan chuckled. "Fine. It was just an idea. I can understand why you feel that way, though. Still, it might be a good idea if we didn't spend too much time here in the future. We don't want to give Carnahan even more of an excuse to bother those folks."

Breckinridge sighed. He knew Morgan was right. The idea of seeing less of Dawn Wind didn't appeal to him.

But, he reminded himself wryly, he couldn't really see *more* of her than he already had.

Breckinridge had been worried that Carnahan's bunch might have gone to the camp and stolen everything, but the place appeared to be untouched when he and Morgan got there.

He began to feel sick that night. By the next morning he couldn't keep anything in his stomach, and the dizziness was even worse than it had been the day before. His head throbbed and spun every time he moved. Morgan hovered around with a worried frown on his face, even though Breckinridge told him to go ahead and check the traplines.

"I don't care about the pelts," Morgan said. "Somebody needs to keep an eye on you, Breck. I wish there was a doctor somewhere closer than a thousand miles away."

"I don't need a sawbones," Breckinridge insisted. "I just got a hard wallop on the head, and it's makin' me feel poorly. That's all. I'll be fine in a day or two."

"Why don't I go to the Crow village and get Dawn Wind to come and take care of you?"

Breckinridge started to refuse that suggestion, then thought about it and said, "Well, if you really think you ought to . . ."

"I'll be back as soon as I can."

True to his word, Morgan was gone less than an hour. When he returned, he had Dawn Wind with him . . . but Running Elk and an elderly Indian had come along, too.

Dawn Wind dropped to her knees beside Breckinridge where he lay on his bedroll. "This is Badger's Den," she introduced the old man. "He is a medicine man of great power." She rested a hand on Breck's shoulder. "I thought you were all right, Breckinridge."

"So did I," he murmured. "I reckon sometimes gettin' hit in the head can catch up to you later on."

Badger's Den built up the fire and tossed some sort of herbs he took from a hide pouch onto the flames. Whatever the stuff was, it burned with a stink bad enough to make Breckinridge wrinkle his nose when he caught a whiff of the smoke. The old-timer took out a rattle and began to shake it as he shuffled around Breck and chanted words that made no sense. Breck sighed and closed his eyes, figuring maybe he could go to sleep in spite of the racket.

Badger's Den stopped and bent over to seize Breckinridge's shoulder in a clawlike hand. He gave it a hard shake that made Breck's eyes pop open. "What the hell!" he exclaimed.

Badger's Den jabbered something. Dawn Wind told Breckinridge, "He says you must not sleep. Evil spirits have crept into your brain, and if you sleep, it will give them a chance to build a mighty fortress. Then all of his medicine will not be able to chase them out. So you must stay awake and give what he is doing a chance to work."

"But I'm mighty tired," Breckinridge protested.

"I have told you what Badger's Den said. If you sleep, you may die."

Breckinridge sighed and muttered some curses under his breath. He said, "All right, all right, I'll try to stay awake. But I ain't makin' no promises."

Badger's Den spoke to Running Elk and gestured curtly toward Breckinridge. Running Elk nodded solemnly.

Dawn Wind smiled a little as she said, "Badger's Den has charged my brother with keeping you awake. Running Elk will take such a responsibility very seriously."

Breckinridge saw how the young warrior was frowning at him and said, "Yeah, I'll just bet he will. He'll take some pleasure in makin' me miserable, too."

"That is possible. He has an idea of how I feel about you, Breckinridge, and it does not make him happy."

"Well, he's your big brother and all. If he knew everything that happened . . ."

"He does not. But the fact that we were together without clothing would bother him less than knowing how fond I am of you. We care less about things of the body than we do about things of the spirit."

Morgan said, "Wait just a dang minute! The two of you were together without—"

"Aw, hush up and let Badger's Den get on with his medicine-makin'," Breckinridge said.

Even though the four people taking care of him made sure he stayed awake, Breckinridge was in and out of coherence for the next day and a half. He might not have been asleep, but he had no idea what was going on at times.

Finally, he looked around, realized it was morning, and saw that Badger's Den was no longer shuffling around him and chanting. He turned his head to look for the old man. The movement didn't cause any pain or dizziness this time. Emboldened, Breckinridge started to sit up.

Dawn Wind appeared beside him and put a hand on his shoulder. "You must rest," she told him. "Badger's Den says the evil spirits are gone from your head and that you will be all right now, but you are still very weak."

"The old-timer . . . is gone?"

"Yes, he returned to the village last night. And Morgan and my brother have gone to check the traps this morning. Running Elk is going to help with the trapping until you are well again, Breckinridge."

"I'm mighty obliged to him for that, but he don't have to do such a thing," Breckinridge said as he lay back on the pile of blankets where he had been resting for the past couple of days. "I'll be on my feet in no time." Something occurred to him now that he was thinking more clearly again. "What about Carnahan? Has there been any sign of him or the rest of his troublemakers?"

Dawn Wind shook her head. "No one has come near the camp. Our hope is that they have finally decided to leave you and Morgan alone."

"Mine, too."

"That is another reason Running Elk stayed. He did not think Morgan should be working the traplines alone." Dawn Wind smiled. "I think you have another partner for the summer, if you want his help."

"That sounds all right to me. We'll have to pay him back some way, though. I don't imagine he'd be interested in a share of the profits."

"Your friendship will be payment enough, I think." She paused. "Also, I believe he intends to keep an eye on you and me. The only reason he left us alone today is because you are so weak. He assumes you will not behave improperly."

"Reckon he's the only one . . . who ever assumed that about me," Breckinridge said. "I'm mighty tired. Is it all right to sleep now?"

"Badger's Den said you could."

"Damn well about time." Breckinridge settled back and closed his eyes. He sighed as he felt Dawn Wind's fingertips lightly brush his forehead. He heard her murmur something as she leaned close to him, but he couldn't make out the words, and sleep claimed him before he could ask her what she had said.

Chapter 17

It was rare for Breckinridge to be sick for very long, and this case was no exception. After sleeping for several hours and then eating a big meal of biscuits and salt pork, washed down by multiple cups of hot coffee, he felt so much energy flowing back into his body that he had to get up and move around. Dawn Wind told him to be careful and not do too much, but Breck could tell that he was almost back to normal.

Morgan and Running Elk returned to the camp late that afternoon with several beaver they had harvested from the traps. When Morgan saw Breckinridge sitting beside the fire with a cup of coffee in his hand, he grinned and said, "I was hoping you'd be up and around when we got back, Breck. How do you feel?"

"A whole heap better," Breckinridge replied. "Good enough to skin those beaver and clean the pelts, if you want."

"We brought 'em in, didn't we, Running Elk?" Morgan said to his companion. "It's only fair that

Breck do some of the work now that he's feeling better, isn't it?"

Running Elk didn't say anything. He just crossed his arms and regarded Breckinridge solemnly, then turned his gaze to his sister. Dawn Wind spoke to him in the Crow tongue. Running Elk grunted in apparent disbelief, then responded to whatever she had said. She told Breckinridge, "My brother thinks I should return to our people's village."

"Maybe you should," Breckinridge said, although his heart didn't really agree with that sentiment. "You've been gone for several days, takin' care of me."

"I feared for your life," Dawn Wind said. "And my life would no longer be complete without you, Breckinridge."

That comment made worry stir inside him. It sounded mighty like she was telling him she loved him. The last woman who had told him that . . .

He shoved the thought away. The past was over and done with and ought not to have anything to do with the present. His main concern about the way Dawn Wind felt was the knowledge that one day he would be moving on. Since leaving home, he hadn't been the sort to stay in a place for very long. That might change someday, when he was older and started feeling like he ought to settle down, but he wasn't ready for that now.

He needed to be careful and not lead her on. He didn't want her to believe they would be together forever. The last thing he wanted to do was hurt her. In the long run, the kindest thing to do would be to make sure she didn't get too attached to him.

Gruffly, he said, "Yeah, you go on back home. I'll let you know if I need you."

Hurt flared in her eyes at his tone and his words. But she said, "You should be careful and take care of your head—"

"I'll be fine," he interrupted curtly. "Thanks for your help."

She regarded him intently for a moment with a mixture of anger and confusion on her face, then nodded and said, "Good-bye, Breckinridge."

"So long," he said offhandedly.

Dawn Wind snapped something at her brother in their language. Running Elk glared at Breckinridge, but there was nothing new about that. Both of them turned and walked away from the camp, heading back toward their village.

Morgan frowned at Breckinridge and asked, "What the hell was that about, Breck? All of a sudden, you acted like you don't give a damn about that girl, and after all she's done for you!"

"That ain't true at all. She just needs to get on with her life and stop worryin' about me."

"She's just afraid you aren't right in the head yet." Morgan snorted. "I have to say, I'm not sure I disagree with her."

Breckinridge turned away. Dawn Wind had told him to take care of his head, and Morgan had just said sort of the same thing. Breck knew, though, that if there was a problem, it didn't lie in his head.

It was his heart he had to worry about.

Thankfully, there was a lot of work to do. That kept Breckinridge's mind off any potential trouble with Dawn Wind. She didn't show up at the camp, and

Breck and Morgan were kept busy working their traplines.

After what had happened, Breckinridge didn't expect Running Elk to show up and help them anymore, but he was wrong about that. The young warrior trotted up to their camp every morning and accompanied them when they went to check their traps. Whenever Breck and Morgan needed to split up, Running Elk went with Morgan so he wouldn't have to be alone in case of an ambush. The two of them quickly became friends and learned how to communicate with sign language and a few words of each other's tongue. Running Elk still didn't seem to like Breck very much, but Breck didn't mind that. He avoided the Crow village, not wanting to see Dawn Wind again. Morgan visited the village at times, but Breck stayed away.

After several weeks, Morgan said over supper one night, "You've got to do something about this, Breck."

"About what?" Breckinridge asked in apparent innocence, although he had a hunch he knew what his friend was talking about.

"About this staying away from the Crows, especially Dawn Wind. Running Elk told me today that she's been sad ever since you ran her off."

"I didn't run her off. And the way Runnin' Elk feels about me, I'd think he would be glad I ain't been havin' anything to do with his sister."

"What are you talking about?" Morgan said. "Running Elk likes you."

"Are you loco? He looks at me like he wants to take his knife and carve my gizzard out!"

Morgan laughed and shook his head. "That's just his way. As far as I can tell, he thinks you're a fine fellow. He just doesn't like the way you've made Dawn Wind unhappy."

"It'll make her a whole lot more unhappy when fall comes and we got to leave these parts and go back to St. Louis." Breckinridge stared into the fire, knowing he shouldn't be doing that because it would ruin his night vision for a while. He was lost in visions of his own, though, visions of the past and of possible futures.

"So that's it," Morgan said.

"What's it?"

"You're still upset about whatever happened with Dulcy."

Breckinridge's gaze snapped away from the flames and over to Morgan. "I told you I don't intend to talk about that."

"You're hurt, and you don't want to risk getting hurt again." Morgan blew out a breath. "All that talk about wanting to protect Dawn Wind's feelings, when it's really yourself you want to protect!"

"Aw, the hell with this!" Breckinridge said as he got to his feet and caught up his rifle. "I'm gonna go scout around a mite."

"In the dark?"

"What better time? Ain't no tellin' what might be lurkin' out there."

"It's not going to change anything, Breck. You can't get away from whatever it is that's bothering you."

Maybe not, Breckinridge thought as he stalked off into the woods, but he could damn sure try to ignore it.

Since the day he'd been shot, they had seen no sign of Jud Carnahan, Gordon Ralston, or any of the other trappers who had turned into deadly enemies. It appeared that Carnahan's bunch had moved on to some other part of this vast valley. There were plenty of creeks teeming with beaver ripe for the taking. Breckinridge believed there was a good chance that he would run into Carnahan and Ralston sometime in the future, possibly back in St. Louis, but he hoped if that happened, it would be far away from Dawn Wind, Running Elk, White Owl, and his other friends among the Crow. They didn't deserve to be in danger because of any grudges held against *him*.

Even though those thoughts were going through his head, his senses were on alert as he circled through the woods around the camp. He kept moving farther and farther out until he remembered that Morgan was back there by himself. They had been trying to stick together, and here Breckinridge had gone off on his own again without thinking, just because he was upset. He turned and was about to start back when he stopped in his tracks.

For a second he wasn't sure what had caught his attention. Then he heard it again: a faint cry floating through the night air, followed by another and then another.

They were coming from the direction of the Crow village.

As Breckinridge stiffened and listened intently, he began to tell a difference in the shouts. Some were angry, some were frightened. But they all told him the same thing.

Something was wrong over there. Terribly wrong.

He didn't stop to think about it. He just plunged through the woods toward the village, heedless of any obstacles that might be in his way. He was willing to risk dashing his brains out on a tree trunk or a low-hanging branch if it meant he could get there sooner.

His first thought was that Carnahan and the other trappers might have attacked the Crows in retaliation for the help they had given him and Morgan earlier in the season. But he didn't hear any gunfire, and he was sure he would have if white men had been responsible for the trouble.

That left Breckinridge uncertain as to what was going on, but he felt sure it couldn't be anything good. As he came closer and heard screams mixed in with the shouts, he was more convinced of that than ever.

He caught sight of a flickering light up ahead, through the trees, and realized it was something burning. Something bigger than a campfire, too. He slowed as he neared the edge of the trees that surrounded the Crow village.

Several of the tipis were in flames. People rushed here and there. A few of them tried to put out the fires, but most were either running for their lives or fighting with other Indians whose faces were streaked with paint. Those attackers belonged to a war party from some other tribe, Breckinridge realized. When he saw one of the raiders lift a tomahawk and get ready to bring down a killing stroke on a Crow defender who had fallen, he didn't hesitate. He snapped his rifle to his shoulder and fired.

The ball smashed through the invader's ribs under the upraised arm and tore through the man's lungs. He dropped the tomahawk and fell to the ground, then writhed for a few seconds as he drowned in his own blood before dying.

Breckinridge bounded into the open. One of the

attackers lunged at him, also swinging a tomahawk. Breck drove the rifle's brass butt plate into the man's face with such force that bone crunched and the raider went backward as if he had run face-first into a stone wall.

Something tugged at Breckinridge's shirt. He realized it was an arrow that had come from behind him. He whirled around in time to see a war-painted figure drawing back a bow to launch a second missile. One of Breck's pistols was already in his hand as he turned. The gun boomed and bucked against his palm as he squeezed the trigger. The double-shotted weapon sent both balls into the raider's chest, shredding it and knocking him backward off his feet. The man released the arrow, but it soared harmlessly high over Breck's head.

He shoved the empty pistol behind his belt, set his rifle aside, and picked up the tomahawk dropped by the first man he had shot. With his knife in his left hand and the tomahawk in his right, he started toward the large tipi at the center of the village, where White Owl lived. Dawn Wind lived with some of the other young, unmarried women, but Breckinridge believed that when the attack started, she would have tried to reach her father.

Two of the raiders spotted him and charged him. Breckinridge stood his ground, and for a long moment he fought them off, the knife flashing in the firelight as he parried and slashed with it and the tomahawk. Then a lunge buried the blade in the chest of one enemy, and a swift stroke with the 'hawk crushed the second man's skull. Breck yanked the knife free, leaped over the corpses, and bulled on toward his destination, pausing only to kill another couple of raiders when they got in his way. He was like an avalanche rumbling through the village, obliterating every obstacle in his path.

He suddenly veered off his course when he saw one of the raiders snatch up a screaming, terrified child. The youngster looked like he was barely old enough to walk. Nearby lay a woman with blood gushing from a hideous wound in her neck. She was probably the child's mother and had been trying to flee with him when she was struck down.

The attacker grasped the child's leg and swung him high, ready to smash him against the ground. Breckinridge slid his knife back in its sheath as he lunged forward. His left hand flashed up and closed around the wrist of the raider's upraised hand. The fury inside him welled up and was channeled through his muscles into that horrible crushing grip. Bones snapped and ground together. Taken by surprise, the raider screamed in agony. His hand opened and the child fell.

Breckinridge caught the boy before he could hit the ground. Then, cradling the child against him, he swung the tomahawk in a backhanded blow that caught the raider in the throat, sheared through muscle and bone, and separated the man's head from his shoulders. It popped into the air as blood fountained from the gaping wound where the head had been attached a second earlier.

Breckinridge had already turned away before the dead invader's head thumped to the ground.

He saw one of the Crow women and thrust the boy into her arms, then resumed his charge toward White Owl's tipi. When he reached it he saw the chief struggling with one of the painted warriors. White Owl was not as young and strong as he once was, and he fell under a glancing blow from the raider's tomahawk. As White Owl slumped to the ground, his attacker lifted the weapon to strike again.

Out of nowhere, a slim, buckskin-clad form leaped between them, hovering over the chief's fallen form. Horror seized Breckinridge as he realized the newcomer was Dawn Wind, trying to protect her father even though it meant her own death as the tomahawk streaked toward her.

Chapter 18

Breckinridge acted faster than he ever had in his life. Too swift for the eye to follow, his arm flashed back and then forward, sending the tomahawk spinning through the air in a perfect throw. The weapon's sharp flint head struck the raider just above the left ear with such force that it cleaved through the man's skull and deeply into his brain. The blow he had aimed at Dawn Wind continued to fall, but as the attacker's body crumpled and twisted, the tomahawk in his hand struck the ground instead, next to White Owl. The corpse toppled onto Dawn Wind, who shoved it aside as her face twisted in revulsion.

By that time, Breckinridge had reached her side. He reached down, grasped her arm, and lifted her effortlessly to her feet. She threw her arms around his massive torso. Her hands didn't meet on his back, but she clung to him anyway and pressed her face against his broad chest.

"Breckinridge!" she cried.

He put his right arm around her shoulders and held her close. At the same time, from his great height he was able to look over her head and turn his gaze from side to side as he searched for any more threats. The battle continued, but it seemed to be breaking up in places. As Breckinridge watched, some of the raiders gave up their attack and ran for the woods with Crow arrows flying after them. The fighting continued to become more sporadic and within minutes had ended completely.

That didn't mean the mournful wails and the cries of pain had stopped, however. Those sounds of misery still filled the air all around the Crow village.

Dawn Wind lifted her head to look up at Breckinridge. "You are not harmed?" she asked. The firelight from the burning tipis reddened her face even more than it already was.

"I'm fine," Breckinridge assured her. "We'd best check on your father."

Dawn Wind looked around at White Owl, suddenly alarmed again. She slipped out of Breckinridge's embrace and dropped to her knees beside her father, who had sat up and started shaking his head groggily. Blood dripped from the cut that the glancing blow had opened on his forehead.

Dawn Wind spoke hurriedly to him. White Owl put a hand on her shoulder and squeezed. Breckinridge could tell that the gesture was meant to be reassuring. He extended his free hand to the Crow chief. White Owl reached up, clasped it, and allowed Breck to help him to his feet. He spoke a few words.

"My father thanks you for saving my life and probably his as well," Dawn Wind said.

"I'm just sorry I didn't get here sooner so I'd have had the chance to kill more of these varmints," Breckinridge said. "Where'd they come from, anyway?"

"They are Blackfeet." When Dawn Wind said the name, she sounded like it tasted bad in her mouth. "Sometimes they drift south in the summer like this and raid the villages of the Apsáalooke and the other tribes who are our allies. They kill and steal horses and take prisoners that they turn into slaves."

"Quite a few of 'em won't ever do that again," Breckinridge commented as he looked around the village. A number of bodies belonging to Dawn Wind's people lay scattered on the ground, but there were more corpses with painted faces.

Running Elk hurried toward them. The young man spoke quickly to his father and sister, no doubt making sure they were all right. Then he turned to Breck and rested a hand on his shoulder.

"Breck'ridge . . . good friend," he said.

Breckinridge put a hand on Running Elk's shoulder and responded, "Running Elk good friend, too."

There was nothing more to be said. From the look on Running Elk's face, it was obvious that any reservations he'd had about Breckinridge were gone, destroyed by the bloody events of this night.

In a way, that might make things more complicated, Breckinridge mused. As long as Running Elk had considered him a completely unsuitable match for Dawn Wind, it had been a little easier for him to stay away. Without the young warrior's disapproval, Breck was going to be even more tempted to spend time here in the Crow village.

Before he could ponder on that, Dawn Wind touched his arm and then pointed toward the trees. Morgan had emerged from them and was looking around with a shocked expression on his face. He spotted Breckinridge, Dawn Wind, Running Elk, and White Owl and hurried toward them.

"Breck, are you all right?" Morgan asked. "What in blazes happened here?"

"A Blackfoot war party raided the village," Breckinridge explained. "I heard the commotion and came to see what was goin' on."

"And I heard some gunshots from back at our camp. I assume that was you?"

"Yeah. Had to ventilate a couple of the bastards."

"I figured you had to be right in the middle of it, whatever it was," Morgan said. "Dawn Wind, are you hurt?"

She shook her head and said, "No. Breckinridge saved my life." She pointed at the corpse of the raider who lay on the ground nearby with the tomahawk still lodged in his split skull. "I have never seen such a throw, not from any warrior of any tribe."

Morgan laughed. "Yeah, Breck's sort of a tribe of his own, I guess you could say. There aren't any more like him back where he came from, or where I came from, either."

Those sort of comments made Breckinridge uncomfortable. He said, "There are plenty of folks here who are hurt. We'd better see about tendin' to 'em."

"You are right," Dawn Wind said. "Starting with my father."

She took White Owl's arm and steered him toward his tipi. Breckinridge, Morgan, and Running Owl began going around the village to check on the wounded and see that the ones in need of care got it. As Breck watched the way Running Elk took charge, he figured the young man would make a fine chief one of these days.

When they had done all they could to help the wounded, they began dragging the Blackfoot corpses out of the village. Breckinridge didn't know what would be done with them, but he didn't figure it would be anything good. The Crow would want to make sure their enemies weren't able to enjoy the next life.

After that grisly chore was concluded, Breckinridge and Morgan stood near the ashes that marked the location of a burned-down tipi. Morgan said, "I get the feeling you're even more of a hero to these folks now, Breck."

"I wouldn't say that. I pitched in and killed a few of those Blackfoot varmints, but that's all."

"And saved the chief and his daughter while you were at it," Morgan pointed out. "I talked some to Running Elk. Well, maybe we didn't actually talk that much, but we understand each other. As far as the Crow are concerned, you're one of them now. You'd be welcome to stay here from now on."

"That was never what I planned to do."

"Sometimes our plans get changed, usually when we don't expect it. Listen, Breck. You've got a smart, brave, beautiful young woman here who loves you."

"I don't know that I'd go that far—"

"She loves you," Morgan repeated. "Anybody with eyes in his head can see that. You could, too, if you weren't so damn stubborn. Now, why would any man in his right mind turn his back on a situation like that?"

"I don't recollect ever claimin' that I'm in my right mind," Breckinridge said.

"Well, then, listen to somebody who is. We need to move our camp over here. If we'd been here tonight when the Blackfeet attacked, some of the people they killed before you got here might still be alive."

Breckinridge thought about the young woman whose child he had saved. Morgan was right. If he had been on hand when the attack began, he might have saved the woman, too.

Of course, it was impossible to know such things for sure, he reminded himself. Each hand in life played out as it would, and there was no way to deal the cards again.

"Maybe it wouldn't be such a bad thing to spend more time here," Breckinridge said. "Seems like even Runnin' Elk was warmin' up to me a mite."

"Of course he is. Like I told you, the Crow consider you one of them now. They probably have some sort of ritual or ceremony to induct you into the tribe officially." Morgan smiled. "Maybe it's even part of their marriage ceremony."

"Now, don't you go startin' on that! You're gettin' mighty far ahead of yourself. I ain't said nothin' about marryin' Dawn Wind."

"Well, you need to start thinking about it," Morgan said. He laughed. "As if you really have anything to say about it."

Breckinridge didn't know about that, but he knew his heart took a big jump in his chest when he looked toward White Owl's tipi and saw Dawn Wind push aside the canvas flap over the opening and step out. She smiled as she came toward him.

There was no way of knowing what was going to happen, Breckinridge thought, but maybe it was time he stopped being so stubborn and found out.

* * *

Even though it was ushered in by fire, tragedy, and death, that was the beginning of an idyllic time for Breckinridge. He and Morgan were given a tipi in the village for their dwelling. Together with Running Elk, they spent the days working the traplines and strengthening their friendship with the young warrior. Running Elk acted now as if he had never disapproved of Breck as a potential suitor for his sister.

After about a week, Dawn Wind took Breckinridge's hand one evening and led him to a newly constructed tipi replacing one of those that had been destroyed. She displayed pride as she showed it to him and said, "This will be mine."

"It's mighty nice," he told her.

"And you will share it with me."

Breckinridge's brows rose. "Now, wait a minute—"

She tightened her grip on his hand and tugged him into the tipi, where a fire already burned in the rock pit in the center and robes were spread on the ground. She turned to him, raised a hand to rest it on the back of his neck, and lifted her face to his. Their mouths met in a kiss that grew quickly in passion and urgency.

Breckinridge didn't try to stop her as she pulled her dress over her head. This was the first time he had seen her nude since that day by the pool. If anything, she had grown even more beautiful during that time.

He was fully recovered from being shot in the head, too. He proved that with plenty of enthusiasm and satisfaction for both of them.

Days spent out in the wilderness with his friends, nights spent in the arms of a beautiful, passionate young woman . . . A fella just couldn't do better than that, Breckinridge thought many times. And since life was so pleasant, the days rolled by almost without notice, turning into weeks and then months. It was only when Breck saw what a large pile of beaver pelts he and Morgan had accumulated and felt the coolness of the air early in the morning that he realized something he had put out of his thoughts entirely.

Fall was coming. It was time to head back down-river to St. Louis.

Chapter 19

Breckinridge wasn't the sort to sit around brooding about anything, but he wasn't looking forward to telling Dawn Wind that he was leaving. So he postponed it as the pile of pelts grew larger and the days grew shorter. Unfortunately, the journey would have to be undertaken before much longer, or it would be too late in the season. Winter might arrive before he and Morgan could reach St. Louis.

Along with Running Elk, the two of them were headed back to the village from their traplines one day when Morgan said, "Breck, we have to talk about what we're going to do next."

Breckinridge nodded glumly. "I know. It ain't somethin' I've wanted to think about, let alone hash out."

Morgan laughed and said, "That's because you didn't realize that I've come up with the perfect solution."

Breckinridge frowned. "What are you talkin' about?"

"I'll take the furs back to St. Louis and sell them for us. You stay here for the winter with our friends . . . and Dawn Wind."

Breckinridge's shaggy brows rose in surprise. "It's a far piece to St. Louis," he said. "You can't haul those pelts back there all by your lonesome."

"Why not? I can load both canoes and tie the second one on behind mine. Since I'll be going with the current I can paddle enough to keep both craft moving. It's not like there's any chance of getting lost along the way, either. All I have to do is keep heading downstream, merging with the larger rivers, until I reach St. Louis."

"I reckon you could find the place, all right," Breckinridge said. "But a fella travelin' by himself is sort of dangerous."

"For a greenhorn, maybe. But that's not really what I am anymore, is it?"

Breckinridge looked at Morgan and had to admit that his friend was right. The lean, hard-muscled, brown-bearded frontiersman he saw was a far cry from the soft, beardless youth Morgan had been a couple of years earlier, when Breck first met him. He had endured considerable hardship and trouble. He might not be a seasoned veteran just yet, but he was getting there.

"And you can't be worried about me trying to cheat you out of your share of the profits," Morgan went on. "Not after all we've been through together."

"It's sort of an insult, you even bringin' that up," Breckinridge said. "I trust you as much as I would any of my brothers. More, I reckon."

"There's a practical consideration to my suggestion, too," Morgan went on. "You can keep all our gear with you, and next spring, you and Running Elk can get a jump on all the other trappers in the mountains. By the time I get outfitted and return, you'll already have taken some pelts."

Breckinridge nodded and said, "Reckon I understand now. You want me to do all the work whilst you rest easy back in civilization."

"That's not what I—" Morgan stopped when he saw the grin on Breckinridge's face. He laughed and said, "Yes, I'll be back in so-called civilization, but you'll be here with our friends . . . and Dawn Wind. Now, tell me . . . who's getting the better end of this deal?"

Breckinridge glanced over at Running Elk and said, "We don't know how Runnin' Elk feels about the idea, or White Owl and the rest of the Crow."

Running Elk put a hand on Breckinridge's shoulder and said, "Breck'ridge . . . stay."

"He's picked up enough English to know what we're talking about," Morgan said. "So that ought to tell you nobody's going to object. You're one of them, Breck. Probably more than I ever will be, although I'm honored to call the Apsáalooke people my friends."

"You make a mighty powerful argument," Breckinridge admitted. "The only part I really don't like is you headin' back downriver by yourself."

"I'll be fine," Morgan insisted. "Why don't you talk about it with Dawn Wind and see what she thinks?"

"I'll do that," Breckinridge said.

He had a pretty good idea how she was going to react when he told her, though.

They were sitting together on the buffalo robes in the tipi they shared as Breckinridge explained the idea. Just as he expected, Dawn Wind threw her arms around his neck and hugged him tightly. She whispered something in the Crow tongue.

"What was that?" Breckinridge asked.

"I am thankful to the Great Spirit for keeping you with me, Breckinridge," she said.

"Now, hold on. I ain't said that I'm goin' along with Morgan's idea."

"Why would you not? It is a good thing for everyone."

"Well, it seems that way . . ."

She leaned back a little and said, "Why do you worry? Why do you always see the worst thing that can happen and not the best?"

She had a point, he thought. When he was younger, his optimism had known no bounds. No matter what troubles came, he had always believed, deep down in his heart, that sooner or later things would work out all right.

The events of the past couple of years, beginning with the trouble that had forced him to leave home, had tempered his outlook considerably. No longer did he believe that his strength and enthusiasm for life could carry him through any ordeal.

But at the same time, he wasn't cut out to be overwhelmed by doom and gloom, either. He still believed in seizing the good things in life. Dawn Wind was right. He couldn't allow the uncertainty of the future to make him turn his back on happiness.

"You've done convinced me," he said. "Morgan will go back to St. Louis with our furs, and I'll stay here."

She nodded and snuggled into the curve of his arm around her shoulders. "It is good, Breckinridge," she said. "We will warm each other through the winter and then welcome the spring together."

That sounded mighty good to him, too.

A surprise was waiting when it came time to load the pelts into the canoes and get ready for Morgan's journey to St. Louis. Running Elk announced that he was going along, too.

"Are you sure you want to do that?" Morgan asked the young warrior. "St. Louis is really different from anything you've ever known here in the mountains."

The two of them were in Dawn Wind's tipi, sharing supper with her and Breckinridge. Morgan looked at Dawn Wind and went on, "Maybe you should translate what I just said for him, so we'll know he understands what he's getting into."

Dawn Wind nodded and spoke to her brother in the Crow tongue. He nodded somewhat impatiently and said in English, "Running Elk knows."

"Civilization stinks a lot worse," Breckinridge said. "It's a heap more crowded, too, and the skeeters there along the river are mighty bad."

Dawn Wind translated that, too. Running Elk waved away the cautionary words. He spoke at length in his language.

Turning to Breckinridge and Morgan, Dawn Wind told them, "He says it is time for our people to learn more about the white man's world. More and more of them are coming here, and the more the Apsáalooke know about them, the easier it will be to live with them in peace."

"He's got a point," Breckinridge said with a shrug of his massive shoulders. "And if Runnin' Elk goes along, you won't have to make the trip by yourself, Morgan."

"I'd be fine," Morgan replied. He was the one who sounded impatient now. "I don't need Running Elk to come along and take care of me."

"I never said that. You two get along good, though. You can keep each other company. This country's so big, it can be mighty lonely for a fella if there ain't nobody else around."

"I suppose that's true. I'm just afraid Running Elk won't like St. Louis once we get there."

"He can stand it until next spring."

Morgan frowned in thought for a long moment, then finally nodded. He looked over at Running Elk and said, "All right, you can come along. The trip *will* be easier with some company, I suppose."

Running Elk never grinned or laughed, but good humor was visible in his eyes, belying his solemn expression as he nodded. "It will be . . . good trip," he said.

"We can hope so," Morgan said.

Later that evening, Breckinridge was walking across the village toward Dawn Wind's tipi when Morgan came up behind him and called his name. Breck stopped and looked back at his friend.

"I've been bundlin' up some of them pelts," Breckinridge said. "We've had such good luck that we're gonna have to work hard to fit 'em all into the canoes."

Morgan laughed. "I know. We certainly can't complain about the number of beaver we've taken this season."

Breckinridge thumbed back his hat and said,

"Yeah, I've heard old-timers say that trappin' ain't what it used to be, that the beaver are gonna run out, but it don't hardly seem possible, does it? The creeks are teemin' with 'em."

"Yeah." Morgan seemed a little distracted. "Breck, I want to talk to you about something, now that we've got it all settled about you staying here and me going back to St. Louis with the furs."

"You ain't wantin' to, what do you call it, renegotiate our partnership, are you?"

"What? Hell, no! We're in this equally and always will be."

Breckinridge nodded. "I'm glad to hear it. What was it you wanted to palaver about, then?"

Morgan leaned his head toward the stream and said, "Let's go and sit down by the creek."

Breckinridge frowned. That sounded like something serious. He wasn't sure he wanted to have this conversation, whatever it was. But he couldn't turn down the request from his best friend.

There was a big log on the creek bank, a short distance from the village, where Breckinridge liked to sit sometimes and whittle in his spare moments. He and Morgan went to it now and sat down. The moon was up, and its silvery light sparkled on the creek's constantly moving surface. A night bird called somewhere in a tree. The air had a chill in it, but not enough to be uncomfortable.

As Morgan took out his pipe and began packing tobacco in it, Breckinridge said, "All right, what's all this about? I got to admit, Morgan, the way you're actin' has me a little spooked."

"Oh, there's no reason to be worried," Morgan said. "We have a deal, and I'll stick to it. It's just that, before we split up for the next six months or so, there's something I want to know."

"About me? Hell, we ain't got no secrets from each other."

"That's just it, Breck. We do. I want to know what happened last fall when you went home. I want to know what happened to Dulcy."

Breckinridge stiffened. Involuntarily, his hands clenched into fists, although he had no desire to hit Morgan or anybody else. He had learned the hard way that a good swift punch wasn't going to solve some problems.

When he trusted himself to speak, he said, "That ain't any of your business."

"I think it is," Morgan insisted. "You're my friend, Breck, and I know that whatever it was hurt you."

"I've done put it behind me." Breckinridge waved a hand toward the village. "Hell, I've got friends here . . . and I've got Dawn Wind."

"And for a long time you tried to push her away because of what happened back in Tennessee. You know that's true. How can you say you've put it behind you when it still hurts too much for you to talk about it?"

Breckinridge stared off into the night and muttered, "You're a nosy son of a gun, you know that?"

"Yeah, I am. But I think it's time you talked about this. Besides, if you think back on it, Dulcy was my friend, too. Not like what you and her had, of course, but I was still fond of her. I want to make sure she's all right."

"She's fine, as far as I know," Breckinridge said. "I ain't seen her since before I headed west again."

"Didn't you take her back there to meet your family before the two of you got married?"

"I did. We didn't have any trouble along the way, neither." Breckinridge sighed. Maybe Morgan was right. Maybe it was time to unburden himself, although he was damned if he was going to sit around and wallow in self-pity. He would tell the story straight and unadorned, with no fancy frills. "The trouble didn't start until after we were back home . . ."

Chapter 20

The Wallace family farm lay about five miles from the settlement of Knoxville. Old Ebeneezer Wallace, Breckinridge's grandfather, had taken up the land in return for his service in the American army during the Revolutionary War.

There he and his wife had raised a large family, and one of his sons, Robert, had taken over the running of the farm when Ebeneezer grew too old and feeble. The patriarch now lay in the family plot along with his wife, several children, and a few grandchildren taken from life too early.

Robert and *his* wife, the beautiful, redheaded, former Samantha Burke, had raised five sons to manhood on this land: Edward, a scholar at heart; Thomas and Jeremiah, stolid sons of the soil; Henry, a hard worker but a bit of a hothead . . . and the youngest, born well after his parents expected no more children, Breckinridge.

Breckinridge . . . was trouble.

He had admitted all that freely to Dulcy, telling her

everything about his rambunctious, often violent past as they journeyed from the frontier back here to Tennessee.

There was no real point in them keeping secrets from each other. He knew perfectly well that she was a widow who had drifted into a life of prostitution after the tragic loss of her husband and young daughter to a fever.

He had never held that against her. Nobody was perfect, after all, least of all the reckless, redheaded giant known as Breckinridge Wallace.

Dulcy was understandably nervous, though, as she sat on the wagon seat next to Breckinridge while he guided the vehicle toward the farm.

She was almost a decade older than him but still a very beautiful woman with rich, dark brown hair, brown eyes, and striking features. There was a small scar on her upper lip just above the right corner of her mouth, a tiny note of imperfection that gave her loveliness a touch of character.

She pushed one of the dark wings of hair back from her face and said, "Are you sure you don't mind keeping the truth about me from your family, Breckinridge? I don't want you to feel like you have to lie for me."

"I don't reckon I consider it lyin' to leave out part of a story," he told her. "Now, you know me. I don't much give a damn what anybody thinks, especially my pa and my brothers."

"What about your mother?"

"Well," he said with a grin, "I got my red hair from her, and it's true she can raise some hell when she takes a mind to, but I can handle her when I have to. There just ain't any need to. You're a widow woman I met at a rendezvous, and that's plenty to tell 'em as far as I'm concerned."

"Thank you, Breck." Dulcy looked down at the wagon's floorboards. "I don't want your family to think any less of you because you're marrying a whore."

Breckinridge lightly slapped the reins against the backs of the mules pulling the wagon. "What you used to be ain't the same as what you are now," he said. "Folks can change. Hell, I ain't quite as dumb as I used to be."

Dulcy slipped her arms around Breckinridge's right arm and leaned her head against his shoulder. She said, "I don't think you're the least bit dumb."

"I probably could've used a mite more schoolin'. Never could hardly bear to sit inside, though, when there were so many interestin' things goin' on outside." He nodded toward the large, whitewashed farmhouse they were approaching. "Anyway, here we be. These fields we been drivin' past are all Wallace fields, and there's the house."

Several dogs saw the wagon coming and charged out to meet them, barking loud and raucous greetings. Breckinridge recognized a couple of the big, shaggy brutes, but the others were new, born since the last time he'd been here. They charged around enthusiastically, spooking the normally placid mules as Breck brought the team to a halt in front of the house.

He looped the reins around the brake lever, put a hand on the edge of the seat, and vaulted to the ground. Two of the big dogs jumped up on him and started trying to reach his face with their slobbering tongues.

Breckinridge let out a booming laugh, wrestled

with the dogs, and said, "Howdy, Sammy! Howdy, Ranger! Dang, it's good to see you old varmints again!"

The farmhouse's front door opened and Breckinridge's mother appeared on the porch. Samantha Burke Wallace was a small woman who had always seemed bigger because of her powerful personality.

She regarded Breck with no apparent emotion and said, "I thought I heard a bear roaring out here, but I see now that it's just you, Breckinridge." Anyone seeing and hearing her would think that he had been gone for a matter of hours, not months.

"Howdy, Ma!" Breckinridge bounded up onto the porch and swept her into his arms. Her feet came off the porch planks as he hugged her. "Dang, it's good to see you again."

"I believe you just said the same thing to the dogs," Samantha pointed out, a little breathlessly because of the way he was hugging her. "Now put me down, you big oaf."

"Yes'm." Breckinridge lowered her to the porch. He turned, held out a hand toward the wagon, and went on, "Ma, I brought somebody with me—"

"Yes, I can see that. Now go help her down. You can at least *try* to be a gentleman."

"Uh, yeah, sure." Breckinridge shooed the dogs aside as he went to the wagon. He said, "I'm sorry, Dulcy, I should've got you down from there first."

"That's all right," she told him with a smile. "I understand that you're happy to be home."

He reached up, took hold of her under the arms, and lifted her down from the seat as if she weighed almost nothing. Then he held her hand—his big paw engulfing her slender fingers—and led her up onto the porch.

"Ma, this here is Dulcy Harris," Breckinridge said. "Dulcy, my ma."

Samantha held out her hand and took the one that Dulcy tentatively offered. "It's a pleasure to meet you, Miss Harris."

Dulcy smiled and said, "Actually, it's, uh, Mrs. Harris." She added quickly, "I'm a widow."

"Oh. Well, I'm sorry for your loss. What brings you to our part of Tennessee?"

Breckinridge said, "I brung her, Ma. Me and Dulcy are gonna be married."

"Is that so?" Samantha didn't look particularly surprised. "Come on in the house, the both of you. Breckinridge, your father and brothers are bound to have heard the commotion, and they'll be on their way in from the fields to see what it's about. Mrs. Harris, can I get you some tea?"

"That would be lovely," Dulcy said.

Samantha took Dulcy's arm and ushered her on into the kitchen, leaving Breckinridge to follow them.

By the time they got there, the back door was opening. Breck's oldest brother, Edward, came into the house and stopped short at the sight of him.

"Breck!" Edward said. He hurried across the room, threw his arms around Breckinridge, and started pounding him on the back. Breck returned the enthusiastic greeting.

He hadn't seen Edward in more than a year, even though he had returned to Tennessee for a visit during that time. As it happened, Edward had been gone from home at that time, coincidentally enough having gone west to look for Breckinridge and inform him that he was no longer wanted for murder. Now Breck was very glad to see that Edward had made it home safely after that trip.

The two of them barely looked like brothers. Edward was slim and studious and had inherited their father's dark hair and saturnine features. He gripped Breckinridge's arms, looked him over, and said, "You haven't shrunk any while you were gone, that's for sure. I think you're even bigger than you were when you left, if that's possible."

"Fresh air and healthy livin' done it," Breckinridge said.

Edward turned to Dulcy. "And who's this?"

"Your brother's betrothed," Samantha said.

Edward's eyebrows rose. "Really? You're getting married?"

"That's right," Breckinridge said. "This here's Dulcy Harris. We're gettin' hitched, all right."

Edward started to shake Dulcy's hand, then suddenly hugged her instead.

"I hope that's all right, since you're going to be part of the family," he said.

"Of course it is," she told him. "I'm glad to meet you, Edward. Breck's told me so much about you." She glanced at Samantha. "About all of you. I . . . I'm so happy to be here."

Breckinridge thought for a second that Dulcy was going to start crying, but she managed to put a smile on her face instead. Then a commotion broke out as Breck's other three brothers came in and there was a new round of introductions, handshaking, and hugging. Thomas, Jeremiah, and Henry were all pleased to meet Dulcy—and a little surprised to hear the news that she and Breck were getting married.

Henry gestured toward Thomas and Jeremiah and said, "I always thought one of these two would be the first to get married and settle down. They've already got the personality of tree stumps, roots and all." He grinned mischievously as he spoke.

Thomas swung a lazy hand at Henry's head and missed deliberately. "Hush up your foolishness, lad," he said.

Another step sounded in the doorway, and they all turned to look at Robert Wallace, the current patriarch of the family. He was smaller than any of his sons but filled with a vitality that belied his age.

"What's this, then?" he asked. A trace of a Scottish burr remained in his voice.

"Your youngest son has brought his intended bride home, Robert," Samantha said.

"Aye?" Robert turned a stern gaze toward Dulcy. "This would be th' lady?"

Breckinridge said, "Pa, this is Dulcy. Uh, Dulcy Harris."

"Mrs. Harris," Samantha added. "She's a widow, the poor dear."

Robert stepped forward and extended his hand. "Welcome to our home, ma'am. Are ye sure you're in yer right mind?"

"Excuse me?" Dulcy said.

"I mean, to be marryin' this great lout of a boy—"

Dulcy had been about to take his hand, but now she drew herself up straighter and gave him a cold frown.

"Your son happens to be one of the finest men I've ever known, Mr. Wallace, and I don't think you should insult him."

"That's so, is it?"

"Yes, it most certainly is."

Robert smiled and said, "Then some of it must be because of yer influence, Missus Harris, and I thank ye for it." He reached out, took the hand she still held out in both of his, and told Breckinridge, "Ye've done well for yerself, boy, if ye convinced such a fine lady to hitch her wagon to yours."

Breckinridge grinned in relief and said, "Thanks, Pa. I'm glad you like her."

"Like her? I think she's splendid!" Robert kept hold of Dulcy's hand and led her to the table. "Sit yerself down, ma'am."

Samantha poured a cup of tea and set it in front of her. "Here you go. You'll be staying for supper, won't you? In fact, I hope you'll stay here with us. You can have Jeremiah and Henry's room. They won't mind sleeping in the barn, will you, boys?"

Dulcy said, "I won't want to put anyone out—"

"Nonsense," Robert said. "'Twould be our honor to have you stay with us. We're all pleased that Breckinridge has made such a fine match for himself."

This time Dulcy couldn't help it. A tear ran down each cheek. With a visible effort, she controlled the emotions that gripped her and said, "I'll be happy to stay, Mr. Wallace. You don't know how . . . how happy I am to be welcomed like this by all of you."

"Now, dear, we just want what's best for Breckinridge," Samantha said. "His rambunctious ways can take some getting used to, but he *does* grow on you after a while."

"Yeah," Henry said, "like a weed you can't get rid of."

Breckinridge pantomimed a sweeping blow at his head. Henry ducked and laughed. He was used to his gibes getting responses like that.

Robert took hold of Breckinridge's arm and asked, "Have ye come home for good, son?"

Breckinridge had been expecting that question, and in truth it worried him more than how his family would react to Dulcy. He had figured they would be as taken with her as he'd been.

With a shake of his head, he said, "No, Pa, we're just here for a visit, and to get married. But after we're hitched, Dulcy and me are headin' west again. I've been out there trappin' beaver, and I plan to go back to the mountains next spring."

"Fur trapping?" Samantha said. "That's no life for a woman!"

"It will be," Breckinridge insisted. "I've got a partner to help me with the trappin', and I'm gonna build a nice sturdy cabin for Dulcy. We're gonna make a life for ourselves out there, Ma. It's the most beautiful place I've ever seen."

"Ye could take up a farm somewhere around here—" Robert began, then stopped himself before he could finish. "Nay, that's not th' sort o' thing ye'd ever want to do, is it?"

Breckinridge shook his head. "No, Pa, it ain't. I'm just too different from you and the other boys."

"Don't include me in that," Henry said. "I'd like to go adventuring one of these days, too."

Robert ignored that and said to Breckinridge, "A peddler came through these parts once. He had a cage attached to the back of his wagon, and in that cage was a bear somebody had captured. A sorrier sight you never saw. The bear just sat there. The man would try to get it to roar at folks and act ferocious, you know, like a show. But the bear wouldn't do it, no matter how much that damn peddler poked at him. 'Twasn't even a bear anymore, to my way o' thinkin'. Just a great mound o' fur and sadness. I don't want that for you, lad." Robert surprised Breck by hugging him and slapping him on the back. "Go on back to the mountains when you're ready, son. Go be a bear."

Breckinridge had to swallow hard. He wasn't quite sure why his throat was trying to close up, nor why Dulcy was crying again or why even his ma had to wipe away a tear. He just pounded Robert on the back and said, "Thanks, Pa. It sure is good to be home, even if it's just for a little spell."

Chapter 21

Although Breckinridge didn't care much for farming, it was different now that he and Dulcy were just visiting. He was more than willing to pitch in and help with the plowing and the other chores around the place. It actually felt good to be working with his father and brothers again, even though he had avoided that as much as possible when he was younger.

Dulcy spent her days with Samantha, and as she told Breckinridge when she got a chance to be alone with him, "It's wonderful to be around another woman again who's not . . . well, one who's interested in home and family, I mean. But it kind of makes me sad, too, because it makes me remember my husband and my little girl . . ."

Breckinridge put his arms around her and said, "You don't want to forget about them, not ever. I know that was a mighty good part of your life, and I hate that you got it taken away from you. That just weren't fair. Dang it, if there was any way I could, I'd go back and put that right, even if it meant you and me never would've met."

"I wouldn't want that," she whispered as she rested her head against his chest. "Everything we go through . . . good and bad . . . it makes us who we are. I guess, in the end . . . we just have to hope that the good more than balances out the bad."

"I reckon the scales are still pretty much even when it comes to the things I done in my life."

"I wouldn't say that, Breck," she told him softly. "I wouldn't say that at all."

One morning at breakfast a few days later, Samantha put a piece of paper on the table in front of Breckinridge. He frowned at it and asked, "What's this?"

"I know you can read well enough to make out what's written there," she said. "Those are the supplies I need for you to pick up at the store for me when you and Dulcy go into town this morning."

"I didn't know we was goin' into town." Breckinridge looked over at Dulcy. "You know anything about this?"

"Listen to me," Samantha said, drawing his attention back to her. "You said that the two of you are going to get married while you're visiting here."

"That's the plan," Breckinridge said with an emphatic nod.

"Well, then, hadn't you better get started working on it? You need to go talk to Gavin Balfour, the minister at the kirk. You'll be having the ceremony there, I expect?"

Breckinridge saw the look of worry that sprang up in Dulcy's eyes. They hadn't really discussed the details of their impending marriage. Breck had assumed that the justice of the peace in Knoxville would perform the ceremony. He realized now, though, that his mother, a devout Presbyterian, would expect them to get married in the church.

"I, uh, reckon we could do that," he said, mostly to placate Samantha until he had a chance to talk to Dulcy about it. He didn't really care how they went about it as long as they got hitched, but he supposed the bride ought to have the biggest say in something like that. He glanced at Dulcy again. She didn't look particularly happy, but she nodded.

"Very good," Samantha said. "You'll be going to fetch those supplies this morning, so after you're finished at the mercantile, you can stop and talk to Reverend Balfour."

"Sure," Breckinridge said. At this point he would have agreed to almost anything to end the uncomfortable discussion.

Later, he went out to the barn to hitch the mule team to the wagon that had brought him and Dulcy to the farm. She surprised him by following him.

"Breckinridge, we have to talk about this," she said.

"Talk about what?" he asked. He didn't figure acting innocent would do any good, but he supposed it was worth a try.

It wasn't. Dulcy said flatly, "This business about us getting married in church."

"Well, that's, uh, where most folks get married, I reckon," he said with a shrug. "And my ma, she's a real spiritual person, I guess you could say. Her family, back where they came from, were all Church of Scotland. The kirk, they called it. She still does, even though it's a Presbyterian church in Knoxville."

"I'm a Baptist, so I don't know anything about that." She lowered her voice. "But I do know that most churches don't look kindly on whores."

He tightened the harness on one of the mules and said, "Now, just hold on a minute. I want you to stop talkin' about yourself like that. Best thing you can do is just forget about everything that happened between the time your family passed on and the time we started back here. Forget about everything except meetin' me, that is."

"But it *did* happen and I can't forget about it," she insisted. "It just wouldn't be right for a . . . a sinner like me to be married in a church."

"I admit I don't know a whole heap about the Bible, but I don't recollect any rules in it sayin' that a widow can't get married again. And as far as bein' a sinner goes . . . ain't nobody ever set foot in a church who *ain't* a sinner. That much I know for damn sure."

She put a hand on his arm and told him, "I appreciate everything you're saying, Breck. I really do. But just because you have such a good heart, that doesn't mean everyone else does. I . . . I'm sure that if your family knew the truth about me, they'd be horrified. Your mother would never allow you to marry me, let alone have the ceremony take place in a church!"

"It ain't up to her," Breckinridge said. "You and me decided to get hitched, and we're the only ones who count."

Dulcy shook her head. "I wish that was actually true, Breck. But I don't want you turning your back on your family for my sake. That's not fair." She started to turn toward the barn's entrance. "And it's not fair to lie to people who have been so nice and hospitable to me. I'm going to tell your mother the truth."

"Dang it!" Breckinridge grabbed hold of her arm to stop her. With his incredible strength, she couldn't move. When she winced a little, he realized he was hurting her and hastily let go. But he rested his hands gently on her shoulders to keep her from doing anything foolish. "You don't need to do that. We've done talked about this, over and over. What you've done in the past ain't who you *are*. My ma's a mighty smart woman. She sees the real Dulcy Harris—and so do I."

"Breck . . ."

"You're just worryin' about nothin'," he went on. "The most important thing in this world, Dulcy . . . well, other than bein' out in the fresh air and seein' what's on the other side of the next hill . . . the most important thing in the world is love. Shoot, come to think of it, maybe that's even more important than them other things I mentioned. Now, I love you and you love me, or at least that's what we've done told each other, and I sure as blazes meant it. Did you?"

"You know I did," she whispered.

"Then there ain't nothin' else that amounts to a hill o' beans." He cupped his hand under her chin and lifted her face to his. His lips brushed gently over hers. She reached up and encircled his neck with her arms, her movements a little jerky because of the emotions within her.

A moment later, as they moved apart, he went on, "Now, let's head for town, pick up them supplies Ma wanted, and go talk to the preacher."

Being at the confluence of three rivers, Knoxville had served as a major jumping-off point for westward migration during its earlier days, and with so many people of all kinds passing through, it had had a reputation as a rough and rowdy settlement during that era.

In the past decade it had calmed down considerably and now was a growing city full of fine frame homes and redbrick business buildings. Emerson's Mercantile was one of those establishments. A number of wagon teams and buggy horses were tied up in front of it when Breckinridge brought his vehicle to a halt at one of the hitch racks. Customers went in and out of the big double doors in a steady stream.

On the way here, they had passed the impressive structure known as the Brick Meeting House, where the First Presbyterian Church held services. Dulcy had looked at the building nervously as Breckinridge drove past. She had asked, "Do you know this Reverend Balfour your mother mentioned?"

"Nope," Breckinridge had replied. "He must've come to be the pastor after I pulled up stakes and headed west. But Ma sounded like she likes him, so he must be all right."

"Maybe he's not *too* strict."

"He's a preacher. Bein' strict is sorta his job, ain't it? But you don't have anything to worry about. He can't help but like you."

Obviously, Dulcy wasn't so sure about that. As Breckinridge parked the wagon and hopped down from the seat, she still wore a worried frown. He reached up to help her climb down from the seat.

They went into the crowded store. Dulcy looked around anxiously as if she didn't care for being somewhere with this many people. Breckinridge could understand that. He didn't consider himself antisocial, but he liked being in places where he could get his breath and didn't have to worry about running into people or stepping on their toes. There had been times out West when he had felt like he was the only human being within a hundred miles, and that had suited him just fine.

Or rather, it had suited him until he met and fell in love with Dulcy. Now he couldn't imagine being that far away from her.

He put a hand under her elbow and steered her past the shelves full of merchandise, toward the long counter in the rear of the store. A stocky, balding man with enormous muttonchop whiskers stood there. He wore a canvas apron and had the sleeves of his woolen shirt rolled up so his hairy, muscular forearms were visible as he crossed his arms over his chest. He didn't seem surprised to see Breckinridge, but he did say, "Breck Wallace, as I live and breathe. I would have figured that you'd be hanged by now, lad."

"Naw, that murder charge against me was dropped, Mr. Emerson," Breckinridge said.

"I was speaking more on general principles." Emerson looked curiously at Dulcy. "Who's this?"

"The lady I'm gonna marry. Dulcy Harris."

"How did you trick an intelligent-looking woman into a mistake like that?"

"Excuse me, sir," Dulcy said, sounding a little annoyed. "I happen to have a very high opinion of Breckinridge. He's a fine young man."

"Aw, Mr. Emerson's just joshin'," Breckinridge said. "He's an old friend of the family." He placed the list his mother had given him on the counter and smoothed it out. "My ma sent me to pick up these things. You'll put 'em on her bill?"

"Of course." Emerson picked up the list. "Give me half an hour."

"Sure thing." Breckinridge turned to Dulcy. "You want to walk around town?"

"I suppose we could do that. Do you think there's time to go talk to the minister?"

Breckinridge rubbed his jaw and frowned in thought. "We might ought to wait until after we've got the supplies to do that. You never know how long a preacher's gonna talk."

They started toward the front of the building, taking their time and looking at some of the goods on the shelves along the way. A counter to one side with some pistols in it caught Breckinridge's attention. He lingered there, admiring the fine craftsmanship of the weapons. The same was true of some knives that were also displayed for sale. He found those things a lot more interesting than the shovels, hoes, scythes, and other farming tools hung on the walls.

Dulcy stopped and looked at several bolts of colorful cloth and some spools of lace. "I need to start thinking about a wedding dress," she said.

"I figured you'd just wear one of the dresses you've already got," Breckinridge said.

"I suppose I will, but I think I could fancy it up a bit with some lace."

"That'd be mighty pretty," he assured her. "I can't wait to see it."

"Oh yes, you will," she said with a laugh. "It's bad luck for the groom to see his bride in her wedding dress before the ceremony."

"Yeah, I seem to remember hearin' somethin' about that. But I never put much stock in it."

"Don't you believe in luck?" she asked.

"I darn sure do. If I hadn't been lucky, I never would've met you."

She smiled, linked her arm with his, and said, "That's a nice thing to say. You've made me feel a lot better about things, Breckinridge—"

They were almost to the front doors. One of them swung inward before they could get to it. A tall, broad-shouldered man filled the opening. He wore a wide-brimmed hat, homespun shirt, canvas trousers, and heavy boots. Breckinridge didn't know him but thought he had the look of a riverman. There was a considerable amount of traffic on the Tennessee River between here and Kentucky, where the Tennessee flowed into the Ohio River. Keelboats and other vessels carried immigrants, supplies, and trade goods westward and had done so for many years.

Because of his familiarity with that, Breckinridge didn't give the man a second glance. He eased aside, taking Dulcy with him, so the newcomer could step past them and they could be on their way.

Instead, the man stopped short, stared at them, and exclaimed, "Dulcy?"

Breckinridge felt her stiffen beside him. She said, "I . . . I'm sorry, sir, I don't know you."

"Sure you do," the man said. His voice boomed out and filled the store. "I'm Bill McConnell. Hell, girl, I was a regular customer o' yours when you were whorin' at Tom Mahone's tavern over in Missouri!"

Chapter 22

Horror filled Breckinridge . . . Horror for Dulcy's sake as he saw how stricken she looked. He'd had a hunch what this riverman was going to say, or at least the general drift of it, but the realization hadn't dawned on him in time for him to stop McConnell from blurting out those words.

Dulcy swallowed hard and managed to say, "You've made a mistake, sir. You've taken me for someone else."

A lecherous grin spread across McConnell's face. "I took you, all right, gal. Every time I had enough coin in my pocket to pay for it! 'Twas money well spent, too. You were one o' the best I ever had." His gaze switched to Breckinridge. "When you're done with this fella, come and look me up. Maybe you'd give me a good price, you know, for old time's sake."

Everyone in the store had stopped what they were doing in order to turn and look at the loud-voiced confrontation near the entrance. Dulcy must have felt those shocked stares. Breckinridge certainly did.

Then, abruptly, Dulcy pulled away from him, covered her face with her hands, and sobbed.

Breckinridge exploded.

He lunged forward, taking the riverman by surprise. McConnell appeared to have been drinking, although he didn't seem drunk. He didn't react anywhere near quickly enough to get out of the way of the punch Breckinridge threw. Breck's fist crashed into his jaw with enough force to send the man stumbling backward out of control. McConnell went through the open door, across the porch, and then toppled into the street, landing on his back practically underneath the hooves of a wagon team.

Breckinridge charged out of the store. Behind him, Dulcy cried, "Breck, no!" He was too furious to pay any attention to her. The object of his wrath was right in front of him. That was all he could see through the red haze of fury that had dropped over his eyes.

Stunned though McConnell was, he realized he was in danger of being trampled by the wagon team and rolled aside to get away from the spooked horses. Breckinridge left the porch in a flying leap that carried him into McConnell just as the riverman heaved up to his knees. The impact knocked McConnell backward again. Breck started punching—wild, looping blows that might have killed McConnell if all of them had landed.

McConnell jerked his head aside and brought up a knee. He sunk it into Breckinridge's belly with enough force to make Breck fold over. McConnell was a big, strong man, too, and desperation forced him to get his wits about him again. He grabbed Breck's shoulders and heaved the redhead aside.

Quite a few of the store's customers had followed

Breckinridge out the door. They clustered on the porch and shouted encouragement to the fighters. McConnell, no doubt feeling himself to be the aggrieved party, scrambled up and went after Breck. He drew back his foot and sank a brutal kick in his opponent's ribs. Breck grunted from the impact, but when McConnell tried to kick him again, he was able to reach up and grab the riverman's boot. Yelling in fury, Breck thrust upward on it. McConnell lost his balance and fell heavily again.

That gave Breckinridge time to reach his feet. So did McConnell. They came together like a couple of maddened bulls, standing toe to toe and slugging away at each other. The powerful blows rocked each man, but they caught themselves and bored in again.

Breckinridge was only vaguely aware of the commotion the battle was causing along Knoxville's main street. People came running from all directions to witness this epic struggle. The combat swayed back and forth until Breck and McConnell were pounding at each other in the middle of the street. Both men were smeared with mud and horse dung. Fists had opened cuts on their faces. Breck tasted blood in his mouth and blinked it out of his eyes. McConnell was in even worse shape. His face was swelling already, his features almost unrecognizable.

He had stamina, though, and absorbed the punishment Breckinridge dished out while delivering plenty of his own. As far as Breck was concerned, the other man's blows were little more than insect bites. He ignored them and kept walloping McConnell as hard and fast as he could.

Eventually, Breckinridge's slight advantages in height, weight, and reach began to have an effect.

McConnell's punches grew weaker, his reactions slower. He blocked fewer of Breck's punches, and each blow that landed accelerated the process. Finally, Breck hooked a left into McConnell's midsection that doubled over the riverman and put his chin in perfect position for the uppercut that Breck started around his knees. The punch landed with a sound like an ax biting deep into a tree. McConnell's head jerked so far back it seemed like it was about to come off his shoulders. His feet left the ground. He crashed down on his back, like a falling tree this time, and lay there motionless except for his heaving chest. His arms were flung out to the sides. He couldn't move them anymore. Air rasped over his bloody, swollen lips and through his now misshapen nose.

Awed silence hung over the street. People stared, clearly shocked to see a brute such as Bill McConnell laid so low.

Breckinridge turned away from the unconscious man. He brought up a shaking hand and dragged the back of it across his mouth to wipe away some of the blood. A sharply indrawn breath hissed at the pain that caused. He lifted his eyes toward the porch in front of the mercantile and took a couple of staggering steps in that direction as he searched for Dulcy.

She wasn't there.

Breckinridge increased his pace. The spectators gathered on the porch hastily got out of his way as he stumbled onto it. Maybe she was still inside the store, he thought. He stomped through the open doors and looked around.

Still no sign of her.

"Mr. Emerson!" Breckinridge said as he spotted the

store's proprietor. The swollen lips made his voice thick. "Mr. Emerson, where is she?"

Emerson shook his head. "I don't know, lad. After the fight started, she ran off down the street, crying." The storekeeper paused, then asked, "Those things McConnell said . . . were they true?"

The look Breckinridge gave him made Emerson take a quick step back. The man held up his hands, palms out.

"I'm sorry, son. I had no right—"

Breckinridge ignored the apology, turned his back, and stalked out of the store. He was starting to catch his breath now. His ears still rung a little from some of the blows McConnell had landed, and his vision was blurry from the blood that had run into his eyes, but he could see and hear well enough. He looked up and down the street, searching for Dulcy, and when he didn't see her, he grabbed a bystander's arm.

"Where'd she go?" Breckinridge demanded. "The gal who was with me, where'd she go?"

The man whose arm he held had gone pale from pain, fear, or both. He stammered, "I . . . I don't know—"

Breckinridge shoved him aside and turned to another man, who flinched back before Breck could take hold of him. "Where'd she go?" Breck bellowed.

He had to confront three more frightened men before one of them pointed a trembling finger and said, "If . . . if you're talking about that pretty lady with dark brown hair, I . . . I think I saw her heading into the tavern down yonder."

Breckinridge looked at the building the man indicated. Its walls were constructed from large, irregular pieces of red and brown stone mortared together, and it had a red slate roof. The sign hanging over its door proclaimed it to be the RED TOP TAVERN. Breck remembered it well. In his earlier days, he had downed quite a few mugs of ale in there.

He stomped toward it now, the crowd parting to let him through. Behind him, several men tried to lift the still mostly senseless McConnell to his feet, but they weren't having much success. Breckinridge didn't care about that. The fight was over and forgotten now.

All he cared about was finding Dulcy.

Some of the people followed him, evidently thinking that something else interesting—or violent—was going to happen. Breckinridge became aware of these human vultures straggling along behind him. He stopped, turned, and snarled at them. That caused the bystanders to scatter. Breck reached out, caught hold of the heavy door's latch, and hauled it open. He stepped into the tavern and paused, his eyes needing to adjust for a moment before he could see what was going on in the dimly lit room.

His heart slugged heavily as he spotted Dulcy sitting on a bench at one of the tables. She was so close to the man beside her that she might as well have been in his lap. She had one arm around the man's shoulder and was using the other to caress his beard as she spoke softly into his ear.

But like everyone else in the tavern, they turned their heads toward the door to look at the redheaded man-mountain looming there.

"What in the blue blazes?" Breckinridge yelled. He started toward the long table where Dulcy sat. The man she had been cozying up to hurriedly abandoned her. The other men at the table scrambled to their feet and headed for the bar, too. A burly, grizzled, mostly bald man stood behind the bar. His name was Mackey, Breck recalled. He reached down, picked up a bung starter from a shelf, and laid it on the bar just in case.

Dulcy stayed where she was. She regarded Breckinridge with a cool stare as he came up to her. She didn't say anything, though, so after a second he exclaimed, "What the hell are you doin'?"

"What does it look like?" she asked. "I'm working at my profession."

"Your profession, as you call it, is bein' my wife!"

"We're not married," Dulcy said.

"We're fixin' to be!"

"No, we're not," she said. Her voice was hard and flat. "It was a mistake to believe that we ever could be."

Breckinridge flung a big hand toward the doorway and said, "Because of what that stupid bastard said in the store? I gave him a thrashin' he'll never forget! I busted up that son of a bitch good!"

"And what did that change?" Dulcy asked. "Did it make me any less of a whore?"

"You ain't a whore!"

"I was. You know that, Breck. Nothing can change that. Not ever."

A feeling of helplessness welled up inside him at her calm, almost icy resolve. He didn't like it. He had always been able to grab hold of his problems and shoot them, punch them, or just shake them until they went away. But as he looked at Dulcy, he realized that none of the things he was really good at would help in this situation.

He had to try to make her see that she was wrong. He said, "You're upset because o' what that fella said, and I don't blame you."

"It was the truth. I said that I didn't remember

him, but I do." She smiled faintly. "He was a good customer. Not as rough as you might have thought he would be."

The image that called up in Breckinridge's mind made him a little sick. He knew perfectly well how Dulcy had lived in the past, but like the fight with McConnell, it was over and done with and didn't mean anything anymore. He could put all those thoughts away and not let them bother him. He'd pondered it some, and he knew it was true. He wasn't fooling himself.

"You ain't gonna make me feel bad about you," he said, quietly now as his rage subsided and the fear of losing her took its place. "You could never make me think I'm makin' a mistake by marryin' you. I done plenty o' things in my life I ain't very proud of, but I figured that by gettin' hitched to you, I'd be makin' a new start. I figured we could just forget everything else and worry about what's gonna happen from now on."

"That's what I *am* worried about." She finally stood up and faced him. "You know what's going to happen, Breckinridge. Some gossip is probably already riding out to your parents' farm to tell them everything McConnell said. By the time we could get there, your mother and father and brothers will all know that I'm a—"

"Don't say it," he rasped.

"A harlot, then. A trollop. A fallen woman. Call it whatever you want. It's the truth, and they're going to know it." She sighed. "I wish now I had told them myself, the way I wanted to. It would have ended things between you and me, just as surely, but at least

I would have known that I was honest with them. They're good people, and they deserve the truth."

"What about you?" Breckinridge demanded. "What do you deserve?"

Dulcy smiled and gestured to indicate the tavern around her and the men who were watching with avid interest. "*This* is what I deserve, Breck. If you can't see that, you're a fool."

He stared at her for a long moment, unable to come up with any words to refute her argument, even though he still believed she was completely wrong. At last he said the only thing that was still in him.

"I love you."

"I love you, too," she said in a voice tinged with sadness, "but it doesn't change a damned thing."

Breckinridge had never run from trouble. He had always been the sort to charge right into it. But he had never faced anything quite like this, either. He stood there, his hands opening and closing, his breath trapped in his throat, a band around his chest that tightened more and more until it seemed to be on the verge of squeezing the very soul out of him.

Then, feeling closer to panic than he ever had in his life, he turned and rushed out of the tavern, stumbling into the road. He put his hands to his head as the blood pounded madly inside his skull. Instinct guided his steps back toward the wagon parked in front of the mercantile.

No one got in his way.

No one would have dared.

Chapter 23

"That was just about the end of it," Breckinridge said to Morgan as they sat on the log next to the creek. Morgan's pipe had gone out while he listened to the story, but he hadn't gone to the trouble of re-lighting it. "I know I went back to the store and found that Mr. Emerson had packed up the supplies my ma wanted and put 'em on the wagon. Then I drove back out to the farm. But you can't hardly prove any o' that by me, because I don't really remember any of it. I remember the look on Ma's face, though, when she first saw me, and I knew then that Dulcy was right, somebody had already been out there and told 'em what happened. She looked at me like she had when I was a little kid and my dog died, only this was a whole heap worse."

Into the silence that settled down over them, Morgan said, "Damn it, Breck, I'm sorry. I wish now I'd just left you alone. I didn't mean to stir up so many bad memories."

Breckinridge laughed humorlessly. "Seems to me that's exactly what you meant to do. But that ain't necessarily a bad thing, so you don't have to apologize for it. It's been like . . . havin' a sore place on my soul that won't go away. It's just been a-festerin' and gettin' worse. It needed to be opened up, so all the bad stuff could be let out." He leaned forward, laced his fingers together between his knees, and nodded. "Now it has."

"You mean . . . you feel better now?"

"I reckon I do. It kind of surprises me, too."

After a moment, Morgan said, "I have to know . . . What happened to Dulcy?"

"Well, here's the thing. My ma and pa and every one of my brothers told me to get on back to Knoxville and fetch her. My pa said he didn't give a damn what anybody thought, he'd gotten to know her and figured she was a fine gal and thought I still ought to marry her. Ma said the same, although I could tell it really did bother her a mite, Dulcy's past and all, I mean. But us Wallaces stick together through thick and thin, and if I wanted to get hitched to her, that was what I ought to do. Edward and the other boys said the same. But I was so tore up inside—not from that fight with McConnell, you understand, I got over that in a hurry—but from the way she just up and give up on us, that it was the next day before I let 'em talk me into it. Last place I'd seen her was at the Red Top, so I went there and found that she'd left a letter for me with Mackey, the fella who ran the place. It said that she was leavin', and that she wouldn't ever cause me no more trouble, and that if I really did love her, I hadn't ought to try to find her."

"But you *did* try to find her, didn't you?"

"Of course I did! I searched high and low all over that part o' the country for weeks." Breckinridge sighed. "I guess I ain't as good a tracker as I figured I was. I never turned up a trace of her, Morgan. She was gone like she hadn't ever been there. Finally, there was just nothin' left to do except say good-bye to my folks and brothers and head on back to St. Louis to meet you, like we'd planned." The brawny shoulders rose and fell in a shrug. "You know everything that happened after that."

"Yeah, I guess I do. I'm sure sorry, Breck. It's not fair, the way things worked out."

"Life ain't fair. Or I reckon maybe it is, on account of sooner or later it r'ars up and wallops everybody in the face, don't it? You just got to shake off the punches and go on." Breckinridge laughed again, and this time the sound had some genuine warmth in it. "I got to admit, havin' good friends like you and Runnin' Elk and White Owl helps. And bein' with Dawn Wind . . . Well, I reckon that's gonna help that sore place inside me go away. I can already feel it gettin' better. Now, you just got to do one more thing for me."

"Anything, Breck, you know that."

Breckinridge slapped his friend on the shoulder, nearly knocking him off the log, and said, "Take them pelts to St. Louis and get a good price for 'em, then come back here in the spring and we'll do it all over again."

The whole village turned out to say good-bye to Morgan and Running Elk. It was a crisp, early fall day as the Crow gathered on the creek bank where the two fully loaded canoes rested. Large bundles of pelts rested in each of the craft. Most of the supplies

Breckinridge and Morgan had brought with them to the mountains were gone, so the travelers would have to live off the land for the most part. Luckily, game was so abundant that they shouldn't have much trouble doing that.

Breckinridge clasped Morgan's hand while Dawn Wind hugged her brother. Breck said, "You two keep your eyes open. We ain't seen hide nor hair of Carnahan's bunch for a long time, but that don't mean they ain't still around somewhere in these parts. The same's true for the survivors of that Blackfoot war party."

"Those Blackfeet are long gone," Morgan said. "Their usual hunting ground is up close to Canada, Running Elk told me, and this is a long way from there. And by now, Carnahan and his men will have plenty of pelts of their own and will just be concerned with getting them back to St. Louis and selling them."

"More than likely," Breckinridge agreed. "Be careful anyway."

"Always," Morgan said with a grin. He clapped a hand on his friend's shoulder. "I figure by the time I see you again, you'll be an old married man. Probably even have a young 'un on the way."

"What?" Breckinridge exclaimed. "I don't know what the hell you're talkin' about."

"Of course not. I'm just saying that it wouldn't surprise me a bit. It's going to be a long, cold winter, though. You and Dawn Wind are going to be spending a lot of time wrapped up in those buffalo robes."

The young woman turned to Morgan in time to hear his comments. Looking a little embarrassed, she hugged him and then said, "Breckinridge will miss you, Morgan. So will I and my father." She laughed. "From the gossip I hear, so will some of the girls in the village. When you return, many will be interested in becoming your wife."

"Now, hold on a minute—" Morgan began with a note of alarm in his voice.

A laugh boomed out from Breckinridge. "So it's all right for you talk about me gettin' hitched, but the same ain't fair for you."

"I didn't say that. It's just that . . . Damn it, I'm too young to settle down!"

"We'll see." Breckinridge slapped his friend on the back, staggering Morgan a little.

White Owl bid farewell to the two young men and gave them his blessing for their journey in a long speech that Dawn Wind translated briefly. Badger's Den chanted a song that would give them good medicine. Then Morgan and Running Elk pushed the canoes out into the creek, climbed in, and took up their paddles. The current caught the craft and edged them downstream. Everyone on the bank waved good-bye.

Dawn Wind hugged Breckinridge's arm and said, "I will miss them. It will be good to see them again when they return in the spring. That is a long time from now, though." She looked up at Breck. "A time I will enjoy spending with you, Breckinridge."

He turned her toward their tipi and suggested, "Let's go get started on that."

By the middle of the day, the two young men had followed the creek to the Bighorn River and entered the larger stream. They paddled north toward the Yellowstone. It had always struck Morgan as a bit odd that in this case north was downstream. It seemed to him that the opposite should have been true, but that was the way the geography had worked out.

They hadn't talked much. Running Elk still wasn't all that comfortable with English, and Morgan had struggled to learn much of the Crow language. They could understand each other when they had a chance to sit down and use more extensive sign language, but out here on the river they settled for a few gestures and an occasional comment called from one canoe to the other.

Ahead of them, the bank on the right side of the stream rose to a thickly wooded bluff. Morgan looked closely at it as the knowledge that this would be a good place for an ambush stirred inside him. He searched the growth for any sign of movement or a bit of sunlight reflecting from the metal of a gun barrel or a knife.

Instead, the landscape seemed empty and peaceful. Morgan smiled ruefully to himself and shook his head. Sure, he had promised Breck he would be careful, but there was no point in worrying all the time. He kept up his steady strokes with the paddle. The canoe glided smoothly over the creek's surface, even loaded down with pelts like it was. It just rode a little lower in the water than it had on the journey up here into the mountains.

The bluff fell behind the two young men. A couple of hundred yards past it, they rounded a bend, and the bluff was out of sight.

Several birds exploded from the tree branches as the three men who had been lying hidden and motionless in the undergrowth for the past hour finally moved again. Jud Carnahan had a satisfied smile on his bearded face as he got to his feet. He looked at

Gordon Ralston and said, "Looks like Wallace and Baxter had a successful season. Those pelts represent quite a bit of money."

"Wallace wasn't with him," Ralston snapped. "I want *his* hide."

"You'll have your chance at it," Carnahan said. "Our friend told us Wallace stayed behind with the Crow. We'll be settling scores there, too, but first I want to deal with Baxter and get our hands on those furs." He looked over at the cold, impassive face of the Blackfoot war chief known as Machitehew, which he had been told translated as *He has evil in his heart.* "We can afford to bide our time with Wallace. Let him settle down and be happy. Then we'll make the son of a bitch wish that he'd never been born."

For two days, Morgan and Running Elk traveled downstream, following the Bighorn to the Yellowstone. By now Morgan had grown accustomed to the spectacular scenery, but every now and then he still realized how beautiful this country was and felt lucky that he'd been able to explore its wonders. Living in his father's mansion back East, he never would have dreamed that someday he would feel this way, but many things had changed over the past couple of years and the way he regarded the frontier was one of them.

On the third morning, he and Running Elk were packing up their camp on a bluff above the river. The bank fell almost sheer to the Yellowstone, but there was a path that led down to the narrow gravel bar where they had left the canoes. Morgan expected to have another good day on the river and perhaps even reach the Missouri by nightfall.

A grove of trees stood about fifty yards from the campsite. The previous evening, Running Elk had killed a deer with an arrow, then dressed out the animal and hung the carcass from a limb of one of those trees. He walked toward it now, intending to hack off enough meat to last them for several days. Morgan shouldered the pack of their dwindling supplies and turned toward the bluff to carry the pack down the path to the canoes.

He had just put his back to the trees when he heard Running Elk's shout of alarm.

Morgan whirled around, dropped the pack, and lifted the rifle he held in his other hand. A gunshot boomed from the direction of the trees. Morgan saw the spurt of flame in the shadows under the branches, as well as a puff of grayish-black smoke.

Running Elk had dropped to one knee as he reached for an arrow in the quiver slung on his back. His motions were too swift for the eye to follow as he nocked the arrow, drew back the bow, and loosed the shaft toward the trees. As he fired, he let out an angry cry.

Morgan didn't know where the first shot had gone, but there was no doubt where the second ball landed. He heard the awful thud of it striking flesh and saw the way Running Elk rocked back and almost fell. The young warrior caught himself and tried to pull out a second arrow, but his movements were slower and more awkward now. Morgan knew his friend had been hit but couldn't tell how bad the injury was. Perhaps worst of all, there was no cover around Running Elk, no place he could seek shelter from the attack.

Without thinking about what he was doing, Morgan raised the rifle to his shoulder, took aim at the place where he had seen a muzzle flash, and pressed the trigger. Its roar blended with a third shot from the trees, and this time Running Elk went over backward as blood spurted in the air from a terrible wound in his throat. His bow and the second arrow fell aside, unfired.

"Nooooo!" Morgan howled. He dropped the empty rifle and pulled his pistol from behind his belt. He didn't fire immediately, though. Instead he started toward Running Elk. He wanted to reach his friend and try to help him—even though, somewhere inside him, he knew it was too late already to do anything for the young man.

He had taken only a couple of steps when something smashed into his right shin with enough force to knock that leg out from under him. He tumbled to the ground and screamed as pain exploded from the wound.

Men emerged from the woods and moved toward Morgan, not advancing in any hurry. His vision was blurred by the agony that came from his injured leg. The figures drifting toward him were like ghosts. Panting hard, he forced his stunned brain to work. He put his free hand on the ground and pushed. He knew he had to get up. If he could hobble to the path and down to the river, he thought, he might be able to reach one of the canoes and get away. When he was halfway up, he saw his rifle lying on the ground nearby, got hold of its barrel, and used it as a lever and then a crutch.

He wasn't thinking straight because of the pain. He realized that as he struggled upright and balanced on his good leg. The blurriness in his eyes receded slightly. He could tell that some of the killers approaching him were white, but others appeared to be Indians. That confused Morgan. Then one of the figures spoke.

"Surprised to see us again, aren't you, Baxter?"

Carnahan. Jud Carnahan was back, and he still had that one-eyed major with him, and now some evil-looking Indians as well . . . Morgan's head swam crazily. He propped himself up on the rifle and backed away from the men closing in on him. Bloodlust was written clearly on their faces. They had killed Running Elk already, and now they were about to kill him.

Breck had been right. They should have been more careful . . .

"That's a good-looking load of pelts you have, boy," Carnahan said mockingly. "Put together with the furs we took, they'll make us a good profit. We should be able to get even more, though. There'll be a lot of you fellows heading back to St. Louis this time of year. They're going to deliver their pelts to *us*. They just don't know it yet."

"You . . . you're nothing but thieves!" Morgan gasped. "Outlaws!"

"Call us whatever you want," Carnahan said. "I prefer to think that we're going to be rich men. Of course, there's more to life than money. There's the satisfaction of settling old scores. And with the help of our new Blackfoot friends here, that's exactly what we're going to do, starting with you and that buck we just killed." A savage grin curved Carnahan's mouth inside the bushy black beard. "Your friend Wallace and his squaw are next."

Fury welled up inside Morgan and erupted from his mouth in an incoherent yell. He had backed all the way to the bluff's edge. There was nowhere else for him to go.

But at least he could die fighting and maybe blow that damned smirk off Carnahan's face. He jerked up the pistol in his right hand.

Several shots blasted at the same time. A terrible blow crashed into Morgan's body and knocked him backward. The rifle slipped out of his other hand. He couldn't hold himself up anymore, and there was nothing underneath him, anyway.

He plummeted the forty feet to the Yellowstone River and struck the water with his back, throwing up a huge splash of water as he went under the surface. Long moments passed as Carnahan, Ralston, Machitehew, and the other men stood on the edge of the bluff and watched. Morgan didn't come up.

Carnahan spat out a glob of phlegm that arched over the river and then dropped into it. "The bastard's dead," he said. "Come on. We have more scores to settle and more pelts to gather."

"And more killing to do," Ralston said.

Chapter 24

Now that he wasn't spending his days checking the traplines, Breckinridge wasn't sure what to do with himself at first. The Crow village would need meat over the winter, of course, so he began devoting himself to hunting, along with some of the young men.

They brought the carcasses of the deer, elk, and antelope they killed back to the village, where the women skinned and dressed out the animals and cut off strips of meat to be dried and preserved for the cold, hungry months ahead.

It didn't take long to get a foretaste of those months, either. A week after Morgan and Running Elk left for St. Louis, an early storm blew in, bringing with it a frigid north wind and snowfall that ranged from several inches in the open to drifts that were several feet deep. The unseasonable storm reminded Breckinridge of the one that had roared down on him and Morgan the previous spring, when they had been ambushed by some of Carnahan's men.

That night as he and Dawn Wind sat beside the fire in their tipi, the young woman said, "I hope Morgan and my brother will be able to find shelter if this storm catches them."

"Yeah, I was hopin' they'd get far enough down the Missouri by the time the first snow rolled in that they wouldn't have to worry about it," Breckinridge said. "Just goes to show you that when you're talkin' about the weather, you can't never tell what's gonna happen."

"That is true of most things, is it not?"

Breckinridge thought about the way his plans had been upended time after time during the past couple of years and chuckled.

"Well, yeah, you could sure say that," he replied. "But I'm sure Morgan and Runnin' Elk are fine. They know what they're doin', and they'll find a place to get in outta the storm." He put his arm around Dawn Wind's shoulders and pulled her closer to him as he listened to the wind blowing outside. "I reckon I'm more worried about how you and me are gonna stay warm tonight."

"That does not concern me," she said as she snuggled against him. "That does not concern me at all."

The storm caught Carnahan, Ralston, the rest of the outlaw trappers, and their Blackfoot allies mostly by surprise, although Machitehew had warned Carnahan that the weather was unpredictable at this time of year.

They took shelter in a canyon that blocked the worst of the wind and built a fire under an outcropping of rock that shielded the flames from most of the snow. Some of the swirling flakes drifted into the fire anyway and melted with a faint sizzling sound.

Some of the men didn't have thick enough coats for this sort of weather. They huddled as close to the fire as they could get for its warmth.

Major Gordon Ralston was one of them. His face was more lean, wolfish, and bitter than ever as he held out his hands toward the fire.

"We should've already killed Wallace and headed back downriver," he muttered.

Carnahan, who was also sitting near the fire, leaned forward. "What was that, Major?"

Ralston hesitated, as if unsure whether he wanted to repeat what he had just said. But then a stubborn look came over his face.

"I said we should have killed Wallace and headed back to civilization before now."

"Are you questioning my judgment, Major? Maybe you think you should be the one giving orders around here, not me."

Ralston didn't respond to that right away. The pause made Carnahan's face darken with anger above the beard.

Then Ralston said, "I'm willing to take your orders, Jud. You know that. But you have to admit, this storm complicates things."

"Not really," Carnahan insisted. "Sure, we haven't gotten back to that Crow village yet . . . but we're richer than we were a few days ago, aren't we?"

In addition to the pelts they had stolen from Morgan Baxter and Running Elk, the group had also taken another load of furs from three trappers they had encountered the next day. Those men had been able to get into some rocks, hunker down, and put up a desperate fight for their lives and their pelts, but in the end, all three had died and the pelts wound up in the possession of Carnahan and his group.

However, that encounter had slowed them down enough that they hadn't been able to reach the Crow village before this storm moved in.

"We're not rich," Ralston said in response to Carnahan's comment. "We won't be until we get back to St. Louis and sell those furs."

"They're as good as money," Carnahan said, "and you know it. In fact, I've been thinking it might be a good idea not to go back downriver at all this winter."

That statement made Ralston and all the other white men stare at him in surprise. More than surprise, actually. Some of them looked shocked and upset.

In a quiet voice tinged with menace, Ralston asked, "What the hell are you talking about, Carnahan?"

Carnahan looked up the canyon as his deep-set eyes narrowed in concentration.

"What if we built some cabins and stayed right here for the winter? We'd be out of the worst of the weather, so we'd be comfortable enough. There's plenty of game around. We wouldn't go hungry. And we're close to the river. Every trapper who comes by would be waltzing right into our hands. We snatch them up, kill them, and add their pelts to our stockpile. When spring comes and more men start traveling *up*river, we'll be waiting for them, too. All their traps and supplies will be ours for the taking. We wipe them out as they come, so we won't have any competition for next summer's pelts. I'm telling you, Major, it won't be long before we have a damn *empire* up here!"

Ralston stared at Carnahan for a long moment, disbelief etched on his face. But then the former officer frowned and said slowly, "You know, that might actually turn out to be true. It's a bold plan, but it could work."

Al Nusser exclaimed, "Hold on a minute! You're talkin' about spendin' the whole winter up here, Jud."

"I know that," Carnahan said calmly.

"We'll freeze our asses off!"

Chet Bagley added, "The rest of us were sort of counting on spending the winter in some nice warm whorehouse back in St. Louis, Jud."

"The whores and the booze will still be there a year from now," Carnahan said. "Think how much more you can enjoy them as a very wealthy man."

Nusser scratched at his brown beard. "It's a mite hard for me to imagine that. I ain't ever been wealthy."

"Then this is your chance."

Ralston inclined his head toward Machitehew and the other Blackfeet, who hunkered a short distance away from the fire and maintained their usual aloofness from the whites.

"What about our, ah, allies?"

"They'd be free to stay or go, as they pleased," Carnahan said. "But they need our help if they want to have their revenge on the Crow."

That was true. Only a dozen warriors were left alive after the raid on the Crow village. Although a Blackfoot warrior considered himself easily the equal of ten men from another tribe when it came to fighting, Machitehew was practical enough to know that another attack on their despised enemies would result in the rest of his men being wiped out. He hated the Crow, but his hatred wasn't strong enough to turn him into a fool. He'd always had plenty of cunning to go along with his ruthless nature.

Carnahan was well aware of that. From the first moment he had laid eyes on Machitehew, when the two groups unexpectedly faced each other across a clearing and hesitated as they tried to decide whether to do battle, Carnahan had sensed a kindred spirit in the Blackfoot war chief.

That was why he had stepped forward, palm outstretched in the universal gesture of peace, and hoped the savage felt the same way. They could kill each other, or they could join forces and become much more dangerous to their mutual enemies.

Of course, at that precise moment, Carnahan hadn't known for sure that they even *had* mutual enemies. But when Machitehew spoke sharply to his warriors and hostilities didn't break out, everyone relaxed a little. Machitehew spoke some English, and he and Carnahan and Ralston soon had their heads together in a council of war.

They understood each other well enough that it hadn't taken Carnahan long to figure out Machitehew and the surviving Blackfeet also had a grudge against the massive youngster named Breckinridge Wallace. Wallace and his friend Baxter had been in the Crow village when the Blackfoot war party attacked, and the big redhead had killed more of Machitehew's men than anyone else and turned the tide of battle almost single-handedly.

Machitehew wanted to kill all the Crow and burn their village to the ground, but he wanted vengeance on Breckinridge Wallace as well.

Although Carnahan deliberately made no mention of it around his rough-and-tumble companions, he was an educated man. He had read treatises on war;

more of them, he suspected, than the former army officer who was his second-in-command. He realized immediately that since he and Machitehew had common goals, it made sense to work together. The Blackfoot war chief shared that instinct, and so the partnership had formed.

So far they had killed Baxter, his Indian friend, and the other three trappers and added a nice pile of pelts to their loot, but they could do so much more, Carnahan thought now. They could afford to bide their time and grow into the most powerful force west of the Mississippi, especially if Machitehew cooperated and helped bring in allies from other Blackfoot bands. If Machitehew didn't want to go along with that, he could be gotten rid of when the proper moment came.

Carnahan could see it all unfolding in his head, like scenes from a play. As he thought about it, his certainty that he was right grew stronger.

Ralston nodded and said, "All right, Jud. I'll go along with this plan of yours . . . for now."

Carnahan returned the curt nod. He would accept Ralston's agreement.

For now.

The major seemed to think that he was indispensable to Carnahan's efforts, though, and sooner or later he might have to be taught just how wrong he was.

The weather remained cold enough that the snow stayed on the ground for several days without melting.

Breckinridge spent most of that time in the tipi with Dawn Wind. Lovemaking occupied some of their hours, of course. Folks had to rest up from that, too, so they had plenty of chances to talk.

They shared stories from their lives, often laughing as they did so. But sometimes solemnly as well, as when Breck told her about the troubles that had brought him to the frontier in the first place.

He even told her about Dulcy, and after he had gotten started on that tale, he worried that it was a mistake. A gal wouldn't want to hear about some other gal her fella had almost married . . . would she?

But Dawn Wind didn't seem to mind. She was sympathetic, and she even assured Breckinridge that he hadn't done anything wrong. Maybe she was just trying to make him feel better. He didn't know about that, but he was grateful to her anyway.

And as he had told Morgan, with everything out in the open now, he felt like he had healed up inside. There might be a scar where life had wounded him, but that was better than a festering sore.

He and Dawn Wind also went out and ranged through the woods near the village. One day when they were out exploring, Breckinridge killed a rabbit with a throw of his knife, and they skinned and roasted it over a fire Dawn Wind built. Food had seldom tasted better, Breck thought, but maybe that was because of the company and the wild, beautiful landscape around them.

The weather warmed, the snow melted, and as soon as the mud left behind had dried up, life was good again, crisp autumn days and clear, cold nights. Breckinridge sat with White Owl one afternoon as the chief made arrows. Breck watched for a while, then began to help out. White Owl showed him what to do, speaking in Crow, which Breck had begun to understand fairly well, but communicating mostly in gestures.

Breckinridge frowned as he began to feel like someone was watching him. Without being too obvious, he glanced up from the arrow shaft he was fashioning from a branch with his knife.

One of the Crow warriors stood about fifty feet away, glaring at him. The man was big for a Crow, broad across the shoulders but also thick through the body. It was rare to see a fat Indian, but this fella almost fit that description. Breck figured a lot of his thickness might be muscle, though. He vaguely remembered noticing the man around the village before but didn't recall ever hearing his name.

Frowning, Breckinridge said to White Owl, "See that fella standin' over there givin' me the evil eye? Who's he?" He repeated the question in the Crow tongue as best he could.

White Owl glanced up, then said in his language, "That is Isáa Sampa." The chief added in halting English, "You say . . . Big Stump."

"Big Stump," Breckinridge repeated, nodding. "I reckon that's a good name for him. He's as thick as a big ol' stump."

The warrior looked coldly at Breckinridge for another moment, then turned and walked away with his back stiff. Breck didn't know what the hell that was all about, but he wasn't sure he cared enough to find out.

Despite that, when he was in the tipi that evening and they had finished the stew Dawn Wind had cooked for supper, he gave in to his curiosity and said, "I was visitin' with your pa this afternoon when I noticed one of the warriors givin' me a strange look. If I didn't know better, I'd say he wanted to lift my hair."

"Do not even joke about such a thing, Breckinridge," Dawn Wind said. "All of the Apsáalooke are your friends."

"I don't think this fella was. White Owl said that in English he'd be called Big Stump."

"Oh!" Dawn Wind put a hand to her mouth in surprise. "I did not think about Isáa Sampa. I am not sure his name would be *exactly* Big Stump in your tongue." She laughed. "But now that I think about it, that would be a good name for him."

"Who is he, and how come he's mad at me?"

"We were children together, and ever since we were young, he has wanted to marry me. For many moons he has said that one day I would be his wife. He had his father offer my father five horses for me."

"What the—" Breckinridge drew in a deep, angry breath. "That ain't hardly right!"

"You think I am worth more than five horses?"

"No, but . . . Well, yeah, but . . . I mean . . . he shouldn't ought to have his pa tryin' to *buy* you!"

"That is often the way things are done among my people. There is no real shame in the two of us lying together even though I am not yet your wife, and a father arranging a marriage for his daughter is accepted by all, as well, even though it is not always done that way."

"Well, ol' Big Stump ain't gonna buy you for no five horses, I can tell you that," Breckinridge declared. "Not for five hundred horses!"

"I do not know . . . I believe if my father was offered five hundred horses, he would be *very* tempted."

Breckinridge might have said something to argue with her, but then he saw how she was smiling at him.

"You're just havin' some sport with me," he said. "You ain't interested in gettin' hitched to Big Stump, are you?"

Dawn Wind shook her head. "I will marry no one except Breckinridge Wallace, if he will have me."

She leaned closer, put her arms around his neck, and kissed him. Breckinridge returned the embrace, sliding his arms around her waist, then picking her up and depositing her on his lap. From a while they simply sat and kissed and snuggled, enjoying the closeness they shared.

Then Breckinridge leaned back, frowned slightly, and said, "Do I have to worry about this here Big Stump comin' after me? You know, to get rid of his competition?"

"Isáa Sampa is no competition for you, Breckinridge. You are not afraid of him, are you?"

"Not hardly! I just don't want to cause any trouble for you or anybody else in the village. You folks have took me in like this was my second home."

"You have been a good friend to us. Do not worry. I will speak to Isáa Sampa. There will be no trouble."

Breckinridge hoped she was right. The only problem was, it seemed like every time somebody promised him there wouldn't be any trouble, things never quite worked out that way.

Chapter 25

Breckinridge didn't see anything more of Big Stump for a couple of days. He knew the warrior had to be around the village somewhere, but if Big Stump was avoiding him, that was just fine with Breck, knowing what he now knew about the man's feelings for Dawn Wind.

Unfortunately, that respite didn't last. Breckinridge was sitting again with White Owl one afternoon, both men cross-legged on the ground, when the chief suddenly looked across the village and frowned. Breck followed White Owl's gaze and saw Big Stump coming toward them. The thickset warrior had an angry, determined expression on his face.

"Breck'ridge Wallace," Big Stump said as he came to a stop in front of Breckinridge and White Owl. He continued in the Crow tongue, "I would speak with you."

Breckinridge had spent a lot of time with Dawn Wind practicing her language, so he was able to understand Big Stump. He put a hand on the ground to brace himself and got to his feet. Breck was a head taller than most of the Crow warriors, but Big Stump was almost as tall. He had to look up only a couple of inches to meet Breck's eyes.

"Isáa Sampa," Breckinridge said with a nod. "I will listen."

Big Stump looked a little surprised at the response. He said, "You know who I am?"

"I have spoken to White Owl and Dawn Wind about you."

Big Stump's hands clenched into fists. "Then you know that Dawn Wind is to be my wife."

"I know that's what you *want*," Breckinridge said. "I also know she's never agreed to that."

"It does not matter. The spirits have told me that we are meant to be together."

"If that was true, the spirits would have told her, too. She's with me." Breckinridge knew that among the Crow, as with many other tribes, an actual ceremony wasn't necessary, so he stated flatly, "Dawn Wind is my wife."

"No!" Rage darkened Big Stump's face. A white man who was so overcome with anger probably would have thrown a punch. Big Stump's reaction was different.

He launched himself at Breckinridge and tackled him.

The attack didn't exactly take Breckinridge by surprise. He knew Big Stump was mad and unpredictable. But the warrior moved faster than Breck expected and crashed into him with considerable force. Big Stump was no lightweight, either. The collision knocked Breck back a step. Big Stump drove hard with his legs, keeping Breck off-balance, and when a piece of firewood rolled under one of his feet, he went down.

Big Stump fell on top of him. The warrior's weight drove most of the air out of Breckinridge's lungs, and an instant later, Big Stump locked his hands together behind Breck's back and tightened his arms in a bear hug. Breck couldn't get his breath. Big Stump was strong, too, strong enough that Breck felt his ribs creaking under the inexorable pressure.

Breckinridge heaved up from the ground and rolled. He hoped that would knock Big Stump loose from him. The warrior's grip never lessened, though. If anything, he squeezed even harder. Breck's body began crying out for air. Red flashes danced in front of his eyes.

He wound up on top. Big Stump wrapped his legs around Breckinridge's knees and held on that way, too. With his arms and legs pinned, Breck had only one way of fighting back. He lifted his head as much as he could and then slammed his forehead into the middle of Big Stump's face.

Blood spurted from Big Stump's nose. He grunted in pain. But he didn't let go. Breckinridge butted him again. This time he felt Big Stump's grip slip slightly.

For a third time, Breckinridge rammed his forehead into Big Stump's face. As the warrior's arms loosened even more, Breck heaved with his arms and shoulders and broke free. He pushed himself up far enough to hook a hard right into Big Stump's midsection.

It was about like punching an actual tree stump, he discovered. Breckinridge's hunch that Big Stump's thickness was more muscle than fat was confirmed. Big Stump didn't even seem to feel the blow. He slashed upward with an elbow that caught Breck in the jaw and knocked him to the side.

Breckinridge rolled over and tried to come up on his knees, but Big Stump had already recovered enough to tackle him again. They tumbled over and over. Big Stump managed to pin one of Breck's arms again, but the other was still free. Breck whipped it around and peppered Big Stump's face with several short, sharp punches. Big Stump rammed a knee into Breck's stomach and brought a fist down on the back of his head. The two men whaled away at each other mercilessly.

They rolled against one of the tipis and got tangled in its buffalo hide wall, bringing down the cone-shaped dwelling. Somewhere nearby, a woman screeched fiercely. She probably lived there, and now Breckinridge and Big Stump were busting up her home. Breck fought his way free of the clinging folds of hide and surged to his feet. Big Stump flailed until he was loose, too, and leaped up.

"Damn it, that's enough!" Breckinridge roared in English. "Stop fightin', you dang fool!"

Big Stump either didn't understand or didn't care. He charged at Breckinridge again, arms outstretched to catch the white man in another brutal bear hug.

Breckinridge didn't let it come to that this time. He didn't try to avoid Big Stump. Instead he stepped forward, pivoted at the waist, and put all the power of his back and shoulders into a straight, pile-driver punch with his right fist. Big Stump was wide open as the blow rocketed in. It landed with a sound that made several of the watching warriors wince. Big Stump's upper half went backward while momentum carried his bottom half forward. That resulted in him slamming down on his back, out cold.

At least Breckinridge hoped he was just unconscious. He worried that he might have killed Big Stump.

As he stood there, though, he saw the warrior's chest rising and falling in a ragged rhythm. Big Stump was alive, just senseless. Breckinridge took a step back and looked around warily in case the fella had any friends or relatives who might want to continue the battle.

Quite a crowd of men, women, children, and dogs had gathered to watch the fracas, but nobody seemed to be too upset. Some of the warriors muttered comments among themselves, evidently impressed by Breckinridge's triumph.

Dawn Wind stood off to one side with a worried frown on her face. Breckinridge didn't know if her concern was for him or for Big Stump, who, after all, had been her friend since childhood. Could be she was worried about both of them, Breck thought.

White Owl walked up to Breckinridge and said, "That was a mighty battle, my friend. It is a shame Isáa Sampa would not listen when you tried to reason with him."

"I hope I didn't hurt him too bad." Breckinridge looked down at the man he had defeated. Big Stump's nose was probably broken, and the blood from it was smeared all over his face. His breathing was raspy but had settled down and was steadier now. Breck shook his head and added, "Well, he wasn't all that good-lookin' to start with, I reckon."

Dawn Wind came over and put her hand on

Breckinridge's arm. She asked in English, "You are all right?"

"Yeah. He's a tough scrapper, but I been in fights with a heap worse. I tried to talk him out of tanglin' with me, but he wasn't havin' any of it."

"Big Stump is a stubborn man. I have told him many times I would not marry him, but he has never given up." Dawn Wind sighed. "Perhaps now he will."

"I wouldn't count on it. If I had my heart set on marryin' you but you weren't interested, I'd sure keep tryin' to change your mind."

She squeezed his arm and said, "Lucky for you I *am* interested."

Breckinridge laughed. "Mighty lucky, as far as I'm concerned."

On the ground not far away, Big Stump began to stir. He moved his head from side to side and let out a groggy groan, but he didn't open his eyes yet. Some of his fellow warriors moved forward to help him.

Breckinridge took Dawn Wind's arm and led her toward the tipi they shared. It would probably be a good idea if they weren't there when Big Stump came around. He wasn't afraid of the warrior, by any stretch of the imagination, but there was no point in provoking another ruckus, either.

The canyon that Jud Carnahan had chosen for his headquarters veered off from another creek about ten miles from the Crow village, plenty far enough that the sound of axes wouldn't be heard as the men chopped down trees and used the logs to fashion cabins. Carnahan had them building three of the structures. One would be his while the rest of the group would split up between the other two. Some of them might resent him having a cabin to himself, but he didn't care about that. He was the leader, and he deserved the privacy.

Not that he intended to spend the entire winter alone. When the time came, that pretty young squaw Wallace had taken up with was going to be his. She would cook for him and warm his blankets at night. Carnahan looked forward to that, but he was a man who could control his appetites. He would wait until the time was right before striking at Wallace and the Crow again.

Not everybody had that sort of patience, though. While Carnahan was supervising the construction of the cabins one afternoon, Gordon Ralston approached him, that blasted scabbarded saber slapping against the ex-major's leg as he walked. Ralston carried the sword like it made him better than everybody else, and that always got under Carnahan's skin.

"I've been down at the Crow village, Jud," Ralston announced without any greeting.

Carnahan turned sharply toward him. "I gave no orders for that," he snapped. "What the hell do you think you were doing?"

"It never hurts to scout the enemy," Ralston replied. "And I thought as your second-in-command, I didn't have to wait for orders for everything I do. A good officer shows initiative."

Carnahan wasn't sure how good an officer Ralston had been. Based on a few enigmatic comments the man had made, Carnahan suspected that Ralston had been booted out of the army. Or maybe he had just deserted and never gone back. There was really no telling.

No point in flogging the matter now. In a rumbling tone, Carnahan asked, "What did you find out?"

"Wallace is still there."

"Did you expect he *wouldn't* be?" Carnahan laughed. "The man's befriended those savages, and he's sharing his robes with a hot-blooded young squaw. He'd have to be a fool to leave, wouldn't he?"

"I suppose," Ralston replied with a shrug. "Not everyone in that village is a friend of his, though. I was watching through my spyglass this afternoon while Wallace had a battle royal with one of the Crow braves."

Carnahan cocked a bushy eyebrow in surprise. "Really? How did the fight turn out?"

"Wallace won," Ralston said, "but it looked like the man gave him quite a tussle."

"Could you tell what it was about?"

Ralston shook his head. "I was several hundred yards away, on the other side of the creek. I couldn't hear anything they were saying. Anyway, it probably would have been in that redskin jabber, so I wouldn't have been able to understand it. Wallace was talking quite readily to several of the savages, so I suspect he speaks their lingo now."

"More than likely. He can't spend all his time bedding that squaw." *Although it would be enjoyable to try,* Carnahan thought.

"At any rate," Ralston went on, "I was wondering when you plan to attack the village again."

Carnahan nodded toward the construction going on and said, "We're still building our cabins."

"We don't have to have them finished before we kill Wallace and wipe out those redskins."

"No, I suppose not, but surely you learned something about tactics at West Point, Major."

Ralston bristled at Carnahan's mocking tone of voice. "Of course I did," he said.

"Then you should know the value of striking your enemy when he least expects it. Relatively speaking, not much time has passed since we clashed with Wallace or since Machitehew and his war party attacked the Crow village. They'll still be wary. But just let the winter set in, and they'll be spending most of the time in their tipis, growing soft and sleepy and complacent. Wallace won't be looking for trouble. *That* is when we strike."

Ralston rested his left hand on the saber's grip and curled his lip as he said, "I'm not sure if I want to wait that long."

"Your revenge will be that much sweeter if you do." Carnahan's voice hardened as he added, "If you try anything before I say we're ready, you'll do it on your own. I won't lose an advantage just to satisfy your bloodlust, Ralston."

For a moment the two men stood there trading glares. Then, abruptly, Ralston nodded. He turned and walked away. Carnahan watched him go and thought that Ralston was going to come in handy for making his plans come to fruition.

But when that was over and done with, it would be high time for the arrogant son of a bitch to die.

Chapter 26

For a few days, Breckinridge didn't see Big Stump around the village. When the man finally showed his face again, both eyes were blackened and his nose was still swollen and sore-looking. It appeared he—or someone else—had tried to straighten the broken nose, with decidedly mixed results.

Big Stump didn't seem to have gotten over his anger, either. He still glared at Breckinridge from a distance. But he stayed away and didn't provoke any more fights, so Breck was willing to settle for that outcome. He went on enjoying life in the Crow village: hunting, fishing, spending time with White Owl and some of the other warriors during the days . . . and spending the nights with Dawn Wind in the warmth of their tipi. If this was what being an old married man was like, Breck thought, it wasn't bad at all.

A couple of weeks later, winter arrived in earnest. The temperature dropped like a rock again, and snow began to fall, often for days at a time without stopping. A thick blanket of white covered the landscape.

In a situation such as that, time had little meaning. Days slipped past and turned into weeks with Breckinridge hardly noticing. The sky was overcast most of the time, which meant darkness descended early. As long as he was spending his nights with Dawn Wind, Breck didn't see that as any reason to complain.

Supplies began to run shorter. There was less dried meat to support the people. Breckinridge accompanied hunting parties that left the village in search of game. They had competition, though, from the wolves and mountain lions. The herds of deer, elk, antelope, and moose had already been thinned out considerably by those natural predators. Even rabbits were harder to find. When spring came, things would be different, but it was still months until spring.

On a morning with a thick, dark gray layer of clouds in the sky that held the potential for more snow, Breckinridge left the village with a small party of hunters, three Crow warriors who had become his friends: Swims Like a Fish, Gray Bear, and Bitter Mouth. The latter was a repudiation of anyone who claimed that Indians lacked a sense of humor. Bitter Mouth was always smiling, laughing, and making jokes, usually at the expense of his friends.

The four men ranged far up the creek toward the Bighorn Mountains. Gray Bear, the oldest of the group and the best tracker, claimed that in this direction they would find a herd of the nimble-footed sheep that gave the river and the nearby mountains their names. He had spotted their tracks the week before but had not had enough time that day to pursue them. Breckinridge and the others started out early this morning, so they would have a chance to find the sheep, kill a couple of the beasts, and haul them back to the village before nightfall. That would provide enough meat to last for a while. With a new storm possibly brewing, though, it was important that they not waste any time.

Breckinridge found himself walking along beside Bitter Mouth. The warrior was more serious than usual, Breck noticed. He asked, "Something wrong?"

Bitter Mouth shook his head. "No. There is talk about you, my friend."

"About me?" Breckinridge said. "Is somebody upset with me? Besides ol' Big Stump, I mean?"

"Isáa Sampa is part of the problem. He talks to many of the men in the village and says that you are not a friend to the Apsáalooke people."

"Well, that's just a dadgum lie! What in the world would make him say such a thing?" Before Bitter Mouth could respond, Breckinridge went on, "I reckon I know. This is still because I wound up spendin' the winter with Dawn Wind."

"That is exactly what Isáa Sampa says: that you will spend the winter with us and then leave when the spring comes. That when the weather is warm and the beaver swim in the streams again, you will no longer care about the Apsáalooke. You will abandon Dawn Wind because you are not a true husband to her."

Anger welled up inside Breckinridge. He said, "Those are damned lies. The Apsáalooke are my friends and always will be. Dawn Wind is my wife. I might have to leave for a while, but I'll always come back."

Emotion led him to speak the words, but as they came out of his mouth, he realized they were true. He would never forget his family, but his home was here in these mountains. He would never leave the frontier for good. He didn't think he could be happy anywhere else.

He tried to explain that to Bitter Mouth, although he had never been that comfortable talking about how he felt. The warrior nodded, and a trace of his customary good humor appeared on his face again.

"This is very good to hear, Breckinridge. For many moons, since Dawn Wind was a girl, many of our people have believed that in time she would marry the son of a chief from another band, to make a bond between us. Either that, or she would marry a great warrior. You may not be the son of a chief, but there is no doubt you are a fighter. You have killed many enemies of our people. When Dawn Wind gives birth to your son, there will be no more talk by Big Stump or anyone else of how you are not a true friend to the Apsáalooke."

"I should hope not," Breckinridge said. "I—Wait." He stared at Bitter Mouth. "What did you just say?"

"That Big Stump will have to . . . what would a white man say? Shut his lying mouth."

"No, before that. About my . . . son."

Bitter Mouth suddenly looked worried. "I should not have spoken," he said. "I do not know that it is true. My wife is friends with Dawn Wind, and she tells me that Dawn Wind has said things to make her believe she is with child."

"Good Lord!" Breckinridge said. He wasn't really shocked to hear that Dawn Wind might be going to have a baby. They had been together so many times during the past few months that the odds were heavily in favor of that development. But being aware of that in his mind wasn't the same as knowing it in his heart.

His first feelings were happiness and anticipation, but then he began to worry that he was too young to be a father. Then he thought that he definitely wasn't smart enough or stable enough to be responsible for bringing up a child. Hell, it had only been a little more than two years earlier that he'd been on the run from the law with a murder charge hanging over his head!

Of course that charge had been false. A lot of things had happened since then, it was true, and no doubt he had learned quite a bit about life. He'd been forced to, in order to survive. He wasn't the same wide-eyed, hair-triggered, devil-may-care hell-raiser he had once been.

That still didn't make him fit to be a father.

But if Dawn Wind really *was* expecting, there wasn't a blasted thing he could do about it. He would have to figure out how to be a good parent.

Maybe she wasn't going to have a baby after all, Breckinridge reminded himself. Bitter Mouth wasn't sure. It was just a hunch his wife had.

Either way, Breckinridge was suddenly even more anxious to get back to the Crow village than he had been earlier. Bitter Mouth grinned as Breck said, "Let's hurry up and find them dang sheep!"

Gordon Ralston grimaced as he lowered the spyglass from his one good eye.

"I don't see the son of a bitch," he said. "I've been watching, and I haven't spotted him moving around anywhere. He has to be there, damn it!"

"Take it easy," Carnahan said. Both men lay in the snow on the far side of a knoll about five hundred yards away from the Crow village. Machitehew, the other Blackfoot warriors, and the rest of the outlaw trappers were waiting behind them, well out of sight.

"I want Wallace dead," Ralston said. "He's the luckiest bastard I've ever seen. I've come close to killing him I don't know how many times, and somehow he always survives."

Carnahan gave the major a narrow-eyed glance and said, "I don't recall sending you to kill Wallace that many times, but we'll leave that alone for now. This is the day to hit that village, and that's what we're going to do."

"I don't see why it's so important that we do it today."

"Look at the sky to the north," Carnahan said. "There's snow in those clouds. The redskins know that as well as we do. They'll be thinking about getting ready to make it through another blizzard. They won't be expecting trouble. Hell, there's a good reason these savages don't usually fight among themselves at this time of year. They'd rather stay in their tipis and try not to freeze to death."

Ralston muttered something Carnahan couldn't make out, then sighed and said, "You're right. We have a better chance of taking them by surprise today. But Wallace had better be there somewhere. I want him to die, and I want my face to be the last thing he sees!"

Carnahan nodded and looked at the sky again. As he did, he felt something cold touch his face. He lifted a gloved hand, brushed away the snowflake, and grinned. He half turned, raised his arm, and motioned to Machitehew and the others.

"Come on," Carnahan said as he got to his feet. "It's time."

"There," Gray Bear said as he pointed at a rocky mound about a hundred yards away. Breckinridge saw at least a dozen bighorn sheep among the rocks as they pawed at the spaces between the big slabs of stone in order to expose the hardy grass in those gaps.

The hunters made sure they were downwind of the mound as they approached, so their scent wouldn't carry to the sheep. Breckinridge had brought his rifle with him, but he had rigged a sling for it so he could carry it on his back. He had a quiver of arrows on his back as well, arrows that he had fashioned with the help and advice of White Owl. His right hand was wrapped around a bow he had made. He was going to try hunting today the way the Crow did it.

That meant the men would have to get closer. Gray Bear warned them that the sheep had excellent eyesight, as well as hearing and sense of smell. It wouldn't be easy getting within range for the bows and arrows the hunters carried. The men used every bit of cover they could find and moved as stealthily as if they were creeping up on human enemies.

Finally Gray Bear held up a hand in a signal to stop where they were. The hunters crouched behind a low screen of brush as they silently withdrew arrows from their quivers and nocked the shafts. They would get only one try. As soon as the sheep knew they were there, the animals would bound away and wouldn't stop running until they were long gone.

Gray Bear had already told the men to each pick a different target. Breckinridge had settled on a good-sized ram with large horns that rose and curled back around its head to point forward. The ram stood on one of the rocks while several ewes hunted for grass below his position, as if he were standing guard over them. Breck felt a slight pang of regret that he intended to kill the ram, but that was the way nature worked. The ram wanted to protect his family. Breck wanted to feed his.

"Now," Gray Bear whispered.

All four men stood up at the same time and drew back their bows. Breckinridge aimed his arrow and loosed it, trusting to his eyesight and instincts. All four missiles flew through the air with deadly swiftness. Several of the sheep threw their heads up in alarm as they spotted the movement, but there wasn't time for them to escape.

Breckinridge grimaced as he saw the arrow he had fired glance off the rock only inches from the front hooves of the sheep he had targeted. The creature leaped high, sailing off its perch to land just below the ewes, still in its protective attitude. If any enemy came within reach, the bighorn would charge it with incredible speed and power.

At the same time, a ewe on another part of the mound leaped up and let out a shrill bleat of pain from the arrow driven into its side, just behind the front legs. The arrowhead must have penetrated the animal's heart and killed it almost immediately, because it collapsed after that single reaction. Several yards away, one of the rams, similarly wounded, staggered and then went to its knees. The sheep struggled to stay upright for a second before toppling over.

The other arrow had missed, like Breckinridge's shaft. In not much more than the blink of an eye, the ewes had whirled and fled over the top of the mound. The rams raced after them. Swims Like a Fish and Bitter Mouth were fast enough to launch a second arrow apiece before the last of the sheep disappeared, but those shots fell short as the rams vanished over the mound with flicks of their lighter-colored rumps.

"Dadgum it!" Breckinridge exclaimed.

Gray Bear put a hand on his shoulder and said, "Do not be ashamed, my young friend. You made a fine shot."

"I didn't hit the dang thing! I came so blasted close, too."

"Yes, you came very close on your first shot at a bighorn sheep. That is an achievement. Bitter Mouth's arrow missed as well—and by more than yours."

Bitter Mouth grinned and shrugged.

"So I say again, do not be ashamed," Gray Bear went on. "What matters is that we downed two of the sheep. There will be food for the village's families."

"And we should not waste any time getting back there with it," Swims Like a Fish added. He pointed to the sky.

Breckinridge looked up and saw the snowflakes beginning to swirl down from the heavens. As he watched, the snow thickened and began to fall faster.

Chapter 27

Dawn Wind sat in her father's tipi, mending some of White Owl's buckskins. Her mother had died some years earlier, and since then White Owl had taken two more wives, both of whom had passed on as well. Now he had declared that he was too old to be married again, a decision that Dawn Wind didn't necessarily agree with. But it was her father's choice to make, and as his daughter she would see to it that he was well cared for. She cooked his meals and mended his clothing.

There would come a time, though, in the reasonably near future, when she would no longer be able to carry out these tasks. She would be too busy caring for someone else. Someone small and helpless who would need all her attention.

She smiled to herself as she thought about the new life within her.

She heard a footstep at the tipi's entrance and looked up from the work in her lap. Her smile disappeared as she saw Isáa Sampa standing there, holding back the entrance flap. Through the opening, Dawn Wind saw that snow had started falling.

"Dawn Wind," Big Stump said, "I would speak with you."

"I have nothing to say to you, and you have nothing to say that I wish to hear." She frowned regretfully. "We were friends once. I wish that could still be true."

He came a step into the tipi and let the flap fall closed behind him. "You have known since we were children that I wished for you to be my wife. Never did you tell me that this would never come to pass."

"Neither did I tell you that it would," she responded. "I am not responsible for the things you believed, Isáa Sampa."

"I think you are." He moved another step closer to her. "I think you enjoyed knowing that I loved and wanted you, whether *you* loved and wanted *me* or not."

The way he loomed over her made him seem even larger. She didn't feel threatened by him, actually. She was the chief's daughter and another warrior's wife— she thought of Breckinridge as one of their people now—and she knew Big Stump wouldn't dare hurt her. She didn't think he would, regardless of who she was. For all his bluster, he had a good heart. But still, he made her nervous.

She looked down at the mending with which she had been occupying herself and said, "I think you should go now. We have nothing to talk about."

"It is not too late," he insisted. "We can still be together—"

She stopped him by saying, "No, we cannot. I am with child. I carry Breckinridge's son or daughter. A son, I think, who will be a fierce warrior."

Big Stump stared at her. She had suspected her

condition for a while, and recently she had become certain of it, but this was the first time she had actually spoken so plainly about it. She carried Breckinridge Wallace's child. That knowledge filled her with a fierce rush of pride.

"So you see," she went on after a moment, "there can be nothing between us except friendship—"

Somewhere in the village, the sound muffled by the tipi walls but still audible, a woman screamed. A second later, the blast of a gunshot followed the cry.

Dawn Wind leaped to her feet. Big Stump turned toward the tipi's entrance. Confusion and alarm masked his broad face. He said, "What—"

Dawn Wind tried to get around his considerable bulk. "I must find my father!" she said as more gunfire erupted outside.

He caught hold of her and thrust her behind him. "Stay here!" he ordered. "I will protect you."

War cries sounded as well as the shots. The village was under attack. The guns told Dawn Wind that white men were involved. Her people's only real enemies among the other tribes were the Blackfeet, and they had few firearms. Her thoughts went to the group of trappers with whom Breckinridge and Morgan had clashed in the past. Could her husband's old foes have returned to strike at him at last?

Suddenly, even as fear filled her, she was glad that Breckinridge had gone hunting today with Gray Bear, Swims Like a Fish, and Bitter Mouth. If he wasn't here, then these evil men, whoever they were, couldn't harm him.

But her child . . . her child was in danger, and she had to make sure she protected that innocent life.

Big Stump stood at the tipi's entrance, clearly torn

by emotion as he hesitated. He wanted to stay here and do everything he could to make sure Dawn Wind wasn't hurt, but at the same time, as the shooting, shouting, and screaming continued outside, he wanted to go help his people fight off the raiders. Dawn Wind saw that and knew what she had to do.

"Go, Isáa Sampa!" she said. "Go and fight for the Apsáalooke!"

He turned his head to look over his shoulder at her. His lips were drawn back from his teeth in a grimace. Their eyes locked for a second, and she saw in his gaze the love he felt for her. Under other circumstances, she would have wished that she could return it.

But now, Big Stump turned back to the entrance, let out a cry of anger, and thrust the flap aside as he pulled his knife from its sheath. He took a hurried step outside—

Then his head jerked back as a shot blasted very close by. Big Stump reeled backward through the opening, lost his balance, and fell. Dawn Wind stared down in horror at the black-rimmed hole in his forehead. Big Stump's wide, dead eyes stared back at her sightlessly. As she watched, a worm of bright red blood crawled from the wound.

More screams from outside shook Dawn Wind from the grip of the shock that had almost overcome her at the sight of Big Stump's body. She bent and picked up the knife he had dropped. She would probably have to defend herself, and that was the handiest weapon.

In fact, she was still tightening her hand around the knife when a burly shape appeared at the tipi's entrance. The white man seemed almost as broad as he was tall, and a long black beard jutted down over his chest. Gray smoke curled from the muzzle of the pistol he held.

"There you are!" he exclaimed. "I was hoping to find you unharmed, girl. You're coming with me."

"No!" Dawn Wind started to back away. She held the knife in front of her.

The white man stalked across the tipi toward her. The arrogant, confident grin he wore was barely visible under the bushy whiskers. His eyes gleamed with something akin to madness.

"You're not getting away," he said. "You might as well put that knife down."

Dawn Wind circled the fire pit. She thought that if she could lure the man after her, then she could make a dash for the entrance. She had always been fleet of foot.

He started around the fire pit, too, but as Dawn Wind lunged away from him, she realized his move was just a feint. He was ready for her. A swift leap brought him back in front of her, close enough to make a grab for her. She slashed at him with the knife as he did so. He blocked the blade with the barrel of the empty pistol, striking it so hard that the impact went up Dawn Wind's arm and forced her to open her fingers. The knife flew out of her grip.

With nothing to protect her now, all she could do was strike futilely at him with her hands as he grabbed her. He was so strong it was like trying to fight off a bear. He swung her off her feet, tucked her under his arm, and strode out of the tipi with her kicking and squirming, all to no avail.

Dawn Wind stopped fighting as horror washed over her at the sight that met her eyes. Bodies were strewn everywhere, bodies of her people, of men, women, and children cut down brutally by bullet, knife, and tomahawk, their lives stolen from them. Dawn Wind screamed as she saw her father lying on his back, his chest a bloody mess where he had been shot several times. Not far away was the body of the old medicine man, Badger's Den, hacked so badly with knives that he barely looked human anymore. All around, blood painted the snow red.

As Dawn Wind watched, stunned, she saw one of the white attackers wielding a sword ram the blade through a woman's body from behind. The tip emerged from her chest between her breasts. Her eyes widened grotesquely large as death claimed her. She collapsed, and her killer callously rested a booted foot on her back as he pulled the saber free.

Then he turned toward Dawn Wind and her captor and said, "That's Wallace's woman. Where is he?"

"I don't know, Major," the bearded man said. "I haven't seen him."

Dawn Wind had never seen anything more frightening than the one-eyed man's face at that moment. He was the essence of pure evil. He said, "Wallace has to be here!"

"It appears that he's not. But maybe this one knows where he is." The bearded man set Dawn Wind on her feet and grasped her shoulders painfully. "Where's that big redheaded bastard?" he demanded.

Dawn Wind's fury overcame her fear. She screamed out her rage and then spat in the man's face. His features twisted in anger. He let go of her left shoulder and used that hand to slap her. The brutal blow cracked across her face with enough force to twist her head around.

"Don't kill her!" the one-eyed man exclaimed. "She has to tell us where Wallace is!"

"No, she doesn't," the bearded man said. A back-handed blow slammed Dawn Wind's head back the other way. She felt consciousness slipping away from her. "All we have to do is keep her alive and take her with us. Then Wallace will come to us."

He punched Dawn Wind in the belly. That doubled her over, making it easier for him to pick her up again and throw her over his shoulder. Blackness washed over her mind, shutting out the terrible carnage around her. She was only vaguely aware of the motion of her head and dangling arms swaying back and forth a little as the man carried her away through thickening clouds of snow.

The snow was falling heavily by the time Breckinridge and his fellow hunters neared the village. They had cut poles from saplings, lashed the legs of the dead sheep to them, and now they carried the carcasses, one man at each end of the poles. They couldn't move very fast that way, but their progress was steady despite the snowdrifts starting to form here and there on top of the several inches that remained from the last storm.

The wind whipped this way and that. Breckinridge caught a whiff of smoke, then it was gone. Smoke was nothing to worry about. In weather like this, fires burned night and day inside the tipis and smoke always escaped through the small opening at the pinnacle of the dwelling.

Something about this smoke, though, made the hair rise on the back of Breckinridge's neck. It didn't *smell* right. Not like just firewood burning, although that was mixed in there as well. He was at the back end of one of the poles, with Bitter Mouth at the front. Breck asked him, "Did you smell that?"

Bitter Mouth looked back over his shoulder. "Smell what?"

"Smoke."

"No, but we are getting close to the village. We will be there soon. You smell the cooking fires, my friend."

Maybe Bitter Mouth was right, Breckinridge thought. The unusual tang he had thought he detected in the smoke could have been meat roasting. Maybe the smell would come again and he could tell for sure.

The next time it was Gray Bear who caught the scent, however. He stopped, lifted his head, sniffed, and said, "That is not right."

"What are you talking about?" Swims Like a Fish asked.

Instead of answering directly, the older warrior said, "Put these sheep down. We must hurry on to the village."

"If we put them down, wolves may get them," Swims Like a Fish protested.

"Now!" Gray Bear barked. He lowered his end of the pole to the ground, and Swims Like a Fish had no choice but to do likewise.

Alarm welled up inside Breckinridge. Clearly, Gray Bear thought something was wrong. Breck asked, "Did you smell the smoke, Gray Bear?"

"The smoke is wrong," Gray Bear said by way of reply. "I have smelled something like it before."

That sounded particularly ominous to Breckinridge, especially in Gray Bear's grim tone of voice.

Breck lowered his end of the pole to the ground and then unslung the rifle from his back. After checking to make sure it was loaded and primed, he broke into a run in the direction of the Crow village. Snow flew up every time his boots hit the ground. The other three men trailed behind him, also running. They readied their bows and arrows as they hurried through the storm.

Through shifting rents in the curtains of snow, Breckinridge caught sight of leaping flames up ahead. His heart hammered wildly in his chest. Those weren't cooking fires. The last time he had seen such large flames, some of the tipis in the village had been on fire during the Blackfoot raid.

He had been told by the Crow elders that the Blackfeet would not return to raid again during the winter. After their previous defeat, they would have retreated to their own hunting grounds to lick their wounds and nurse their sour hatred. Breckinridge had assumed that White Owl and the other Crow knew what they were talking about, since they had been battling the Blackfeet for generations.

But what if they were wrong? What if the survivors from that war party had been lurking in the area all along, waiting for a good opportunity to strike at their traditional enemies once again?

That possibility roused fear inside Breckinridge. Fear for Dawn Wind . . . and for the baby she might be carrying.

His long legs carried him even faster as he bounded over logs, weaved around trees, charged up ridges, and then leaped down the far sides. He left his friends behind. They couldn't keep up with a maddened Breckinridge Wallace.

As the wind gusted, more puffs of smoke practically slapped him in the face. The sickly sweet smell that was just hinted at earlier was strong now. That was human flesh burning, Breckinridge knew. Something terrible had happened.

He burst out of some snow-mantled trees at the top of a rise. A long, gentle slope lay before him, and at the bottom of it was the Crow village, next to the partially frozen-over creek. Flames leaped from several of the tipis as fire consumed them. Other dwellings, already destroyed, were ugly black splotches against the snow. Dark shapes scattered around were bodies, Breckinridge knew. His stunned gaze went to the tipi he shared with Dawn Wind.

It was ablaze. He thought he could hear the roar of the flames even from where he was, although that might have been just his imagination.

"Noooo!" he bellowed, and then he charged down the slope, straight toward a scene that might have been ripped from the bowels of hell.

Chapter 28

The crackle of the flames filled the air, along with mournful, raw-throated wails from women who knelt next to the sprawled bodies of their husbands and children. When Breckinridge reached the village, he stumbled to a halt and looked around.

Whoever was responsible for this massacre was gone. Breckinridge saw no enemies. At least, not any who were still on their feet.

But here and there lay the bodies of white men killed in the fighting, along with a few painted warriors he recognized as belonging to the Blackfoot tribe. That made no sense, Breckinridge thought. He knew the faces of the white men. They had been members of Jud Carnahan's party. Had Carnahan joined forces somehow with the Blackfeet?

That was the only explanation that made any sense, although Breckinridge didn't see how it could have come about. He didn't waste any time pondering it, though. He shook himself out of his stunned reverie and hurried to the tipi he shared with Dawn Wind.

The dwelling had burned down to ruins. The ashes

still gave off a great deal of heat, and he knew he couldn't walk among them, but he stood at the edge of the charred circle and searched frantically with his eyes for his wife's body.

He didn't see anything like that. Relief washed through him, although it didn't really do anything to temper the fear and dismay he felt.

He turned and shouted into the snowfall, "Dawn Wind! Dawn Wind, where are you?"

There was no answer.

Breckinridge tightened his grip on the rifle and turned toward White Owl's tipi. If Dawn Wind wasn't here, it was possible she had been at her father's dwelling when the attack began. Breck's long strides carried him to the tipi, which still stood.

A pair of legs clad in buckskin leggings and high-topped moccasins stuck out of the entrance. Breckinridge caught his breath for a second, then re-alized there was no way those muscular limbs could belong to Dawn Wind.

He yanked the hide flap aside and saw Big Stump lying there cold and dead. The thickset warrior had been shot once in the forehead.

Breckinridge felt a pang of regret at the sight. True, he had battled against Big Stump and wanted the man to leave Dawn Wind alone, but she claimed he was a decent man at heart, and Breck was inclined to believe her.

He bent down to peer through the opening. Dawn Wind wasn't in the tipi. Again Breckinridge felt a mix-ture of relief and apprehension. If she wasn't here, where was she?

The men who had been with him had reached the village by now. Breckinridge heard a grief-stricken shout and turned to see Bitter Mouth kneeling beside the body of a woman. He grabbed her, pulled her up into his arms, and rocked back and forth on his knees as he cradled her limp form against him. Breck didn't recall her name, but he knew she was Bitter Mouth's wife . . . the one who had hinted that Dawn Wind was with child.

That thought prompted him to dash back and forth amidst the burned tipis, the mourning women, and the bodies of the dead. Some of the women lay facedown, and they looked enough like Dawn Wind that he had to turn them over to be sure none of them were her.

He didn't find her, but his heart twisted painfully anyway at the death and destruction carried out here.

Someone would pay for this, he vowed. He would see to that. And he would start with those bastards Carnahan and Ralston.

Gray Bear came up to him and asked, "Have you found your wife, Breckinridge?"

He swallowed hard and shook his head. "She don't appear to be here. I . . . I don't know where she could be."

But an answer to that had begun to form in the back of his head. An answer so terrible he didn't want to even consider it, but now that he had searched the village for Dawn Wind without finding her, he had no other choice.

The raiders must have taken her with them.

A shout from Swims Like a Fish distracted Breckinridge from that awful prospect. He looked around to see the warrior pointing along the creek. Breck gripped his rifle tighter as a dozen warriors trotted toward the village.

Then he relaxed slightly as he recognized some of them. They were Crow, he realized. Survivors of the attack who must have pursued the raiders.

He glanced around to say something to Gray Bear but saw that the older man was no longer standing beside him. Gray Bear had gone over to one of the bodies and dropped to a knee beside it. Breckinridge bit back a curse. The dead man was White Owl. The Crow chief had been shot to pieces.

Gray Bear rested a hand on White Owl's shoulder and murmured, "I am sorry, old friend. We will find the men who did this."

"I was thinkin' the same thing," Breckinridge said.

He left Gray Bear there mourning his friend and went with Swims Like a Fish to meet the warriors returning to the village. Several of them had been wounded, but not badly enough to keep them from going after the attackers.

"Where did they go?" Swims Like a Fish asked.

One of the warriors shook his head. "Along the creek toward the river. But the snow was too heavy. We could not follow them. Their tracks filled in too quickly."

"Blast it, they must've gone one way or the other when they got to the river," Breckinridge said. "You couldn't tell which way?"

The warrior looked at him coldly. "That is what I just said, Breckinridge Wallace. We would not have returned if we had been able to pursue them, though they outnumbered us and some of us are wounded."

"Could you tell . . ." Breckinridge had to pause to take a breath. "Could you tell if they had Dawn Wind with them?"

Another man said, "They were seen taking several

captives with them. Some women, some children. I do not know if Dawn Wind was among them."

"She has to be. She's not here in the village, and I didn't find her body."

Breckinridge forced his voice to remain calm and level as he spoke, even though what he really wanted was to throw back his head and roar in anger.

"What about the men who did this?" Swims Like a Fish asked. "There are bodies of white men and Blackfeet in the village. Did they attack together?"

The first man who had spoken nodded and said solemnly, "The white men came first with their rifles and pistols, but the Blackfeet were right behind them. I myself saw the Blackfoot war chief called Machitehew, who led the other raid on our people. But the war chief this time was a white man."

Breckinridge held out a hand, well below his shoulder level, and said, "A fella about this tall, with big shoulders and a long black beard? He would have had another man with him, taller, lean like a wolf, a patch over one eye?"

"Both of these men came among us and killed our people. They are as evil as Machitehew, whose very name means that his heart is filled with evil."

"Yeah, that's Carnahan and Ralston," Breckinridge muttered. "They won't get away with this."

"How do you know that?" Swims Like a Fish asked.

"Because before this is over, I'm gonna kill both of those bastards, and that son of a bitch Machitehew, too," Breckinridge said.

Dawn Wind didn't think she had been unconscious for long. When awareness seeped back into her brain, she was still draped over the bearded man's shoulder, bouncing and swaying as he stomped along through the snow.

She started to lift her head but then stopped. She decided it might be better if her captors didn't know she had regained consciousness.

Unfortunately, a jolt of pain that originated low in her belly stabbed through her, and she couldn't hold back the cry that escaped from her mouth.

It wasn't just the pain, either. The location made her think something might be wrong with the child she carried, and that thought terrified her.

The man carrying her stopped. He swung her down from his shoulder and set her on her feet. Her legs tried to fold up underneath her. She would have fallen if he hadn't had a tight grip under her arms.

"So you're awake, eh?" he asked her. Before she could respond, he warned her, "Don't spit in my face again, squaw. I don't like that. And you won't like what I do when I'm not happy."

The pain had eased a little, but not enough to reassure Dawn Wind that nothing was wrong. Fear still filled her. Since she was feeling a little steadier on her legs, she tried to pull away from him. He laughed and tightened his grip on her until she trembled from the cruelty.

"What's your name?" he demanded.

She spoke in the Crow tongue, telling him that he was the lowest, most craven dog that had ever slunk upon the face of the earth.

He gave her a hard shake and said, "I know damn well that you speak English. Now tell me your name!"

In a low, hate-filled voice, she said, "I am called Dawn Wind."

"You're Wallace's woman. Don't bother trying to deny it. I've seen you with him. Where was he today?"

"You will never find him. But he will find you."

"That's what I'm counting on. My name's Jud Carnahan. You've probably heard him talk about me."

Dawn Wind didn't say anything, but he was right. She had heard Breckinridge speak of this man Carnahan numerous times, and he had never said anything good about him.

The rest of the group had stopped when Carnahan did. When Dawn Wind glanced around, she saw quite a few white men, none with even an ounce of mercy on his face. Among them was the tall, gaunt man with the patch over his eye. Major Ralston, Breckinridge had called him, she remembered.

There were also several Blackfoot warriors in the bunch, all with faces painted for war with red and black streaks. They looked just as coldhearted and vicious as the white men.

Dawn Wind was not the only prisoner, either. She saw four other women and a handful of children, all clustered together, standing with their heads down in obvious terror.

The Blackfeet probably intended to take the women back to their hunting grounds as slaves. The children might be taken into the tribe, or they might live out their lives as slaves, too. None of it would end well for any of them—Dawn Wind was sure of that.

Of course, the white men might insist on keeping the women to use them, in which case their lives would be even shorter, as well as more brutal and degrading. She would find some way to end her own life, Dawn Wind vowed, before she would submit to the lusts of these monsters.

"I'd still like to know where Wallace is," Carnahan went on.

Dawn Wind thought rapidly. She knew perfectly well that Breckinridge had gone hunting today with three other men from the village. They would return before the day was over and see the death and destruction that had been visited upon the band of Crow. Breck would search for her among the victims, and when he realized that she was not among the dead, he would come looking for her. She was certain of that.

But if she could make Carnahan believe that Breckinridge wasn't anywhere around here, he would have a better chance of taking the raiders by surprise.

She lifted her head, jutted her chin out defiantly, and said, "He is gone. He went back downriver to spend the winter with his own people."

Carnahan frowned at her for a couple of seconds, then abruptly laughed.

"Try another story, gal," he said. "He was seen in the village just a few days ago."

"He left yesterday," Dawn Wind insisted.

Carnahan shook his head. "I don't believe you. If he was going back East, he wouldn't have waited until winter had set in to do it. He would have gone when his friend Baxter did. Not that he and that young buck who was with him ever made it down the river."

The implications of Carnahan's words sunk in on Dawn Wind's stunned brain. Without thinking about what she was doing, she grabbed the front of his coat and shouted, "What did you do?"

"With Baxter and that young fellow with him, you mean?" Carnahan laughed again. "Oh, we killed them and took their pelts weeks ago. We've been jumping the other trappers when they try to leave this part of the country and adding their furs to our pile. I'm going to be the king of this country, Dawn Wind, didn't you know that?"

Grief squeezed Dawn Wind's heart like a cruel hand. She was shaken to her core. Not only was her father dead at the hands of these animals, so was her brother. She had gone along from day to day, living her life, being happy with Breckinridge and looking forward to the future, and all along Running Elk had been dead and rotting . . .

The pain slammed into her guts again. Her knees buckled. Carnahan kept hold of her right arm and tugged her along as the group started moving once more. She tried to walk but did more stumbling than anything else.

"I don't suppose it really matters where Wallace was today," Carnahan said. "He'll be along soon enough, looking for his little squaw."

"And when we get our hands on him," the one-eyed man said, "he'll die screaming. I'll see to that myself."

Dawn Wind struggled to hang on to even a shred of hope. She had faith in Breckinridge, but the sorrow she felt at the deaths of her father and brother, as well as her friend Morgan and all the others of her people who had been slaughtered in the attack on the village, was almost too much for her to withstand. It overwhelmed her, numbed all her senses. She didn't even feel the cold as she stumbled along through the snow.

There were two things she could cling to, however. Two things she hoped would allow her to survive this ordeal.

One was the hope that her baby was still all right, despite the pain she felt.

The other was her longing to see these men die at the hands of Breckinridge Wallace.

And if he didn't manage to kill them, she would find a way to do it herself . . .

Chapter 29

Breckinridge didn't waste any time getting ready to set out on the raiders' trail. He had his rifle, his pistols, and his knife with him, along with powder horn and shot pouch.

He also had the bow and the quiver of arrows. The few supplies he'd had in the burned tipi were gone, so he didn't worry about them.

He had what he needed to kill his enemies. That was all that really mattered.

Bitter Mouth came up to him and said, "You are going after those men?"

"Yeah, in just a few minutes."

The warrior nodded. "I will come with you."

"Your woman is dead," Breckinridge said, knowing his words were blunt but not seeing any other way to express it. "You need to stay and mourn her."

"No, I need to come with you and help kill the men who did this," Bitter Mouth replied. His customary good humor was gone now, banished from his face— and his soul—perhaps forever.

Breckinridge understood the way his friend felt. If

he had found Dawn Wind dead when they got back to the village, he would have set out for revenge, too. He couldn't deny that opportunity to Bitter Mouth.

"All right," he said. "I'll be leaving soon."

"I will be ready," Bitter Mouth said.

Gray Bear and Swims Like a Fish walked up in time to hear that grim declaration. Gray Bear said, "We are ready, as well, Breckinridge. We spent the day hunting sheep with you. Now we will hunt men."

"Although they are more animals than men," Swims Like a Fish added. He gestured at the destruction around them. "Not even wolves would do something like this."

Breckinridge agreed. It took a special sort of evil to carry out such an atrocity, and animals didn't really have that in them.

Humans did, though. Some of them were the worst predators of all. Jud Carnahan and Gordon Ralston certainly fell into that category.

The bodies of the slain villagers had been picked up by their loved ones, who were now preparing to lay them to rest. Breckinridge and the warriors who went with him wouldn't be there for those rituals. Their concern was with the living, not the dead.

Gray Bear reported that four more women and five children were missing from the village. It was assumed that they had been taken captive, along with Dawn Wind.

The bodies of the white men and Blackfoot warriors who had been killed in the attack would be dragged into the woods and left for the wolves and mountain lions. They deserved no consideration or dignity in the eyes of the Crow, and Breckinridge couldn't argue with that. He might have pitched the corpses into a ravine, but that was as far as he would go, and then only if there was time—which there wasn't.

Several of the men who had pursued the raiders earlier volunteered to accompany Breckinridge and the others. Breck told the wounded ones to remain in the village and have their injuries tended to. He wasn't trying to be kind. He just didn't want them slowing him down.

The final group totaled ten men, including Breckinridge. He could only guess at the size of the force they were going after, but he knew he and his companions would be outnumbered. He didn't care about that.

If there had been a hundred enemies or even a thousand, Breckinridge would have charged straight into them to save Dawn Wind.

At the same time, he had to be smart, he warned himself as he and the others started along the creek toward the Bighorn River. He couldn't afford to give in to emotion and get himself killed. That wouldn't do Dawn Wind and the other captives any good.

For once he needed to be smart instead of reckless. There was a time to throw caution to the winds, but he might have to be patient and wait for it.

That was going to be hard. Damned hard.

The snow was still falling as they tramped along. In places it had started to pile up in deep drifts. It covered the ice that had formed along the edges of the creek.

Even though Breckinridge had been upset that the first group of pursuers had turned back earlier, he could understand why they had. There were no tracks to follow. The snow had covered them all.

He tried to keep a close eye on both sides of the creek, looking for any sign that the raiders might have veered away from the stream with their captives.

Gray Bear pointed to the trees they passed, which grew thickly along the banks, and said, "See how the snow is undisturbed on the lower branches? No one has brushed past them."

"I'm glad you're with us, Gray Bear," Breckinridge said. "I can use all the help I can get when it comes to trackin'."

"We will find them, my friend," the older man said. "We will never stop searching until we do."

Dawn Wind had lost track of the time. It seemed like many hours had passed since the attack on the village, perhaps even days. She knew logically that wasn't the case. They had covered quite a few miles from the Crow village but hadn't been traveling for days.

At least the pain in her belly had subsided gradually. It was just an intermittent dull ache now. Worse was the cold, which had overcome her previous stunned state and by now had crept into every muscle and bone in her body.

She had been inside her father's tipi when the attack began, so she wasn't dressed to be trudging along in a snowstorm. Nor were the other captives, some of whom appeared to be half-frozen by now. The children were having an especially hard time of it, shivering and stumbling as they were prodded along by their captors. Dawn Wind wanted to comfort them, but there was really nothing she could do.

Anyway, Jud Carnahan still had hold of her arm most of the time, keeping her close to him.

At one point, maybe to distract herself from her misery as much as anything else, she said to the bearded man, "Why do you hate Breckinridge so?"

"He has only himself to blame for that," Carnahan replied. "The first time we ever met, I offered him and Baxter the chance to throw in with us. They were too good for that, though. Instead they tried to steal from us."

"I do not believe that! Breckinridge Wallace is not a thief."

Carnahan laughed and said, "Well, actually, you may be right about that, girl. My friend the major hates Wallace even more than I do. It's possible he was responsible for what happened. I believe he has a grudge against Wallace going back to something that happened in St. Louis, before we all headed west. But what I do know is that Wallace has been getting in my way ever since, and when a man does that he's my enemy, now and forever."

Dawn Wind looked around. The group was scattered out. Major Ralston was somewhere behind her and Carnahan, she thought. He wasn't close enough to have heard what Carnahan had just said—not that it made any difference. Carnahan wasn't afraid of the one-eyed man, although perhaps he should have been. Just thinking about Ralston made Dawn Wind feel even colder inside.

"What are you going to do with us?" she ventured to ask.

"Right now we're going back to my camp," Carnahan replied. "We'll probably all stay there until the weather improves. I don't know what Machitehew will want to do after that. More than likely, he'll decide to go back where he came from and take his men with him. That'll be up to him."

"What about . . . the prisoners?"

"He can take the children with him. I've no use for the pups. Maybe he'll turn them into good little Blackfeet, for all I care. But you'll stay with us, and at least some of the other women will, too. My men wouldn't stand for anything else, and we still outnumber Machitehew and his savages."

Carnahan had hold of her arm, and he must have felt the shiver that went through her at his words. That prompted a laugh from him.

"Don't worry, girl," he went on. "I won't turn you over to Ralston and the others. You're the bait in the trap for Wallace. I'd rather keep you nice and healthy. That's why you'll be staying right by my side."

Maybe that should have relieved some of Dawn Wind's fear. Carnahan probably meant it that way. But it didn't.

They had reached the Bighorn River earlier, turned south, and proceeded along it for miles. It was rough going, especially in the drifting snow. They reached another creek and followed it, leaving the river behind. After another freezing, exhausting eternity, Carnahan pointed to the dark mouth of a canyon up ahead on the left.

"That's going to be your new home for a while," he told Dawn Wind. "It may be pretty primitive, but I promise you, it'll be better than being out here in this snowstorm."

Dawn Wind didn't say anything. She just kept her head down and trudged on beside her burly captor.

The whole group entered the canyon. Almost immediately, the biting wind was blocked for the most part, which was a relief. The snow still fell, but it swirled down more gently inside the canyon, which was about a hundred yards wide. Sheer walls, eighty or ninety feet tall, rose to rugged rimrock. Trees and bushes grew in the canyon, sticking up from the snow-covered ground.

Night would fall early because of the storm and the thick overcast. Shadows had already begun to gather in the canyon. Dawn Wind could still see well enough to pick out the dark shapes looming ahead of them.

They were cabins, she realized. To her eyes, they looked odd, since she was used to tipis, but she had visited trading posts in the past and had seen the sort of structures favored by the white men. She counted three of the buildings, one set a short distance apart from the other two.

"That's mine," Carnahan said as he pointed to the cabin by itself. "And yours, for the time being, anyway. Who knows, once Wallace is dead, you may decide you want to stay with me and be my woman. I'm not as bad as you probably believe I am, you know. I can be gentle when I want to, especially with such an attractive morsel as yourself."

Dawn Wind suppressed another shudder. Was this man actually insane enough to believe that she would ever be with him willingly? That she would give herself to the man who planned to kill her husband?

Thankfully, it would never come to that. Either Breckinridge would kill Jud Carnahan—or she would.

The white men herded the other prisoners into one of the two remaining cabins. Some went in there with the captives while the rest took the other cabin. Machitehew and the Blackfeet had made lodges from the brush and took shelter there.

That left Dawn Wind and Carnahan. He held tightly to her arm while he used his other hand to open the door of his cabin. He pushed her into the dim room and followed her inside, then heeled the door closed behind him.

Embers still glowed in a crude fireplace on one side of the single room. Carnahan poked them to life and fed in wood shavings that caught fire and curled into tiny flames.

He worked skillfully at the fire until he had a nice little blaze going. The reddish light from the flames spread and brought with it a faint but welcome warmth.

"Take a look around and get used to it," Carnahan told Dawn Wind. "You're not going to be leaving for a while."

By the time Breckinridge and his companions reached the Bighorn River, the light was fading rapidly. Gray Bear was not the only skilled tracker in the group, and their consensus was that the men they were following had stayed with the creek this far.

"But we cannot continue to track them and have any hope of success in the dark," Gray Bear told Breckinridge, "especially with no moon and stars because of the storm."

"Are you sayin' we ought to camp here and wait for mornin'?" Breckinridge asked. He was tense and tight all over from worry.

Gray Bear nodded. "This is what we must do," he said. "Some of the men brought buffalo robes. There are enough for all of us. We will be cold, but we will not freeze."

"By tomorrow mornin', any sign that's left will be gone," Breckinridge objected. "The snow and the wind will see to that."

"Any tracks are already long gone," Gray Bear pointed out. "Following the creek was simply a guess based on the direction they were headed the last time they were seen, as well as the terrain. There has been no really good place for them to strike off in a different direction."

Breckinridge rubbed his jaw and frowned. "They went either upriver or down," he said. "I'd bet my hat on that. You think that come mornin' we might be able to tell which way?"

"It is possible. But there is *no* chance in the dark."

"Then we make camp," Breckinridge said with a curt nod.

Stopping now meant that Dawn Wind would have to spend at least one night with Carnahan, Ralston, and the rest of that no-good bunch. It wouldn't do her any good, though, for him to wander around aimlessly on a dark, snowy night and get lost, maybe fall in a ravine and break a leg or even his damn fool neck.

Carnahan wouldn't hurt her, he told himself. He had already started to consider the possibility that maybe Carnahan had taken Dawn Wind in order to lure Breckinridge after them. Carnahan might be planning a trap of some sort. If that was true, sooner or later he would need Dawn Wind alive. Her safety was the best card Carnahan had to play.

"Let's clear off some ground under the trees," he suggested. "Maybe get a fire goin'. Blast it! I didn't think to bring any food."

"I have enough jerky for both of us," Swims Like a

Fish said. "If it takes us several days to find our quarry, perhaps we can find some rabbits to roast. Or even a sheep."

Breckinridge thought about those bighorn sheep they'd been forced to leave behind when they realized something was wrong at the village. Losing them was a shame.

But there had been much worse losses today, losses that might take a long time to heal, if ever. Bitter Mouth hadn't said a word since they left the village. He was lost in his sorrow and anger and might never find his way back to the happy-go-lucky man he had been.

By the time full night had fallen, Breckinridge and the other men were huddled around a tiny fire, buffalo robes wrapped around their shoulders. They gnawed on jerky and downed handfuls of snow and thought their own dark thoughts.

It was going to be a long night.

Chapter 30

Under considerably different circumstances, the same thought was going through Dawn Wind's mind. The fire had warmed up the inside of the cabin quite a bit, but frigid gusts of wind still clawed their way through every gap in the log walls. She shivered now and then as she sat on a crude bench next to an equally rough-hewn table.

Carnahan brought a blanket over to her and wrapped it around her shoulders. The warmth was welcome, but if he thought she was going to thank him for the gesture, he was going to have a long wait for any such expression of gratitude.

The only thing she would tell him would be for him to go to hell. She didn't actually believe in such a place of eternal punishment, but white men did.

Carnahan had a pot of coffee boiling. Dawn Wind shook her head when he offered her a cup. He brought her some salt pork and a biscuit. She turned her head away from the food.

"If you're thinking you're going to get away from me by starving yourself to death, you can forget about that," Carnahan said. "It would take too long, for one thing. This business with Wallace will be over before you'd have time to die from not eating. Besides, it would be foolish. Why punish yourself for something that's not your fault? This war is between me and Wallace. You just happened to get caught in the middle."

She didn't look at him or say anything. After a moment he sighed and went away, leaving the food on the table in front of her. She wanted to snatch it up. Her belly was painfully empty, clenching on itself, and she knew that eating would relieve some of the chill and exhaustion she felt.

Even more important, the child growing inside her needed sustenance. Dawn Wind was still afraid that the rough treatment she had endured had injured the baby, but she had no way of being sure about that, one way or the other.

For now, she had to proceed on the assumption that the child was still all right. For that reason, if for no other, she had to take care of herself.

No matter how much she hated Jud Carnahan and didn't want to give him the satisfaction of her cooperation.

Still without looking at him, she picked up the piece of meat and began to gnaw at it. She pretended she didn't hear his chuckle from the other side of the room.

The cabin door opened, letting in a blast of cold air and snowflakes, along with Major Ralston.

"Sentries are posted," he reported.

Carnahan turned sharply away from the fire and snapped, "Damn it, Ralston, knock before you come in here."

A sneer twisted the one-eyed man's mouth. He said, "I just thought that after the tiring day we've all had, you wouldn't be having any sport with the squaw just yet."

Carnahan took a step toward him. The man's jaw clenched in apparent anger, making his beard jut out even more. For a moment Dawn Wind wondered if the two of them were going to come to blows. If they fought, she might be able to use that to her advantage and escape from the cabin.

Yes, escape into a canyon where two dozen more cutthroats waited, and beyond that nothing but a dark night filled with falling snow and freezing temperatures.

As much as she hated to admit it, even to herself, she knew that if she fled from her captors tonight, they probably would find her body in the morning, frozen stiff.

Unless Breckinridge was somewhere nearby, and they found each other in the storm. But that would require a miracle, and Dawn Wind decided that she couldn't afford to wager her life—and the life of her unborn child—on such a slim chance.

Carnahan must have made a decision, too—not to force the issue with Ralston. He grunted, shook his head, and said, "I want the men on guard to stay alert. I know it's cold, but no huddling up and dozing off. For one thing, they might freeze to death if they did, and for another, we can't rule out the possibility of Wallace finding us. The odds of it are very small, but I don't want the bastard taking us by surprise."

"The men know that," Ralston said. "We'll be ready for him when he shows up." He glanced at Dawn Wind.

"I just hope he doesn't decide the redskin bitch isn't worth the trouble."

She looked away from him. She didn't want to meet his gaze. His eyes looked too much like a snake's eyes, full of cold, reptilian malice.

With a dismissive tone in his voice, Carnahan told the major, "Let me know right away if anything happens."

"Of course." Ralston turned and stalked out of the cabin, closing the door quickly behind him to keep more of the warmth from escaping.

Carnahan came over to the table. "I saw the way you looked at him," he said to Dawn Wind. "You're afraid of him—and well you should be. I'm afraid of no man who draws breath, but if I was going to fear anyone, it might be Gordon Ralston. But you don't have to worry. I'll never let him near you."

That was how it started, Dawn Wind thought as she stared down at the rough table. Carnahan intended to play her fear of Ralston against her and win her over that way. It wouldn't do him any good. But at some point she might have to let him think that it was working.

She pulled the blanket tighter around her shoulders and wondered if there would ever again come a time when she wasn't cold and tired and hurting.

Under the circumstances, Breckinridge wouldn't have been surprised if he didn't sleep much that night, but the fact that he was basically a large, healthy animal came in handy again. He was able to put aside all the discomfort and worry and fall into a deep, dreamless sleep as he curled up in one of the buffalo robes.

He woke when the sky was gray with the approach of dawn. It didn't lighten much as the men hunkered on their heels underneath the trees and gnawed on strips of jerky.

The snow had stopped sometime during the night, but the clouds were still thick and dark. There might be more snow later, Gray Bear said as he squinted up at the overcast.

But for now, it was at least light enough to see, so after their meager breakfast the men set out to search for any signs of the raiders. Because they didn't know which way their quarry had gone, they had to split up into two groups, one heading upstream and the other downstream.

Breckinridge went upstream with the party led by Gray Bear. The men moved slowly along the riverbank. The snow was almost a foot deep, and it was deeper in the drifts, of course.

The snow had not only piled up on the branches and on thick clumps of needles, it clung in places to the rough-barked trunks of the pines. Gray Bear studied the trees intently as the searchers passed them. He explained to Breckinridge that a man's shoulder or arm might brush against a trunk and dislodge some of the snow, leaving a visible mark if someone knew what to look for. The same was true of the low-hanging branches.

"I don't know how much trouble Carnahan would go to when it comes to coverin' his trail," Breckinridge said. "I've got a hunch he wants me to find him so he can settle the score between us. That might be why he took Dawn Wind."

Gray Bear nodded solemnly. "If he wants to kill you, it makes sense that he would take what is most precious to you. He probably did not know that you would be away from the village yesterday."

"Yeah, I reckon that likely ruined his plans. But he's smart enough to think of some other way to get back at me. That's why I think he may be settin' a trap."

"I have seen no sign yet," Gray Bear said, "but the day has barely started."

Time passed, and as it did, Breckinridge felt the frustration growing inside him. Every hour that went by was another hour Dawn Wind spent in the hands of those devils.

It was difficult to tell because of the gloomy day, but he thought it was late in the morning when they came to another creek angling off from the Bighorn River. Gray Bear raised a hand to signal a halt and then pointed at one of the trees as he said to Breckinridge, "Look there."

Breckinridge saw that the snow on the trunk had been disturbed at just about shoulder height. His pulse quickened as he thought about what Gray Bear had said earlier.

"That means they came this way," he said.

"An animal could have brushed against the tree, but I do not believe that is the case," the older man said. "We should send a runner back to the other men and find out if they have found any sign. If they have not, they should join us."

"That means waitin' here most of the day," Breckinridge objected.

"We are too few to rescue the captives alone."

Breckinridge seethed inside, but he knew Gray Bear was right. As much as he wanted to go thundering up that creek in search of his enemies, it wasn't the right play.

"Maybe I should do some scoutin' while the rest of you wait for the others," he suggested.

Gray Bear shook his head gravely. "Your decision is for you alone to make, Breckinridge, but I would not advise it."

Breckinridge muttered some curses under his breath but then nodded.

"We'll wait," he said. "But whoever goes to fetch the others better not waste any time gettin' there and back."

The youngest of the other three warriors in the group, a man called Beaver Tail, volunteered to run back and find the others. He took off at a trot through the snow. Breckinridge knew it would be the middle of the afternoon at the earliest before he returned with the rest of the warriors.

Waiting had always been one of the hardest things Breckinridge had to do, and he knew it wouldn't be any easier this time. Being patient went against his nature to start with. His concern over Dawn Wind and the other captives would just make it worse.

While Beaver Tail was gone, Breckinridge and Gray Bear ventured up the creek to search for more signs, but only for a short distance. Gray Bear found several more places where the snow on trees or rocks had been disturbed and was more convinced than ever that their quarry had gone this way.

So was Breck. He could almost feel Dawn Wind up there somewhere in the rugged terrain, the danger she was in and his desperate need to rescue her drawing him on.

One of the men killed a rabbit with an arrow and

built a fire to roast it. Breckinridge ate distractedly, even though he wasn't hungry, because he knew the fresh meat would give him strength and stamina and allow him to continue the search.

Later, he sat on a rock and tried not to think about what might be happening to Dawn Wind. Gradually he slipped into a reverie that threatened to turn into a stupor.

His head jerked up sharply, though, when he heard someone calling in the distance. He looked along the river to see Beaver Tail hurrying toward him, along with Bitter Mouth, Swims Like a Fish, and the rest of the group that had gone downstream.

Swims Like a Fish clasped arms with Gray Bear and said, "Beaver Tail says you have found sign."

Gray Bear turned and waved a hand along the creek. "They went up this stream, I believe. You found nothing?"

Swims Like a Fish shook his head. "No sign of anything. This is the right way. I can see that, too."

"Then what are we waitin' for?" Breckinridge said. "Let's go get those varmints!"

Before it's too late, he added silently. He wasn't much of a praying man, but he sent up a fervent hope that Dawn Wind was still all right.

There was no bunk in the cabin, only a bedroll, but that didn't matter to Dawn Wind because she was accustomed to sleeping on buffalo robes and wouldn't have been comfortable in an actual bed. The night before, she had taken the blanket Carnahan gave her and curled up in a corner, ignoring his suggestion that she join him in the bedroll.

For a moment she had thought that he might try to force her into his blankets with him, but then he had glared at her and growled, "Suit yourself."

She was relieved by that, but sleep proved to be elusive. As the fire burned down, she lay there staring into the thickening darkness and wondered where Breckinridge was. By now he would be on her trail, more than likely, but she hoped he would hole up somewhere and wait out the night and the worst of the storm.

Finally, exhaustion claimed her and she dozed off, but her sleep was shallow and unsatisfying. Restless, she woke up several times while Carnahan was moving around, but she saw that he was just feeding more wood into the fire to keep it from going out.

On each occasion, she fell asleep again. It was early morning before she woke up fully.

Across the room, Carnahan snored in his bedroll.

Dawn Wind lifted her head and looked around. She saw a line of faint gray against the door and knew it was growing light outside. Her muscles were so cold and stiff they didn't want to work at first, but she forced her arms and legs underneath her and lifted herself from the puncheon floor.

On hands and knees, she hesitated, unsure whether to crawl toward the door or toward Carnahan. She knew the man wore a knife. If she could get her hands on it, she could cut his throat.

But if she could reach the door, she might get away, and if the rest of Carnahan's men were asleep, she could slip into the nearby woods. Ralston had said something the night before about guards, but Dawn Wind believed she could elude them.

She began crawling slowly toward the door, moving as silently as she could.

She kept glancing over her shoulder toward Carnahan, but he continued snoring and didn't move. She was about halfway to the door when he let out a snort and rolled onto his side.

Dawn Wind froze, and not from the temperature this time. She waited in the gloom, unmoving, until she heard Carnahan's deep, regular breathing. Only then did she resume inching toward the door.

After what seemed like an eternity, she reached it and was lifting her hand toward the latch string when a soft footstep sounded behind her. Carnahan's big hand reached over her and clamped around her wrist. Dawn Wind cried out in pain and surprise as he jerked her to her feet.

"You're not the only one who can sneak around, girl," he told her as he pulled her against him. He turned and shoved her toward the table. "Thought I was asleep and you could slip out, didn't you? If you're not careful, I'll start to believe you don't appreciate my hospitality."

Dawn Wind caught herself with a hand against the table. "I should have killed you!" she said through clenched teeth.

"You might have tried, but that wouldn't have worked out any better for you. Make yourself useful. Go stir up the fire. It's cold in here."

Dawn Wind thought about telling him to stir it up himself, but then she decided that the chore would give her something to do, at least. Glaring, she went to the crude fireplace and used a broken branch to poke at the embers and get them glowing brighter. She bent over and added shavings until flames flickered up in several places.

A glance over her shoulder showed her that Carnahan had turned his back toward her. He stood at the table, clearing his throat and shaking his head as he tried to wake up for good.

Dawn Wind closed her hand around a chunk of split firewood a foot long and several inches thick. She picked it up, took a firm grip on it with both hands, and spun around suddenly to lunge at Carnahan. She lifted the firewood and brought it down as hard as she could on the back of his head.

Chapter 31

The chunk of wood landed with a dull thud. Carnahan grunted and slumped forward. He caught himself with both hands on the table, but as he did so, Dawn Wind hit him again and then a third time, putting all the strength that desperation gave her into the blows.

Carnahan fell forward across the table.

Dawn Wind dropped the firewood, whirled around, and dashed for the door. She yanked it open and plunged outside into the gray light.

She didn't realize until it was too late that she should have taken Carnahan's knife and plunged it into his heart while she had the chance. Flight had been uppermost in her mind, though.

She had taken only a few steps when arms like iron bands clamped around her and swung her off her feet.

"What the hell!" Gordon Ralston exclaimed. "Where do you think you're going, you redskin whore?"

It was still gray and shadowy inside the canyon because of the overcast and the fact that the sun hadn't come up yet, but there was enough light for Dawn Wind to see the one-eyed man's face as he leered at her. Her arms were pinned to her side so she couldn't strike at him, so she kicked frantically with her legs, instead.

To no avail. Ralston laughed harshly and maintained his cruel grip on her as he turned toward the cabin. His sour breath was right in her face. It gagged her as he said, "We'll just take you back where you came from. I'm sure Carnahan wouldn't be pleased if you were to run off."

Dawn Wind had left the door open behind her. Carnahan stumbled into the opening and rubbed the back of his head where she had struck him with the firewood. His mouth was open. Evidently he intended to raise a shout of alarm.

That angry bellow died on his lips when he saw that Ralston had recaptured Dawn Wind.

"Good work, Major," he rumbled. "Bring the stubborn little fool back in here."

Carnahan stepped aside so Ralston could carry Dawn Wind into the cabin. He lowered her onto the floor beside the table and stepped back.

"She's a pleasant enough armful of squaw," he said. "I hope you're planning on giving the rest of us a turn with her before this is over, Jud."

"I didn't think you cared that much about women, Major," Carnahan said.

"Oh, the pleasures of the flesh have their place, certainly. It's just that there are more important things in life, after all."

Carnahan grunted. "Like money and power—and vengeance. The girl's not a squaw to me right now.

She's a lure to bring Wallace into our hands, nothing more."

"I agree," Ralston said with a nod. He rested a hand on his sword's pommel. "We'll discuss her ultimate fate when that problem has been dealt with."

Carnahan looked like he didn't intend to discuss anything with the major. He was in charge, so he would give orders, instead. That was the impression Dawn Wind had as she rested one hand on the table to brace herself while she watched the two men.

She was bitterly disappointed that her attempt to escape had failed, but that didn't mean she was going to give up.

Carnahan changed the subject by asking, "Any problems during the night?"

"None," Ralston reported. "There was no sign of Wallace or any of the savages from that village. The snow may have covered our tracks too well for them to follow us."

"I wouldn't count on that. Anyway, even if it's true, Wallace will move heaven and earth to find that girl. He'll be searching for her, and he's bound to find this canyon sooner or later. I want men hidden in the rocks at the mouth of the canyon, and impress upon them, Major, that if they do anything to give away their position and warn Wallace, they'll have to answer to me."

Ralston nodded curtly. "You want him and whoever he brings with him to be allowed into the canyon, is that it?"

"Yes, and then we'll close the door behind them." A grin split Carnahan's face under the beard. "Wallace can come in . . . but he'll never go back out."

"I'll give the orders," Ralston said. He started to

turn toward the door but then paused. "Is it safe to leave you with the redskin, Jud, or do you think she'll attack you again?"

That gibe made Carnahan's grin disappear. In a tight, angry voice, he said, "She won't cause any more trouble. You can count on that." He looked at Dawn Wind. "Do you understand, girl? It's not an absolute necessity that you remain safe and sound in order to trap Wallace."

Dawn Wind looked down at the table and remained stubbornly silent. She wasn't going to promise that she wouldn't try to escape again. If she got a chance, she would flee from this canyon—and she would leave Carnahan dead behind her.

She wouldn't make the mistake of leaving him alive again.

Carnahan let out a bark of humorless laughter. "See to the preparations, Major," he ordered.

This time Ralston left the cabin without saying anything else.

"And you," Carnahan went on to Dawn Wind, "make yourself useful. Get a pot of coffee on to boil and make me some breakfast. Or does a savage like you know how to boil coffee?"

Breckinridge had taught her how to make coffee. She said, "I must have snow to melt for the pot."

"We'll get it together. And if you try anything else, you'll regret it."

At this point, the only thing she regretted was that she hadn't killed this man when she had the chance.

The creek that Breckinridge and the others were following upstream twisted and turned through the rugged landscape as it ran down out of the Bighorn Mountains. Breck began to think it never ran straight for more than a hundred yards at a stretch.

That meant there were plenty of places where they couldn't see very far, which was worrisome. He voiced that concern to Gray Bear.

"We could be walkin' into an ambush," Breckinridge told the older man as he gestured toward the rocky, wooded slopes around them.

"We could," Gray Bear agreed, "but there is no other way to follow the trail."

Breckinridge scraped a thumbnail along his red-stubbled jaw, then tugged at his right earlobe as he frowned in thought. After a moment he said, "I ain't so sure about that. There's a ridge up yonder to the left that's runnin' in the same general direction we're goin'. If a couple of fellas could get up there, they might make better time. And they'd have the high ground if any trouble broke out."

Gray Bear signaled a halt and turned to gaze toward the ridge Breckinridge had mentioned.

"This is true," he admitted. "But to do such a thing would mean splitting our forces."

"Yeah, it's a risk. But we're already facin' long odds. Might be worth it to take a chance."

"It will be a hard, dangerous climb. Who would attempt to reach this ridge?"

"Me and one other fella," Breckinridge said. "That's what I was thinkin'."

"I will come with you," Bitter Mouth volunteered without hesitation.

The grieving warrior had said very little during the journey. Normally the most talkative of the Crow, sorrow had silenced his tongue. Breckinridge looked at Bitter Mouth, saw his cold-eyed determination, and nodded.

"That's all right with me."

Gray Bear looked at the sky and said, "There are perhaps two hours of daylight left. Will you try to rejoin us tonight?"

"Only if we find anything between now and nightfall," Breckinridge replied. "If we see any signs of trouble up ahead while it's still light, we'll try to get a warning to you, so keep an eye out for any signal from up yonder. Maybe we can send up some smoke."

"It is well," Gray Bear agreed.

The two men split off from the main group of searchers and began climbing the hill that sloped down almost all the way to the creek, leaving only the narrow bank they had been following. The ascent was a steep one, but there were trees to help them when they needed to grasp something and pull themselves up or lean against a trunk to rest for a moment. The growth was thick enough that Gray Bear, Swims Like a Fish, and the others were soon lost to sight below.

The fact that Bitter Mouth was silent now was probably helpful, because both men needed their breath for climbing. The air was thin and cold, and even with Breckinridge's enormous lung capacity, he was gasping a little by the time they reached the base of the ridge.

He bit back a groan of dismay as he tilted his head back and looked up a sheer rock face that rose for at least a hundred feet. From down below, the rugged rimrock had been visible over the tops of the trees, but he hadn't realized the approach to it was so impossible. Not even a mountain goat could climb that cliff.

"We'll just have to move along the base and hope we can find a place where we can get up there," Breckinridge told Bitter Mouth. The grim-faced warrior nodded in understanding.

It was tough going. The ground sloped steeply under their feet and was littered with rocks. A misstep could mean a bad fall that would send them tumbling down head over heels, probably to smash against a tree trunk.

They had to move slowly and carefully, and that frustratingly deliberate pace gnawed at Breckinridge's guts. He needed to find Dawn Wind and assure himself that she was all right.

Carnahan and the others wouldn't hurt her, he told himself over and over. She was the bait in the trap. They needed her alive.

But did they, really? She could already be dead, and as long as he didn't know that, he would continue searching for her. Besides, knowing the evil to be found in the hearts of Carnahan and Ralston and most of the other trappers, not to mention Machitehew and the other survivors from the Blackfoot war party, Breckinridge wouldn't put anything past them.

He shoved those thoughts out of his brain. Dwelling on them wouldn't do any good. He concentrated on finding a way to the top of the ridge.

It didn't help that the light was bad, even though it was still a good while until nightfall. The thick, dark clouds blocked the sun so thoroughly, and the cold was so pervasive, that Breckinridge was starting to feel like life would never be bright and warm again.

Finally, he spotted what looked like a thin dark line wavering its way up the cliff face. As he and Bitter Mouth came closer, he realized it was a crease in the rock, a natural chimney of sorts. Whether they could follow it to the top, Breckinridge didn't know, but it was the only promising possibility they had found so far.

"Look there," he said as he pointed it out to Bitter Mouth. "Reckon we can give it a try?"

"We have no other choice."

That was the way Breckinridge felt about it, too. When they reached the bottom of the crease, he studied it intently. It was about six feet deep and half that wide. The walls were irregular, narrowing in places and studded with rocky projections. It didn't run straight up and down but rather at slight angles that bent back and forth where the rock had been sundered under some ancient geologic stress.

Breckinridge figured he and Bitter Mouth could climb it, although with his broad shoulders and deep chest, he might have a little trouble squeezing through here and there. Bitter Mouth was slender and could make it.

For that reason, the Crow warrior said, "Let me go first." He stepped into the crease, found footholds and handholds, and began pulling himself up.

When Bitter Mouth had ascended perhaps ten feet, Breckinridge started up after him. Back home in Tennessee, he had climbed trees and ridges almost before he could walk, so he knew how to find the grips he needed and test them out before he trusted his weight to them. He rose through the crease in slow but steady fashion and didn't encounter any trouble until it made its first bend back in the other direction, maybe twenty feet off the ground.

Bitter Mouth negotiated that turn without a problem, but he paused above it and called down, "Be careful, Breckinridge. There will not be much room for you. Do not get stuck."

"I won't," Breckinridge promised. "If I have to scrape a little hide off to get through, I dang sure will."

He began turning, pressing the front of his body against the rear of the crease to do so. He reached above the bend, found a knob of rock he could close his hand around, and pushed up with his feet. The sides of the crease pinched against his shoulders. He found another handhold and pulled harder. The crease narrowed even more. His jaw clenched and his breath hissed between his teeth.

He didn't like this feeling of being closed in. With a grunt of effort, he forced his way past the bottleneck and felt relief surge through him as his shoulders popped free.

"I'm all right," he told Bitter Mouth, who was gazing down at him worriedly. "Keep goin'."

The warrior resumed the climb. Breckinridge followed. The next bend in the crease was easier, but the one after that was even tighter than the first. Breck had to heave and strain against the rock walls. He was putting so much strength into the effort that he began to think he might pop right out of the crease, like a seed being squeezed out of a piece of fruit. If that happened, it would be a long drop to the ground, followed by an even longer tumble down the lower slope.

He wasn't sure but what he actually did leave some skin behind before he got through that one. But he was above it at last, and Bitter Mouth told him, "Only one more."

Breckinridge blew out some breath and nodded

as it fogged in front of his face. His hands were about frozen from contact with the cold rocks. His fingers were getting numb and clumsy, and he knew he wouldn't be able to climb for much longer. He braced himself with his legs and shoulders so he couldn't slip and blew on his hands, trying to warm them up with his breath.

After a few moments he told Bitter Mouth, "Let's go."

They resumed the climb. The last bend in the natural chimney was tight, but not as bad as the one Breckinridge had just made it through. He twisted and pushed through this one, then hauled himself up the final fifteen feet.

Bitter Mouth disappeared over the rim. Breckinridge pulled himself up and over the edge and then rolled onto his back, utterly exhausted. Weather and exertion—and worry—were taking a toll, even on him.

After a few seconds, he lifted his head and looked around. Bitter Mouth sat nearby, also catching his breath. The ridge was about a quarter of a mile wide. On its far side, it gave way to a jumble of rocky spires and crevices that looked to be impassible by anyone except one of those mountain goats Breckinridge had thought about earlier.

Breckinridge sat up and looked over the edge. He caught a glimpse here and there of the creek as it meandered along, but the trees along its banks concealed the stream for the most part. As far as he could tell, the ridge followed the creek fairly closely, although some of its bends weren't as sharp.

Nor was the growth as thick atop it. He and Bitter Mouth could make better progress up here than the others down below could, Breck thought.

"You ready to get movin' again?" he asked after a few minutes.

"We do not have much time before night falls," Bitter Mouth said. "We should cover as much ground as we can."

"Damn right," Breckinridge said as he pushed himself to his feet. "Dawn Wind and them other captives are up ahead of us somewhere, and I sure as hell don't want to leave 'em in the hands of those bastards for another night if I don't have to."

Chapter 32

The night had been a long one for Dawn Wind, but the day was even longer. She was torn with worry . . . worry that Breckinridge would not show up to rescue her . . . and worry that he *would*, only to be killed by Carnahan and Ralston. If she could be certain that he would live a long and happy life without her, she would almost surrender her own life to bring that about.

But she couldn't guarantee that, and anyway, it wasn't just her own life that would enter into such a bargain. There was also the life of the child she was carrying to consider. She had to protect that child above all else. She knew Breckinridge would understand her feelings.

Carnahan left her alone for the most part, after he realized she wasn't going to respond to any of his comments about the life they might share once Breckinridge was dead.

The monster was attracted to her, Dawn Wind realized, but she couldn't bring herself to try to use Carnahan's lust to her advantage. Not yet, anyway.

Several times during the day, Major Ralston showed up at the cabin to deliver reports to Carnahan. There had been no sign of Breckinridge or anyone else from the Crow village.

"Machitehew is getting restless," Ralston told Carnahan late that afternoon. "He wants to take his warriors and the prisoners and head back where he came from. He says that travel is just going to get worse as winter goes on."

Carnahan grunted and said, "He's probably right about that. I want him here until Wallace has been dealt with, though."

"Then that redheaded bastard had better show up in the next day or two, because I'm not sure you can convince the Blackfeet to stay any longer than that. They got what they wanted. They dealt out misery to their old enemies the Crow, and they have some captives to turn into slaves. They're ready to go home."

Carnahan waved a hand dismissively as he sat at the table. Ralston shrugged, turned, and left the cabin.

Carnahan looked at Dawn Wind, who sat on the floor near the fire, and said, "Maybe Wallace has decided he's better off without you, girl. You ever think about that?"

Dawn Wind ignored him. She knew his words were a lie. Breckinridge would never abandon her. He would come for her.

Unless he was already dead.

Darkness closed down over the rugged landscape. It was as black and impenetrable as it had been the previous night, but at least the snow wasn't falling anymore. The air was cold and a slight breeze was blowing.

Breckinridge and Bitter Mouth paused on the ridge to hunker under a stunted pine and eat some jerky. They debated trying to start a fire but decided not to. For one thing, Breckinridge hadn't decided whether he was going to stop for long, even though night had fallen.

"As long as we're careful and don't fall off the edge, I don't see why we can't keep movin' once we've rested for a while," he said to Bitter Mouth. "We're not followin' sign up here, anyway. Carnahan and the others must have a camp somewhere in these parts. If they've got a fire goin', we ought to be able to spot it from up here."

"I am willing to continue," Bitter Mouth replied. "That may be our best chance of taking them by surprise."

Breckinridge smiled, even though his companion wouldn't be able to see it in the dark.

"I was just thinkin' the same thing. Carnahan's probably got a trap set for us, but maybe we can come at him from a direction he ain't expectin'."

With that settled, they finished their sparse meal, ate some snow to wash it down, and then continued moving carefully along the ridge.

Despite the fact that both men had keen eyesight, the darkness was so thick they practically had to feel their way along in order to avoid the dangerous drop-off to their right. The ridge was plenty wide, but if it had any ragged edges that angled in sharply with no warning, that might cause a problem. Breckinridge and Bitter Mouth couldn't afford to be in a hurry.

That was particularly galling since every instinct in Breckinridge's body was crying out for him to find and rescue Dawn Wind just as soon as possible.

They pushed on into the frozen darkness. Breckinridge couldn't have said for how long. But he knew when he sensed something different.

He lifted his head and said, "Ssst!" to Bitter Mouth. Breckinridge stood absolutely still and drew in a deep breath of the frigid air.

"I smell it, too," Bitter Mouth whispered. "Smoke."

"Wood smoke," Breckinridge replied, equally quietly. "From a good-sized campfire. Actually, doggoned if it don't smell like a chimney burnin'."

Was that possible? he wondered. Could there be some sort of cabin out here in the middle of the wilderness?

He thought about how much time had passed since the last time he had seen Carnahan, Ralston, and the others. They had had plenty of time to build a cabin, or even several cabins, he realized. All they needed were axes and plenty of trees, and those things were available.

Carnahan might have himself a damn *stronghold* up here, Breckinridge thought. He probably believed there was no chance Breck could get to Dawn Wind without being caught.

Before much longer, Carnahan was going to find out how wrong he was about that.

"How close you reckon that smoke is?" Breckinridge asked Bitter Mouth.

"Hard to say. The wind is not strong tonight. The smoke could have drifted for quite a distance. Perhaps a mile or more."

"Maybe. Anyway, all we can do is keep going. Just take it slow and careful-like."

"That will not be easy." For the first time, Bitter Mouth's iron self-control slipped a little. Breckinridge could hear that in his voice as he said, "My heart cries out for vengeance."

"Mine, too, my friend. We'll have it, along with justice for all those folks Carnahan and his bunch murdered."

The smoke smell gradually grew stronger as Breckinridge and Bitter Mouth pushed ahead warily along the ridge. Breck knew they were going in the right direction.

He was slightly in the lead, tasting the footing with each step, when suddenly there was nothing under his right foot except empty air. He caught his breath as he swayed forward and strained with every muscle to pull himself back.

He might have been able to save himself from a fall, or he might not have, but just then Bitter Mouth caught hold of his buckskin shirt and hauled back on it. Both men toppled to the ground.

Breckinridge's heart slugged heavily in his chest. He didn't know how bad the fall would have been if he had plummeted from the brink, but some sixth sense told him it wouldn't have been good. After a few moments of lying there to catch his breath, he sat up and then got on hands and knees.

"Stay where you are," he whispered to Bitter Mouth. "I'm gonna see if I can tell what's ahead of us."

"Nothing, I think," Bitter Mouth whispered back.

Breckinridge had a hunch his friend was right about that. He inched forward, sweeping a hand back and forth across the ground in front of him.

Within a couple of feet, he felt the edge under his fingers. He eased a little closer and reached out. His hand found nothing but emptiness. It spread out in front of him like a pitch-black sea.

No, wait . . . In the distance to his left was *something* . . . a faint glow . . . a few tiny, dancing specks of light . . .

Glowing bits of ash from a fire, Breckinridge realized, rising on a column of hot air. More than one, in fact. But no flames were visible, which meant the fires were contained. There were fireplaces down there, and that meant cabins. Two or three, he guessed, based on what he could make out.

He backed away from the edge, reached out, brushed a hand against Bitter Mouth's shoulder. Leaning close, he breathed, "Looks like a big canyon, best I can tell. There are cabins down there. I can smell the smoke and see some ashes floatin' in the air, but no flames, so they're not open campfires."

"Cabins?" Bitter Mouth replied. "This man Carnahan wishes to live here?"

"I reckon he's gonna spend the winter, and he figured he might as well be comfortable while he's doin' it. It'd be a good place to keep prisoners, too."

Bitter Mouth didn't reply for a moment, then, "What will we do now?"

"We need to get down in there and see if we can find Dawn Wind."

"We cannot."

Breckinridge started to bristle at that. "What in blazes—"

"We cannot climb down into a canyon in darkness like this. We would fall and probably kill ourselves. Then there would be no one to help the prisoners."

The warrior sighed. "I want to kill our enemies every bit as much as you do, Breckinridge, but we must wait until morning when we can see what is down there. And then one of us should go back and let Gray Bear and the others know what we have learned."

Bitter Mouth's words made perfect sense, but Breckinridge didn't want to hear them. He was close to Dawn Wind now. He could feel that certainty in every bone of his body. She was somewhere down in that canyon and he had to go to her.

But once again, a small voice of caution in the back of his head spoke up, warning him that he couldn't do anything to rescue her if he was dead. They needed to wait for morning, as Bitter Mouth said, even though that meant leaving Dawn Wind in Jud Carnahan's hands for a second night.

"All right," he whispered, "but if anybody carries word back to Gray Bear tomorrow, it ain't gonna be me. Now that I'm this close to Dawn Wind, I ain't leavin'. I just wish there was some way to let her know that I'm here . . ."

Dawn Wind could tell that Carnahan was growing more impatient. That evening, the bearded man paced back and forth in front of the fireplace, his hands clasped behind his back and a scowl on his face.

Dawn Wind sat at the table and kept her head down and her face carefully impassive, even though she wanted to laugh at Carnahan's discomfiture. It wouldn't do to make him angry.

She had survived so far, and she was determined to stay alive until Breckinridge came for her.

Carnahan abruptly stopped pacing and swung around to glare at her.

"I was goading you earlier," he said, "but now I really am starting to wonder if Wallace decided not to come for you after all."

"Life will unfold as the great spirits wish," she said calmly. "There is little we can do to influence them, other than trying to live as they might wish."

Carnahan let out a bark of laughter. "Your great spirits aren't going to help you, girl. Even if they exist, they don't give a damn about us. They threw us into this world and left us here to live or die on our own, according to how strong we are. That's what my life has taught me."

"Then I almost feel sorry for you," Dawn Wind said. "Almost."

Carnahan snorted and resumed stalking back and forth in front of the fireplace.

After a while, Dawn Wind went to her corner, wrapped the blanket around her, and curled up on the floor. The wind wasn't howling through the cracks between the logs tonight, as it had been the night before, so it wasn't as cold in the cabin.

If she had been here with Breckinridge instead of Jud Carnahan, she might have even considered her surroundings cozy and comfortable. She had assumed that when she and Breck spent their lives together, they would do so in a tipi, but perhaps he would prefer to live in a cabin like this, she thought now. White men liked solid buildings.

She lost herself in musing about what their lives would be like, spending the years to come in a sturdy cabin, Breckinridge going out each day to trap and hunt, while she remained at home to care for their home and all the children they would have. It was a very pretty dream, easy to get lost in . . .

And dream it became, as she slipped off to sleep.

Once again, weariness from the day's efforts enabled Breckinridge to sleep better than he expected to.

However, he was still tired, stiff, and sore when he woke up early the next morning. He had hoped to see the dark clouds breaking this morning, but they hung stubbornly in the sky, as thick and threatening as ever.

Breckinridge and Bitter Mouth had drawn back well away from the edge of the canyon before making a crude camp under some trees. When both men were good and awake and there was enough gray light in the sky for them to see what they were doing, they crept forward to the brink and risked a look down into the canyon. Breck took his broad-brimmed hat off as he did so, to lessen the chances of drawing attention to his presence.

The mouth of the canyon was a couple of hundred yards to their right. An equal distance back the other way were three cabins, two set fairly close together, the other a short distance apart.

There were crude lodges built of brush down there as well. Bitter Mouth pointed them out, grimaced, and mouthed the word *Blackfoot*.

Breckinridge nodded. The remaining members of Machitehew's war party had thrown in with Carnahan; there was no doubt about that now.

As he and Bitter Mouth watched, faint movements in the rocks around the canyon mouth caught Breckinridge's eye. He studied them more closely, pointed them out to Bitter Mouth, and then motioned for the two of them to withdraw again.

When they were away from the edge, Breckinridge whispered, "Carnahan's got men in those rocks at the canyon mouth. I reckon that's the trap he plans to spring. He's hopin' the rescue party will advance into the canyon, then his men will fall in behind them and catch Gray Bear and the others in a cross fire. We got to keep that from happenin'."

"I will go back, find them, and warn them," Bitter Mouth said. He surprised Breckinridge by smiling faintly. "I know you will not agree to leave this place."

"You're damn right about that. Dawn Wind's down there, and I ain't leavin' until I've figured out a way to rescue her."

"Wait until I get back with the others," Bitter Mouth suggested. "We will attack the men at the mouth of the canyon. That will draw the others away from the cabin. Then you can climb down and find her."

Breckinridge thought about that for a moment and then nodded. He was no real tactician—his usual plan was to charge in like a big old bull and lay waste to whomever he was fighting—but he recognized that Bitter Mouth's idea was a good one.

"Go ahead," he told the grim-faced warrior. "But don't waste any time. While you're gone I'll do some scoutin' and find a good way down into the canyon, so I'll be ready when the time comes to move."

Bitter Mouth nodded. He reached out and squeezed Breckinridge's arm.

"Good luck, my friend. Before this day is over, you will be reunited with Dawn Wind . . . and I will have my vengeance and be reunited with my wife."

Breckinridge nodded and clasped Bitter Mouth's shoulder in return. Bitter Mouth got to his feet and trotted back the way they had come, fading quickly into the gray dawn light.

He was gone by the time Breckinridge realized what his friend had meant by that last statement.

Bitter Mouth intended to die in battle today.

Chapter 33

Breckinridge crawled back over to the rimrock and stretched out there, then watched as the light grew stronger and men began to move around, down in the canyon. Several of them emerged from the two cabins that were close together. They tramped around in the snow and seemed to be hunting for firewood. That guess was confirmed when they returned with their arms full of broken branches.

Other men, these carrying rifles, left the cabins and headed toward the canyon mouth. They were going to relieve the men who were standing guard in the boulders there, Breckinridge supposed.

He was right about that, too. Several minutes later, roughly the same number of men returned from the canyon mouth. Among them was Major Gordon Ralston.

Breckinridge's hands clenched into fists as he recognized the former officer. There was no mistaking the lean, wolfish figure with the patch over one eye and a scabbarded saber hanging from his belt. Breck had a mighty low opinion of Ralston, but evidently the man took his turn standing guard and Breck had to give him credit for that.

Instead of heading for the cabins where the men had emerged, Ralston walked toward the building standing apart. Before he could get there, a warrior came out of one of the crude lodges and called to him in a harsh voice. Breckinridge couldn't make out the words, but he could tell that the Blackfoot didn't sound happy.

The warrior strode up to Ralston. The two of them stood there talking for several minutes. Now and then one of them made a curt gesture, usually returned by the other. Judging by that, Breck figured the discussion wasn't a very friendly one.

Gray Bear had told him the Blackfeet were led by a well-known war chief known as Machitehew. The Crow had battled him before, during previous raids, and he had been recognized during the attack on the village.

Breckinridge had a hunch that was Machitehew talking to Ralston now, and the war chief sure wasn't happy about something.

Finally, Machitehew flung out both hands abruptly and dismissively, turned his back on Ralston, and walked away. Breckinridge saw Ralston's hand stray toward the sword for a second.

Ralston's impulse may have been to yank out the saber and plunge it into Machitehew's back, but if that was true, he controlled the urge. Instead he continued on to his destination, the cabin that sat apart from the other two.

When he reached the door, it looked like he started to go straight in, but then he paused and knocked. That was an indication the cabin belonged to Jud

Carnahan. Sure enough, a moment later someone inside jerked the door open, and Breckinridge saw Carnahan's long, bristling black beard.

If Carnahan was in there, Breckinridge thought, there was a good chance Dawn Wind was, too. He hadn't seen any sign of her or the other captives, but they had to be here somewhere. Since Dawn Wind was the bait in the trap, it was likely Carnahan would keep her close to him.

That thought made a shiver go through Breckinridge. He wanted to get down off this canyon wall somehow, bust into that cabin, and see for himself. He wanted to kill Carnahan, Ralston, and all the others and then take Dawn Wind into his arms and promise he would never let her be hurt again.

He warned himself that his best chance of being able to do that was to stick to the plan. He had to wait for Bitter Mouth and the others to get here.

But in the meantime, he could look for a way to get down from the rimrock into the canyon. If he couldn't find one, they would have to come up with some other idea.

But whatever it took, he and Dawn Wind would be together again before this day was over, Breckinridge vowed.

"I thought you should know, Machitehew just told me that he and his men are leaving," Ralston said as he stood at the door of Carnahan's cabin. "He said they were going today and taking the prisoners with them." Ralston nodded past Carnahan toward the inside of the cabin where Dawn Wind was. "Including Wallace's squaw."

Carnahan's bearded face darkened in a scowl. "The hell he is," he declared. "I don't care what that savage wants. I'm not finished with him and his men yet."

Ralston shrugged and said, "He'll probably back down when it comes to the squaw. We can divvy up the other females. But if he really wants to leave, I don't see how you can stop him short of killing him. You don't have anything left to bargain with, now that he's raided that Crow village and gotten what he wanted."

"He has other enemies, doesn't he? I can promise that we'll help him wipe them out, too, as long as he stays to help us with Wallace."

"And once that's done . . . ?"

Carnahan smiled coldly. "Well, then there won't be any reason *not* to kill him, will there?"

Ralston nodded slowly. "I convinced him not to leave until after I'd talked to you. I take it I can promise him our help in any other grudges he's carrying?"

"Promise him any damn thing in the world," Carnahan snapped. "Just keep him here."

He turned and went back into the cabin, closing the door firmly behind him.

Dawn Wind looked up from the corner where she sat. She felt poorly this morning. There was a dull ache deep in her belly. She didn't know what was causing it, and she didn't want to think too much about what it might mean.

To distract herself from all the worrisome possibilities, she said to Carnahan, "I heard what the major said. You cannot trust a Blackfoot. He will always betray you. That is why they wage war against all the other tribes."

"I don't trust Machitehew." Carnahan went to the fireplace and held out his hands toward its warmth.

"I'll kill him if he tries to double-cross me. But as long as he doesn't, I'll make use of him."

"And when he is of no more use, you will kill him. I heard you say so yourself."

"What of it?" Carnahan said.

Dawn Wind cocked her head a little to the side and said, "What is it that fills a man so full of evil?"

"You're talking about me?" Carnahan jabbed a thumb against his massive chest. He laughed. "I'm not evil."

"You cannot think you are good, as much innocent blood as you have spilled."

"Now, you see, you're making two wrong assumptions there. I don't think I'm good *or* evil, because those two things don't actually exist. There's weak, and there's strong. That's all there really is. And that leads right to your other wrong assumption, that there's such a thing as innocent blood. Nobody's innocent."

"A child—"

"Just hasn't had the chance to figure out which path he's going to take. That makes him ignorant, not innocent. As for me, I knew early on that I was going to be strong. My folks taught me that. My ma was a damned whore, and my pa beat her to death for it. Then he marched all five of us kids down to the Ohio River and started knocking us in the head and throwing us in the water from a high bluff. He got to me last because I was the youngest."

Carnahan paused and chuckled as if he were sharing some pleasant reminiscence before he went on, "I suppose the old bastard never gave any thought to the chance I might pull his pistol out of his belt, stick it in his face, and blow his brains out. I was barely big enough to lift the damn thing. But I managed. He went backward off that bluff into the river with the others. I threw the pistol in after him."

Dawn Wind stared at him, horrified by the story. When she could speak again, she asked, "How old were you?"

"Five, I think. Maybe six. Young enough that folks didn't question me much when I said that something bad had happened to my family and I didn't understand it. I understood it, all right. I was the only one left, so that made me the strongest. Seemed pretty simple to me."

"How . . . how did you . . . ?"

"How did I get by at that age?" Carnahan said. "Another family took me in. Nice, churchgoing folks. Had a daughter a couple of years younger than me. They raised me until I was fourteen. Then I cut their throats one night, had my way with the girl, and left them all behind in a burning cabin when I set out on the road. I've been on my own ever since. That's the way I like it."

She looked down at the floor and couldn't suppress the shudder that went through her.

"Or maybe I just made all that up," Carnahan said with a laugh. "The thing of it is . . . you don't know, do you? But maybe you understand a little better now why you need to cooperate with me. You'll be a lot better off in the long run that way, I promise you."

Dawn Wind *didn't* know if the terrible story he had just told her was true or not, but she was certain of one thing.

She would be better off dead than being forced to stay with Jud Carnahan.

Breckinridge made his way along the top of the canyon wall, staying well back from the rim most of the time so he wouldn't be spotted if any of the men down below happened to glance up at just the wrong moment. He approached the rim now and then to search cautiously for some way he could descend.

It would be better if he could reach the canyon floor behind the cabins, he decided. There was more cover that way.

The canyon wall was almost sheer in most places. A few roots and rocks stuck out here and there. Breckinridge might have been able to climb down, but it was a lot more likely he would slip and fall.

A broken leg or a busted neck would ruin all of his plans. After the harrowing climb up to the top of the ridge, he'd had enough of such things for a while.

The canyon was about half a mile deep, gradually narrowing until it ended in a steep, talus-covered slope that rose to another looming cliff. Breckinridge studied the slope and thought that he might be able to get down that way, although he would have to be very careful.

If he slipped in the snow or one of the rocks turned under his foot and made him fall, he would slide a long way and bring down a bit of an avalanche with him. Such a commotion would attract attention, that was for sure.

As far as Breckinridge could see, though, that was the only possible way he could get down there to where Dawn Wind was. That meant he had to risk it.

Now it was a matter of waiting for Bitter Mouth, Gray Bear, and the other Crow warriors to arrive and launch their attack on the sentries at the canyon mouth. When Breckinridge didn't intercept them to stop and warn them, they would go ahead with the plan.

He settled down to wait, which had never been easy for him and certainly wasn't now. From where he was, near the back end of the canyon, he could catch only glimpses through the trees of the cabin where he believed Dawn Wind to be. He wished he could look through those log walls and make sure of her presence.

As he sat there on a spot he had brushed clear of snow, something darted past his vision at the corner of his eye. He turned his head to look closer and saw another bit of white dance past on the cold breeze.

It was *snowing* again, damn it.

Breckinridge watched while the snow began to fall faster and heavier. The past couple of days, the clouds had loomed darkly and ominously overhead. Gray Bear had commented yesterday that there would be more snow before this was over.

The old warrior had been right. When Breckinridge looked toward the mouth of the canyon, he saw that it was veiled in white, obscured by the falling snow.

Maybe this was a good thing, he told himself. Those sentries wouldn't be as likely to see Gray Bear and the others sneaking up on them until it was too late. If more snow collected on that talus slope, though, that could make it trickier for him to get down without falling.

If he was able to rescue Dawn Wind, should he

bring her back here so they could try to climb out of the canyon the same way he intended to enter it? Breckinridge pondered that question. It would be a lot harder coming back up than it would be going down, he thought. And he couldn't bring *all* the captives that way, especially those little kids.

But Dawn Wind wouldn't want him to leave them behind. He knew her well enough to be certain of that.

The best he could do might be to send her out of the canyon while he attacked Carnahan's bunch from behind. Wiping out the renegades was really the only way to be sure that all the captives would go free.

The snowstorm made it impossible to tell what time it was. Breckinridge didn't know how long it had taken Bitter Mouth to get back to the rest of the group, nor how much time they would need to reach the canyon once Bitter Mouth explained the plan to them. But it seemed to him like they ought to be here by now!

Breck clenched a big right fist and patted it quietly into the palm of his left hand. He was ready for action.

At first he almost didn't hear the faint popping sounds in the distance, but then he recognized them as rifle shots and his head jerked up. The attack had started.

Breckinridge surged to his feet and slung the long-barreled flintlock rifle on his back, along with the bow and the quiver of arrows. He didn't want to drop any of his weapons if he happened to fall during the perilous descent.

Snow swirled around him as he ran toward the slope. He could see some of the trees but not the cabins. If he couldn't see very well, then neither could the men in the canyon. Anyway, all of them would soon be busy fighting off the attack when they realized their trap had failed to spring.

Breckinridge stepped out onto the loose rock. His heart was in his throat as he began the descent. His footing shifted underneath him and he held his breath for a second until he caught his balance again.

He hoped his friends were all right, but he knew they were willing to fight and die to rescue the captives, just like he was.

He covered five feet, then ten, as the guns continued to go off at the mouth of the canyon. Men's startled shouts blended with the rifle blasts. The cries darted through the wind-whipped snow, here and then gone.

Breckinridge held his arms out to the side for balance as he took another step. Then one of the things he had worried about happened.

One of the rocks shifted under his weight, and he was thrown off too much for him to recover in time. His balance deserted him. He landed on his rear end in a hard, undignified fall.

But it was dignity be damned as more rocks began to slide and Breckinridge went with them. He flung his hands out, but there was nothing to grab. As a cloud of snow flew up around him, he slid out of control toward the canyon floor, taking what seemed like half the mountainside with him.

Chapter 34

Dawn Wind kept an even closer eye on Jud Carnahan after that bloody tale he had told her. She had been afraid of him before, but now she worried that he might go completely insane at any moment. She had no trouble at all believing that he had told her the truth about his background.

And even if he hadn't, what sort of madman would make up such a terrible story as *that*?

Carnahan looked at her from time to time and chortled, obviously well aware that he had spooked her. He took pleasure in her fear. That was one more reason Dawn Wind's instincts told her he had been truthful about his past.

Sometime during the day—it was difficult for Dawn Wind to keep track of the time, shut up in this cabin the way she was—Carnahan went to the door and opened it to peer down the canyon.

"I don't understand what's taking Wallace so long," he said in a peevish tone. "He's had enough time to find us."

"When Breckinridge gets here, you will wish he had not found you."

Carnahan swung around to glare at her. "You're just trying to keep your hopes up, girl. He'll stand no chance against me and my men *and* Machitehew's warriors. Even if he brings some of your people with him, they'll be outnumbered. We already wiped out most of the warriors in your village."

"You sound proud of that."

"Pride doesn't have anything to do with it. The only thing that matters is strength. When word gets around the mountains about what happened, no one will dare cross me ever again. There'll be nothing standing in the way of the empire I'm going to build up here."

He was not only insane, he was a fool, Dawn Wind thought. If all the tribes were to join forces and rise against him, he and his men would be blown away like bits of dry grass before a strong wind.

But what if he continued to recruit more trappers and more allies from the hated Blackfeet? What if he built more cabins and fortified this canyon? There might come a time when he *would* be powerful enough to exert his will, at least on this part of the mountains.

If that day ever came, it would be terrible to behold, she thought.

Carnahan closed the door, which cut down on the chilly, whistling drafts, but a short time later he went back to it, as if drawn by some compulsion. He opened it, looked out, and exclaimed, "By God, it's started to snow again!"

Dawn Wind looked past him through the door and saw the white flakes floating down thickly from the dark gray sky. If that kept up for very long, it would add several inches to the snow that was already on the ground, she thought.

She shivered as another gust of wind blew through the cabin. Carnahan stepped outside. She heard him say something to one of the others, and a moment later Ralston replied, "I'll go on back out there and make sure they've got their eyes open. In this snow, it'll be harder to see Wallace and the others coming."

"Be careful," Carnahan warned. "Don't let yourself be seen, Major. If you spoil the surprise we have planned for Wallace, I won't be happy."

"Don't worry about that," the one-eyed man snapped. "I know what I'm doing."

Carnahan just grunted, but he managed to pack contempt into the sound. Dawn Wind could imagine the angry look on Ralston's face as the major walked off.

Carnahan came in and closed the door again. It was dim inside the cabin. The flames in the fireplace gave off some light, but there were no candles or lamps. He was a dark, hairy bulk in the shadows. Like a bear.

Dawn Wind would have almost preferred being trapped in here with a bear.

More time passed. Probably not much, but it seemed like a lot to Dawn Wind. Carnahan got up from where he had been sitting at the table and stomped over to the corner where she sat.

"On your feet, girl," he ordered.

"What do you want? I can make coffee or food—"

"I don't want coffee or food. I'm tired of waiting for Wallace to get here so I can settle things with him. I told you all along I wanted to keep you safe . . . but that doesn't mean you have to be untouched."

A chill colder than that from the wind went through her. She tried to scoot farther away from him, but she couldn't go very far, hemmed in by the walls the way she was.

"Leave me alone," she said. "It will profit you nothing—"

"I told you, the only profit I'm really interested in is power. You can't stop me. Wallace can't stop me. I'm going to do whatever the hell I want with you."

"I . . . I am with child!" she blurted out. Some men might be disgusted by the idea of forcing themselves on a pregnant woman.

She should have known better where Carnahan was concerned. He just threw back his head and laughed.

"Do you think I care about that, girl? Now, do like I told you and stand up, or I'll drag you over to that bedroll—"

He stopped abruptly and turned his head toward the door, then stood stock-still and listened. A grin split his bushy face.

"Hear that?" he said. "Gunshots! Wallace is here!"

Dawn Wind heard the faint reports from the direction of the canyon mouth, all right, and with each one, her heart sank. Breckinridge had been trapped. She wanted to believe that he would fight his way free and come to save her, but the odds were against him . . .

"You and I can have our fun later," Carnahan said. "I'm going to be in on the finish of that redheaded bastard!"

He swung around, grabbed his coat and hat from

the table, and shrugged into them as he went to the door. He picked up his rifle, which was leaning against the wall, and flung the door open. Dawn Wind watched, her fear growing, as he started to step out.

Then without thinking about what she was doing, she leaped to her feet and threw herself after him, crying, "No!" All she could think about at this moment was trying to protect the man she loved from whatever horrible fate this monster had in store for him.

She leaped on Carnahan's back and wrapped her arms around his thick neck. She tried to twine her legs around his waist, but he was too big.

Carnahan grunted, sounding more like he was annoyed than anything else. He reached up and back with his free hand, grabbed hold of her, and ripped her away from him almost effortlessly. In doing that, he half turned away from the door and threw her toward the table like a child discarding a rag doll.

Out of control and unable to stop herself, Dawn Wind crashed against the table. Carnahan whipping her toward it like that had turned her around. The edge of it rammed deep into her belly.

Pain shot through her. She tried to catch hold of the table and keep from falling, but splinters just dug into her hands and she slipped to the floor anyway. Agony made her curl into a ball.

"It'll be even better this way," Carnahan said from the doorway. "When you and I get together, you'll know that Wallace is dead."

He stepped out into the snow and disappeared, leaving Dawn Wind on the floor beside the table. She struggled to hang on to consciousness as she felt something hot and wet underneath her.

It was blood, she realized. Despair flooded her being.

Then it went away along with everything else as blackness swept over her.

As snow flew around his head and filled the air, Breckinridge had a hard time breathing. Falling rocks pelted him. His hat had flown off when he fell. He got his arms over his head to protect it as much as possible.

At the same time, he drew in his legs, so he began to roll like a ball down the slope.

The tumbling descent lasted only a few seconds, but to Breckinridge it seemed much longer. When he landed hard at the bottom of the slope, he allowed his momentum to carry him into another roll, then came out of it on his feet.

He stumbled away from the rock slide as several more good-sized stones thumped against his back and legs. Then he was out of range of the falling rocks and paused for a second to take stock of himself.

Amazingly, he didn't seem to have broken any bones, although he would probably be black-and-blue all over from the pounding he had taken.

Equally surprisingly, he still had all of his weapons and they were intact. The bow hadn't snapped, and the arrows were still in the quiver.

He drew in a deep breath and looked around. Carnahan's cabin was about a hundred yards away, visible in the falling snow even though the rest of the canyon beyond it wasn't.

That was where Breckinridge hoped to find Dawn

Wind. He loped toward it as the flat, booming sound of gunfire continued at the far end of the canyon.

When he came closer, he could make out the other two cabins as well. No one seemed to be around them, but if the other prisoners were there, guards probably were posted where Breckinridge couldn't see them.

He would worry about that later, after he had found Dawn Wind, he told himself. None of the cabins had any windows in the back, so no one inside them could see him coming from this direction.

He swung to his right and reached the corner of Carnahan's cabin. Pressing his back to the rough log wall, he drew both pistols from behind his belt and looped his thumbs over the hammers. Holding the weapons ready, Breckinridge slid along the wall toward the front.

When he got there, he risked a look around the corner. No one was in sight. It appeared that the cabin's front door was standing wide open, though, and that struck Breckinridge as strange.

His heart pounded heavily and he couldn't seem to get his breath as he steeled himself to move. Then, as fast as he could, he lunged along the front of the cabin in two long strides and wheeled through the open doorway with the pistols thrust out in front of him. He thumbed back the hammers as he leveled the guns.

The cabin was empty.

Breckinridge shifted slightly. Snow that had blown in through the open door crunched under his boots. He stiffened.

The cabin wasn't empty after all. A dark shape lay huddled on the floor next to a crude table. Breckinridge's heart froze as he made out the familiar buckskin dress in the dim light that came from outside and from a small fire in the fireplace.

"Dawn Wind!"

He wouldn't have recognized that croaking sound as his own voice. He lowered the hammers on the pistols and sprang forward. His eyes widened in horror as he spied the dark pool spreading around her.

Breckinridge dropped the pistols on the table and fell to his knees beside her. His big hands gently clasped her shoulders and lifted her, turning her so that he could see her face. Lines of pain had been etched into her features.

He cradled her against him, heedless of the blood smearing his clothing. "Dawn Wind!" he said wretchedly. "Dawn Wind!"

Her eyelids flickered and then came open.

Hope shot through Breckinridge. Dawn Wind wasn't dead. She looked up at him and gradually focused on his face.

"Breck . . . in . . . ridge," she whispered. "I knew . . . you would . . . come for me."

"You just rest easy," he told her. "I'm here now, and you're gonna be all right."

"The . . . child?"

"It's fine, just fine."

Breckinridge knew that was probably a lie. His eyes searched Dawn Wind's body and saw no signs of a gunshot or stab wound. The blood soaking into the puncheons appeared to have come from under her dress. There was no way she could be bleeding that badly and have the baby be all right, he thought.

But telling her that wasn't going to do any good. His main goal now was to see that she got out of here safely. He wanted her to live, above all else.

In her condition, there was no way she could climb the talus slope. Nor could he carry her up that treacherous route. She would have to leave this canyon through its mouth, and there was only one way that would be possible.

Carnahan, Ralston, Machitehew, and everyone else who stood in his way had to die.

Something else occurred to Breckinridge. He leaned closer to Dawn Wind and asked, "What about the other captives?"

"They are . . . in the other cabins. You must . . . save them."

"I intend to," Breckinridge promised her. He looked around, saw a blanket on the floor nearby, and reached out with one hand to snag it. He wadded it up into a makeshift pillow and slipped it underneath her head as he lowered her carefully to the floor. "I got to go tend to things."

Somehow she found the strength to catch hold of his hand and squeeze it. She said, "You will . . . kill that man . . . Carnahan?"

"I reckon you can count on that," Breckinridge said.

Chapter 35

The cabins disappeared into the swirling snow behind Carnahan as he trotted toward the canyon mouth. He had to be careful; he didn't want to blunder right into Wallace and the rest of the search party, trapped in the cross fire between the guards he had posted.

He wasn't the only one thinking that. From behind him, Al Nusser called out, "Better be careful, boss."

"I know that, damn it," Carnahan snapped. "Have your guns ready. We'll take them by surprise and finish the job of wiping them out."

He thought about ordering that Breckinridge Wallace be taken alive if possible, so Carnahan himself could have the pleasure of finishing him off, but that was too risky. Wallace needed to die, no matter who took his life.

Carnahan could get his satisfaction from spitting on the big redheaded bastard's corpse.

Before heading for the ambush at the canyon mouth, Carnahan had fetched the rest of the men from the other cabins, except for one man left behind to guard the other captives. He had chosen Chet Bagley for that job, since Bagley wasn't much of a fighter. He ought to be able to keep those redskin women and kids under control, though.

Carnahan didn't believe that Dawn Wind would be going anywhere, the shape she was in. He hoped he hadn't hurt her too badly. He still intended to take his pleasure with her when this was all over.

A frown creased Carnahan's forehead. They ought to be getting close to the mouth of the canyon, he thought.

Something came out of the snow and struck the coonskin cap on his head, sweeping it right off his tangled mane of dark hair. Startled, Carnahan came to an abrupt halt. He turned around and picked up the cap.

"What the hell?"

An arrow was embedded in the raccoon head Carnahan had left on the hide when he fashioned the cap.

A thud sounded, followed instantly by a grunt of pain. Carnahan looked over and saw Nusser gazing down in shock and horror at the arrow protruding from his chest.

A second later the trapper's knees buckled and he pitched forward, driving the arrow even deeper into his body as it struck the ground.

War cries came from up ahead. Buckskin-clad figures emerged from the clouds of snow. More arrows whipped through the air.

The Crow search party hadn't been caught in the trap after all. Instead, they were bringing the fight to Carnahan and his men.

"Fall back!" Carnahan bellowed. "Fall back!"

They would fort up in the cabins, he thought, and then those damned redskins would see what a bad mistake they had made.

Breckinridge hated to leave Dawn Wind, but there was still a battle to be won. Her breathing was fairly steady and regular now, and the pool of blood didn't seem to be growing.

All he could do was hope she would be all right. But she sure as hell wouldn't be if Carnahan and his bunch emerged triumphant.

He picked up the pistols and ran out of the cabin. As he did, he saw the other cabins sitting off to the side and turned toward them. He would get the other captives and tell them to gather in Carnahan's cabin. The other women could look after Dawn Wind.

As Breckinridge approached, a man stepped out of the nearest cabin and pointed a rifle at him. Breck raised the pistols, but he held off on pulling the triggers when the man suddenly cast the rifle aside.

Breckinridge recognized Chet Bagley, who had done most of the cooking for Carnahan and the others. The balding, round-faced man held out his hands and cried, "Don't shoot, Wallace!"

Breckinridge kept his pistols aimed at Bagley as he approached, even though he didn't believe the man would try any tricks.

"I don't want any more of this," Bagley said miserably. "I . . . I never knew how terrible Carnahan and the others were when I signed on with them. You've got to believe me, Wallace. I just wanted to be a fur trapper. I'm not a killer!"

Breckinridge nodded toward the cabin and said, "Are the other captives in there?"

"Yes, all of them. Carnahan left me to watch them."

"Get them and take them over to Carnahan's cabin. Dawn Wind is in there, and she's hurt. You protect her and the others and maybe I won't kill you."

"Of course. I . . . I'll keep them safe. I give you my word on that."

Breckinridge glanced toward the Blackfoot lodges. "Where are Machitehew and the rest of those varmints?"

Bagley shook his head and said, "I don't know, I swear I don't. Carnahan and the rest of the men headed for the canyon mouth. The Blackfeet probably went with them."

Breckinridge nodded. He hoped Bagley was right about that. He wanted all of his enemies in one place.

Easier to kill them that way.

Major Gordon Ralston had been with the four men hidden in the rocks on the western side of the canyon mouth when an arrow had come out of nowhere, skewering the neck of the man standing next to him. Blood gushed from the man's mouth as it dropped open in pain.

Ralston had just warned the men to be extra alert now that the snow had started falling so thickly, obscuring their vision. Wallace and the others shouldn't have any idea they were walking right into a trap, but still, it wouldn't hurt to be careful.

As the dying man collapsed and more arrows began whistling through the air, Ralston realized instantly that Carnahan had been wrong all along. Somehow, the rescue party had sniffed out the ambush, and now they were attacking the men who should have been the jaws of the trap.

As if to confirm that, a grim-faced Crow warrior bounded out of the snow and plunged a knife into the chest of another trapper. The blade went in and out of the hapless victim's body several times, faster than the eye could follow.

Ralston ducked just in time to avoid an arrow that knocked his tricorne hat off his head. The rocks were full of shadowy, struggling figures now. Death cries rang out. Ralston reached for his saber, intending to sell his life dearly, then changed his mind and turned to flee instead.

That brought up bitter memories of running from the enemy, that moment of weakness that had cost him his military career and any pride he had left. Once broken like that, a man could never be made whole again. All that remained was the rage he felt at the world—and himself.

But if he had to die, it would be at a time and place of his own choosing. With luck, that might not be today, in this desolate canyon. If he could reach Carnahan and the others, he could warn them and they could still wipe out Wallace and those accursed Crow.

Even as he turned, an arrow buried itself in the back of his left thigh. That leg went out from under him, dumping him on the rocky ground. He tried to stand up but couldn't force himself to do it.

Instead he crawled into a small gap between two boulders and lay there panting in pain as he listened to the war cries and the screams of dying men.

* * *

Breckinridge saw the figures running toward him from the white curtains and skidded to a halt in the snow. He lifted the pistols but hesitated until he got a better look at the men.

He recognized some of the outlaw trappers and the Blackfoot warriors just as they spotted him blocking their retreat. One of the white men yelled in alarm as they tried to stop and bring their weapons to bear.

Breckinridge pressed both triggers.

The pistols boomed and bucked in his hands as flame and smoke spewed from the barrels. The heavy lead balls, double-shotted in each gun, scythed through the air and cut down three men, striking with sounds like a butcher driving his cleaver into a big shank of meat.

Breckinridge cast the empty pistols aside and dropped to one knee as he grabbed the bow slung on his back and brought it around in front of him. He plucked an arrow from the quiver, nocked it, pulled back the bow, and loosed.

Driven by his great strength, the arrow went all the way through one of the outlaw trappers still on his feet. The flint head, smeared with blood and flesh now, stood out almost a foot from his back. He dropped like a stone.

Breckinridge already had another arrow nocked. He let fly and saw this shaft sink into the belly of a Blackfoot warrior. The man folded up around it and collapsed.

Breckinridge was just one lone man. He probably couldn't have stemmed the retreat on his own. In another moment the enemy would have rolled over him.

But just then the pursuers from the Crow village

caught up to Carnahan's men and the remainder of Machitehew's war party. Chaos erupted in the snow.

The battle quickly became a whirling melee of one-to-one fights, although Breckinridge was often taking on two or more of the enemy at a time as he waded into the ruckus. He had tomahawk in one hand and knife in the other as he laid waste to his foes. Blood flew in the air and turned the snow crimson.

One of the largest of the Blackfoot warriors suddenly confronted him, also armed with tomahawk and knife. Breckinridge didn't know it, but this was the war chief Machitehew. He attacked with a ferocity that Breck hadn't seen from any of the others.

For long seconds, it was all he could do to fend off the furious assault. He blocked all the blows he could, but Machitehew's tomahawk got through once and glanced off Breckinridge's left shoulder.

Even at that, the impact was powerful enough to make his left arm go numb. His own tomahawk slipped from his fingers.

Breckinridge had to duck as Machitehew continued that stroke into a vicious backhand. Armed now only with the knife and the rifle slung on his back that wasn't going to do him any good, he knew he couldn't fight off another flurry of blows like that.

He didn't even try. Instead he lowered his head and plowed into Machitehew, using his great size and strength to knock the war chief back off his feet.

Machitehew landed in the snow with Breckinridge on top of him. Breck drove his knife into the Blackfoot's body, angling the blade up to try to reach the heart. Machitehew spasmed and struck a blow with his own knife. Breck felt it bite into the back of his left shoulder.

He pulled out his blade, ripped it again into Machitehew's chest. Blood sprayed hotly from the war chief's mouth as his breath gusted out of him. Again Breckinridge hammered the knife into him.

Machitehew's head was raised, the cords in his neck standing out from the strain. They suddenly went slack. His head fell back limply and his eyes were wide and unseeing. Breckinridge rolled off him.

The fight was almost over, Breckinridge saw as he staggered to his feet. A few struggles were still going on, but the canyon floor was littered with the gory corpses of Carnahan's men and the Blackfoot warriors. Breck looked for Carnahan himself but didn't see him.

Gray Bear and Swims Like a Fish, both bleeding from minor wounds, came up to join him. They watched as the last few of Carnahan's men were dispatched. No quarter was asked or given.

"My friend, you are bleeding," Swims Like a Fish said to Breckinridge.

"So are you," Breckinridge said.

Gray Bear pointed and said, "You still have a knife stuck in your back."

"Oh." Breckinridge gave a little shake of his head. "Didn't notice. Reckon one of you fellas could pull it out?"

Swims Like a Fish performed that task. Breckinridge grimaced a little as he felt the blade slide out of his flesh. Feeling had returned to his left arm. It hurt like the devil, but he moved it around and said, "Appears it'll be all right."

"Our people?" Gray Bear said.

Breckinridge turned and pointed toward the cabins. "They're back yonder, all right as far as I know. One of Carnahan's men is with 'em, but he surrendered and I promised him he wouldn't be killed if he cooperated."

The two Crow warriors didn't look too happy about that, but they nodded.

"It will be so," Gray Bear said. "What about Dawn Wind?"

"She's hurt," Breckinridge said grimly. Now that the heat of battle was subsiding in him, worry over Dawn Wind welled up inside him again. "I got to go to her—"

He turned and had started to take a step toward the cabins when another figure loomed out of the still-falling snow and lunged awkwardly at him with an incoherent cry of hate. Breckinridge caught a glimpse of the cadaverous face, the eye patch, and the gleaming saber that was about to drive into his chest.

Before the blade could strike home, another figure darted in front of it. Bitter Mouth staggered, transfixed on the saber wielded by Major Gordon Ralston. When he fell, his body pulled the sword out of Ralston's hand.

Ralston had an arrow in his leg, Breckinridge saw as he leaped over his fallen friend. He had limped up here in a futile effort to strike one final blow, to kill Breck at last. But he would never get another chance to do that.

Breckinridge's hands closed around Ralston's throat and squeezed. Ralston kicked as his feet came up off the ground. More blood flowed from the wound in Breck's shoulder as the powerful muscles heaved and bunched.

With a loud crack, the former officer's spine snapped in two. He went limp all over. Breckinridge snarled as he pulled Ralston's face close to his and looked into an eye from which the life was fading swiftly.

Then Ralston was dead and Breckinridge threw him aside like so much trash.

He turned back toward Bitter Mouth to find that Gray Bear and Swims Like a Fish were already kneeling on either side of him. Gray Bear looked up at Breckinridge and said, "He is gone, my friend. He gave his life to save yours."

"Damn it," Breckinridge rasped. "He didn't have to do that."

"I believe he did," Swims Like a Fish said. "He died when his woman did, back there in the village. Never again would he have been the warrior, the man, he once was. Better to leave this life doing a good thing for a friend."

"I'll never forget him," Breckinridge said. "But I'm gonna remember him grinnin' and makin' some joke."

"He would like that," Gray Bear said as he rose wearily to his feet. He clasped Breckinridge's arm. "Go to your woman, my friend. We will make sure everything is all right out here."

Breckinridge nodded and turned toward the cabins. He took a step and then another.

And then he was running.

Chapter 36

Breckinridge pushed aside the tipi's hide flap and stepped out into the warm sun. Its caressing rays felt good. He was glad that spring was finally here, after the winter he had just spent here in the Crow village . . . the darkest winter of his life.

Not just because the sky had been overcast most of the time and the village had remained snowbound for weeks on end. Those things were bad enough, but Breckinridge had experienced much worse.

He was not alone in that, either.

A soft step sounded behind him. Dawn Wind said, "The sun is shining today. This is good."

Breckinridge turned to smile at her. "The world is beginnin' again," he said.

"For some. I am happy for my people."

She didn't look happy, though. Her face was still as thin and drawn as it had been for months now, and the same pain and grief were visible in her eyes. She started to turn away, but Breckinridge took hold of her arm and stopped her.

"Don't you reckon it's time you and me started over, too, the same way the plants and the animals are doin'?"

She looked up into his eyes and slowly shook her head. "I wish we could, Breckinridge," she said. "But we both know it is not to be."

She had regained her health after losing the child, but she had lost weight steadily ever since and Breckinridge had never seen a smile on her face, not once. She never came right out and said that she blamed him for what had happened. He knew that feeling lurked in her heart, though.

And knowing it was like a knife in his guts, day after day.

"There are many beaver in the streams," she went on now. "You should go and trap them. Already there are other white men in the mountains who have come to take the pelts. Go and be one of them."

"I can't go off and leave you—"

She smiled sadly and shook her head. "You are not with me now, Breckinridge. Can you not see that?"

He could. He could see it plain as day. And that just made the pain worse.

He might have tried to argue with her, even though he knew it would be a waste of time and breath, if he hadn't noticed Swims Like a Fish hurrying toward them. Judging by the expression on the warrior's face, something unexpected had happened.

"Breckinridge," Swims Like a Fish said as he came to a stop, "white men in canoes are paddling up the creek."

"Not the first ones we've seen this season," Breckinridge replied. "Sure won't be the last, neither. There's some mighty good trappin' in these parts."

That was true . . . now that the evil was gone.

"One of these men we have seen before," Swims Like a Fish insisted. "But not this year."

"What are you tryin' to say?"

"It is your friend Morgan, Breckinridge. Morgan Baxter."

Dawn Wind gasped. Breckinridge felt like he'd been punched. She had told him what Carnahan had said about killing Morgan and Running Elk and stealing the pelts. Breck had given some thought to going and looking for their bones once the winter was over, but he didn't really expect to find them.

Now Swims Like a Fish was telling him that Morgan was alive. That didn't seem possible. Breckinridge grasped the warrior's shoulders and said, "Are you sure?"

"I saw him myself, in a large canoe with several other men. And there were other canoes and more men with them. It was Morgan, my friend. I am certain. But you can go and see for yourself." Swims Like a Fish pointed. "They are nearly here."

Breckinridge looked down the stream and saw four canoes gliding over its surface as the men inside them stroked with their paddles. One man in the lead canoe wasn't paddling. He seemed smaller, shrunken. But there was something familiar about him . . .

Breckinridge broke into a run.

Men were stepping out of the canoes and pulling them onto the bank when Breckinridge got there. One of the men reached back to help the small, frail figure out. Breck came to an abrupt halt.

It was Morgan. Pale, sickly-looking . . . but Morgan Baxter, beyond a doubt.

Another shock went through Breckinridge when

he looked down and saw that Morgan's right leg ended just below the knee. In its place was a wooden peg that made Morgan's gait awkward as he walked up the bank, leaning on the man who had helped him from the canoe.

"Morgan . . ." Breckinridge said in an awed half whisper.

Morgan smiled and said, "Hello, Breck. You figured you'd never see me again, didn't you?"

Breckinridge swept down, arms wide, ready to grab Morgan up in a bear hug. Then he stopped short and said, "Uh . . ."

"You're not going to hurt me," Morgan said as his smile widened into a grin. "Come here, you big buffalo."

Breckinridge let out a whoop, enveloped Morgan in his embrace, and lifted the smaller man from the ground. Morgan reached around Breck and pounded him on the back.

Finally, Breckinridge put him down and said, "How . . . I thought you was . . . This don't make any sense!"

"Sure it does," Morgan said, growing more solemn. "Let's find some place to sit down, and I'll tell you all about it."

"I'm sure Carnahan believed I was dead," Morgan said a short time later as he and Breckinridge sat on the same log where they had sat while Breck told him about Dulcy. "I held my breath and stayed underwater as long as I could and let the river carry me on downstream. I knew that was the only chance I had—and it wasn't a very good one."

"But you made it," Breckinridge said.

"I did. After a while I crawled out of the water and tried to figure out what to do next. I didn't think I stood much of a chance of getting back here, but I thought maybe if I went downstream I'd run into some other trappers and get them to help me. That's what happened. I broke off a tree branch to use as a crutch and hobbled downstream for a couple of days before I came on a camp. The fellows there patched me up and splinted that broken leg. They didn't want to turn around and take me back to St. Louis, but I promised to pay them more than double what they could have made from a season of trapping, so eventually they agreed."

"They took you all the way back down the Missouri."

"They did," Morgan said, nodding. "And by the time we got there, my leg was in such bad shape that the doctor had to take it off. It was a near thing. I almost died, they tell me. But I wasn't going to do that, as long as I had a score to settle."

"With Carnahan," Breckinridge said, his voice flat and grim. "I hate to tell you this, but the bastard seems to have gotten away. We wiped out the rest of his men. Well, except for Chet Bagley, who I told to skin outta this part of the country as fast as he could if he wanted to live."

"Major Ralston?"

"Dead." Breckinridge held up his hands. "Broke his neck my own self."

"Good," Morgan said. "He had it coming."

"I've got the pelts they stole from you and Running Elk, as well as the ones they took from the other fellas they killed." Breckinridge scratched his jaw. "I thought I might sell 'em and give most of the money to the families of trappers who disappeared out here in the mountains. Wouldn't seem right just to keep it."

Morgan nodded solemnly. "Yeah, I can see that. We don't know who all Carnahan and his bunch murdered, but we can make some pretty good guesses." He paused. "What about that Blackfoot war party?"

"All dead. I done for their war chief Machitehew, too."

"Somehow I'm not surprised."

Breckinridge frowned and said, "You didn't look too surprised when I told you Carnahan got away, neither."

"That's because I wasn't. I saw him in St. Louis, Breck."

Breckinridge couldn't help himself. He came to his feet and his hands clenched into fists.

"He made it all the way back down there alive?"

Morgan nodded. "Yes. I was sitting in Red Mike's one night, when I was putting together a party to come out here, and Carnahan walked in. This was about six weeks ago. I was going to get my gun out and shoot him then and there, even though I probably would have been hanged for murder, but Mike told him to leave. I tried to go after him . . ." Morgan smiled. "I'm afraid I'm not very fast on my feet these days. By the time I reached the street, he was gone."

"What was he doin' in there?"

"I asked Mike that same question. He said he'd heard that Carnahan was putting together a trapping expedition, but Mike didn't want him recruiting in there. I'd already told Mike, you see, about what Carnahan did out here. Mike won't take sides in many disputes, but he said he wouldn't have a snake like that in his place."

Breckinridge rubbed his jaw and then said, "So Carnahan's alive and headed for the mountains again, eh?"

"He may already be here. What do you think we should do about that, Breck?"

"I ain't sure you're in any shape to do anything."

Morgan stiffened. "I'm still a lot tougher than I look, damn it! I'm getting better all the time at getting around on this blasted peg leg. If you think I can't keep up or carry my weight, you're wrong. All I want is a chance to show you."

Breckinridge had sat back down on the log. Now he turned his head to gaze toward the tipis. Dawn Wind stood beside the one they had shared—without touching—for the past six months. Her body was slim and straight and inflexible. She had her arms crossed over her chest, and Breck could tell she was looking at him, too.

Then she lowered her arms, turned away, and disappeared into the tipi.

Breckinridge drew in a deep breath and let it out slowly. He nodded to Morgan and said, "Let's go find Carnahan and kill the son of a bitch."

Turn the page for an exciting preview!

Johnstone Justice. What America Needs Now.
*Bestselling authors William W. Johnstone and
J. A. Johnstone have thrilled readers with the epic struggles
and hard-fought triumphs of the pioneering Jensen family.
Now this great American saga continues—
with the next generation of Jensens . . .*

JENSEN PROUD. JENSEN TOUGH.

It's the dawn of a new century. But on the vast
Sugarloaf Ranch not much has changed since
legendary gunfighter Smoke Jensen and his wife,
Sally, tamed the land two decades ago. Raising cattle
is still a dangerous business—and just as deadly
as ever. When Smoke is injured swapping bullets
with some cow thieves, Sally puts out a call for help
to Matt, Ace, and the rest of the Jensen clan.
But time is running out. The bloodthirsty rustlers
are ready to strike again—and there are lots more
of them. And the Sugarloaf's last defense is
Smoke and Sally's next of kin . . .

Enter the Jensen twins. Denise and her brother
Louis have just returned home from their schooling
in Europe. Louis is studying to be a lawyer and is
too sickly to defend the ranch. But Denise is to
the manor born—she can ride like a man,
shoot like her daddy, and face down the
deadliest outlaws like nobody's business.

THE JENSEN BRAND, the explosive new series
by WILLIAM W. JOHNSTONE
with J. A. Johnstone!

On sale now, wherever Pinnacle Books are sold.

Live Free. Read Hard. www.williamjohnstone.net

THE JENSEN FAMILY
FIRST FAMILY OF THE AMERICAN FRONTIER

Smoke Jensen—*The Mountain Man*
The youngest of three children and orphaned as a young boy, Smoke Jensen is considered one of the fastest draws in the West. His quest to tame the lawless West has become the stuff of legend. Smoke owns the Sugarloaf Ranch in Colorado. Married to Sally Jensen, father to Denise ("Denny") and Louis.

Preacher—*The First Mountain Man*
Though not a blood relative, grizzled frontiersman Preacher became a father figure to the young Smoke Jensen, teaching him how to survive in the brutal, often deadly Rocky Mountains. Fought the battles that forged his destiny. Armed with a long gun, Preacher is as fierce as the land itself.

Matt Jensen—*The Last Mountain Man*
Orphaned but taken in by Smoke Jensen, Matt Jensen has become like a younger brother to Smoke and even took the Jensen name. And like Smoke, Matt has carved out his destiny on the American frontier. He lives by the gun and surrenders to no man.

Luke Jensen—*Bounty Hunter*

Mountain Man Smoke Jensen's long-lost brother, Luke Jensen, is scarred by war and a dead shot—the right qualities to be a bounty hunter. And he's cunning, and fierce enough, to bring down the deadliest outlaws of his day.

Ace Jensen and Chance Jensen—*Those Jensen Boys!*

Smoke Jensen's long-lost nephews, Ace and Chance, are a pair of young-gun twins as reckless and wild as the frontier itself . . . Their father is Luke Jensen, thought killed in the Civil War. Their uncle Smoke Jensen is one of the fiercest gunfighters the West has ever known. It's no surprise that the inseparable Ace and Chance Jensen have a knack for taking risks—even if they have to blast their way out of them.

Chapter 1

The Sugarloaf Ranch, Colorado, 1901

A thin sliver of moon hung over the mountains bordering the valley, casting such a feeble amount of light that it did little to relieve the pitch blackness cloaking much of the landscape.

A rustlers' moon, Smoke Jensen thought.

"Are they there?" Calvin Woods whispered next to Smoke. "I can't see a blasted thing!"

"They're there," Smoke told his foreman. He raised the Winchester he held in both hands but didn't bring it to his shoulder just yet. A shot would spook the men who had been stealing his cattle, and he didn't want them to take off for the tall and uncut before he had a chance to nab them. "Hold your fire . . ."

Hidden in the trees along with Smoke and Cal were half a dozen more Sugarloaf hands, all of them young and eager for action, like frisky colts ready to stretch their legs. One reason cowboys signed on to ride for the Sugarloaf was the prospect of working for Smoke Jensen, quite possibly the most famous gunfighter the

West had ever known. They figured just being around Smoke upped the chances for excitement.

That was true. Even though Smoke had put his powder-burning days behind him more than two decades earlier and settled down to be a peace-loving rancher, things hadn't quite worked out that way. Trouble still seemed to find him on a fairly regular basis, despite his intentions.

That was the way it was with Jensens. None of them had ever been plagued with an abundance of peace and quiet.

In recent weeks, for example, Sugarloaf cattle had begun disappearing on a regular basis. Only a few at first, then more and more as the thieves grew bolder. Smoke was in his fifties, and it only made sense to believe that he might have slowed down some. Some might have figured he wasn't the same sort of pure hell on wheels he had been when he was younger.

Those rustlers were about to find out how wrong they were to assume that.

"There to the right," Smoke whispered as he looked out across the broad pasture where a couple hundred cattle were settled down for the night. "Coming out of that stand of trees."

"I see 'em," Cal replied, equally quiet. He had started out as a young cowboy, too, twenty years earlier. Back then, the reformed outlaw known as Pearlie was the Sugarloaf's ramrod, and he and Cal had become fast friends. Pearlie was also a mentor to Cal, who'd learned everything there was to know about running a ranch. When it came time for Pearlie to retire, it was only natural for Cal to move into the foreman's job.

He still looked a little like a kid, though, despite

the mustache he had cultivated in an attempt to make himself seem older. However, no one on the crew failed to hop when he gave an order.

On the other side of the pasture, several riders moved out of the trees and rode slowly toward the cattle. It was too dark to make out any details about them or even to be sure of how many there were. But they didn't belong and there was only one reason for them to be there.

Calling out softly, slapping coiled lassos against their thighs, they started moving a jag of about a hundred head along the valley, toward the north end.

"I've seen all I need to see," Cal said. "Let's blast 'em outta their saddles."

"I'd rather round up a few of them if we can," Smoke said. "I'd like to know if they started this wide-looping on their own or if they're working for somebody."

"You got suspicions?"

"No . . . but if there's a head to this snake, I'd just as soon know about it so I can cut it off." Smoke leaned his head to indicate they should pull back, although it was doubtful Cal saw the gesture in the thick shadows. "Let's drift on back to the horses."

"If we go chargin' out there, we'll scatter those cows all over kingdom come," Cal warned.

Smoke chuckled. "They can be rounded up again."

Silently, the men moved through the trees until they reached the spot where they had left their horses and swung up into the saddles. Over the years of his adventurous life, Smoke had learned to trust his gut. He'd had a hunch the rustlers might strike again that night, so he, Cal, and some of the hands had gone out to a likely spot for more villainy where they could stand watch and maybe catch the cattle thieves in the act.

"Are you gonna give those varmints a chance to surrender, Smoke?" Cal sounded like he hoped the answer would be no.

"Yes . . . but not much of one. They'd better throw down their guns and get their hands in the air in a hurry. Otherwise . . ." Smoke didn't have to elaborate.

All the cowboys would be checking their guns before they rode out into the pasture.

He gave instructions. "We'll swing around and come up behind them. I'll hail them. If they start the ball, you fellas do what you have to. Like I said, it would be nice to take some of them alive, but I'd much rather all of you boys come through this with whole hides. Now let's go."

With Smoke and Cal in the lead, the men rode slowly through the trees until they reached the edge of the growth. The dark mass of the cattle was to the left, moving away as the rustlers pushed the reluctant animals along. Smoke and his companions moved out into the open and started after them, still not hurrying but moving fast enough to catch up to the plodding cattle.

The sounds made by the cattle and the hooves of the rustlers' horses were enough to muffle the advance of Smoke and his men. At least Smoke hoped that was the case. The rustlers hadn't panicked yet, at least.

The group from the Sugarloaf closed in.

Smoke had his Winchester in his right hand and the reins in his left. He looped the reins around the saddle horn, knowing he could control the rangy gray gelding with his knees. With both hands gripping the rifle, he shouted, "You're caught! Throw down your guns!"

Instead of surrendering, the rustlers yanked their horses around. Spurts of gun flame bloomed in the darkness like crimson flowers as they opened fire.

In one smooth motion, Smoke brought the rifle to his shoulder, aimed at one of the spurts of orange, and squeezed the trigger. The Winchester cracked. He barely felt the weapon's recoil. Working the lever to throw another round in the chamber, he shifted his aim, and swiftly fired a second shot then kneed his horse into motion and charged toward the rustlers.

Around him, Cal and the other Sugarloaf hands galloped forward, yelling and shooting.

The thieves scattered in all directions, abandoning the cows they were trying to steal.

Although it was difficult to see much, Smoke and his allies continued aiming at the muzzle flashes of their enemies. Of course, the rustlers were doing the same thing. The air was filled with flying lead.

Smoke always hoped his men would come through such an encounter unscathed but knew better than to expect it.

He made out one of the fleeing rustlers and closed in on the man, who twisted in the saddle and flung a shot back at him. Smoke felt as much as heard the slug rip through the air not far from his ear. That was good shooting from the back of a running horse. He leaned forward to make himself a smaller target and urged his mount to greater speed.

As he drew close to his quarry, the rustler turned to try another shot, but Smoke lashed out with the barrel of the Winchester. It thudded against the rustler's head and swept him out of the saddle. Both horses galloped on for a few strides before Smoke was able to swing his mount around. Elsewhere in the big pasture, gunfire still crackled.

He swung down from the saddle and let the reins drop, knowing the horse was trained not to go anywhere. Keeping his rifle pointed at the dim figure on the ground, Smoke approached him. The fallen rustler didn't move.

Smoke ordered, "Put your hands in the air!" but there was no response. Wary of a trick, he lowered the rifle and drew the Colt on his right hip. The revolver was better for close work. Almost supernaturally fast with it, he was confident he could put a bullet in him before the varmint had a chance to try anything.

"On your feet if you can, and keep your hands where I can see 'em!"

The rustler remained motionless. He appeared to be lying facedown. Smoke hooked a boot toe under his shoulder and rolled him onto his back.

The loose-limbed way the man flopped over spoke volumes. The fall from the running horse had either busted the rustler's head open or broken his neck, more likely the latter. Either way, he sure looked dead.

Or he was mighty good at playing possum.

Smoke backed off and holstered the Colt. He'd go back later and check on the rustler. At the moment, his men needed his help elsewhere.

He mounted up quickly and rode toward the sound of the guns, which had become intermittent. The shots died out completely as Smoke approached several dark shapes that turned into men on horseback as he got closer.

He had his rifle ready, but he recognized the voice that called, "Smoke? Is that you?"

"Yeah, Cal, it's me. Are you all right?"

"Fine as frog hair. How about you?"

"A few of those bullets came close enough for me to hear, but that's all. How about the other fellas?"

"Don't know. Randy and Josh are with me and they're all right, but I can't say about the rest."

"And the rustlers?"

"We downed a couple. Don't know about the rest of *them*, either."

Smoke said, "The fight seems to be over. Let's see if we can round up the rest of our bunch."

"Then we can round up those cows," Cal said. "They scattered hell-west and crosswise, just like I figured they would."

"But they're still on Sugarloaf range," Smoke pointed out. "Those rustlers didn't succeed in driving them off."

"They sure didn't!"

Smoke drew his Colt and fired three shots into the air, the signal for his riders to regroup. Over the next few minutes they came in. One man had a bullet burn on his arm, but the others were unhurt . . . until the last two horses plodded up. One man rode in front, leading the other horse.

Smoke could make out a shape draped over the second horse's saddle, and the sight made his jaw tighten in anger. "Who's that?" he snapped.

"I'm Jimmy Holt, Mr. Jensen." With a catch in his voice, the young cowboy said, "That's Sid MacDowell behind me. He . . . he cashed in his chips. One of those damn rustlers drilled him right through the brisket. I ain't sure Sid had time to know what happened."

"Might be better that way," Smoke muttered. "What about the rustlers? Did any of them get away?"

"I think one of them did," another cowboy reported. "I'm pretty sure he was hit, but he managed to stay on his horse. Do you want us to see if we can trail him, Mr. Jensen?"

"The best tracker in the world couldn't follow a trail on a night like this, and I've known a few who could lay claim to that title." Smoke shook his head. "No, we might see if we can find any tracks in the morning, but right now, some of you boys start gathering those cows and the rest of you come with me and Cal. I want to see if any of the rustlers are still alive."

For the next half hour, Smoke, Cal, and a couple other men rode around the pasture, hunting for the bodies of the rustlers. Smoke hoped to find at least one of them only wounded and still able to talk, but as thief after thief turned up dead, that hope began to fade.

Finally they rode over to the man Smoke had knocked out of his saddle. Smoke knelt beside him, struck a lucifer, and saw by its flaring light that the rustler's wide, staring eyes were sightless. The unnatural twist of his head told that his neck was broken. Smoke had tried to take him alive, but fate had had other ideas.

Smoke straightened and told Cal, "You can bring a wagon out here in the morning and collect the bodies . . . if the wolves haven't dragged them off by then. Haul 'em into Big Rock to the undertaker. I'll pay to have them put in the ground if they don't have enough money on them to cover the cost."

Cal nodded. "Should I get Sheriff Carson to take a look at them?"

"Wouldn't hurt. Chances are some of them are wanted. You fellas might have some reward money coming to you."

Cal rubbed his chin. "I'm not sure I'd want to take blood money. On the other hand, the world's probably better off without these varmints, and that's worth something, I guess."

"Up to you." Smoke wouldn't be taking any reward money. Between the Sugarloaf's success and the lucrative gold claim he had found many years earlier, he was one of the wealthiest men in Colorado, although no one would ever know it to look at him. He still dressed like a common cowhand.

"We'll make sure none of those cattle ran too far when they spooked, then head back to the bunkhouse," Cal said. "How about you?"

Smoke had already turned his horse. He said over his shoulder, "I'm headed home."

Chapter 2

The small ranch house that Smoke had built when he and Sally first settled on the Sugarloaf had been added onto many times over the years, until it was a big, sprawling, two-story structure surrounded by cottonwoods and oaks. He always felt good when he rode up to it. He couldn't help but think about all the fine times he and his wife and their children had had. More often than not, the house had rung with laughter.

As he approached the house, he saw that a lamp still burned in the parlor despite the late hour. The glow in the window was dim enough he knew the flame was turned low. More than likely, Sally had waited up for him. That came as no surprise.

Movement on the porch caught his eye. Out of habit—one that had saved his life on occasion—his hand was close to the butt of his revolver. He relaxed, though, as he recognized Pearlie's tall, lanky figure.

"Thought I heard shots up yonderways a while back," the retired foreman said as he came down the steps from the porch. "You must've had a run-in with those wide-loopers."

"We did." Smoke dismounted. "They figured on chousing off a hundred head. We changed their minds."

Pearlie reached for the reins of Smoke's horse. "I'll take care of that for you. I ain't forgot how to wrangle a cayuse. How's the kid?"

Even though Cal wasn't that far from being middle-aged, he would always be a kid to Pearlie. The two of them had shared many adventures, had been through tragedy and triumph together, and were fast friends.

"Cal's fine," Smoke assured him. "We lost one man. Sid MacDowell."

"Blast it! I didn't really know the younker—Cal hired him, not me—but he deserved better 'n a damn rustler's bullet."

"That's the truth. We tried to even the score for him, though. Five carcasses are still out there for Cal to haul into town in the morning."

"Didn't manage to take any of 'em alive?"

Smoke shook his head. "Nope. And one got away, although he might've been wounded. We'll do some tracking in the morning and see if we can turn up another body."

"Even if you don't, killin' five out of six practically wipes out the gang," Pearlie said.

"Only if there were just half a dozen of them to start with," Smoke pointed out.

"No reason to think otherwise, is there?"

"Not really," Smoke admitted. "If the rustling stops now, I reckon we can assume that was all. But if they were just part of a bigger gang—"

"We'll probably know that soon enough, too,"

Pearlie said in a gloomy voice. He started toward the barn, leading Smoke's horse, and added over his shoulder, "Miss Sally's waitin' up in the parlor."

Even though Smoke was tired and the smell of gun smoke clung to him, he was smiling as he stepped into the house.

Wearing a soft robe, Sally was sitting in one of the rocking chairs beside the table where the lamp burned. She was reading a book, but she set it aside on the table and looked up with a smile as he stepped into the parlor.

She was on her feet by the time he reached her. Her arms went around his neck and his arms encircled her trim waist. Their mouths met in a passionate kiss that had lost none of its urgency despite the time they had been together.

He lifted his lips from hers and said, "You ought to be in bed getting your beauty sleep . . . not that you need it."

That was certainly true. There might be a few more small lines on Sally's face, and if you looked hard enough you could find a strand of gray here and there in her thick, lustrously dark hair, but to Smoke she was every bit as beautiful as when he had first laid eyes on her in the town of Bury, Idaho, all those years ago.

Smoke knew he hadn't changed much, either. If there was gray in his hair, its natural ash blond color made that sign of age hard to see. Most men on the far side of fifty were past the prime of life, but not Smoke Jensen. He was still as vital as ever, his muscular, broad-shouldered frame near to bursting with strength. He attributed that to fresh air, sunshine, clean living, and being married to the prettiest girl alive.

"I didn't see any bloodstains on your clothes when you came in," Sally said, "so I assume you're all right."

"How do you know there was even any trouble?"

"You went out looking for it, didn't you? If there's one thing Smoke Jensen is good at, it's finding trouble."

He chuckled. "I'd like to think I'm good for more than one thing."

"Well, we might find out about that in a little while, but first, tell me what happened."

Smoke grew serious as he said, "Those rustlers made a try for the stock in the big pasture up north of Granite Creek, just like I had a hunch they might. We killed five out of the six of them and probably wounded the one who got away. No telling how bad." He paused a moment. "But Sid MacDowell was killed in the fight."

Sally took a step back and put a hand to her mouth. "Oh, no. Sid was a fine young man. I'll have to write to his mother and sister down in Amarillo."

Smoke hadn't known that the young cowboy had a mother and sister in Amarillo, but he wasn't surprised Sally was aware of it. She made it a point to be a good friend to every member of the ranch crew.

"We'll send them the wages he had coming, and more besides," Smoke said. "Of course, that won't make up for losing him."

"No, but it's all we can do, I suppose."

He changed the subject by gesturing toward the book on the table. "What are you reading?"

"Charles Dickens' *A Tale of Two Cities*. It's very good."

"Maybe I'll read it one of these days," Smoke said.

She reached for the book. "There's something else in here you'll want to see right away." She opened the volume's front cover and took out a small, square sheet of yellow paper. "Late this afternoon, right after you and Cal and the others rode out, a boy from town brought me this telegram that had just come in."

"Telegrams are usually bad news," Smoke said with a slight frown.

"Not this one, I'm happy to say. Denise Nicole and Louis Arthur are coming home!"

Smoke's frown disappeared. He reached for the flimsy and scanned the words printed in block letters by the telegrapher in Big Rock.

ARRIVING BIG ROCK 27TH STOP
COMING HOME FOR GOOD STOP
LOVE TO YOU BOTH STOP LAJ AND DNJ

Smoke's heart beat faster as the news soaked in on him. His kids were coming back to the Sugarloaf, and according to the telegram Louis had sent, they would be staying. That was enough to quicken the pulse of any man who loved his children and missed them when they were away.

For most of their lives, Louis and Denise had indeed been away from the Sugarloaf. Twins, they had been inseparable as youngsters, and when sickness had threatened Louis's life and forced Smoke and Sally to seek treatment for him in Europe, Denise had gone along. Sally had taken the children back east to her parents' home, and then John and Abigail Reynolds had sailed across the Atlantic and delivered Louis to top specialists in France.

Through their efforts, the boy had been saved, but his health had remained precarious enough that he had remained in Europe to be closer to the medical help he might need.

That wasn't the only reason the twins had stayed in Europe, living on an estate in England owned by Sally's parents. They had traveled all over the continent and soaked up all the education and culture available to them. Smoke's mentor, the old mountain man called Preacher, thought such behavior was plumb foolishness, and to be honest, at times Smoke felt sort of the same way, but it seemed important to Sally and her folks, so he had gone along with the idea. He missed his kids, but he wanted what was best for them.

They had come back to Colorado for frequent visits to the Sugarloaf, and each time Smoke had harbored the hope in the back of his mind that they might decide to stay. Judging by the telegram in his hand, it looked like that might finally come to pass.

"It'll sure be good to have the kids around again," he said as he placed the telegram on top of Mr. Dickens' novel.

"I'm not sure we can think of them as children anymore," Sally said. "They're twenty years old. They're grown, Smoke."

"Twenty's not grown."

"Think of all the things *you* had done by the time you were twenty years old."

Smoke scowled. He had killed more than two dozen men and been forced to battle for his life countless times. He had married a woman, fathered a child, lost them both to vicious murderers, and avenged their deaths by tracking down those killers and blasting them to hell. He had been a wanted outlaw and worn a lawman's badge.

Yes, it was safe to say that Smoke Jensen had grown up fast. Too fast.

But his children hadn't lived that sort of life, thank God. Instead of dodging the law and shooting it out with gunmen, they had spent their time in clinics and universities and concert halls. They had learned mathematics and natural science and literature instead of how to track an enemy and reload a gun in the heat of battle and stay calm with bullets whipping around their heads.

Smoke was glad they hadn't had to endure such hardships. To his way of thinking, that easy life meant they were still kids. Nothing wrong with that.

Instead of arguing with Sally about whether or not the twins could be considered grown, he said, "The twenty-seventh is only a couple days away. Can we be ready for them by then?"

"There's no getting ready to do," Sally said. "I keep their rooms just like they've always been. They can move right in."

"It's been a while since we've seen them. I wonder if they've changed much."

"Probably not. Louis Arthur will still be handsome and Denise Nicole will be as beautiful as always."

Smoke smiled. "I don't doubt it." They had always been beautiful to him, even as red-faced, squalling babies.

Louis Arthur was named for two of Smoke's oldest friends, the gambler and gunman Louis Longmont and Preacher, whose real name was Arthur. The name was also a way of honoring Smoke's first son, the one who had been murdered, who was named Arthur as well. Along with the old Reynolds family name Denise, Nicole, Smoke's first wife, had inspired the middle name given to his daughter.

Smoke would never forget his first family, the one that had been ripped brutally from him. That tragedy had forged his steel-hard determination to see evildoers brought to justice, and he was more than willing to deliver that justice from the barrel of a gun whenever and wherever necessary.

He wasn't one to dwell on the violence of the past, though. It was more his nature to look ahead to the future with optimism and a friendly smile.

Sally put a hand on his arm. "Would you like a cup of coffee before we go upstairs?"

Smoke slid his other arm around his wife's waist again, feeling the supple warmth of her body under the robe, and smiled "No, I reckon not. If I'm going to be kept awake for a while, I'd rather it was by something else besides coffee."

She laughed and linked her arm with his as they turned toward the parlor entrance. They had gone up only a few steps when she said, "Do you think the rustling is over?"

"I hope so. There's no reason to think otherwise, but we'll just have to wait and see. I can trust Cal and the others to keep a close eye on the stock and let me know if any more turn up missing."

"I hope that's the way it turns out. I'd hate to have a bunch of trouble going on just as Louis Arthur and Denise Nicole finally come home to stay."

"Yeah," Smoke agreed. "Jensens and trouble just don't mix."

She laughed and swatted him lightly on the shoulder, and they continued on their way upstairs to their bedroom.